AF084826

THE FRENCHMAN

Jack Beaumont is the pseudonym of a former operative in the clandestine operations branch of the French foreign secret service, the DGSE. He joined 'the Company' after being an air force fighter pilot and later flying special operations and intelligence missions. In 2021 his debut book, *The Frenchman*, quickly became a bestseller and is now published internationally and in translation. *Dark Arena*, his second book, continues the story of French spy Alec de Payns. Beaumont's background gives his novels a level of authenticity that few other spy thrillers have been able to achieve.

For more information and updates, follow him on Instagram on @jackbeaumont_official

Also by Jack Beaumont

Dark Arena
Liar's Game

PRAISE FOR

The Frenchman by Jack Beaumont

'A richly detailed cloak-and-dagger thriller reminiscent of the novels of John le Carré . . . I hope Jack Beaumont, whoever he is, writes a follow-up.' ***The Australian***

'A superior thriller.' ***Courier-Mail***

'Subterfuge, secrets, betrayal, torture, traitors, elaborate set ups, extraordinary secret agents . . . There's authenticity on every page.' ***Herald Sun***

'Taut and terrific.' ***Gold Coast Bulletin***

'A gripping thriller with an extremely authentic feel . . . highly recommended.' ***Canberra Weekly***

'Beaumont reveals a world of international espionage that's at once exhilarating, morally repugnant, and deadly . . . An action-packed spy thriller with an authentic feel.' ***Kirkus Reviews***

'*The Frenchman* is, in the way of many thrillers, a disturbing reminder of how fragile our modern world is and how easy it might be to upend the world order. It is a spy thriller that only an insider could have written.' ***The Blurb***

'*The Frenchman* is one of the finest examples of the spy genre in recent memory. Suspenseful, masterfully plotted, and completely riveting.' **Nic Pizzolatto, creator of HBO's *True Detective***

THE FRENCHMAN

JACK BEAUMONT

CORVUS

First published in Australia in 2021 by Allen & Unwin

First published in eBook in Great Britain in 2025 by Corvus,
an imprint of Atlantic Books Ltd.

First published in paperback in Great Britain in 2026 by Corvus,
an imprint of Atlantic Books Ltd.

Copyright © Jack Beaumont, 2021

The moral right of Jack Beaumont to be identified as the author of this work has been asserted by him in accordance with the Copyright, Designs and Patents Act of 1988.

All rights reserved. No part of this publication may be reproduced, stored in a retrieval system, or transmitted in any form or by any means, electronic, mechanical, photocopying, recording, or otherwise, without the prior permission of both the copyright owner and the above publisher of this book.

No part of this book may be used in any manner in the learning, training or development of generative artificial intelligence technologies (including but not limited to machine learning models and large language models (LLMs)), whether by data scraping, data mining or use in any way to create or form a part of data sets or in any other way.

This novel is entirely a work of fiction. The names, characters and incidents portrayed in it are the work of the author's imagination. Any resemblance to actual persons, living or dead, events or localities, is entirely coincidental.

10 9 8 7 6 5 4 3 2

A CIP catalogue record for this book is available from the British Library.

Paperback ISBN: 978 1 80546 553 9
E-book ISBN: 978 1 80546 554 6

Printed in Great Britain by CPI Group (UK) Ltd, Croydon CR0 4YY

Corvus
An imprint of Atlantic Books Ltd
Ormond House
26–27 Boswell Street
London
WC1N 3JZ

www.atlantic-books.co.uk

Product safety EU representative: Authorised Rep Compliance Ltd., Ground Floor, 71 Lower Baggot Street, Dublin, D02 P593, Ireland. www.arccompliance.com

MIX
Paper | Supporting responsible forestry
FSC® C013604

TO MY WIFE AND CHILDREN

AMIN

The expert standing on the stage thanked the presenter, signalling an end to the session on solid-fuel propellants. Amin rose to his feet with two hundred other scientists and engineers as the lights came up on the conference floor. The large doors of the ballroom in Singapore's Pan Pacific Hotel swung open and he moved towards them. As he reached the exit, a ruddy-faced Australian radar engineer approached him. Amin knew John Vaughan from other conferences but, despite the Queenslander's friendliness, Amin had always kept his distance, trying to limit his social exposure.

'Shit, mate, did you understand any of that?' John shook his head. 'I was a passenger for most of it.'

Amin chuckled. 'It's a small club, the rocket world.'

'Fancy an early beer?' asked the Aussie. 'The boys found a bar needs propping up.'

Amin glanced at his watch.

'Sorry, I have some work to finish in my room.'

He caught the elevator to his room on the eighth floor and secured the interior mechanical bolt. Pulling the curtains, he shut out a view of the marina and fished a disposable cell phone from his wheelie case. It was 1.59 p.m., one minute until his daily call. He assembled the battery and SIM card into the Samsung he'd bought at Changi Airport, and at 2 p.m. Singapore time he selected 'Dan'—a name in the middle of a contact list of nonsense numbers—and hit the green button.

The phone chirped as the call relayed to the Colonel, the man in charge of Amin's project section. A silver-haired man with a thick neck who never wore a military uniform, he'd introduced himself the day before Amin turned twenty-six and made his proposal: *Use your PhD to help build Pakistan's missile capability and you'll be paid more than your peers and work at the highest levels in the best labs.* It seemed like a perfect birthday present, even if the trade-off was a profession he couldn't talk about and a life controlled by Pakistan's secret intelligence service, the ISI. Not that a government employee could ever ask if they were being overseen by the ISI; persons being controlled by the ISI were not emboldened to ask questions about it. But after working on missile development for six months, some of the engineers told him that his phone and internet were probably monitored, as were his interactions with friends. He considered this a small price to pay. He got to travel, he wore nice suits and expensive watches, and the pay was good—it had taken his father, a senior bureaucrat in the Ministry of Finance, thirty years of service to earn what Amin was making before he was twenty-nine.

It wasn't until he met Anita that he'd started to question the compromises. Amin had disclosed his relationship with her, as required for classified workers, but the Colonel seemed to know about his new girlfriend already. Amin told his new love that he worked in a university research lab on the outskirts of Rawalpindi, without mentioning what he was actually working on. Anita worked at a classified scientific facility called the MERC, and they came to an unspoken agreement early in their courtship: don't ask—don't tell. Perhaps, Amin pondered once after he'd drunk too much wine, the Colonel was relaxed about Anita because he *knew* they didn't discuss work? Perhaps he knew, because phone and internet were not all he monitored?

Amin grew increasingly restless with the arrangement. He didn't like lying to his girlfriend—now wife; he didn't like it when the Colonel showed him photos of Anita from university, with her Western friends, or when he disclosed that Anita's father was a secret alcoholic. When Amin tried to push back, the Colonel explained the facts of life: *This is not a job you walk away from—but you'd be smart enough to understand this, yes?*

Yes, thought Amin as he sat on the hotel bed, waiting for the call to connect with Islamabad. He was smart enough to have worked that out.

'Amin,' came the smooth voice of the Colonel, when the call connected. 'What news?'

Amin was accustomed to these communications. When he travelled he made the same call every day and it usually lasted twenty seconds. Sometimes the Colonel would ask a pointed question about gyroscopic stabilisers or satellite guidance systems. He always asked who had spoken to him and his response.

'An Australian engineer, John Vaughan,' said Amin when the inevitable question was posed. 'He invited me to go for a drink. I said no.'

As the Colonel ended the call, Amin's iPhone began to buzz along the desktop. He'd switched it to vibrate in the seminar, and now it just rattled on the wood veneer. He checked the caller ID; it was Anita.

'Hello, my love,' he said, happy to hear from her. Since marrying, he was prone to homesickness.

'Amin, you have to come home,' she said. 'Please! It's urgent.'

'Slow down. What's happening?'

'It's Mama—she's sick,' said Anita. He could hear the fear in her voice now. Amin's mother-in-law was a healthy woman; any sign of ill health would be a shock to her family.

'I'm on the two o'clock flight tomorrow,' he said. 'There's a round table tonight.'

'No,' she said desperately. 'Mama might not make it through the night. We need you here *now*.'

'Okay, okay,' said Amin, sensing panic.

'There's a flight from Changi at six,' said Anita, almost shouting. 'I've emailed you a ticket. You *cannot* miss that flight, Amin.'

Amin frowned. Anita was a scholarship science student who completed her PhD in Britain before joining the best scientists in Pakistan at the MERC. She didn't yell, she wasn't easily flustered—and she was very, very careful with money. She didn't just pay for an earlier flight when her husband was already booked on one courtesy of the government. Amin knew something very serious was driving this conversation. He looked at his watch. 'I'll try to make the flight. Don't worry.'

'Don't just try,' she snapped. 'Do it! I need you here.' She hung up.

Amin had never heard her like this before. He opened his laptop, retrieved his e-ticket from Anita's email and clicked the option to have it sent to his phone. It was now 2.10 p.m. Then he opened his ProtonMail account and saw a new email in the inbox from Marcus Aubrac. It said: *Meet for a drink?*

Aubrac was a French aerospace consultant whom he'd first met in Vienna, at a conference like this one. Amin remembered it well. It was held in a grand old hotel that had been modernised while still retaining its imperial aura. They'd bumped into one another at the breakfast buffet, exchanged pleasantries and shared a table. More conferences, a few drinks at the bars, with Marcus never asking for anything. In fact, it had been the Frenchman dropping tidbits about Israeli guidance systems and Russian quantum computing in their missile defence. Amin liked Marcus's worldly grasp of missile technology—plus they had fatherhood in common. Amin must have talked too longingly about the advantages of raising his son Javed in Europe, because one afternoon, at a bar in Brussels, Marcus asked him outright what he'd be prepared to do to have a new life in Paris. It had been one of those precipice moments. After a long silence, Amin had finally said, 'I gather this is not a hypothetical question?'

Marcus replied that he worked for the French government, and he was in a position to offer a pathway for Amin and his family to gain French citizenship and new identities.

'And what does France want in return?' Amin asked.

The answer was updates on his missile development and any collateral he might be privy to.

Over the next two weeks they'd worked out a deal, down to timelines, possible employment opportunities in Paris and the safety of Anita's and Amin's extended families. They organised a meeting schedule, always at an international conference and always on the afternoon of the final day. Aubrac had advised him to use a burner phone, to use an encrypted email service such as ProtonMail, and explained how to wipe the history on his laptop—always seven times—to avoid having his ProtonMail discovered by the snoops at Amin's lab.

They became close, swapping tales of wives and children, work pressures and the eternal annoyance of politics. Amin assumed Aubrac wasn't Marcus's real name, but the details of his life—even if disguised by false names—rang true. There was something magnetic about the Frenchman—aged in his mid-thirties, he was handsome, with a lightly tanned face and sandy hair. His well-cut suit hinted at an athletic build, and although he was over six foot tall his movements were those of a more compact man. If Amin had seen Marcus in a public place he'd have assessed him as a professional tennis player dressed for an office job.

Now Amin looked away from Aubrac's email; he keyed a number on his burner phone and sent a text to the number provided in the email. The Frenchman responded quickly with his own text: *Queen's Inglish pub, two-thirty.*

Amin shut down the ProtonMail site, wiped his history and collapsed on the bed. His stomach was clenched like a fist; his pulse banged in his temples. Something was very wrong.

Aubrac had taught him some basic hygiene habits to avoid detection by the Pakistani secret services. First and foremost was to remain calm and never behave like a man who thinks he's being followed, so for a few minutes he just stared at the ceiling, breathing slowly through his nose, until the jitters had passed. Then he rose and packed his wheelie suitcase, grabbed his blazer and headed for the elevators with his suitcase.

He walked into the pub, one block south-east of the Pan Pacific, just before two-thirty and went to the end of the bar. There were twenty other customers in the pub but he couldn't see Aubrac. That wasn't unusual—Marcus Aubrac usually entered a meeting place after him. He ordered a lemonade and before it landed on the bar Aubrac arrived, smiling as usual, dressed in a light-grey suit, no tie.

'*Bonjour*, Amin,' said Aubrac, his pale eyes crinkling with affection.

Amin shook the Frenchman's hand, trying to match his ease.

As they took a table, Amin realised he still didn't know what to say. He reflected on the deal he had made with Paris—two years' worth of inside engineering data on the RA'AD II extended-range missile development, and Amin and his family would receive new identities and French passports. He was five months short of the two years, which would have given Javed the greatest gift—to grow up as a citizen in a rich European country. On his walk to the bar he'd toyed with the idea of asking Aubrac for the help of the French secret services. Could they find out what was up with his wife and her family? But he couldn't bring himself to ask. He worried that telling Aubrac might result in the French cutting ties with him. The French were not known for sentimentality. He would just have to return to Pakistan on the evening flight and see for himself what was going on.

'I just wanted to let you know I've been called back to Pakistan,' said Amin, mustering a regretful smile. 'My mother-in-law is very sick. I have to be at Changi in an hour.'

Aubrac looked briefly at his watch. 'Family first, my friend,' he said, gesturing to the barmaid for a beer.

Amin noticed a pretty young woman at the bar staring at Aubrac with a gaze that required no interpreter. As usual, Aubrac pretended not to notice.

'So, you have anything of interest for me?' asked the Frenchman.

Amin shook his head. 'The new fuel loads and compositions are locked in for now and the testing engineers take over for a while. I'll start seeing telemetry in two, maybe three weeks.'

Aubrac nodded. 'Keep the development and testing teams separate. That's smart.'

Avoiding eye contact with his friend, Amin stood. Aubrac appeared to hesitate. Amin thought the Frenchman was on the verge of asking if everything was okay, but he merely said, 'Well, I guess it's goodbye, Amin.'

'Yes, my friend,' said Amin, emotion welling up.

'I'll see you at the Paris conference?'

Amin nodded and then he grabbed the Frenchman's hand in a double grip. 'Farewell, Marcus.'

They parted with a smile but after two heavy strides, Amin stopped and turned. '*Adieu*, my friend,' he said to a person who'd been privy to his deepest fears and ambitions and yet had never revealed his own name. The two men looked at each other for a moment longer than was normal, then Amin wheeled his suitcase out into the Singapore sunshine.

■

The flight landed at Islamabad International Airport just after 2 a.m. Amin collected his suitcase and headed for the taxi stand, a strange nausea gripping his stomach. He'd brooded on the flight, wondering about Mina, his mother-in-law, and what could have stricken her. There was a lengthy queue outside the bustling airport terminal, and as he took his place behind a sweating businessman, a black Nissan Maxima pulled up in the taxi zone. A man alighted from the passenger seat, large and athletic. Amin knew him as Johnny—one of the Colonel's staffers.

His stance was threatening but he smiled. 'The Colonel sent us to pick you up,' he said, reaching for Amin's suitcase. 'Let's go.'

The driver leaned across and opened the rear door, and Johnny leaped in the back with Amin after depositing the suitcase in the boot. They accelerated into the traffic, the smell of American aftershave thick in the car.

'Where are we going?' asked Amin as they left the terminal building. 'The hospital?'

'Later,' said Johnny, lighting a cigarette and cracking his window. 'The Colonel wants a chat first.'

They motored east, presumably towards Noor Khan, the Pakistan Air Force base that was home to the missile research program and the Colonel's office. As they closed on the west of Rawalpindi, the driver took an off-ramp and circled under the freeway so they were travelling south and around the outskirts of the sprawling city.

'I thought we were going to see the Colonel,' said Amin. 'He's not at Noor Khan tonight?'

Johnny shrugged and lit another cigarette. They veered off the main road onto a street with little lighting and a high security fence to the left. The only vehicles visible seemed to be security.

Amin was about to protest that he thought they might be lost, when he saw a security checkpoint in the distance. Now he recognised the street. He'd driven Anita here once, when her car was in the workshop. He'd dropped her at the checkpoint and the guards had called for a golf cart to come down and pick her up. Even with his security clearance, Amin wasn't allowed in this facility.

Acid churned in his stomach as they swept through the checkpoint. This was not right.

'Why are we here?' he asked, craning to scope his environment. 'This is the MERC, isn't it?'

Johnny smiled. 'MERC? I have no idea what you're talking about.'

They pulled over beside a large white building, and were met by a plainclothes man—ISI, Amin guessed—at the side portico. The man searched Amin before walking him to an elevator. Amin wondered if he was going to faint; he couldn't seem to get enough air.

'We going down?' asked Amin. His throat was dry and he was aware of sweat prickling on his forehead.

Johnny and the ISI man ignored the question.

The elevator stopped at B5. Amin walked out first, and turned right at the guard's direction. The concrete walls were a pale green, made putrid by the weak fluoro lighting. The corridor smelled of damp and bleach. Behind him, Amin heard a throat clearing, and he turned—the ISI man had his hand on the doorknob of an unmarked room. Amin walked back to him like a man in a dream.

As Amin entered the dimly lit room, two thugs grabbed him, threw him into a steel-framed chair and shackled his ankles and forearms to it.

'Hey,' he yelled, struggling, but he knew the truth—he was going nowhere.

He looked around as he tested the straps on his arms. The room smelled of industrial cleaning fluids and cigarette smoke. The Colonel sat on the other side of a wooden desk, smoking and silent. There were four chairs arranged in a box formation.

In front of him, Anita was strapped to her own chair, duct tape sealing her mouth. Javed stared back at him from the interrogation chair at his ten o'clock.

'Why are my family here?' Amin asked the Colonel, his voice high and frightened.

The Colonel exhaled smoke through his nose. 'Perhaps we should try to answer that question?'

Amin shook his head, trying to shake away the reality—he'd played with the French devil and he'd lost. 'It's me you want, and I'm here. Let them go. Javed is seven. He's just a boy.'

'And boys turn into men,' said the Colonel, his voice flat. 'They can develop all sorts of hatreds against their country, especially if their father is a chatterbox—a well-paid chatterbox, yes, Amin?'

Amin's thoughts were a jumble; his breath rasping in fast, shallow pants as panic flooded through him.

The Colonel nodded at the thug in a black business shirt who'd thrown Amin into the chair. The man walked to a table behind Anita and turned on a lamp, revealing a battery-powered drill. Black Shirt picked up the drill, and walked around to stand in front of Anita. Her eyes grew huge as the thug hit the trigger, testing the spin of the drill bit. The motor whined.

'This Frenchman,' said the Colonel, as the drill slowed. 'Who is he?'

'I don't know,' said Amin, shaking his head. He'd imagined what it would be like to be caught, but he'd never thought about what he would say.

'Don't know?' The Colonel smiled. 'You don't know who he is? Or you don't know a Frenchman?'

Amin opened his mouth to reply but no sound came out.

'I'll give you a clue. He's a tall, handsome blond man with nice suits. Speaks with a French accent.'

'Aubrac,' croaked Amin. 'Marcus Aubrac, from Paris.'

'What does he do?'

'Aerospace. More on the finance and investment side, but well informed.' Observing Anita's eyes, which were wide with terror, he added, 'My wife knows nothing about this.'

The Colonel stood, dropped his cigarette and ground it into the concrete floor. Then he walked over to Amin. 'What did he want from you?'

'Not much,' said Amin.

The Colonel nodded at his sidekick, who brought the drill to full revs then kneeled and drove the bit into the top of Anita's bare foot. She arched her back as the drill bit exited the sole of her foot in a flurry of blood and flesh. Amin struggled against his restraints as the thug withdrew the spinning drill bit. He looked at Javed, whose face was flooded with tears, his accusing eyes boring into his father.

'Stop, please!' Amin begged. 'I'll tell you everything.'

The Colonel returned to his desk and lit a cigarette as Anita's blood ran across the concrete. 'Okay, so talk.'

'I told Aubrac about the fuel loads, and the weight and the range of the RA'AD II.'

'The test telemetry?'

Amin shook his head. 'I couldn't download it. I memorised the summaries, though, and I believe that was enough for the French to reverse-engineer the performance.'

'How did he contact you?'

'ProtonMail,' said Amin.

'And then?'

'He'd give me a burner phone number to call—it was always different.'

The Colonel nodded. 'And then?'

'We'd meet at a bar or a cafe, always on the afternoon of the final day of the conference.'

'What did you tell him about the project?'

Amin hesitated, unsure what the Colonel was asking.

The Colonel nodded, and the thug revved his drill and drove it into Anita's left ankle; she passed out before the drill could stall inside her ankle joint. Another man stepped forward with a bucket of water and threw it on her, waking her up to her own pain as Black Shirt yanked the drill out of her ankle and revved it again.

'Tell me what you want to know!' yelled Amin.

'You discussed the purpose of the missile range extension?'

'Yes,' said Amin. 'I told him it was designed to strike Tel Aviv.'

The Colonel leaned on his forearms, looking at Amin. 'From *where*?'

Amin paused. He was going to die, he realised, and so was his family.

The thug revved his drill and started working on Anita's right kneecap. She arched against her chair, stifled screams muffled behind the tape. Amin could smell loosened bowels—Javed's.

'Have you told him where you work?' the Colonel persisted.

Amin nodded. 'Yes, they know about Noor Khan.'

'What about this facility we're in? Do the French ask about it?'

Amin's bottom lip trembled. He could no longer look at his son.

'Do they call it anything other than the Pakistan Agricultural Chemical Company?' asked the Colonel, referring to the name on the building.

Amin gulped. 'They call it the MERC.'

'I see,' said the Colonel, his face set in a rictus of disappointment.

He stared at Amin for several long seconds as the muffled sounds of a panicked seven-year-old boy emerged from behind duct tape. Then the Colonel nodded at the man in the black shirt, who moved to Anita, took the drill to full revs and drove the bit directly between her eyes, deep into her forehead. The blood spurted briefly and then ran freely down Anita's pretty face, her limbs briefly jerking as the life ran out of her, her features frozen in agony.

Amin sobbed openly, unable to look at his dead wife. He turned back to his son, whose dark eyes were wide with terror and disbelief. The Colonel nodded and Black Shirt moved to stand in front of Javed. He revved the drill.

'No!' said Amin, as the drill hit the top of Javed's left foot, splattering skin and bone as it disappeared into the flesh. 'Ask me anything. I'm telling the truth. *Please.*'

The Colonel raised his hand briefly to stop Black Shirt. 'The French know the missile is designed to reach Tel Aviv, but do they know from *where*?'

Amin took a deep breath. 'They know it could be fired from Iran.'

The Colonel stared deep into Amin's wet eyes. 'You told the Frenchman that we're working with the Iranians?'

Amin nodded.

'Very good, Amin. Now we're getting somewhere.' He nodded at the thug, who revved his drill and aimed it at Javed's kneecap.

PARIS

Alec de Payns sensed a presence and looked up from his screen. Dominic Briffaut's PA stood in his office doorway. 'Boss wants to see you.'

De Payns stood and followed the middle-aged woman down the corridor to the elevator.

When they arrived at Briffaut's upstairs office she held the door for him.

'This,' said the boss, pushing a piece of paper across his desk.

De Payns looked at the page. It was a report from a source in Pakistan, the romantically named CRS 00218. The source had a robot's name, but he had a 'B' grading inside the DGSE, France's foreign secret service, which signified the highest level of trust and reliability that could be attributed to a human. Only documents, videos and images could be graded 'A'.

The report from CRS 00218 claimed that the missile engineer Amin Sharwaz, thirty-six, his wife—government scientist Anita Sharwaz, thirty-three—and their son Javed Sharwaz, seven, had been killed the previous week by torture at the hands of the ISI, probably with a power drill, at the Pakistan Agricultural Chemical Company (aka the MERC) in Islamabad.

De Payns sat heavily in the visitor's chair, stunned by what he was reading. He flashed back to their final meeting at the bar in Singapore. Amin had been in a hurry to get to the airport because of a family emergency, but there was something more, something almost haunted about the engineer whom he'd come to regard as a friend. His voice had been constricted and there had been little eye contact. De Payns had spent seven years at the DGSE, six of those years in the Y Division—the DGSE's highly secretive section responsible for clandestine activities. He knew how to read people and was very attentive to sources who might be watched over by the ISI. He recalled Amin's use of the French *adieu*—a deliberate usage, since they communicated in English. The finality of the word had not escaped de Payns. Amin was 'off' and de Payns had been incredibly careful leaving that bar in Singapore and making his way back to his hotel. He suspected Amin had spilled to the ISI—told them he was trading missile secrets for a life in Paris.

And now he saw the picture more clearly—Amin's employers had some suspicions, used leverage to get him back to Pakistan, where they'd tortured the family to death. De Payns guessed the wife and child would have been tortured in front of the traitor, prompting him to tell them everything, before he himself was subjected to the slowest and most painful death.

De Payns threw the report on Briffaut's desk and exhaled loudly as he looked at the ceiling. De Payns had dealt with hundreds of sources whose motives were mercenary and who behaved in a purely transactional way. But Amin was different; they'd become close. In a different life they would have been friends.

'I know you liked this one,' said Briffaut, gesturing to the report. 'But back to business—along with the source being dead, you're now blown.'

'You're right,' said de Payns, shaking off the shock. 'I'll start disassembling the Aubrac ID. It'll be disappeared by tomorrow lunchtime. Clean slate.'

Briffaut looked at him, his face expressionless. 'No, don't do that. They mustn't know we have a source on the other side. I'm guessing they'll try to set up a meeting, pretending to be Amin. If they do, we'll put you into a trapped meeting and we'll see who they are.'

In other words, de Payns was going to be used as live bait.

He looked at his boss and nodded.

■

He left early from the Bunker, the headquarters of the DGSE's Y Division in Noisy, a suburb east of Paris. The Bunker was inside an old fort and was deliberately separated from the main HQ of France's foreign intelligence service, the Centre Administratif des Tourelles, colloquially known as the Cat. The Cat was housed in an imposing Napoleonic building on Boulevard Mortier, in the twentieth arrondissement, a total contrast to the cloistered walled fort of the Y Division.

He caught two trains and was outside his apartment building in Montparnasse shortly before 6 p.m., having performed basic hygiene measures to ensure he wasn't being followed. As he let himself into the small but beautiful apartment, he heard the splashing of kids in a bath. Romy intercepted him at the kitchen entrance and gave him a hug, while keeping her food-covered hands off him.

'Excellent timing,' she said. 'Boys are in the bath—can you deal with them?'

Throwing his keys on the counter, de Payns kicked off his shoes and entered the bathroom, where the younger of his sons—four-year-old Oliver—was standing in the bath pointing at Patrick with a loofah, demanding the return of a Smurf toy that the six-year-old was hiding.

'Hi, Dad,' said Patrick, putting on a great show of insouciance about the Smurf.

'Give it to *me*!' yelled the younger boy, wielding the loofah like a sword.

De Payns kneeled, noticing mud on his youngest son's knees.

'I'll take that,' he said, taking the loofah and putting it on the bathroom counter. 'That's your mother's—this is what you need.' He plucked a washcloth from the bath water.

As he started scrubbing Oliver's legs, a terrible dread welled up in him as he felt the tiny, perfect knee of his son. Amin had a son; he'd shown de Payns photos of the boy, flipping through them on his phone as only a doting parent could do, showing twenty-five pictures when four would have sufficed. Holding his own son's leg in his hand, guilt washed through him like a tidal wave. His chest constricted and he felt himself struggling for breath as he fought against the mental image of Amin's son and wife being tortured with a power drill. He leaned back from the bath, hitting his head on the cabinet, and he was aware of Patrick calling out, 'Mum!'

Footsteps, and Romy's face hovered above him, framed with wisps of blonde hair.

'You okay, honey?' she asked, calm but concerned, her cool hand strong on his jaw.

De Payns shook his head almost imperceptibly.

'Really bad?' she asked in a whisper, and de Payns nodded, tears forming in his eyes.

'*Fuck*,' she murmured, and helped him to his feet.

■

He jumped off the Metro at Jussieu, beside the university campus, and found a bar set back from the main tourist strip. It was a low-slung student dive which could do with a clean. He found a table in the unpopulated far corner, and ordered a Scotch. The conversation with Romy could have been handled better, but after his small breakdown there was nothing else he wanted to do but drink until he felt numb.

The middle-aged barmaid brought him the glass and he drained it, relishing the burn in his throat and the hit of smoky flavour. He asked for another, and a beer, and was feeling almost good by the time he headed for the exit. Fishing a pack of Marlboros from his windbreaker, he lit one and observed the street—crowds of students going to restaurants, leaving bars. He walked a block and a half west and found another local bar, this one with an Irish theme, and stood at the end of the mahogany counter. He drank three shots of Jameson and washed it down with a tap beer, trying to find a way through his predicament. How guilty should he feel about the death of Amin's family? And if Javed could fall prey to the ISI, what did that mean for Oliver or Patrick? What about Romy? Who could save them, if not de Payns?

He left the Irish bar and found another—a quiet establishment for quiet drunks. Even the music—Django Reinhardt's greatest hits—was more like musical wallpaper than entertainment. He drank for a few more rounds, three whiskies to one beer, replaying memories of a smart and fun-loving Pakistani engineer who'd thought he was doing the right thing for peace in the Middle East, while also creating a pay-off for his family. And his son had been tortured for it, probably right in front of him.

After the ninth drink, he knew he was shaking his head and mumbling too loud. When the woman behind the bar approached him she raised one finger and de Payns agreed. Only one more.

He left the bar carefully, gasping slightly at the chill air. He lit a Marlboro, observing the streetscape. It looked clean. He couldn't safely return to his family home in this state—drunken mistakes didn't carry any discount; they could get people killed just as easily as the sober mistake. So he picked up a bottle of Johnnie Walker at a market and wandered in a daze until he found himself outside a seedy private hotel. The woman at reception rented him a room and he fell on his face as he opened the door. Collapsing on the bed he felt an emotional weight that the whisky had only sidestepped, not resolved. He wanted another drink but didn't have the energy, and he fell asleep wondering where the off switch for the bedside lamp was.

■

He might have quit his job that week, but for the niggling need for retribution, something felt strongly among the whole Y Division at Noisy. Besides, the entire rationale of the Company—as the DGSE was known to its employees—was to engage in human intelligence, to get close to targets, earn their trust and inveigle oneself into their world. If that meant feeling the wolf's breath on your neck, then that's what you did.

There was an aeronautical engineers convention in Paris in two weeks and de Payns set the meet for the last day of the conference, as usual. Amin's email address was still active and someone was operating it, judging by the response written in precisely the way de Payns had taught Amin. All the communications protocols were correct—Amin must have given them up. Clearly someone at the ISI wanted to keep the liaison operating long enough to get a look at Marcus Aubrac, while the French were keen to see who the Pakistanis sent to photograph—or kill or kidnap—the operative who'd been running Amin. Failures could be turned to their advantage, the French reasoned, so long as they had an officer who was smart and strong enough to play his part.

The Company spent two weeks preparing the Marriott Rive Gauche for the operation, while de Payns stayed away from the hotel. If the Pakistanis came with muscle, they had to be shut down quickly. If they came to photograph Marcus Aubrac, the Company needed its own photographic and eyes-on verification of the ISI operators. The French had to know who they were dealing with before judging how much danger their agent was in and what they were going to do in response. It was a game—one that both sides were playing with their eyes wide open. De Payns and Briffaut had decided there was a high probability that the Pakistanis knew that the French were aware that Amin was dead. Heck, thought de Payns, they might have deliberately planted the news with the source named CRS 00218 in order to get a good look at de Payns. The mission team would be positioned carefully to look for the Pakistani watchers and undertake their own counter-surveillance. But more important to de Payns was knowing that his mission team would foil a kidnap or an assassination, even as he walked into the wolf's mouth.

The mission was complicated for de Payns not only by the friendship he'd developed with Amin but by the hotel's proximity to his family's apartment in Montparnasse. The Marriott Rive Gauche was on Boulevard Saint-Jacques, only a ten-minute walk from Patrick's school. It felt too close to home, especially given how ruthlessly the ISI had exploited Amin's greatest weakness—his family. Usually de Payns operated overseas; the prospect of engaging with the ISI so close to home had him on edge.

He watched a Netflix movie with Romy the night before the operation, his bare feet on the coffee table and nursing a glass of riesling. He didn't say much—usually he kept up a running commentary, which Romy would quell with a few *shut up*s. She was doing a PhD on political economics, with a complicated thesis about east–west wealth discrepancies within Europe, and de Payns would usually tease her by attributing a Marxist or Anarcho-syndicalist motive to the most stupid character in a given movie. If he was having fun, he could drive her to throw something at him. But tonight he was nervy and she knew it. Rather than ask him about it, she switched off the TV set and took him to bed shortly after nine o'clock.

■

They sent an email after lunch on the final day of the conference, and the stand-in for Amin texted the burner phone number about ten minutes later. De Payns returned the text, suggesting they meet at Café L'Ecir, not far from the hotel, at 5 p.m. De Payns caught the Metro in from the north-west, making three changes of train, before emerging at Glacière Metro station at 4.45. He climbed the stairs to the northern side of the Boulevard Saint-Jacques and walked towards the meet through the early office-leavers.

He was wired up with radio equipment, the battery pack and transmitter strapped to his ankle, wired into a receiver for the earpiece that was attached under his shirt. He put in his earplug and pressed the 'talk' button in his pants pocket.

'Y—check?'

'Y—good copy,' came the reply.

Satisfied the system was working, he signed off with 'Aguilar—copy' and then went to radio silence.

De Payns' team was sitting in vans, planted in other shops and sitting in the cafe as patrons. When operating inside French territory, the Company usually handed over to the DGSI, the French internal security services, equivalent to the FBI or MI5. However on short operations the DGSE would usually work undeclared, as they were on this day. The DGSI were more like the police, and they operated with an arrest and prosecution mandate, whereas the Company might monitor a terrorist for a year and never interdict. Besides, the paperwork required to involve the domestic security services was too laborious for what amounted to a two-hour operation. De Payns relied instead on three of his regular mission team operators—tough people whom he'd worked with in Beirut, Damascus and Cairo. He knew they would intercede if the Pakistanis turned nasty.

He strolled in the late afternoon sunlight that streamed through the overhead trees, passing a Franprix supermarket on his right, aware of a team around him though he was unable to see them.

Stopping at the pedestrian crossing, de Payns caught a glimpse of the cafe through the trees and walked towards it. His senses were on high alert despite his calm demeanour. Agreeing to take part in an operation so close to his family was difficult to justify to himself—and it would be impossible to explain to Romy if she knew.

De Payns found a table inside with a view of the door, the street and the outside tables, and ordered a Kronenbourg. The clock above the bar showed 5 p.m. exactly.

His beer arrived and he acted like any other customer, looking at his phone and sipping at his drink. He was too well trained to look for his team. Even a quick glance of recognition would be picked up by an experienced watcher. He waited and he drank in a painful charade of waiting for a dead man—a man he'd liked—but no one showed. This wasn't unexpected. The Pakistanis had probably never intended for someone to meet de Payns in person; what the ISI wanted was his face on camera.

The earpiece crackled briefly. 'For Y from Jéjé,' came Jéjé's voice. 'I have two guys at the north corner dressed in blue jeans, cheap leather shoes, dark jackets. Looks like they're waiting.'

'Copy from Danny,' came Danny's voice. 'One grey Peugeot in front of the cafe, dark windows, rego 648 RGU 75. One guy waiting inside and looking. Nothing else.'

De Payns didn't respond or change his demeanour. He'd spent half his adult life being followed.

At 5.21 p.m., with no one approaching him in the cafe, he left and walked to the Saint-Jacques Metro. He took two lines, emerging in the middle of Paris. He found a seat in a cafe on the edge of the Place de la République and waited there for ten minutes, then started to walk north-east, counting in his head. When he reached two hundred and sixty, he climbed the stairs with the tourists, turned right at the top and jumped on the back of a motorbike which started immediately and sped off into the traffic.

After ten minutes of expert riding through selected choke points and one-way streets, he was dropped at the Champ de Mars, the large park stretching from the Eiffel Tower to the École Militaire. He walked across to its south-east corner and descended to the Metro, taking two trains to the Gare d'Austerlitz area of Paris. It was almost dark when he emerged, and he walked straight to the Company's changeover house to the west of the station's impressive facade, in a secondary street tucked behind a precinct of bars and restaurants. He walked up to the apartment, opened it using the combination lock, and punched in his security code on the keypad inside the door. It looked like a typical Paris apartment, with a kitchen, living room and two bedrooms, one of which contained the lockers used by the Company's Y Division operatives. De Payns opened his locker and deposited his watch, phone and wallet in the manila envelope with *Marcus Aubrac* printed on a white label. As he decompressed, he could feel the nerves buzzing inside him and he leaned forward with his arms on the locker, breathing deeply to gain composure before stripping off his Aubrac clothes and stashing them in the locker. He took a quick shower, working through every step of the operation and every person he saw. It was possible there was no one from the ISI in or around that cafe. It was possible the whole thing was a psychological ploy, the Pakistanis signalling that they'd already resolved their traitor problem and could now afford to play games with the vaunted DGSE, right there in Paris, on their home turf. Maybe those men in the car were engaged on some other business entirely? Where had they gone after de Payns left? Were they the only ones? Were they official spies, attached to the Pakistan embassy, or were they 'undeclareds', living anonymously in Paris or flown in directly from Islamabad? He cycled faces in his mind, counted steps and audited his memory for mistakes. He pushed himself towards paranoia without getting lost in it, knowing that extreme attention to detail was the difference between success and failure.

Dressed in his jeans, windbreaker and running shoes, he was Alec de Payns once again, and he stepped into the night via an alternative door, leading to the street behind the building, and caught a train west through the fifth arrondissement and into Montparnasse. As he climbed the stairs to the apartment, he made a decision—when he stepped through the door, the Amin operation was over and so was his guilt. Tomorrow was a new day.

He opened his door and smelled fish curry.

'That you, Alec?' came Romy's voice from the kitchen.

'Hi, honey,' said de Payns, a smile spreading across his face. 'I'm home.'

. . . TWO YEARS LATER

CHAPTER
ONE

As far as workplaces go, it wasn't bad. The Mediterranean in July, ten hours out of Cagliari, sailing to Palermo. A glass of beer in each hand and weaving through a gaggle of Germans to get back to his table. De Payns ducked around a dancing drunk who was Living la Vida Loca and arrived at his table. Michael Lambardi looked up from his corner of the ferry's top deck bar, grabbed his Peroni and muttered *santé* before his moustache cut the head like a guillotine.

'That's better.' Lambardi smiled, setting his glass on the table.

The early evening was starting to colour the sky purple and the ferry smelled of sunscreen and spilled beer. The bar contained the contrasts of what Europe had become—loud, happy Germans at the neighbouring table, hand-wringing Belgians trying to lip-read the news on a muted TV, and a couple of sullen Turkish gentlemen hunched at a table by the windows, making a big point of not drinking. De Payns wasn't a great fan of the Teutons, but they at least knew what a bar was for.

'So, Alain,' said Lambardi, as de Payns leaned back in his white plastic chair, 'will these documents work?'

De Payns looked at Lambardi. 'They'll work.'

'Hundred per cent?' asked the Italian.

'Just like the first ones,' said de Payns, taking a sip of his own beer.

Lambardi was an Italian migration agent in his early forties, with a body that couldn't decide if it was heavily muscled or going to seed. De Payns had procured for Lambardi a bunch of Croatian ID cards a month ago, which gave the Italian's clients unimpeded passage into France and Europe. As an *officier traitant* of France's external intelligence service, de Payns was trying to get close enough to his new friend to find out who Lambardi was dealing with and why so many of his clients ended up in France with the smell of Semtex in their prayer mats. He'd infiltrated the Italian's world and joined him drinking around the bars of the Sicilian capital, helping him out where he could, building affinity and listening to the struggles of Italian men when they divorce.

Earning Lambardi's trust wasn't so hard, because with his Marseille-based cover as Alain Dupuis, a migration consultant, and his access to travel documents, de Payns was of use to the Italian. They both liked drinking and looking at pretty women, which were common pastimes in Palermo during summer. But de Payns felt the danger of this assignment. One of Lambardi's clients, according to the Company, was Sayef Albar, a splinter group of AQIM, the North African branch of al-Qaeda. They were resourced and organised and had a homicidal hatred of France. They'd behead de Payns' children in front of him if they knew his real identity. Lambardi wouldn't fare well, either.

De Payns casually scanned the bar and looked out the window, where a couple of Japanese kids climbed on the deck rail of the ferry only to be slapped off by their mother.

Lambardi cleared his throat. 'The reason I ask, Alain, is that, as you know, my next traveller—'

'And his friends,' de Payns interjected.

'And his friends,' agreed Lambardi, 'don't look European, so the Croatian cards . . .'

De Payns smiled. The Croatian ID cards were top-shelf forgeries, accepted at any EU port. But de Payns had something better for the Italian.

'I took the liberty,' said de Payns. 'The package waiting for me in Palermo includes five French passports.'

Lambardi paused, doubtful.

De Payns leaned in. 'I'm serious. Your clients can land in Paris as French citizens.'

De Payns was playing on greed. The fees Lambardi could charge for the passports would override paranoia. And paranoia was relevant—AQIM was not an outfit to double-cross. But while greed would get Lambardi on the hook, coercion would be how they'd reel him in. When it came time to perform the *devoilement*—the moment when a target is told that he now works for Paris—Lambardi had to be right where the French secret services wanted him. He had to be shitting himself. When de Payns' team had photographs and video of Lambardi receiving those passports and selling them to AQIM, the Italian would have nowhere to turn. He'd be scared of going to prison in Italy, but even more scared of what the terrorists would do if they saw those pictures.

Lambardi turned his attention to his smartphone, stood and weaved to the toilet. De Payns crossed his legs and poured his beer into the carpet beside his right ankle. He had to stay sharp. As he inveigled his way further into Lambardi's life, he had expected Sayef Albar security to emerge. He assumed those two Turks in the bar were watching him. They had probably staked out de Payns' office, a serviced space two blocks back from Palermo's harbour, although he hadn't yet detected a tail when he took a room in one of the scores of private hotels in Old Palermo. There were so many ten-room hotels in the city that he could dodge the tails by hopping from one to another, if he was careful. And Alec de Payns was careful like a cat.

Lambardi's apartment was another story. It was in the city's west, and the Sayef Albar security people had an irregular overwatch on the flat and were probably intercepting Lambardi's calls and emails. De Payns fully expected that when he tried to get Lambardi alone at his apartment and have him filmed accepting the French passports, the terrorists would be listening with enhanced audio in the neighbouring apartment or have two men in a van on the street. The French mission team supporting Operation Falcon knew there were no bugs in Lambardi's apartment; they'd checked when they set up the cameras. But there might be an emergency signal system for Lambardi to use if he detected a threat. And although the French mission teams had access to the best techs, de Payns had been unable to get his hands on Lambardi's phone to have it checked and perhaps trapped.

De Payns was mindful of Sayef Albar but he was not overly worried. A man he knew well was sitting in the far corner of the bar, chatting with German tourists. His real name was Guillaume Tibet, but in the intelligence world he was known as Shrek. He was short and solid and his hand-to-hand skills came from Wing Chun kung fu, making him devastating in a fight. The fact that he'd been plucked from an academic and writing career to join the external intelligence services meant he exuded an air of bespectacled innocence.

Shrek was only one part of the mission team—the rest of its members would be waiting at the Palermo ferry terminal and they'd leapfrog one another in vans, on foot and on a motorbike along the route to Michael Lambardi's apartment. If Lambardi—codenamed 'Commodore' by the Company—wanted another drink, the mission team would deploy people around the bars to check for Sayef Albar operatives. If Lambardi wanted to go straight home, the team would coalesce around his apartment, watching the terrorists' surveillance. The whole operation would work like a ballet and be undetectable even to experienced field people.

To ensure the set-up was clean, de Payns had to wait for final confirmation from the mission team in Palermo. De Payns had received a last-minute request to join Lambardi for a meeting in Cagliari, and so there'd been no communication with his team since he'd left Marseille to travel to the Sardinian capital. The mission team used *démarqués* phones, purchased in shitty suburbs with no ID attached, to coordinate among themselves. But once in the field, the support team had no electronic connection with the phone of 'Alain': this phone had been registered with the false Alain ID and was connected only with the legend that went with the identity. When an operation was in-field, the two different worlds—the support team and de Payns—never intersected. There was no communication between them.

De Payns had other ways of contacting his team. Called *liaisons clandestines*, they included dead letterboxes and unobservable visual signals. One of these involved *gommettes*, or stickers—on a wall-mounted poster that advertised Peroni, the support team would leave a round white sticker in the final half-hour before the ship docked in Sicily. If the white *gommette* was on that poster, the op was on.

Lambardi reappeared at the table, and for a split second de Payns thought he caught a pair of eyes look at him then dart away. They belonged to a tall, swarthy man in his mid-thirties who was entering the restrooms that Lambardi had just exited. *Just the blue rats*, de Payns assured himself, a reference to the paranoia that can haunt field operators. The man was most likely a polite Pakistani who didn't want to make eye contact.

The revs lowered on the ferry engines and the vessel tipped forward. De Payns took a quick breath and glanced over his shoulder at the beer poster.

In the bottom right-hand corner was a white *gommette*. Palermo loomed and the game was on. Falcon was go.

CHAPTER TWO

Michael Lambardi wanted to drink, so they headed for Bar Luca, their regular watering hole. They dodged tourists who were drinking and lounging around in the famous glow as dusk settled on Old Palermo. The day's breeze had died down and the warm air was infused with seafood, wine and music—typical of the Mediterranean. De Payns sensed Shrek behind him, but didn't look, as they worked their way through the summer crowds.

Lambardi turned to him. 'Let's do this tonight,' he said, then moved with the foot traffic across Via Francesco Crispi into the bar and restaurant district.

'Do what?' de Payns asked, feeling the reassuring weight of the CZ 9mm handgun in the outer pocket of his Adidas pack. He didn't make a habit of carrying arms when operating under an assumed identity, but the trip from Cagliari to Palermo with Lambardi had been a spontaneous decision and the support team hadn't had time to establish the usual safeguards. So he'd collected the CZ from a dead drop at Cagliari's Bonario cemetery before meeting Lambardi at a cafe with some rich Nigerian clients.

'The passports,' said Lambardi, breathless as he marched across Crispi.

De Payns accelerated and got alongside the Italian's right shoulder, keeping his voice low as they passed sidewalk tables loaded with French and Austrian drinkers. 'I don't have them on me, Michael. They're at the office.'

'We'll drop by,' said Lambardi. Spying a gap between the taxis and minicabs, he darted across the road.

'You're slow for a Frenchman,' Lambardi teased when de Payns joined him on the other side several seconds later, to the accompaniment of a loud dose of Sicilian horns. Lambardi set off again, veering left down a street on which waiters and accordion players smoked cigarettes outside cafes loud with tourists—he was heading for de Payns' office.

De Payns carried no comms or tracking device. He would just have to follow where Lambardi led, trusting in his mission team to have his back.

'We can settle this tonight,' said Lambardi as they turned into the side street where de Payns' office was located. This was not the way de Payns had planned to do the handover. The operation was intended to culminate at Lambardi's apartment, where de Payns would deliver the passports and record the footage.

'I thought we were going to the bar,' said de Payns.

Lambardi kept walking. 'We'll get the passports and I'll get the money for you.'

De Payns grabbed the Italian by the shoulder. 'You know how it goes, Michael. We do it my way, or we don't do it.'

Lambardi shrugged his hand away. 'You'll get three million euros for those passports, but I don't carry that kind of money on me.'

'So what's the point in fetching the passports now?' asked de Payns as they neared the suite of offices.

'Murad will have the money,' Lambardi told him. 'He'll love this deal.'

De Payns was startled. 'Murad?!' he hissed, not wanting to say the name of the Sayef Alber commander too loudly. 'He's in Palermo *tonight*?'

'Sure,' said Lambardi.

'Where are you meeting him?' asked de Payns.

'You kidding me?' the Italian slurred. 'He finds me.'

■

Bar Luca was a bar-cafe in Palermo's old town that had started life as a wine merchant's warehouse six hundred years ago. It was dimly lit, low in the ceiling and heavy on the beams. But the lighting meant its sandstone walls glowed golden. Hanging from the ceiling beams were Knights Templar and Knights of St John paraphernalia, a tribute to the era when the fighting orders ruled the eastern Mediterranean. De Payns scanned the bar as he took a seat at Lambardi's favourite table, in front of the 1960s Wurlitzer jukebox. When they'd first visited Bar Luca more than a month ago, de Payns had panicked slightly, thinking Lambardi knew his real name and its obvious connection to the Knights Templar—Hugh de Payns, founder and first Grand Master of the Order of the Knights Templar, back in the 1100s. But Lambardi wasn't interested in Crusader lineage nor the de Payns family's part in it. He was there for the table service—the owner, Luca, employed good-looking ladies and Lambardi liked one of them in particular.

Lambardi waved at the bar for two beers as de Payns put his Adidas pack between his feet. He was reassured by the presence of the CZ but not comfortable about the passports he was now carrying. He'd managed to keep Lambardi out of his office, insisting that they meet back at the bar. He'd collected the passports and returned to Bar Luca, but he felt vulnerable knowing Murad was around. Still, despite the risks, he was reluctant to call off tonight's operation. The chance to trap Lambardi and lure

Murad into the open was not to be missed. He would normally have used his time alone in the office to warn the support team with a visual signal—a light or something reflective—or ask for a physical contact with the chief of the support team, which would require an orange *gommette* or a hand in his hair. However, the stop at the office had not been planned and de Payns had to hope that the support team would understand something was wrong and provide him with what backup they could.

De Payns scanned the bar, looking for threats. The two Turks from the ferry bar had a table beside the door—they were most certainly Sayef Albar heavies. Margaux, the curvy waitress, was laughing at Lambardi's attempts to charm her. She was way above Lambardi's pay grade but de Payns hadn't told him that yet. Neither had Margaux, who liked the big tips he gave her.

Keeping a smile on his face, de Payns walked to the jukebox, slapping the pockets of his Levi's for change, which allowed him to turn back. 'Any coins?' he asked Lambardi, aware that in a sea of drinking tourists, two sets of dark, sober eyes were aimed at him.

Lambardi leaned back in his chair and tried to get his fingers into the pocket of his shorts. As he pulled out a handful of coins, de Payns saw movement to his left—the tall Turk was on his feet and walking towards the toilets. With his gaze focused on Lambardi, de Payns watched from the corner of his eye as the tall Turk, his burgundy shirt worn untucked to hide his handgun, paused at the start of the corridor where the toilets were and spoke with someone concealed in the shadows. De Payns moved back to his seat and the tall Turk broke away from his conversation, turned to face Lambardi and cocked his head. Michael Lambardi had been summoned.

De Payns' heart rate jumped slightly. This was the first open contact between Lambardi and his handlers—the Italian knew who they were.

Lambardi stood and leaned in to de Payns. 'Got those passports, Alain?'

De Payns breathed out, keeping an unconcerned look on his face while his mind did cartwheels. The operation that would see the passports handed over and the transaction videotaped at Lambardi's apartment was not going to happen. It was going down now, at Bar Luca, and it was being run by the Turks and someone hiding in the corridor. The CZ was an option for de Payns, but only ever in self-defence. The French secret services didn't do shoot-outs. The DGSE's trademark was cool, ruthless, untraceable.

De Payns lifted the Adidas bag onto his lap and patted it. 'Right here.'

Lambardi's tone was apologetic. 'I have to go alone.'

De Payns looked over at the tall Turk.

'Come on,' the migration agent urged. 'By the time this is over, we'll have three million euros, my friend. I promise.'

De Payns didn't like it. He shook his head slowly, wondering how to turn the situation around without revealing himself. As he paused, the main door of the bar opened and Shrek, his face hidden by a blue cap pulled low, entered. He was not a tall or handsome man and was very good at seeming innocuous.

De Payns avoided looking at his colleague and kept his eyes on Lambardi. 'You really want to do this, Michael?' he asked. 'You're a little drunk.'

'Pfft!' said Lambardi. 'You French are so serious.'

In his peripheral vision, de Payns could see Shrek leaning on the bar and ordering a drink. To Lambardi he said, 'It has to be tonight? It feels rushed.'

'It's okay for you, Alain, but I need the money.'

'You need it this badly?'

Lambardi reached for the backpack. 'Try getting divorced in Italy. They nail you to a fucking cross, *amico*.'

De Payns pulled back slightly and unzipped his pack, revealing the yellow manila envelope with the French passports. His training emphasised that an *officier traitant*—an 'OT'—always kept control. No target ever led a DGSE operative around by the nose.

'We do this together,' said de Payns in a low voice, 'or I don't do it at all. Tell your friends I'm an arrogant French bastard.'

The tall Turk bristled with impatience. Lambardi, looking desperate, said, 'Please, Alain. I need this, or you and I are in big trouble.'

De Payns drew Lambardi's small leather waist pack towards him across the table, folded the manila envelope and pushed it into the bag. But he didn't return the waist pack.

'Once they have what they want, you have no leverage,' said de Payns. 'You tell them I don't do business in bar urinals with people I don't know. They can give you the money, and you and I can do our deal at your flat. I know and trust you, Michael. But this Murad? He's your problem, *mon pote*.'

Lambardi chewed his lip. The tall Turk edged forward.

'I'm telling you, Michael, if they are serious, they'll respect what you're saying. Unless you want me to have a word?'

As de Payns made to stand, Lambardi looked like he was going to shit himself.

'No, no,' said the Italian. 'I'll handle it! You stay there.'

Lambardi walked into the hallway with his minder and de Payns felt the shorter Turk eyeballing him from his perch by the main door. By the way he was seated, de Payns assumed there was a handgun in the small of his back. De Payns sensed movement from Shrek at the bar, his right hand moving to his right eye and scratching once beneath it. Then he took off his cap and placed it on the bar. The hair on de Payns' neck stood on end. Shrek had just given the escape and evade signal—the eye scratch meant, 'I see you', and the cap off the head simply translated as 'no more cover'. In other words: *This is over, get the fuck out.*

De Payns raised his beer and scanned the bar—who was in the game and who wasn't? His body was coiled, Creedence Clearwater Revival asked, *Have you ever seen . . .* and Margaux approached the table with a cloth. De Payns stood and, with Margaux as cover, lifted his pack and placed Lambardi's leather bag inside it. As he turned towards the main entrance, the shorter Turk rose and blocked his way, torso angled for quick access to his handgun.

De Payns turned and headed instead for the restroom hallway, holding his pack in front him, keeping the 9mm CZ in easy reach. As he moved into the hallway he could hear the rustling of the Turk's footsteps directly behind him. There were two toilet doors on his left, but it was the glass door at the end of the corridor that had de Payns' attention—through it, in the shadows of the rear loading area, there was movement. And in the door's reflection he could see the Turk's hand going to the small of his back. De Payns turned to deal with it, but as he did a hand gripped the Turk's jawbone from behind and a fist slammed into the man's neck. The Turk dropped to the floor and Shrek turned and walked straight back into the bar, as if returning from a quick visit to the toilet. Blood pumped from a pen-sized hole in the Turk's neck as he went through his death throes.

De Payns turned and quickly walked to the end of the hallway, his heart thumping and his hand inside the pack, still unsure what the mission team had seen. Why was the operation being called off? He pushed through the glass door and into a small loading area. A silver-grey Mercedes SUV was parked side on, wheels on the kerb, its dark windows obscuring the occupants. Was that Lambardi in the back seat? De Payns couldn't confirm it. As he approached the Mercedes it rocked. There was a popping sound and then the rear window of the car darkened. Someone on the inside had lost a lot of blood and tissue. De Payns' hand went instinctively to the CZ as the Mercedes revved and accelerated out of the car park, a face staring from the front passenger window as it sped away.

De Payns was stunned, the adrenaline pumping, breaths coming short and sharp. He looked back through the bar door to where the Turk was flat on his back in the hallway, as yet undiscovered. He threw the pack over his shoulder and set off quickly into the night, joining the throng of tourists in the early summer evening. He was dressed for it, in jeans, polo shirt and a pack, his black cap reducing silhouette recognition that watchers might pick up. His heart pounded as crickets chirped and accordion music drifted on the sweet evening breeze, with the smell of marinara and cigarettes. He scanned parked vans and glanced at reflections in plate-glass windows, watching for the watchers. His spatial awareness was finely honed as he aimed for a landmark a few blocks inland, where he could sanitise himself with an IS, an *itinéraire de sécurité*. This would clear him from the mission zone and let him know if he was being followed. Having quit his mission zone, he would head straight to his exfiltration, planned back in Paris. Just before leaving Sicily, he would put his *gommette* at the emergency exfiltration *plan de support*—usually a public display such as a bus stop advertisement—which would be checked later by the support team to make sure he'd left the country. Only when they sighted de Payns' *gommette* would the team also leave. No *gommette* would mean something happened to him, and they would stay to find out what. If he could get off this island in one piece, his next port of call would be the debriefing in Paris.

As he walked south on the Via Principe di Scordia, an image dominated his thoughts—the face that had peered from the front window of the Mercedes. De Payns was pretty sure it was the polite Pakistani man who'd waited for Lambardi to leave the WC on the ferry from Sardinia. He'd been on that ferry, and therefore he'd been in Cagliari. And he was clearly the boss.

As he calmed his breathing, two things became clear. Michael Lambardi was dead. And de Payns had just survived a run-in with Murad.

CHAPTER
THREE

De Payns walked south of the restaurant precinct and past a car dealership on Via Roma. He took his Nokia from inside his pack, removed the battery and put the SIM in his back pocket. Via Roma suited him because it was one-way for traffic, making it hard for cars to follow him and allowing him to focus on pedestrians.

He walked a zigzag route that would eventually bring him to the Church of St Peter and St Paul three blocks west. The ramifications of the night's events were serious—two people dead in a popular public place. One of them was face up on the floor outside the toilets of a bar. That would bring the police and, because Sicily was an island, the airports and ports could be shut down if the police thought it was a professional job. And what about Sayef Albar? If they had the two Turkish thugs on foot and a vehicle waiting out the back of Bar Luca, then they had at least five people in the field, probably six including Murad. De Payns reckoned that translated to at least two vehicles doing the rounds of the streets and checking out hotels and bars.

Murad had known about those passports and had accelerated the timeline to avoid the trap de Payns had set. If de Payns and his team were worried about walking into a trap, that's what they would have done—change the meet, change the parameters, change the time, take control and see what happens. But why was Lambardi killed? Either Murad had been spooked when de Payns walked into the loading zone, or they were always going to kill the migration agent. And if they were always going to kill him, did that mean the Company's mission was blown?

The exit plan was to cleanse himself and put his sticker on the *plan de support*—a noticeboard at the ferry terminal—before the ferry departed. But if there was a leak from inside the Company, as he now suspected, the *plan de support* was compromised. To go ahead with it would bring the watchers and hinder his exit. Instead, he decided, he'd move through an IS to clear himself of tails. If he still wasn't satisfied, he'd go into hiding and ask the Company in Paris to exfiltrate him.

A group of Dutch tourists strolled past him and a slightly intoxicated straggler smiled and said something in English. De Payns smiled back and answered in French. The Dutchman went straight into perfect French, telling de Payns about the bars they'd just visited and the seafood restaurant they were heading for. They made small talk, de Payns walking on the building side of the footpath, giving him a view of the approaching traffic. No Mercedes, no tall Turkish thug.

The group closed on the crossroads of Roma and Cavour, and de Payns turned left onto a four-lane, leafy boulevard with two-hundred-year-old buildings on each side. The older ones didn't exceed four storeys, while some of the newer apartment buildings were higher. American jazz floated from an old apartment above him while Algerian rap bellowed from a passing car. Via Roma was bathed in a golden glow, the last embers of the Mediterranean sunset illuminating the street. Ahead he saw a silver Mercedes 4x4 flashing across the street, but it didn't slow. There were thousands of silver SUVs driving around Europe in the dusk, de Payns reminded himself; it could have belonged to anyone.

He walked north for twenty minutes and ducked into one of Old Palermo's medieval lanes, which became narrower and more winding as he progressed. Vespas and Japanese scooters were parked against ancient apartment walls, and he pricked his ears for the echo of footsteps behind him, but all he could hear was the blaring of a television and women raising their voices.

At the end of the lane was a small square with a narrow church fronting it. He'd discovered this place during a walk he'd taken six weeks earlier, when familiarising himself with the city and looking for a good place to do an IS. It was perfect for what he wanted—the front door was ajar and he walked into a candlelit church. A priest in short sleeves spoke with two elderly women off to his right, and de Payns kept walking along the left of the pews, through a side door and down the corridor to another door. He opened it and looked out to a street on the next block. Many old churches in European cities covered one block, but they'd been built around over the centuries. Once you'd passed through and were out the other side, you could disappear into the surrounding streets while the followers in vehicles had to go the long way around the block. If walking followers really wanted to stick with you, they were walking through a *point de passage obligé*—a choke point they had to move through—and were hence declaring themselves.

Palermo was in darkness as de Payns emerged onto the street and immediately crossed the road to enter another small street. His IS validated that he was not being followed, and he walked eastwards for ten minutes, towards the port. The bars became louder, the footpath patrons drunker as he neared the bay. He veered south slightly to a 'rupture' route at the Palermo Centrale. De Payns had discovered the 1870s railway station as he'd walked to the Botanical Gardens to assess a huge Moreton Bay fig tree used as a dead drop. He liked the Centrale because there was an entry that passed through a post office—creating another *passage obligé.*

The post office was lit up although the services booths seemed to be closed. De Payns pushed through the doors and walked across the lino floor towards the exit. As he did, he kept his peripheral vision alert for followers and parking cars. He seemed clean. The exit took him directly onto the Centrale platforms and he walked down one towards the police station in the main building. There were no more than thirty people milling around but it was enough to create a distraction for a follower, when you factored in the alignment of the pillars. He stuck with the flow of people and, having passed the police station entry, turned hard left into the main entrance foyer. From there he skipped down the main steps and disappeared into the dark streets, heading east for the ferry terminal and for home.

He paused at the pedestrian traffic lights at the impressive boulevard of Via Crispi. To his left, the hulking dark blue shape of a ferry loomed at the terminal. He asked a woman walking beside him with two children if it was the Naples ferry and she confirmed that it was, adding that it departed in thirty minutes.

De Payns veered off to the right as the pack of tourists moved left onto a large concrete apron leading towards the ferry. Keeping to the shadows, he walked towards the berths south of the ferry terminal. The lights played on the smooth water and de Payns smelled diesel and sewage. It was always like this—when he was anxious, he smelled *everything.*

An African man fished and smoked on the wharf, a bottle of wine keeping him company. De Payns walked away from him, southwards around the curved quay. When a large trawler was between him and the fisherman, de Payns took the pieces of his phone from the pack and threw them in the harbour. He paused and positioned himself for a *see but not seen* look around his environment. It was important not to look furtive. A disco beat pounded out of a bar and bounced on the water. He walked south again, broke down the CZ and disposed of it in separate pieces into the greasy Mediterranean.

He kept walking away from the fisherman towards a rubbish bin in the shadows back from the quayside. He pulled two of the passports from his pack, tore them up as best he could given the plastic and the chips in them, and deposited the pieces in the bin. With his eyes on the fisherman he walked towards another bin fifty metres up the wharf. There he destroyed two more passports. Just twenty metres further along was a commercial dumpster, in near darkness. He ripped up the last passport and threw it in the dumpster, along with the envelope and Lambardi's waist pack. He'd usually make a better spread of a destroyed document, making it almost impossible to find or identify, but time was short—he had to get on that ferry.

He walked back along the quay to the ticket office, emerging into the fragrant evening air a few minutes later with his ticket. From there he headed to the large timetable board affixed to the side of the administration building. De Payns reached into his pack and grabbed a red sticker with a cross marked through it, then placed the red sticker at the bottom right of the timetable. The support team would see that sticker and understand that de Payns was okay, but the operation was paused and he was leaving.

De Payns looked over his shoulder as he walked across the wharf apron towards the ferry. He could see a slow-moving vehicle's roof above the concrete bollards that surrounded the port precinct. A loudspeaker made a beeping sound, followed by a male Italian voice making an announcement; then the same voice in English announced the night sailing to Naples. Passengers were advised to please board the vessel immediately.

As he reached the ferry's stern ramp, the seamen were readying to raise it and commence the night sailing. Relieved, he was about to board when above him an old Italian leaned over a railing and barked at the seamen to stop. De Payns glanced to where the older man was pointing, and saw a vehicle pulling to a stop a hundred metres or so across the wharf apron. A door opened, and the top of a man's head was visible. Then he was hurrying towards the ferry, accompanied by two more men. De Payns tried not to stare but he needed to identify them—they looked local. Probably not Sayef Albar, he concluded, but maybe police?

He turned away, handed his ticket to the purser, walked up the ramp and turned back to the quay, where his elevated position revealed that the two men were younger, and they were hugging the older man in an affectionate farewell. The older man turned and walked up the ramp, carrying an overnight bag.

As the stern ramp started lifting into place, de Payns felt slightly relieved but entirely unrelaxed.

CHAPTER
FOUR

The cabin was an outside double, giving him a view of the starboard decks through a window rather than a porthole. De Payns hadn't realised there was a choice, but now counted himself lucky to have a cabin with an alternative exit should someone come through the door.

Having showered, he sat in the darkness, sitting on one of the single beds but leaning against the wall so he could see the deck when he looked sideways through the curtains. The arrival time in Naples was shortly before 7 a.m., and he was sure no one from that silver Mercedes had followed him onto the ferry. If they really thought Alain Dupuis was a problem, the Sayef Albar operators would use their limited resources to surveil Palermo's hotels and the airport—the ferry terminus at Naples would probably not be a priority. Taking the ferry gave him the night to think through what he was going to do. He had no phone, no credit card, no gun. The red sticker with the cross through it was a signal from de Payns—he was on his own, expected to reappear at the Bunker without Company assistance.

He pulled his pack from the floor and turned on the cabin's bedside light. He upturned the pack and an apple and a muesli bar in its wrapper fell onto the grey blanket, along with his wallet and sunglasses, a half-pack of Marlboro Lights and a cheap plastic lighter. He took two bites of the apple and, as he chewed, stood and looked in the mirror of the vanity basin. He was fairly well preserved for thirty-eight; the pale eyes still lively, the sandy blond hair short and swept back and his skin still glowing with outdoors activity rather than being ravaged by the sun. His bare torso showed a couple of scars, and his arms and back contained a map of fights and high school rugby accidents etched into the skin. The white line down his left forearm came from the surgeons' attempt to put his shattered arm together after a motorbike accident in his last year of boarding school, and the wounds at the base of his spine were reminders of the surgery he underwent after injuring his back as a fighter pilot in the air force. But for someone who was almost forty, he thought, he had at least retained enough muscle to look after himself in a fight.

His wife, Romy, used to tell him that she liked his youthfulness, which she was sure came from him doing what he enjoyed. By which she meant his time in the air force flying fighter jets. By which she meant she was sick of his subsequent intelligence career and the strain it was putting on their marriage. By which she meant, he wasn't so boyish anymore, which was basically true. He sometimes wondered how he'd got to be like this—reserving his light-heartedness and laughter for when he was drinking with his colleagues, the only people he truly felt safe with. He'd heard this was an occupational hazard but he hadn't known what it meant until he realised that his DGSE buddies were the ones who saw the real him while his wife was seeing someone else. It was a professional trade-off that ended in suicide for some and alcoholism for others. Divorce was the rule, not the exception.

He finished the apple, grabbed his smokes and made for the deck outside his room. He torched the cigarette and exhaled the smoke like he was blowing his stress into the sea. The warm breeze from

Africa washed over him; the swish of the sea against the ferry was hypnotic. To his left, a bunch of drunk English tourists hee-hawed over something on a smartphone. He smoked methodically, relaxed by the rolling swell and the fragrance of the Med in summer. It had been a long road to get here, and he wasn't even that old. His journey into the Company started after the Kosovo War, when he was based at Villacoublay Air Base outside Paris, flying special forces and intelligence personnel into the Balkans to find war criminals. It was an uncertain time in his life, when he'd left fighter jets because of his back injury and was trying to establish a new reputation in the TBM 700—a powerful, nimble turboprop plane that could take off and land on very short air strips. He flew without name or insignia on his suit. He flew low at night, without flight plans in VFR mode, relying on sight rather than instruments, sometimes with the IFF identification transponder switched off, or its 'Mode C' deactivated, meaning the control towers on the ground couldn't ascertain his altitude. His destination would often be relayed to him only after they'd cleared the Adriatic. He was told to ignore the usual rules of aviation, and de Payns once landed in three feet of snow at Sarajevo, at two in the morning, without clearance and in total darkness. It was dangerous, stressful work and he loved it.

He ended up in intelligence because of the general who was the passenger on so many of his clandestine flights. The general was conducting a DGSE operation to find Serbian war criminals, and one of the flights involved a top-secret meeting in Podgorica. De Payns smiled now at the passing sea, thinking back to that fancy lunch where the Serbians hadn't realised the general spoke their language and thus was aware that the translator the Serbs had supplied was lying to the French. There were eight men at lunch around that rectangular table in the hotel's huge dining room, and after they'd eaten the general had whispered to de Payns: *At my signal, you drop your napkin. And when you pick up the napkin, look under the table—if they all have guns on their knees, put the napkin on the table; if they don't have guns, put the napkin on your knee.*

De Payns dropped his napkin and looked—all the Serbs had guns on their knees. He put his napkin on the table and the general started to talk in Serbian, letting the Serbs know that for the last eighteen months the French had been listening in to their private discussions.

Then the two Frenchmen had stood and walked out to the driver waiting in the Audi A8 and were whisked to the plane at high speed. They took off for Mostar without lights and flew at low altitude to avoid detection by the Serbs.

That early informal work with the Company had been noticed, probably by the general himself. And after his second spinal surgery, when de Payns was grounded for a while, he was asked to apply to the DGSE. After a tough year-long induction course, a new career had unfolded.

He took one last look up and down the ship's deck, then returned to his cabin, where he washed his hands and hit the lights.

De Payns lay awake in the dark, thinking about an old source of his that he had managed to entice to turn on his country. And how, when the source was caught, the first response of his own secret service was to harm his wife and son. It seemed likely that the episode had resulted from a leak in Paris. And now de Payns wondered about the operation that had gone wrong in Palermo. Had it too been subject to a leak? And, if so, was the same person involved?

He had to avoid leaping at shadows, he warned himself, as he consciously slowed his breathing and waited for the day.

■

Shortly after 7 a.m., de Payns walked with the crowds down the rear ramp and onto firm ground at the western side of Naples harbour. He moved with the families onto the concrete quay, joking and smiling with the kids around him while scanning for watchers. The sky was overcast but the air was warm. In front of him was the service road that buses and taxis used to drop passengers at the terminal buildings, parallel with a main city boulevard, though separated by concrete barriers. To his left were mid-nineteenth-century maritime buildings, and to his right Vesuvius overlooked the bay. He walked towards the service road, past parked taxis and people greeting each other and putting their bags in the back of cars. A bus's diesel hummed as tourists waited for the driver to pull their suitcases out of the belly of the vehicle.

Nothing out of place. Only tourists. No one unattached. No loitering vans. Any watchers would have stood out. De Payns had reversed his windbreaker jacket, so that what was black yesterday was cream-coloured as he left the ferry—a *desilhouettage*. He'd usually do that in a rupture—a disappearance act once a follower had been 'put to sleep'. But he was feeling edgy, and he stayed in the middle of two groups as they walked off the quay and across the main road at the pedestrian crossing. He walked north along the Corso, stopping at a *panetteria* that had its entry on a cross street just around the corner from the Corso. He bought a cup of coffee and a cornetto, while waiting for followers to barrel around the corner and realise they'd lost the Frenchman. But no one came. In the normal run of events, an *itinéraire de sécurité* that took him out of the mission zone, followed by an effective rupture that lost any residual followers, would have been enough. It would have meant a return to being a relaxed 'tourist' on the street. But Operation Falcon had ended badly and he was on high alert.

He scanned the still-quiet street as he stepped onto the pavement, sipping his coffee. He seemed to be clean. After a ten-minute walk, de Payns turned east into the precinct of railway stations and bus terminals and walked to the vast entrance of Napoli

Centrale. Inside the double doors, Naples' main railway station was buzzing. He moved to the cigarette machine and bought a packet of Marlboros with change, ensuring there was no one either on the ground level or the mezzanines looking down on him. The Centrale had a modern interior of the type that would have surveillance cameras. It was something that couldn't be avoided in most European train stations, especially in the major terminals that serviced trains from other countries. De Payns pulled on his cap and, crossing the concourse, waited in the ticketing queue behind an Italian woman who yelled into her phone. He put on a smile as he reached the counter.

'One to Marseille—standard, thanks,' said de Payns, speaking in English to further misdirect any tails.

'To Marseille leaves at nine twenty-five. One stop, Milan,' the woman told him.

De Payns paid for the ticket in cash and wandered to the platform, where he found a seat that let him see both ends of the platform, then lit a smoke. It was one of the guilty pleasures of Italian train travel that they still allowed smokers on the platforms.

His carriage was second-to-last and had only ten other passengers in it—mothers with kids, Nonna and Poppa and a bunch of schoolgirls who seemed to be returning from a weekend in Naples.

As the train pulled from the station, he thought about what had happened in Sicily. How far back had the Sayef Albar people been on to him? That polite Pakistani he saw on the ferry to Palermo—was that a hand-off from Lambardi to his handler? And was the handler Murad? Sayef Albar must have been told that de Payns had French passports. Had Lambardi been ordered to confirm this?

De Payns realised he'd been holding his breath. He let it out in a hiss. He suspected his adversaries knew more than him, and he didn't like it; he had to build up his own side of the story. How had Shrek known to call off the operation? Was his Alain

Dupuis identity compromised? Had Shrek got out of Bar Luca without the cops or the terrorists grabbing him? Where had they slipped up?

If he had ten questions, the Company would have one hundred. The DGSE was famously hard on its field operatives when they came home to debrief. As one of his old instructors had warned him, building a genuine cover is only part of the puzzle; the other part is getting your story straight for the debriefers at the Cat. The administration people wanted to know where the money was spent and the managers wanted to know who the officer met. The intelligence officers—the DR, or *Direction du Renseignement*, the Intelligence Directorate—wanted to know exactly what words and phrases were used in conversations, and the specialist groups might sit in and pepper an agent with questions about nuclear triggers, bioweapons or whatever the operation had touched on. But most of all, if an operation initiated by the Company was called off and someone had been killed, the senior levels would arrive with their ambitious hangers-on and an OT would spend all day with four or five people trying to outdo one another with their suspicions. Such was the French secret services: *Pas vu, pas pris; pris, pendu*—not seen, not caught; caught, hanged.

His version of events would have to pass muster with two different masters. The first was Christophe Sturt, the director of the *Direction du Renseignement*. The DR was home to highly educated and ambitious analysts and managers whose requests for information were the initial triggers for missions such as Operation Falcon. Sturt would feel ownership of Falcon, and so would de Payns' other master, the director of the *Direction des Opérations*, Anthony Frasier. Frasier would make an appearance because someone had died, in a foreign country, on an operation he was legally responsible for. He would have the right to chair the debrief, but his 2IC—the head of Y Division, Dominic Briffaut—would run the blow-by-blow questioning. Briffaut was a former army special forces operator who had switched to the DGSE twenty years ago. He could be hard on his operators, but was also very protective.

But if his masters had a plethora of questions for him, de Payns had one big question for them: Was there a traitor inside the Company?

CHAPTER FIVE

De Payns wandered the concourses of the Milano Centrale, an hour to kill waiting for his train to Marseille. The Italians had created a new railway terminal in the middle of a nineteenth-century building, somehow retaining the original architecture around a labyrinth of shops and escalators as modern as Frankfurt's. It felt light and clean, but within a domed cathedral of polished marble and massive curved skylights.

Grabbing a takeaway coffee, he headed for a side entrance where he could have a smoke, drink his coffee and see who was around. He walked to an alcove at the side of the main entrance and stood under a large analogue clock watching the taxis and the buses leaving and arriving. Two women in cafe-worker shirts were also in the alcove, and as de Payns lit up they crushed their smokes and headed back to work.

De Payns sipped at the coffee and thought about his family. Romy couldn't call him when he was operational because he didn't carry his personal phone when he worked. Six months after they were married, he'd explained this to Romy—separating himself totally from his family while he was in the field was a mandatory sanitation exercise to preserve her and, later, the kids. When he took on a fictive ID, he was someone else during the mission, and this fictitious person would not know Romy de Payns. She could call as much as she wanted but his cell phone would be in a cupboard in the DGSE safe house, with its battery next to it. They'd talked it through over a few wines, and he'd explained that if the temptation ever arose to send an email to her from a cyber cafe, it would be a huge mistake—one he would never commit. If he was under surveillance when he sent such an email from the field, it would give the bad guys the real ID of the operative and reveal the fact he had a family. And in de Payns' world, family was leverage. Family was a vulnerability.

Romy was solid, like him. And like him, she'd spent her teenage years in a boarding school developing independence and discipline that matched her husband's. With two children to protect, there was now no greater advocate of secrecy in France's national security apparatus than Romy de Payns. In many respects she was more solid than her husband, especially when combining parenting with the demands of the DGSE.

There was a catch. Romy had gone back to university when their youngest, Oliver, started day care. Her PhD was going to be awarded in ten days' time, on a Saturday night—the date had been seared in his brain because Romy's parents were coming to Paris and they were all going out for a boozy dinner after the graduation ceremony.

De Payns nodded to himself as he exhaled a plume of smoke. The marital trade-off had always fallen in his favour. In the de Payns household, the Company came first. But this was one date that had to be honoured for Romy. This was her night. He took another sip of coffee and a man paused in front of him, pulling out a cigarette.

'*Bonjour*,' he said, and asked de Payns for a light in French. De Payns tensed—the stranger looked military, from the bull neck and regulation haircut to the way he held his cigarette long-wise inside his furled fist.

'Do I know you?' asked de Payns, smiling.

'Manerie wants to see you,' said the man, serious but not threatening.

De Payns' mind spun. He only knew one Manerie, and if this was the same Manerie it was not a friendly call. 'And you are?'

'I'm the help,' said the man. 'But you can call me Jim.'

'Maybe you have the wrong person?' suggested de Payns, scanning the apron for vans.

'If you're Aguilar, I have the right person.' This was de Payns' pseudo, only ever used inside the Company.

'Aggi Hula?' echoed de Payns, keeping the smile on his face. 'You Algerian?'

'No, but I'm used to getting my way.'

'I bet you say that to all the boys.'

'The director won't see the humour in that,' said Jim. 'But maybe I will when you're in the back of a van with a hood over your head, and I'm reminding you that I tried to be nice.'

De Payns decided this Jim had definitely been a paratrooper, perhaps in the Legion. He smiled and tossed the cigarette lighter to the bulky Frenchman.

'Director will meet you at your seat in ten minutes,' said Jim, lighting his smoke and tossing the lighter back to de Payns. Then he walked away. As far as tradecraft went, it wasn't bad. A watcher would have seen a fellow smoker getting a light and moving on. He didn't linger and monologue. His body language said 'stranger'.

De Payns stayed calm as Jim moved out of sight. Manerie meant Philippe Manerie, the director of the security side of the DGS—the internal affairs division of the Company. The DGS was feared by de Payns and his fellow officers because it represented the potential for either a speedy end to one's career or a long stay in one of the DGS's basements after passage through a French security court. France was haughty and somewhat cynical about the ways of the world, but she abhorred a traitor. There were French people of a certain age who would spit on your shoes for the mention of Vichy France. The DGS represented that attitude and more.

De Payns was tired and questions bounced in his mind—was Jim real or bullshit? Was this actually DGS or someone from another service trying to make him talk? An approach, or a test? The kind of test the DGS performed often.

If the approach was real, why would they contact him in the middle of his exfiltration, against every basic rule of security, rather than find de Payns at the Bunker in Noisy? But if it was bullshit, how had they found him? Was he followed, or did someone who knew the exfiltration plan talk? Someone in his team?

De Payns had a choice—to escape quickly and use an unplanned itinerary, or go to the 'Manerie' meeting to see the face of the person, report it and, if it was an approach, do a counter-manipulation.

He was tired but he was still nosy. De Payns checked his ticket and crushed his smoke under his heel. Then he headed to platform 18.

CHAPTER SIX

He walked the platforms parallel to his train, looking for watchers and traps. Then he walked the length of his train to Marseille. It wasn't the high-speed train he'd caught from Naples, but the windows were large and he could see clearly into the cabins. At his carriage, he clocked the fold-out yellow signs saying that the train was being cleaned, but he noticed Jim and a middle-aged man in a dark suit waiting for him inside the carriage. Philippe Manerie looked over the tops of his spectacles through the window. No expression, no mannerisms. A blank slate. A perfect DGS executive. De Payns recognised the face because he'd seen it across the office and in official biographies. But he'd only met him once before, a long time ago, on a night flight into Mitrovica, when de Payns was flying TBM 700s into northern Kosovo. The face that now stared back had once been his passenger, surrounded by people who looked like Jim.

De Payns boarded the train and walked to his seat. Manerie was seated directly across the aisle and Jim in the seat behind de Payns'.

'Aguilar,' said Manerie. The director leaned over and offered his hand. 'Philippe Manerie.'

De Payns shook. 'Director.'

'Excuse the cloak and dagger; I don't make a habit of it.'

De Payns smiled. He knew Manerie's reputation for surprise meetings and interventions. He was nicknamed Jack, because he sprung up like *Jack-dans-la boîte.* He was dressed like an accountant but carried menace like a waft of aftershave. If even some of the rumours about his special forces career were true, he was not someone to be played with.

'I hear Falcon wasn't completed,' said Manerie, his face trying to make a smile. Like de Payns, he had the blue eyes and high cheekbones of the northern French.

De Payns shrugged. 'Not sure I know what you're talking about.'

Jim snorted and Manerie turned and looked at his henchman with a smile. 'I told you he was solid, *non*?'

'*Oui*,' said Jim, genuinely amused.

De Payns let it go. People like him didn't get into conversations about operations with those who didn't need to know. If you weren't in the room at Noisy, then you weren't in the loop. You messed with that rule and people got hurt.

'We're all in the Forty-four, *ami*,' said Manerie, referring to the French external intelligence service's initial raising out of the 44th Infantry Regiment. 'But let's move along from Falcon and get to what *is* my business.'

De Payns shrugged. At the front of the carriage a cleaner's phone sounded. She leaned her mop against the bulkhead and took the call.

'You know what I do,' said Manerie, 'so you know that while I may not work at Noisy, I am very interested in the crumb trails from the Bunker.'

De Payns didn't like the man's tone. The DGS was the office that monitored counterespionage efforts against the DGSE. It was the office that tried to weed out those who were compromised or were being blackmailed to work against France. It also caught traitors who were just doing it for the money.

'Can I help you, Director?' asked de Payns.

'You can help France,' said Manerie. 'Is that something you'd like to do?'

De Payns' face tensed for just a split second but Manerie saw it.

'I didn't mean it like that,' said Manerie, holding up the peacemaker's hand. 'I acknowledge your service to France. You are not the issue.'

De Payns sensed his neck muscles straining and he leaned back into the seat, forcing himself to relax.

Manerie rested his hand on a leather zip-up satchel beside him on the seat. 'I referred to Falcon because we have a problem, *non*?'

De Payns breathed out.

Manerie continued. 'Has it occurred to you that we are compromised?'

De Payns looked through the window and watched a railway employee walk down the platform. He tried to disassociate himself from what was coming but in his head a voice was screaming, *Who fucked us in Sicily?*

'I take your silence as agreement,' said Manerie. 'You probably want some answers yourself?'

De Payns turned back and looked at him. 'How did you find me?'

Manerie smirked. 'Well, that's one question.'

'Here's another,' said de Payns, looking for facial and vocal reactions. 'Why intrude on my way back to Paris, before being sure that I'm not being watched? Why put me in danger by revealing my real identity?'

'Jim, did you use Alain's name outside the station?' asked Manerie, talking to Jim but looking at de Payns.

'No, Director.'

'Jim, have I used Alain's name in this carriage?'

'No, Director.'

'Jim, you've conducted hundreds of overwatch operations in your career—what is your assessment of this meeting?'

'We're clean, Director,' said Jim.

Manerie eyeballed de Payns. 'In the army we had a saying that went something like: *Don't shit on another man's security arrangements until you're one hundred and ten per cent certain of your own.*'

'I don't know what you're talking about,' de Payns lied.

Manerie made a pained face. 'Don't you? You're bitching at me for catching you before you get to Paris, and yet Operation Falcon is on my radar because it's clearly been compromised.'

De Payns wanted to protest that it wasn't his fault, but Manerie would know that. He was here because de Payns was Falcon's *chef de mission.*

Manerie leaned in. 'I have a proposal for you, Aguilar, that I strongly recommend you agree to.'

'Really?'

'As of this moment, you'll report to me on any meeting or conversation you have at the Bunker, or with anyone who works from the Bunker. Understood?'

'I don't know this Bunker.'

'It's in Noisy,' Manerie snarled. 'It looks like an old fort from the outside but many interesting people work there.'

'Sounds like fun,' said de Payns, his mind focused on where the director was going with this.

'Yes, very interesting people, some of whom are probably working for our enemies.'

De Payns could feel his nostrils flaring. The jabber of the cleaner speaking into her phone echoed into the silence between them. 'You want me to spy on Noisy?'

Jim and Manerie stared at him.

Finally, Manerie nodded slightly. 'Would this be a problem?'

'I work for France,' said de Payns.

'But, *bien sûr*, these are people you trust with your life,' said Manerie. 'Can you help me with this problem without loyalties clouding your judgement?'

'I don't work for you,' said de Payns.

Manerie nodded slowly and reached for his satchel. 'Perhaps we need to define our relationship, *non*?' He reached into his satchel, pulled out an 8×10 black-and-white photograph and handed it over.

De Payns looked down and saw a picture of himself in a pale business shirt and dark chinos. It was a sunny day so he was wearing sunglasses. There were cups of coffee on a table in front of him and on the other side of the table was a dark-haired forty-something Caucasian male in a polo shirt. A sticker on the bottom right of the photograph indicated an address in Amsterdam and a date. De Payns handed back the picture.

'So you saw the date?' asked Manerie, feigning concern as he tucked the photograph into his satchel. 'I also have the declarations for that week.'

'I'm sure you do,' said de Payns.

'And no declaration from you, yet this man in the picture is Mike Moran, who works for British SIS.'

De Payns wanted to say, *He's a friend of mine*, but that would open up too many other options for Manerie. The DGS had him—he'd met with a person of interest and not made a *compte rendu d'entretien*, an official declaration of contact. Total disclosure was a basic condition of employment in French intelligence.

'I'm not interested in Moran,' said Manerie. 'I assume your conversation with him was advancing France, perhaps even some shared history between your families?'

De Payns nodded; Manerie obviously knew that the Morans were friends of the de Payns.

'But,' continued the director, 'we have a failed operation in Sicily. Are you not curious about that?'

De Payns shrugged.

'And we have, what is it, *five* French passports?'

'Sounds about right,' said de Payns.

'Where are they right now?'

'Destroyed and sitting in three rubbish bins at Porto di Palermo.'

Manerie stared at him. De Payns stared back.

'So,' said Manerie. 'Dead people, failed operation, missing passports and suspicions of a mole. Your file doesn't suggest you're a man who'd be happy with that.'

De Payns breathed out. 'They're not missing, they're destroyed. By the book. What do you want me to do?'

Manerie smiled. 'Jim will get a *démarqué* phone to you and he'll create a *plan de liaison*, with a dead mailbox.'

'Are we looking at anyone particular?' asked de Payns, feeling sick.

'I want you to consider the people you'd never really suspect,' said Manerie. 'I want to hear your suspicions before anyone at the Cat hears them.'

'I trust everyone I work with.'

'Of course, of course,' said Manerie, trying for a jovial tone. 'But I'm not friends with any of your colleagues. For me it's just a question of: *Who knew everything? And who fucked us?*'

'That's a small group,' said de Payns, as the cleaners departed the carriage and took their yellow sign with them.

'Very small,' said Manerie. 'As an example, how well do you really know Guillaume Tibet? This is just an example, of course . . .'

De Payns' breath caught in his throat. Was the man serious? He looked away for fear the director might guess that de Payns wanted to kill him.

'Act as planned in Paris, okay?' said Manerie. He stood and grabbed de Payns by the shoulder. 'All for France, right?'

After Manerie and Jim departed, de Payns sat there, stunned. The director of security at the DGS had warned him to keep an eye on his own team—and Shrek in particular.

CHAPTER
SEVEN

There was a time in his career when de Payns would have buckled under if Manerie cornered him and forced him into fealty. Even he was surprised that he'd stonewalled the DGS man on Falcon. De Payns was a product of France's elite boarding school system and the French air force. His grandfather was one of the first to join de Gaulle's Free French Forces when de Gaulle was trapped in London, trying to keep Free France alive. He understood chains of command and narrowly held information. The fact he'd quoted the rule book at a person who could destroy his career and make him unemployable gave him a sense of empowerment and also unease. He was right not to acknowledge Falcon to an outsider, but it was the wrong person to withhold information from.

The Airbus banked over the southern reaches of Paris and lined up for landing, on time for the 12.30 arrival from Marseille. He'd been jittery in that city, which was unusual since he'd spent so much of his DGSE training there. Marseille now felt too much like Palermo—just another dangerous Mediterranean city with all those small lanes, grand boulevards and thousands of windows and balconies hiding an army of watchers. By the time he'd left the train at Marseille Provence Airport he was on the verge of a blue rats episode, where a spy sees only watchers and senses only followers. Every person on the street—from kids playing to the oldest grandmother—could be part of the game. To fight it, he'd resisted doing any more IS routes, no more ruptures.

Now, as they approached the runway in Paris, he tried to clear his head. He knew the reputation of the DGS, but the suddenness of Manerie's appearance and the bluntness of his request was a shock. *Shrek?!* It didn't seem possible. He remembered the first time he'd worked with Shrek. An opposition party figure from Syria was hiding out in Libya, wanting all sorts of gifts from the French government in exchange for information about the Syrian economy, weapons programs and intelligence activity—all the usual bargaining chips that Middle East politicians and generals used to get foreign governments on their side. Shrek had been on the mission team, not the least because of his academic background in the area of Mesopotamia and Asia Minor and the 'Stans'—Kazakhstan, Uzbekistan, Turkmenistan. De Payns and Shrek had formed a friendship at the Bunker during the briefings and they bonded over their love of beer and a shared Templar lineage. While France was the home of the Enlightenment and European liberalism, it was still a nation of secret societies, old family ties and undeclared oligarchy. The Templars were the oldest and most powerful of France's secret societies and many people in de Payns' world claimed a Templar lineage. His friendship with Shrek would have been nothing more than a professional association if it hadn't been for the after-events of the Libya operation. The Syrian politician was conditionally accepted by France, but during the intelligence debriefings the Syrian must have picked up on a line of questioning and realised that his past actions were going to expose him, which would force the French to drop him. He'd obviously decided to cover his tracks and eliminate those who could divulge criminality to the DGSE, because a week after the debrief a French honorary consul was assassinated in Beirut. She was a banker who also worked for the DGSE and was popular at the Company. As it transpired, she had been the Syrian politician's private banker and knew all his offshore accounts and various trust structures. She'd been executed to keep the politician a 'cleanskin' in the eyes of the French.

The DGSE detained the Syrian politician at Évreux Air Base while they decided what to do with him. New assets who backwashed their histories in order to appear 'clean' to the Company were usually executed or fed to their rival factions. But before he could be dumped, he was found hanged by his bedsheets in his cell. Shrek had been the last person to visit him and the legend grew of the genius academic who'd hypnotised the Syrian into suicide, making him believe it was the only way he could spare his family. Mind control, puppet mastery—the man who could peel the onion from the inside. Shrek had never confirmed it, not even to de Payns or the rest of the clan, which included Templar and his other close colleagues, Rocket and Renan. He'd smile like a shark, wink and say something like, *Who wouldn't want a power like that?*

Shrek was inner circle, blood brother. Fingering him for treason was outrageous.

De Payns moved with the summer tourist crowds at Orly, wearing jeans and a polo shirt, and carrying a small backpack across one shoulder. He caught the Orlyval shuttle train to Antony station and waited a few minutes before the fast RER train arrived. He took the first carriage and looked down the platform to see who was watching, jumping sideways into the carriage only when the doors hissed. He left the train at St Michel–Notre Dame and emerged into a mild summer's day in Paris. Crossing the road with the crowds he reached the left bank of the Seine and dropped down onto the Port de Montebello, the riverside walkway that might have been the best-used river path in the world. He headed east, making for the Pont de la Tournelle. To his left, across the river, was the burned-out Notre-Dame cathedral—now covered in a massive tarpaulin—and in front of him were swirling tourists, the gendarmes moving among them to ward off the pickpockets and bag-snatchers who plagued this part of Paris.

A Canadian woman waved her smartphone at de Payns and made the international gesture of *Can you take our picture?* De Payns smiled and took the phone, walking around the newlyweds so he could catch a glimpse of who was behind him. He smiled, took the shot with the cathedral as the backdrop and wished them luck.

In de Payns' career, many hours were spent alone on the streets, using his thinking and internal voice to keep himself safe and on-mission. One of the things that consistently occurred to him was the fact that he was living in a different world, with different players, from those around him. He even had a different soundtrack, if he was wired into the support team with his micro earpiece. It reminded him of a movie called *The Matrix*, in which most people lived life on one plane while a tiny group operated in a world parallel to the common reality. It wasn't glamorous or cool. It was mentally isolating and had pushed many agents away from the one thing that pegged them to reality—their family. Being back in Paris brought on these feelings in overwhelming waves.

He continued east, moving with no hint that he was trained. In contrast to how spies were depicted in the movies, de Payns' job was to put the followers to sleep, which was best done by behaving like anyone else on the streets of Paris. He did this by habit—he was already sure he wasn't being followed, but putting followers to sleep had to be practised at all times. As he did so, he attempted to keep his family at the back of his mind. Oliver, his five-year-old son, was a forty-minute walk away, enjoying his last days of true childhood before starting school after the summer break. His eight-year-old—Patrick—was probably working on a video game in a bedroom that looked like a clothes-bomb had hit. It was also the end of Romy's full-time mothering role; with the PhD in her back pocket and Oliver at school, she would be returning to the workforce, even if only part-time. They had discussed some of the risks, which mainly revolved around Romy being used by a foreign agency for an approach of some kind. He'd trained her to be suspicious of every new face, especially the friendly ones, and her computer habits were now decidedly OCD. But she didn't want to be micro-managed, so de Payns settled for painting the big picture and letting her make day-to-day decisions. He believed that if she was happy, she was more likely to go the distance with what was a less-than-ideal marriage from her perspective. As he walked beside the Seine he felt his family's presence but also their distance, but he couldn't dwell on it.

The wide stone stairway loomed and de Payns climbed it. When he reached the top he turned left to cross the bridge. The traffic was one-way, so if there were followers with a van or motorbike, the vehicles would have to circle around the long way to keep eyes on de Payns, and he'd get to see every vehicle as it approached.

On the other side of the bridge, he stepped onto the Île Saint-Louis and slow-walked with the tourists for two blocks onto the old Pont Marie.

Still no followers.

On the northern side of the Pont Marie he veered right into a series of narrow lanes that took him eastwards again, alongside the Jardin de l'Hôtel de Sens and into the maze around the Rue de l'Hôtel-de-Ville, a series of medieval streets that became more nonsensical the further east he walked. This area had once been used by the Company to attune agents to the signature sounds of footwear on Paris streets. The echoes rang like a bell and even the rubber soles of de Payns' sneakers made a lingering sound. If there was anyone behind him, he'd have heard it by the time he turned north onto the Rue Saint-Paul.

At the Place de la Bastille he did a broad loop around the square, at the centre of which stood the massive July Column, commemorating the revolution of July 1830—a strange idea of revolution, since the revolt simply replaced a Bourbon king with one from the Orléans line. De Payns moved with the pace of the sightseers and confirmed yet again that he was clean. He looked at his watch—it was 2.26 p.m. Across the square was the Café Français, which, if he wanted to come in to the debriefing, he'd have to enter at the half-hour. This was the plan that Manerie wanted him to follow, as if nothing were amiss.

He sauntered towards the cafe's blue canvas awnings, aiming to be inside and at a table at 2.30 precisely but knowing he had a –1/+2 minute window.

The place was crowded with Americans and Australians, and de Payns looked around for a place to sit before moving to one of the multi-coloured tables outside. He sat where he could watch the square and also look in the cafe's main window, where he saw a male patron with a green golf cap resting on his table. The waitress approached him quickly, probably thinking that de Payns' clothing was the sign of a foreigner who would tip too much. He ordered a coffee and leaned back, giving himself a view of the golf cap through the window. Before the waitress could return, the man sitting beside the cap put it on his head and walked out of the Café Français. De Payns dropped a few euros on the table and followed.

They walked with a space of thirty metres between them, the man in front dressed in jeans and a black T-shirt with no markings. They headed north, taking a zigzag route through the streets of Paris, playing what the Company called 'the tourniquet', a game of turnstiles where the job of the officer running the tourniquet was to clear the participant through at least three DGSE checkpoints by two operatives from the Company, called 'Candles'. The Candles were in radio communication with each other via small wireless earpieces, and their job at each checkpoint of the pedestrian route was to watch for followers. When de Payns was cleared of followers, the tourniquet vehicle would swoop and pick up their officer.

After fifteen minutes the man leading him took a right off the Rue de Charonne, and de Payns found himself in a narrow lane with an idling silver Citroën C-series. The man with the green cap kept walking and the rear left door of the car popped open. De Payns got in and the car accelerated down the lane.

There was a red-headed man de Payns didn't know in the passenger seat. At the wheel was his friend Gael, better known as Templar.

'Nice work, my friend,' said Templar as they emerged from the lane into the mainstream traffic.

'How are you?' asked de Payns, not using his name. 'Where are we going?'

'To see the boss,' said Templar.

CHAPTER EIGHT

De Payns and Templar kept it light during the eight-minute drive to the Cat. Templar—a former Marines paratrooper—could have used the Périphérique, the ring road around Paris, to get them to their meeting faster, but instead he'd taken a zigzag route around the Père Lachaise cemetery, and from his old friend's mutterings into a micro earpiece, de Payns guessed a motorbike was behind them and doing parallels. De Payns didn't know the man in the passenger seat and he took his cue from Templar: *Quand tu ne sais pas, fermes ta gueule.* When you don't know, shut up.

They used the secured vehicle entry at the Cat, on Boulevard Mortier. The Citroën's licence plates were scanned by cameras, and when the armoured doors swung open Templar drove the car into a bomb-proof box with cameras pointing up from the floor. Now they were trapped until the DGS guardians decided otherwise. A voice over the speaker system told the occupants of the car to wind down their windows and the two men in the front seats handed their IDs to one of the two blue-suited DGS men who approached. Templar told them that de Payns was without ID, so the second DGS man produced an iPad with a camera hooked on the top and took a photo of de Payns' face, which was then scanned. The process took seven seconds and the DGS man was close enough that de Payns could smell the gun oil of his MP5, but not so close that he could grab the weapon.

'OT number?' asked the man with the iPad, referring to the *officier traitant* number that was issued to a DGSE operative when first commissioned. When de Payns' answer matched with the DGS file, the security doors opened in front of the car and they drove into the compound.

There was a below-ground car park, where a lot of vans and motorbikes were housed, but Templar drove them alongside the lawn quad in front of the main three-storey stone building and around the side of DGSE headquarters to an outdoor car park.

The three of them walked into the employees' area off to the side of the Cat's secured reception. De Payns noticed the unintroduced man was physically fit, slightly taller than de Payns' own one hundred and eighty-two centimetres, and carried a sidearm under his left armpit, making him a right-hander.

They entered the officers' anteroom. De Payns walked to his safe, entered a PIN and retrieved his lanyard. There was a rule at the Cat: no swipe card, no entry. If you lost your swipe card it invited drawn-out interrogations from the DGS, who immediately suspected the employee of being compromised. It didn't matter how you lost it, the replacement would see one hundred euros missing from your next pay packet—but only if the DGS allowed you to regain your clearance.

They swiped through the security gates, overseen by DGS guards, and rode the elevator to the third floor. There was none of the buzz and work atmosphere of the lower floors, where the DR—the intelligence section—and the administration people operated. Those people were not allowed to meet de Payns or members of the Y Division. No one could access the Y files or see the true identities of the Y operatives. To the DR analysts, Alec de Payns was known only by his OT number. The DR analysts were not even allowed to read a Y agent's 'R' reports. Those contained personal observations and incriminating information gleaned by the agent and they were reserved for the eyes of the BER—the 'area' executive—and locked in his or her safe. The analysts could only read the 'O' reports from Y agents; they contained the open or objective information, and on reading them it was unlikely that an analyst could detect who had provided the secret information or what the agent had done to secure such intelligence. In the parlance of the Company, there was no R in O—which came out in French as *no air in eau*.

They paused at a small kitchenette in front of a wood-panelled door. The red-headed man told Templar he was getting the managers and he moved out of sight.

'You okay?' asked Templar, taking a capsule from the rack and placing it in the coffee machine.

'I'm fine,' said de Payns, though his head was swampy with fatigue and he was preoccupied with the approach from Manerie.

'Haven't seen Shrek yet,' said Templar, his heavy-featured face impassive under a mat of short black hair. 'I mean, not in Paris.'

De Payns knew Templar wanted to hear about Palermo, but he couldn't discuss it before going through the debrief. He took the proffered coffee as two men came around the corner. Christophe Sturt, the DR director, looked sharp in his four-thousand-euro suit and that famous grooming that required weekly visits to the barber. Directors of the DR were generally very well educated, and had done a few '*postes*' as the declared DGSE representative in embassies. They were always a pure product of the system, a person who could say *France* as if she were his wife. Sturt was accompanied by his deputy, Charlotte Rocard, the BER–Europe, technically responsible for the oversight of Operation Falcon. De Payns smiled at Rocard but inside he was bristling. Charlotte Rocard, apart from having sartorial tastes almost as expensive as her boss's, was an aggressive teacher's pet who had no field experience in her CV. She was known for showing little interest in Y Division operations, until Sturt was in the room and then she became an expert.

They all filed into the panelled meeting room, dropping phones into a box held by the attendant. Lafont bolted the security door and joined the group, so there were five other people taking their seats around the oval conference table. Directly across from de Payns sat the director of the DO, Anthony Frasier, a large middle-aged man with a crown of thin black hair pushed straight back from his clean-shaven face. To his left sat Dominic Briffaut, the head of the Y Division; his big lumpy knuckles would make him the senior manager of no office in the DGSE other than Y. He assigned the operatives and authorised the planning of the operations. Every other department—Technical, Administration, Intelligence—dealt with the enemy at arm's length, but Briffaut's people lived among France's adversaries. He was known to give his people the benefit of the doubt, but he visited hell upon those who abused his trust. He also had a big sense of humour—Briffaut's ethnic background was obviously West African but when polite Franks asked him where he was from, Briffaut took great delight in telling them he was from Alsace. Which was true. He even had the terrible accent to prove it.

'Aguilar,' said Frasier, nodding at de Payns.

De Payns nodded back. Frasier had used de Payns' pseudo, which was the policy at the Y Division. While other divisions knew de Payns and his colleagues only by OT numbers, internally they were referred to by pseudonyms: Templar, Shrek, Aguilar. There was only one official source in the French bureaucracy where the OT numbers, real names and pseudo titles were recorded in one place. The three most senior officers of the DGS—which included Manerie—held a hard copy of that information.

'Let's start this,' said Frasier, who liked to pretend he was always in a hurry, but who missed nothing. He pushed a piece of paper across the desk to de Payns. 'That anything to do with us?'

The sheet was a Reuters printout, with the previous day's date and headlined: *Two Murders in Palermo, Italy.* Police had found a Mercedes-Benz SUV burned out in the Palermo shipyards in the early hours of the morning; it contained a body, as yet unidentified. Sicilian police were also seeking witnesses to the murder of a Turkish national in a popular cafe-bar called Bar Luca, in Palermo's old town.

De Payns leaned back in the leather boardroom chair, knowing his words were being recorded. He breathed out and told himself to relax, that he'd just play it straight. He only had to tell one lie. Nine years in the DGSE, seven of them at Y, enduring all sorts of privation and being the good agent who never took black money and never lied to the Company. He'd earned the right to one fib, especially one that was being forced on him. When this debrief was over he would write his report and he'd go home and have a bath, kiss his kids and have a glass of wine with Romy. Heck, he might not even have to lie because they might not even ask.

'So just to confirm,' started Frasier, 'have you spoken about Operation Falcon with anyone prior to this meeting?'

'Of course not,' said de Payns. 'I travelled directly to the Cat and detected no surveillance. I've discussed Falcon with nobody.'

'Okay,' said Frasier, his gaze flinty. 'Tell us about Sicily.'

CHAPTER NINE

He wrote quickly and without flourish, just as his instructors had taught him so many years ago. *No piece of writing from an* officier traitant *should betray any personality. We should have no sense of who you are based on your writing style.* That meant short sentences with one idea confined to one sentence. No art, no personality. The screen was linked to an internal computer but all de Payns could see was a screen, a keyboard and a mouse. No slot for USB sticks, no DVD drive and no functionality for 'print'. The only way into this system was to open his DGSE account.

He wrote in third person, through nine sections that started with Modalities and ended with Intentions, and took in such niceties as Manipulations, Directives and *Connaissances Nouvelles Acquises*, Newly Acquired Knowledge, to which de Payns was tempted to append: *We now know there's a mole in the Company who fucked us.* But he didn't write that. Instead he wrote that Sayef Albar had a paramilitary wing operating in Italy; that it was prepared to pay around six hundred thousand euros for a real French passport; and it had at least one Italian national assigned to its cause. He avoided referencing the Reuters report that Frasier had tabled. Intelligence reports avoided *a priori* knowledge, so he didn't surmise the actual fate of Michael Lambardi. He could only report the facts as he saw them in the conduct of Operation Falcon—if the Sicilian police identified the body in the burned-out Mercedes as Michael Lambardi, then the Company could add the information to its file.

He wrote important nouns and names in capitals. He covered the overnight in Cagliari, where he'd joined Michael Lambardi (referred to as Commodore by the DGSE), and the subsequent ferry crossing to Palermo as well as the events of that early evening. He listed his exfiltration, his multiple *itinéraires de sécurité* and ruptures, and he declared every conversation he'd had from the moment he left his 'office' in Marseille to the second he sat at the debriefing table with the directors and heads of sections. He told the truth about the passports—they were destroyed in Palermo and discarded in three wharfside rubbish bins. He played it straight, except for the conversation with Manerie and Jim, which was a small gap in his exfiltration that would be incredibly hard to verify unless someone at the Cat knew where to ask.

He had now officially lied for a DGS man. De Payns had entrapped and manipulated so many people in his career that to be in the grip of Manerie's coercion because of the Amsterdam photograph was both humbling and confusing. If there was a mole in the Y division, de Payns wanted to find it. But if the price was spying on Shrek? Or spying on his own directors? These people were beyond the abstractions of national loyalty—they were the only reason he could do his job, and also be a husband and father, without losing his mind.

And yet the debrief had been unsatisfactory. Frasier wanted to know what parts of Falcon were compromised; if his people had any traps on them that they could drag back to Paris. His main concerns about the passports were ensuring Murad's crew would neither have them to use, nor be able to reverse-engineer them and confirm the supplier of documents was the French government.

Sturt was different—ever the politician, he rested his elbows on the boardroom table and asked non-questions such as: *So you didn't hand over the passports for our cameras? So I guess you'd call the operation a failure? So you left behind a corpse in a bar and a packet of French passports at the docks?*

The fact that the operation had veered off-course was de Payns' fault. He was the *chef de mission* and he technically should have called off the passport transaction when Lambardi tried to change the time and place. But the reason that Lambardi wanted those passports there and then—because Murad was in Palermo—presented France with a much bigger opportunity. Eyes-on, personal interaction was the most powerful *connaissance* available to a service like the DGSE. De Payns had taken the risk, knowing that the Company did not even have a photograph of Murad.

While Frasier and Sturt had reluctantly accepted the trade-off in risk, Sturt's deputy, Charlotte Rocard, asked him to specify the 'product' from Falcon. *What do we have now that we didn't have before this operation?* De Payns listed a possible sighting of Murad, the elusive commander of Sayef Albar's Europe operation; confirmation that al-Qaeda considered the going rate for a genuine French passport to be around six hundred thousand euros; and evidence that Sayef Albar had an operation in Sicily, not just a representative such as Michael Lambardi.

When the debrief was over, de Payns helped the Company's artist sketch a facial likeness of Murad, or the man he thought was probably the Sayef Albar commander.

He finished typing and reached for his coffee, realised it was cold. Then he hit 'save', logged out of his DGSE account and switched off the computer screen. It was now 5.53 p.m. He'd written his report in a little over two hours, which was relatively fast. He stretched, picked up his pack and made for the elevators. He wanted nothing more than a smoke and to shuffle around the house aimlessly for a few days. The deaths at Bar Luca and the requirement to recall them in minute detail were exhausting. The elevator's down-arrow chimed and someone cleared their throat. He turned and saw Dominic Briffaut, still strong in the neck and back, despite being well into middle age.

'Could we have a word?'

It wasn't a request. Briffaut held the elevator door, and when they were both inside he hit the button that would take them to the management's parking level.

They said nothing in the elevator, as per the protocol. They walked through the underground garage to an area adjacent to the mechanics' station, Moroccan hip-hop pounding out of a Bluetooth speaker. Briffaut paused beside a fire hose and grimaced at the music.

'They could use that at Guantanamo,' he mumbled, pulling a pack of Camels from his inside jacket pocket and offering one to de Payns.

'The ID people at the DO are freaking about those passports,' said Briffaut, lowering his voice as a man and woman exited the elevator and walked to a blue BMW. 'They're unusable?'

'I don't know how often the bins are cleared,' said de Payns. 'But I never handed them over. I certainly destroyed them.'

Briffaut nodded.

'We sure Commodore is dead?'

De Payns looked at him. 'I didn't verify it. I couldn't.'

There was silence between them—Briffaut hadn't cornered him for a smoke and de Payns waited for him to get to the point.

'Now it's just you and me,' Briffaut said at last, 'who fucked us down there? Any idea?'

De Payns shook his head. 'Perhaps Commodore was always a useful idiot for Sayef Albar . . .' He let the sentence hang.

'Or?' asked Briffaut.

'Well,' said de Payns, exhaling a plume of smoke at the underground plumbing, 'I wonder . . . Did the conversation go, *You didn't bring the passports—bang, bang you're dead*? Seems like a wasteful way to deal with useful idiots.'

'Or,' said Briffaut, 'Murad said to Commodore, *You're drunk, you don't have the passports and now this French consultant is walking towards us. Too-hard basket.*'

'What if Murad's final words to Commodore were more like, *You brought a French spy into our circle. You're dead*?'

They gave each other a look.

'I've opened an investigation; the director needs a report,' said Briffaut. 'Tell me if anyone's crawling up your arse, okay? You don't have to take that shit on your own. Promise me?'

'Promise,' said de Payns.

They smoked in silence before Briffaut sighed. 'I need you at Noisy tomorrow. Two o'clock.'

De Payns looked away.

'Sorry about the timing,' said Briffaut. 'I know you need some time with the family, but you can't duck this one.'

'What is it?' asked de Payns.

'I don't know much,' said Briffaut. 'Marie Lafont has an operation—I think they're looking at Pakistan.'

De Payns took that in. Marie Lafont was the new head of Counter-Proliferation at the DR, having already made a splash under Christophe Sturt as the BER of the Arabic desk. She was smart and classy, and she liked to be associated with success—she wouldn't be initiating an operation as a fishing expedition, it would be *victory at all costs*. But a story dogged her—she'd allegedly once trained for the Y Division but had flamed out. She'd failed to show up for training one morning and when the DGS went looking they found her phones, wallet and car keys on the coffee table in her apartment and no sign of a struggle. The police discovered her days later on the Pont de Poissy, in a fetal position, convinced that the watchers had infiltrated her phones and her apartment. The blue rats had claimed her before the training was even finished, but Y's loss was the DR's gain.

'I see,' said de Payns. His eyelids were drooping with fatigue. 'You know I have other IDs to tend to, and two of them have meetings coming up. I can't be the only candidate for Lafont's operation?'

'The only one Lafont asked for, and Sturt agrees,' said Briffaut, dragging on the smoke. 'So you're up. But I'll tell you what, let's get through the next couple of months and I'll find you some extra leave, okay?'

De Payns didn't argue. Taking extra leave in the French secret services was more theoretical than it was actual. But the offer of it was an acknowledgement you were overworked.

'I'll hold you to that,' said de Payns, smiling.

'Oh, and make sure you get to the Bunker by midday, okay?'

'Midday?' asked de Payns.

'Yeah,' said his boss, tapping his temple. 'Head check.'

CHAPTER
TEN

The rain started as de Payns emerged from Austerlitz Metro station. He walked several blocks to the changeover house and let himself in with his security protocols. He moved past the apartment's small kitchen to a wall of lockers, stopped at Number 9 and entered his code. The door sprung open and he pulled out a manila envelope with the name *Alain Dupuis* on the front. He placed the Alain Dupuis SIM, wallet and wristwatch in the envelope and returned it. Then, from an unlabelled envelope he removed a Nokia phone in three pieces, a set of keys, a wristwatch and a wallet. The life of Alec de Payns, in one envelope.

He entered the small bathroom and washed his face, relishing the sensation of cold water on his skin. He had one last IS to perform before he was clean enough to walk into the family home. At the end of missions, this was the IS that agents wanted to skip, but they all knew it was potentially the most crucial. This was the 'last mile' that they'd been trained for at Cercottes, the DGSE farm outside of Orléans where Action Service and Y Division people were trained. This was the final ring of security that kept the bad guys from their families, and it had to be done with absolute precision.

He travelled on the Metro, pulling the pieces of the Nokia and SIM from his pocket and assembling it. The screen came to life, and the Nokia screen showed him a message was waiting. It was from 'R', asking if he would be home for dinner. It had been sent the day before. He thumbed in *yes*, and looked up and down the carriage. He walked in the rain without an umbrella—umbrellas were too easy to follow; so easy that most secret services used them as signals and nothing else. He travelled on the left side of the street, from where he could look into the front seat of the parked cars. He zigged and zagged and ended up outside his apartment at 7.38 p.m.

The de Payns' apartment was in a classic nineteenth-century Parisian building with a high-security main entrance, good locks on the doors and a small underground car park. By habit, de Payns circled the building, doing a final look around before entering, checking the letterbox and using the stairs to reach the second floor. Outside his apartment, he leaned his forehead against the door, breathing in the typical smells of mealtime in France's largest city. He could identify Tunisian, Lebanese, Indonesian and Tamil cooking, but no stewed rabbit or steamed mussels. He felt himself start to relax.

He inhaled deeply and turned the key in the lock, then slipped quickly through the door and shut it, a security habit he couldn't shake. Down the hallway, he could hear Romy's voice. By her animated tone, he guessed she was talking to a female friend on the phone. Probably her old school friend Renée, or her thesis supervisor, Marie.

He rounded the corner and saw her stirring something on the stovetop. She still stirred him, this compact, sexy woman—even now, dressed casually in jeans and a T-shirt, her blonde hair pulled into a hasty topknot—and always doing two things at once. He kissed her on the cheek and she smiled, gestured that she was just winding up the call. De Payns threw his keys and phone on the counter and grabbed a bottle of riesling from the fridge. He poured two glasses and made for the sofa, sinking deep into it with a sigh.

The wine was good and the TV news was on, but muted. One of his wife's multi-tasking habits. A woman on the screen announced a story and an update scrolled along the bottom of the screen: *France will explore new trade deal with Iran—Macron.*

Romy rang off, brought her wine over and kneeled on the sofa to kiss him on the lips. When she pulled back, de Payns saw the smile that reached her green eyes.

'I cooked for two—we must be psychic,' she said, rubbing a thumb along his forehead.

De Payns smiled. From their first dates, when he was still a fighter pilot, they'd attributed even the smallest coincidence or happenstance to their psychic connection.

'You okay?' she asked.

'Tired,' said de Payns. Something was niggling at him. He knew what it was but he didn't want to dwell on it. Not now. 'How are the kids?'

'Ready for the holidays to be over,' said Romy. 'Oliver is counting the sleeps until school starts. He's drawn a calendar and everything.'

De Payns chuckled, trying to keep the good vibes going. But he couldn't do it. 'Who was that on the phone?'

'My new friend,' said Romy. 'Ana, a mother from Oliver's preschool.'

De Payns nodded. 'Ana? When did you meet her?'

'I've seen her a few times at the park and at preschool,' said Romy, tensing. 'She's invited us for drinks.'

De Payns' pulse thumped in his temples. 'So, she's married?'

'I don't know.'

'What's her surname?'

'Alec!' Romy's pretty face darkened.

'So, she has your number but we don't know her name?'

Romy stood. 'You agreed to not do this. We *agreed*! You set the rules but you don't manage my every move.'

'Who initiated the conversation?' asked de Payns, now committed.

Romy picked up her glass and walked to the kitchen, shaking her head. 'It's preschool. The kids *initiated* a friendship.'

She swallowed some wine and stirred the pot.

De Payns kicked off his shoes and picked up the remote.

'Don't,' said Romy. 'Please. Not the TV.'

Putting down the remote, he turned back to her.

'We just got talking because Oliver and Charles are friends. I don't think anyone initiated the conversation.'

'Charles? Are they French?'

'I don't know. Turkish, maybe.'

De Payns raised his eyebrows.

'Okay, they look Arabic, but they're very French. She has no accent.'

'Where do they live?'

'I don't know.'

De Payns nodded. 'What was the approach?'

Romy shook her head.

'Has she asked about your husband?'

'No . . . maybe I've offered.'

'What have you offered?'

'That you're away on business.'

'With the Ministry?' asked de Payns, referring to his chosen cover as an administrative person working at the Defence Ministry.

'No, I didn't offer that; she didn't ask.'

'Did she see the car?'

Romy appeared to be struggling to control her anger. 'I know this stuff's important, Alec—I'm very serious about it. But you have to show some trust.'

'So?'

'We may have talked at the car.'

'Did you see her car? Her numberplate?'

Romy shook her head. 'No. I don't know if she has a car.'

De Payns tried to smile. 'If bad people ever wanted to coerce me to act against France, they would probably do it through my family. That's all.'

It was the wrong thing to say, he saw it in her eyes immediately.

'You mean, that's what *you* do to people? Get to their families?'

An icy silence settled, before it was shattered by a shriek.

'Papa!' came the high-pitched sound of a five-year-old boy. De Payns saw a flash of Batman pyjamas and then Oliver was upon him. As he fell sideways on the couch with his younger son in his arms, he thought of Michael Lambardi and wondered what would become of his kids.

CHAPTER
ELEVEN

The Company's shrink didn't have her own rooms at the Bunker in Noisy. She used one of the senior manager offices that sat vacant until an expert from the Cat or the military was brought in to brief a Y team. It was a modern office in an old building, which was the plight of the French security apparatus. The ceilings were high and patterned but the furniture could have come out of an Ikea catalogue from 2003. Bare desk, an Olivetti electric typewriter on a small wheeled trolley, a landline phone and a safe in the corner. No smartphones, no wi-fi, no data switches, and the only computer screens were hooked into an internal system. The Bunker was an 'air bridge' facility. There was no email or internet connection and cell phones didn't work, even if one could be snuck past the DGS security people. Even hard copy was limited—it was against French law to take written material out of a DGSE facility, unless you were at least a director or two-star general, and then only if you were accompanied by an authorised person.

De Payns sat on a sofa and watched the shrink, known only as Dr Marlene, organise her leather compendium. She was in her late forties, trim, with a black bob and very bright red lipstick.

He assessed her as neurotic and more concerned with status and appearance than love or sex. If he wanted to leverage her, he would use flattery, probably focusing on her intellect or superior taste.

'So, Alec. May I call you Alec?'

'Sure,' he said, reaching for his coffee in a white mug emblazoned with the golden cockerel of the French rugby team.

'I like your mug. You're a rugby player?'

'I played at school.'

'Which school?'

'Saint-Joseph of Reims.'

'That was your grandfather's school?'

De Payns paused. The shrinks were going to do this again. Raise the fact that, when he was fifteen, he secretly enrolled himself in the Jesuit boarding school once attended by his paternal grandfather in order to escape a toxic home environment—one dominated by the ceaseless fights between his highly independent English mother and traditional French father.

'Yes, it was my grandfather's school, and no, my father didn't know I was enrolling.'

She smiled at him, and he waited for the inevitable comment about how most teenagers are sent to boarding school against their will; they didn't enrol themselves. But Dr Marlene seemed to get it.

She switched topic. 'How many firearms incidents have you been involved in?'

'Four.'

'When?' she asked, jotting this on a pad. He noticed she had small handwriting.

'Two in Kosovo, one in Tunis, one in Lebanon.'

'Discharges?'

'Two were discharges—one from my sidearm, one from my colleague's. The other two instances were me threatening an adversary with my sidearm, and one time I had a Beretta nine-millimetre held to my temple.'

She smiled. 'No discharge, I gather?'

'Thankfully, no.'

'What about violence? Seen any deaths in your career?'

'As an air force pilot, there were many. Not so many in my intelligence career.'

She raised an eyebrow.

'There was Sicily, two nights ago, I guess,' said de Payns. He suppressed a smile. One of the things they asked him when he was being inducted to the Y Division at Cercottes was whether he could kill kittens. And then they took him into the room where the kittens were! Asking him now about violence seemed a little redundant.

'Palermo, wasn't it?'

He gave her a look.

'Palermo's in my briefing,' she said. 'Can you tell me what happened?'

'A couple of thugs were shadowing a person I befriended in Palermo. When I tried to leave a bar, one of the thugs followed me and was reaching for his pistol.'

'You saw this?'

'I saw him going for the small of his back, saw the pistol in the reflection of a glass door.'

'What happened?'

'I turned to confront him and he had a hole in his neck.'

They looked at each other for two seconds.

'A hole?' she asked, breaking her gaze and writing. 'You mean, like . . .'

'A hole with blood coming out of it. Big enough for a pen or a chopstick.'

Dr Marlene nodded. 'So, was there someone close by who had a pen or a chopstick?'

'There was a man.'

'A man?'

'Yes,' said de Payns, 'from the bar.'

'Did you know the man?'

'Yes.'

'Can you tell me his name?'

'No,' said de Payns.

'You can't, or you won't?' she asked.

'Both. I can't tell you his name.'

'Was it Guillaume?'

'Why ask me if you already have a name?'

She placed her pen on the compendium and pinched the bridge of her nose. 'I'm not here to play games, Alec. I'm here to assess you.'

'How am I doing?'

'Well, you tell me.'

'A thug got a hole in his neck before he could shoot me,' said de Payns. 'On balance I'd say I'm happy, when you consider the alternative.'

'What about this contact of yours, this target?'

'Commodore,' said de Payns.

'Yes, him. How did he fare in this incident?'

De Payns shrugged. 'It was dark and I assumed he was in a car.'

'And?'

'And there was a show of blood and viscera on the inside of the rear window.'

'Leading you to believe . . .'

'That Commodore had been shot. Possibly in the head.'

Dr Marlene sat back. 'Let's assume Commodore is dead, that you saw him being killed. How do you feel about that? I mean, you developed a friendship with him, *non*?'

'He was going through a nasty divorce. He needed money, kept telling me how men in Italy are really screwed in a divorce.'

'How did you respond to that?'

'It was a leverage, the need for money. We work on MICE—money, ideology, coercion and ego. You have to find one to work with, and money was his.'

'What about his divorce?'

'I told him that Italy couldn't be that bad, but he said the man has to pay all the court costs and then punitive child support. He was stressed about seeing his two kids.'

'Do you think about him?'

'Sure,' said de Payns, wanting to steer away from this. 'Kids aren't part of the life, but then again, I guess they are. I like coming home to my own kids, but Commodore chose his friends, I didn't.'

'Did you do enough?'

'For France?' asked de Payns.

'No, for Commodore. Do you have regrets?'

That stumped de Payns. Would someone seriously ask a spy if he had regrets? The entire profession was regret-management. 'If he was killed, it was by his own side. I didn't select his friends,' he repeated.

She seemed satisfied with de Payns' answer, and flipped her compendium to a file at the back.

'Your sense of focus is very strong, yes?'

'I'm sorry?' replied de Payns, confused by the change of subject.

'At the age of twenty you were cleared by the air force for combat training on the Mirage 2000.'

'That's a long time ago.'

She pushed on. 'Fighter pilots focus on what's in front of them and they shut out everything else.'

'I used to shut my eyes,' he said, pretending to shudder. 'Too much speed, too many Gs.'

She allowed herself a brief smile. 'My point is that in your current job you're still shutting out everything except what's in front of you.'

'Perhaps.'

'It comes at a price,' she said. 'You know that, right?'

'I'm not sure . . .'

'Most people's jobs don't involve the risk of being shot in the back. You can talk about it if you want. Talking about something like that would be normal.'

De Payns smiled. 'I thought you were here to assess me? Now we're going to talk?'

He was misdirecting because he didn't want to discuss his own personality. What he called his *shut down* was a state that he'd practised since school—the ability to block out everything that was redundant and extraneous and bring one hundred and ten per cent to the task at hand. It was what had made him a good rugby player despite not being the most muscle-bound student at his school. Dr Marlene was right; it was the quality that elevated him so quickly to fighter jets. He owed everything to that ability and the price he paid was exhaustion, emptiness, social isolation. A sortie out of Dijon Air Base might last a total of four hours; an operation in the DGSE could last between a week and a month. The mental strain was acute. Sometimes he wanted to sleep for a week; other times he wanted to stand in a bar and get shit-faced, both alone and with the clan.

Both, but neither.

'How are you sleeping?' she asked.

'With one eye open,' said de Payns.

Now she laughed. 'How's your marriage? Does she accept what you do?'

'She accepts what I do and that's the only reason I have a marriage,' said de Payns. 'She needs this chat more than I do; she can't talk about this with anyone.'

De Payns was surprised at himself for bringing Romy into the mix. It was unusual for him to be candid about his marriage with the shrinks and Romy was forbidden to discuss details beyond saying that her husband worked for the Defence Ministry. She had no wife or girlfriend to unburden herself to. She was not allowed to see a counsellor, was not allowed to reveal anything about her own husband.

Marlene nodded. 'Panic attacks?'

'No.'

'Blackouts?'

'No.'

'Rage, aggression? Unwarranted, I mean.'

'No.'

'Road rage?'

'It's Paris, not Copenhagen,' he said. 'If you're calm on Paris roads, you're on drugs.'

She flipped the compendium shut. 'Final question—how many hours do you sleep each night?'

'Seven and three-quarters,' he said.

'You seem fine,' she said standing. 'Tired, but fit. My number's in the Company system. You ever want to talk, let me know.'

He shook her hand and watched her leave the office, wondering if perhaps he should have told the truth about his sleep problems. She might have some pills for that.

CHAPTER TWELVE

De Payns sipped on his third coffee and nibbled on the edge of a macaron that Zac, the Y Division armourer, had offered him from a Tupperware box. Armourers always had interesting hobbies and Zac's was baking. Zac was an ex-Legionnaire who ensured that the firearms and other devices distributed to Y Division operatives actually worked when they needed to. De Payns was standing in Zac's basement workshop watching him work on a suppressor held in an elaborate vice.

'So, Zac,' he asked, after they'd dealt with Paris Saint-Germain's injury woes and Macron's new petroleum tax, 'what do you know about a tough guy called Jim, guards someone high up in the DGS?'

Zac smiled as he turned away from the vice, his bespectacled face becoming even more youthful. 'So, you've met Jim Valley?'

'Valley?'

Zac nodded. 'Former Marines special forces, I believe. Deployed under Manerie in Africa.'

De Payns had another bite of the macaron, the sweetness of the biscuit failing to subdue the smell of gun oil. 'He's a good guy?'

Zac chuckled. 'Well, Aguilar, like you said—he's a tough guy. Better a friend than an enemy.'

De Payns caught the elevator back to his office and leaned back in his chair, observing the nondescript office, the safe in the corner and the view through the sash windows over the wooded areas of eastern Paris. He had eleven minutes before his meeting started and he closed his eyes, calming his thoughts.

'My father had died,' said a woman's voice.

De Payns sat up straight, slightly startled. Marie Lafont stood in the doorway.

'I didn't flame out of the Y Division training,' she said, folding her arms and leaning against the doorjamb. She was wearing a pleated skirt with an expensive-looking silk shirt.

'Okay,' said de Payns, coming back to earth.

'There's a story doing the rounds, isn't there, that the DGS found me curled up on a bridge because I couldn't handle the blue rats?'

'Perhaps I heard that,' said de Payns.

'My father had a stroke, he was on life support. The rest of the family wanted to unplug him.'

'I didn't know that,' said de Payns.

As if she hadn't heard him, she continued, 'I needed a few days out of Paris. I should have told the Company.'

De Payns didn't know what to say.

'But what would I have told them? *Hey, I'm going drinking for three days? It'll get messy, guys. You might like to look the other way.*'

De Payns laughed and eased back in his chair. If you drank to get sane, you were one of the gang.

'I'm briefing the op,' she said, looking at her watch. 'Want to walk me over?'

■

The meeting was a small one. Some operations briefings could run to twenty people jammed into a secure room, but there were five in this one. There was Briffaut—who'd discarded his suit jacket—and Mattieu Garrat, his deputy at the Y Division; they sat together at the pointy end of the oval table. Lafont sat opposite de Payns with her 2IC—Josef Ackermann, the deputy-BER of CP—beside her. Ackermann had a mournful, elongated face—hence his nickname of 'Mantis'. He was also a former university lecturer in chemical engineering, and his expertise in counter-proliferation operations was invaluable.

The sticker on the front of the file in front of de Payns read *ALAMUT.* That's what they were calling the operation. He flipped the cover to reveal the administration sheet—dates, authorisation numbers, signatures and the collections of letters that indicated the DR was running Alamut, in pursuit of more intelligence requested by the Counter-Proliferation desk. The DGSE name and logo did not appear on any of the operational documents. If you didn't know what all the letters and numbers meant, then you probably didn't know what you were looking at. De Payns found himself mentioned under CDM—or *chef de mission*—his OT number inside crosshatches. The crosshatches meant his OT number was an official designation of the DGSE and it was the only identifier to be used during or in reference to the operation. There was a list of six designations on the administration sheet—the only person not in attendance was the DR director, Christophe Sturt.

Marie Lafont introduced Alamut as a reconnaissance and intelligence operation that revolved around a facility in Pakistan. Although the building had the words *Pakistan Agricultural Chemical Company* painted on the outside, among Western intelligence operatives it was called the MERC, a rough translation being Material and Energy Research Centre.

Lafont switched on the projector suspended from the ceiling above the table, which also dimmed the lights. The screen showed an aerial shot of the MERC—it looked like a compound of around fifteen squarish concrete buildings arranged in a campus around one main building.

'The SVR has some great shots of the MERC compound,' said Lafont, starting with a joke about the leakiness of Russia's foreign intelligence service. 'This is in the south-western outskirts of Islamabad, eighteen kilometres from the city. It's serviced by a suburb nearby that we believe houses the scientists and engineers from MERC.'

She cycled through a few photos taken from different angles but none of them were very good. The 1990s-era buildings were contained in parklands and there was a security fence around the compound and a security gate.

'Despite signing the Chemical Weapons Convention in 1993, which was supposed to prohibit Pakistan's bioweapons ambitions,' said Lafont, 'we believe their bacteriological weapons program is reaching maturity, probably from this facility. The declared purpose of this compound is agricultural research, but we doubt that's its primary role. For a start, it seems the people who work there have dedicated their lives to the centre.'

'How do you mean?' asked Briffaut.

'Employees are obliged to report everything, from the briefest chance meeting to the most innocuous phone call.'

'Sounds like intel rules,' Briffaut noted. 'So it's run by the ISI?'

Lafont nodded. 'The employee's family and social life is monitored and they have to give up their passports for fifteen years. It's certainly the ISI playbook.'

De Payns kept his eyes on Lafont, aware that some of the other attendees were now looking at him.

She continued. 'Current intelligence points to bacteriological agents being developed at MERC. We've only had a third-hand glimpse through some Russian sources, but if these are accurate, we're looking at a bioweapons facility in Islamabad, so this is where the Y Division comes in.'

Briffaut and de Payns exchanged a glance.

'We need means of access to the MERC,' said Lafont. 'We'd like their internal organisation chart, their lines of work and research, their current projects and their financing. If there is information on potential weaponisation and targets, that's a bonus. But for a start, we need to know what they have, what they want to make and how far they are from achieving it.'

Briffaut leaned on the table and put his fingertips together, a clear sign that he wanted a smoke. He looked at de Payns. 'You have three months to get us initial results.'

'I'm on it,' said de Payns.

'Of course you are,' said Briffaut. 'But we're talking about Pakistan, so let's do this softly softly, okay?'

CHAPTER
THIRTEEN

Alamut was a Persian castle from which the Assassins—a secret group of medieval warriors—launched their attacks on various Middle Eastern rulers, Islamic and Christian. The naming of the operation for a sect that engaged in political assassination seemed a little presumptive to de Payns, when he had more prosaic matters to attend to. As the *chef de mission* of Alamut, de Payns was responsible for designing the operations, seeking sign-off from Briffaut and collating the resources to execute. The first operation in Pakistan would be a technical environment of the MERC structure and its personnel—essentially a search for COMINT, or communications intelligence, which could be done without 'contact'. If the technical environment yielded enough information to proceed to an operational environment, operatives would be put in the field, and then—if that yielded someone interesting, with good potential for MICE leverage—they would move to a contact environment on a target. That's when someone like de Payns was sent to meet, befriend, manipulate and turn the target. Contact was never attempted until the other environments had been established. Contact should always feel seamless to the target—if one day you wake up with a new best friend after one week, he might not be your friend.

It would have to be human because the computer systems at MERC were inaccessible to the Company without more information, such as email addresses of employees, IP addresses or a network signature. Those clues were not visible to the DGSE—another reason to believe that the MERC was controlled by the ISI.

De Payns' team would have to determine one or more human targets to approach; de Payns guessed the target would be senior, but at the outset, the Company didn't even have a name.

De Payns spelled these things out to the three other people in the meeting room: Gael Py, Brent Clercq and Thierry Suquet.

He didn't have to recite the basics to these experienced people, but it was the protocol for briefing on an operation. 'I want a low-key observation platform around the MERC. Count the cars and trucks, log the rego plates, assess the hierarchy and get them on camera.'

'We looking for anyone in particular?' asked Py, his nickname, Templar, thanks to the Crusader tattoo on his back. 'We got a POI?'

'No,' said de Payns. 'We'll log traffic in and out of the MERC compound and assess the best human asset, the one who gives the Company the best chance of access.'

De Payns didn't want to rely on luck. He counted himself lucky that the mission team was headed by Templar.

'This was from a drone?' asked Templar, sorting through the photographic prints of the MERC aerial shots. He sat to de Payns' right at the long briefing desk, his oversized upper body straining through his lightweight sweatshirt. He was one of the best support team operators in Europe, an expert in tricky exfiltrations, workable disguises, breakouts and ambushes. If someone needed to be secretly plucked from the street of a major city and rendered to a safe site, Templar was your man. The only thing he couldn't do was lie convincingly, which was why he was never assigned approaches and manipulations. He'd be the only support team that de Payns would have on this first mission. The other two operatives would be techs from Y-9—the Bunker's technical espionage section.

'The briefing didn't tell us if a drone took the photos,' said de Payns, feeling like he could have done with another twelve hours' sleep. 'Anyone have an idea?' he asked, looking from Templar to Clercq, the head of Y-9. Clercq was a grey-haired forty-something who dressed in cargo pants, sneakers and a polo shirt. He was a smoker with silly jokes but he had a fast brain and careful instincts, and de Payns always liked having him on board. Beside him, in jeans and a sweatshirt, was his colleague Thierry Suquet. At twenty-five he could have passed for a university student—in fact, he had been plucked from an engineering PhD at a polytechnic university in Toulouse—but despite his youthful appearance he was an experienced field operative who had worked in clandestine roles all over Europe and the Middle East.

Clercq pointed his pen at the photograph that showed a main entrance road to the MERC. 'We'll situate our IMSI catchers somewhere on the road to the centre. It will be not too far, not too close. We'll identify phone numbers associated with a few vehicles, based on people we find interesting. We'll refine it as we go, as it becomes clearer. That okay?' IMSI was the international mobile subscriber identity, which identified phone network users by country and cellular network. The IMSI was subdivided into a global format of country code, network code and sequential number. It was unique and all stored on a SIM card.

'Hopefully one of them will be more interesting than others,' said de Payns.

Templar said, 'If that works we'll follow and identify them, and go from there.'

De Payns nodded; the plan was to scan for cell phone signals using a 'spinner', and then try to work back and discover the owners of the phones and who they were talking to. If the MERC campus was jammed or was a non-device/non-transmission zone, then it was a good bet that the scientists and engineers would reach for their phones and fire up as they exited at the end of their working days. Once the Alamut team had identified a person of interest and their phone, Templar would follow them and find out further details.

De Payns wanted the reconnaissance phase of the operation to use one small team and be completed inside two weeks. 'It will just be the four of us in-country.'

'In one car?' asked Clercq.

Yes,' said de Payns, opening a second package. 'The cover will be scouting for a film in beautiful Pakistan.'

De Payns pulled a sheet of paper from the pack. It listed the personnel in the briefing room and their assigned ID for Operation Alamut. A single source of truth about false IDs was essential, because when an agent was questioned, or their bona fides checked while they were operational, any verification done by the Company had to be made on the right IDs.

All four people in the briefing room would travel on fictive IDs, with passports, and they needed credible backstories for why they were in Pakistan and why they were lurking around an alleged bioweapons factory. The legends had been established by the DO at the Cat, and each Alamut team member had to do their own work-ups on their legends. A good legend wasn't just committing life details to memory. To sustain a legend the operative needed believable predicates for when they were stopped by police or intel, or just asked questions by a hotel concierge or a taxi driver. New IDs were supported with LinkedIn and Facebook accounts, but the operatives were also expected to find a disused apartment and have mail sent to them there, to reinforce their false credentials.

De Payns looked down the list and saw that they were all existing IDs, so his team would have to do some gardening and ensure their addresses were viable, that mail was being delivered there, and that their social media was up to date. De Payns would again be using his Clement Vinier ID, that came with a business front, Capital Films.

Templar asked if he would be going into Islamabad to establish the *équipement de ville,* which was the design of the *jeux de rendez-vous* and *points de passage obligés* that the Company used to check for surveillance of their OTs when they were in the field. The *jeux de rendez-vous* were a set of clandestine tools that allowed the team to *see* one another with no collusion visible to outsiders. They included hand symbols and coloured *gommettes*, but also included where to meet up in case of emergency, meeting points for transmitting documents clandestinely, dead drop boxes and agreed timings.

De Payns shook his head. He and Briffaut had agreed on a fast, four-man recon and technical surveillance operation, and while they'd use basic tradecraft to check for surveillance, there'd be no ISs or tourniquets. They'd need vehicles with no connections to the French government, and they'd have to be careful sneaking the spinning machine in-country and driving around with it. Pakistan's secret police and ISI both operated with impunity. There were no legal consequences for a Pakistani intelligence agent getting it wrong and seizing on French filmmakers inside their country.

Looking at his watch, de Payns stood up. The initial meeting was over. There'd be more, and the DA—the administration people at the Cat—would come up with final budgets and disbursements. Daily living money would only amount to less than twenty euros per meal, if an OT was not in contact with a target. And even then, you needed to bring back a receipt. It was a vexed issue, because in many circumstances asking for a receipt could complicate an already-complicated situation. As the operatives often joked, the DGSE had forgotten to put the Aston Martin in its staff packages.

De Payns collected his materials as the team filed out. He noticed Templar waiting by the door.

'Seen Shrek?' asked Templar.

'No,' said de Payns. 'Not since Falcon.'

'I think he's been doing ISs,' said Templar, voice low. 'And not just down south.'

'Here?'

Templar looked at de Payns and dropped his voice to a whisper. 'I hear he was trapped in Saint-Denis, kept pulling out of the IS.'

'Shrek plays it safe, that's all. Especially after that thing with DGSI.'

Two years earlier an officer of the DGSI—the internal French security service—had walked into his house in Paris to find Russian GRU agents holding his wife and daughter. The event had been a wake-up call to people like de Payns, Shrek and Templar—always check the last mile; never relax your security.

Templar didn't look convinced. 'He finally cleared the IS at midday, apparently.'

'He's safe?'

'Safe, yes,' said Templar. 'But we all need a drink, *non*? You up for it?'

'Text me,' said de Payns, as he moved past his friend's bulky frame.

A drink with Templar would involve red wine and Jack Daniel's, but the hangover would be worth it. He needed to be somewhere he could relax, among people he trusted with his life. He needed to be in a cocoon and get totally shit-faced.

CHAPTER
FOURTEEN

Jim Valley was waiting for him as he reached street level of the Port-Royal RER station. Port-Royal gave de Payns about five blocks of walking before he reached his apartment, giving him space to see if he was being followed. Now Jim was here. The former soldier made a show of putting on his cap, which translated to *follow me*. It was 5.46 p.m., on a beautiful Paris evening. De Payns wanted to get home. But he followed Jim, who led him along an avenue of horse chestnut trees into the Jardins des Grands Explorateurs.

Jim sat at an unoccupied park bench overlooking the La fontaine de l'Observatoire and de Payns sat beside him. They both reached for cigarettes.

'So, anything for the director?' asked Jim, tapping his cigarette on the pack.

'Nothing,' said de Payns, lighting up. 'Our friend isn't back.'

'Not what I heard,' said Jim, his heavy features slightly obscured by aviator sunglasses. He wore a black, lightweight windbreaker of the type Templar wore when he was armed.

'He's not in the Bunker yet,' said de Payns.

'What are they saying about Falcon?'

'Confused, mostly. The DO is conducting an internal investigation.'

'Do they suspect you?'

De Payns laughed. 'No, Jim. Not me.'

Jim lit up and waited until two high school kids had walked past before saying, 'So?'

De Payns shrugged. 'There's three theories.'

Jim numbered them on his fingers. 'One, we have a mole. Two, we fucked up. And three?'

'Sayef Albar has a more sophisticated operation than we first suspected.'

'That's number two.'

De Payns looked at him. 'These operations are not a jigsaw puzzle, Jim, with all the pieces slotting neatly into place. It's more like juggling plates.'

'War is shit and then you die,' said Jim, pulling a cheap flip phone from his windbreaker pocket and sliding it to de Payns. 'That's *démarqué*. The only number you need is under Q.'

De Payns took the phone and slipped it into his jeans pocket. 'The drop?'

'Rue de Bretonvilliers, number one-seventy,' said Jim. De Payns knew the street; it was on the Île Saint-Louis. 'In the courtyard is a letterbox for the complex. You use the box for twenty-eighteen. No key, you just curl your finger under the slot and flip the latch. Think you can handle that?'

'Got it,' said de Payns, controlling his annoyance.

'Drops will be on Monday or Thursday, mornings. If there's a white *gommette* on the advertising poster at the corner of Quai de Béthune, we're armed. Okay?'

De Payns nodded, still not looking at Valley.

'And the director will want some progress, so can you give me a date that you'll talk with our friend?'

'Tell him within the next forty-eight hours,' said de Payns.

And without another word Jim was on his feet, walking away.

■

The de Payns' apartment was off the Avenue du Général Leclerc, a trendy but not too expensive part of the Montparnasse district. The main window of the living room opened onto a Juliet balcony that rode slightly higher than the trees. It wasn't large enough for a chair, but de Payns liked to sit on the windowsill, feet on the balcony, looking over the treetops to the north, at the monolith of the Montparnasse Tower. The tower resembled the black slab in *2001: A Space Odyssey*. Too conspicuous in the Paris context, something that ran against his instincts.

'Could you get Patrick from karate?' asked Romy from behind him in the kitchen. She'd been talking about her family coming to town and the graduation ceremony. He'd barely heard a word. He swallowed his mouthful of above-average Bordeaux, stubbed out his cigarette and turned back to face the room. Romy wore faded jeans and a tight tank top. Some Parisiennes were winter women, and others were summer. Romy was definitely summer.

'And we need butter,' she said as he grabbed her by the waist and kissed her neck. She didn't spill a drop from the measuring jug she'd filled with milk. De Payns lingered against her shapely derriere but she batted him away, warning him not to be late for Patrick.

The streets were busy as he walked around the block to the old church hall where sensei John—a West African man in his late twenties—was finishing up with a karate class of about thirteen primary school kids. They were stretching on the mats, following the sensei's lead. Patrick was on the far side of the group, where a pile of heavy bags and headgear was stacked, and de Payns saw that his son had noticed him but didn't break his concentration from the teacher. He also felt eyes on him. Turning slowly, he locked gaze with an Arab woman of around forty, with no hijab and dressed like a Parisienne. She was with another group of parents but she smiled at de Payns and walked towards him.

'Alec, I think?' she said, as she reached him. She was confident and well spoken, with no accent. She was also very attractive. 'You're Patrick's dad, right?'

'Yes,' said de Payns, forcing a smile.

'My boy is Charles. He and Oliver are friends at preschool.'

De Payns recognised the tone women took with men whom they assumed knew nothing about their child's daily life.

'Ana,' she said, offering her hand.

'Pleased to meet you,' said de Payns, and they shook. 'Is Charles in this group?'

'No, five is the minimum age for John's class, but Charles turns five in a couple of months. Romy said Patrick was in this class and I should come down and check it out.'

'I don't think I've met Charles yet—or maybe I know him from his surname?' said de Payns.

'Homsi,' said Ana without hesitation. 'Charles Homsi.'

It sounded Lebanese but de Payns avoided the cliché. 'Syria?'

'Ha!' she said, perfect white teeth lighting up her face. 'Well done, Alec. My husband is going to like that.'

By the time the kids had finished their stretches and were running to their parents, de Payns knew the husband's name was Rafi and he was an engineer with a big firm in Paris, and that the Homsis also lived in the Montparnasse area, slightly north of the de Payns.

He was still thinking about Ana a while later, when the family was eating dessert. 'I met Charles's mother tonight,' said de Payns, while the boys hacked at their bowls of ice cream. 'When he turns five, he wants to do karate with sensei John.'

Oliver looked surprised. 'But Charles already does taekwondo.'

De Payns could sense Romy glaring at him and he forced himself to tamp down his suspicions. He wasn't going to interrogate his son.

As the moment passed, his personal Nokia phone buzzed against his leg. He glanced at it. There was a text message from 'T' which simply said: *S is thirsty. Big Nose 2100?*

CHAPTER
FIFTEEN

The Croix de Rosey wasn't a bar that Paris guidebooks recommended to tourists. It was in Le Marais district on the right bank, but it was off the main boulevards, set back in a small street that ran north–south from the Seine—no outdoor tables, no cute umbrellas advertising Campari. As he walked down the cobbled street towards a glowing Kronenbourg sign, de Payns was reminded of what inner Paris must have looked like before various kings and emperors cleared the slums. There were smells and sounds in these streets that had taken centuries to create.

He pushed through the heavy mahogany door at 9.01 p.m. and took in the scene—a bar that might have been built in the 1700s and perhaps updated two or three times, the last of which was probably 1972. Low beams, a combo of accordion player and guitarist in the corner and a series of round tables spread around in the dimness. Framed photographs on the walls—black-and-whites of Catherine Deneuve, Charles de Gaulle, Jean-Luc Godard and Alain Prost. An eclectic mix of French heroes for a bar that didn't have a brand or an image.

'Ah, Alec,' said Tomas, the thick-set Austro-Frenchman who ran the Croix. He was in his seventies and wore the full apron that had been the barman's uniform in Paris until beards and neck tattoos took over. He'd fought for France in Zaire and kept a length of steel pipe under his bar for the drunks, and a cut-down shotgun alongside it for evictees who returned with reinforcements. His big face supported a big nose, but his patrons kept that to themselves.

'One,' said de Payns, pointing at the Kronenbourg lever. 'And a shot of Goose, thanks, Tomas.'

Tomas put a glass on the bar and poured Grey Goose vodka into it, before turning to the beer handles. 'I'll have what he's having,' said a voice from behind de Payns' left shoulder.

De Payns turned and found himself face to face with Shrek.

'You're too quiet when you walk,' said de Payns, shaking his friend's hand and slapping an arm around his back. 'I swear to God, you'll give me a heart attack doing that.'

'Is that three?' asked Tomas, nodding past Shrek. They turned and saw Templar, taking off his windbreaker and sitting at their usual table—close to the main door but with a view down the hallway to the WCs.

'That's three beers, two vodkas and one Jack Daniel's,' said de Payns.

Tomas chuckled, showing a couple of broken teeth. 'You boys are serious tonight?'

'You're lucky Rocket and Renan aren't here,' Shrek chuckled.

They sat at the table and threw in their coins that bore the Templar knight seal. As long as the coins sat on the table the clan were bound never to discuss what was said between them with another soul. De Payns raised his glass and said, '*Patriam servando, victoriam tulit.*' The other two repeated the motto and they all drank. The phrase was inscribed on the back of the Order of Liberation medal, commissioned by the Free French in London in 1940. The Free French were conceived as a secret society and were infused with influence from that most famous secret society, the Order of the Knights Templar. The head of the Free French Order—Charles de Gaulle—held the title of Grand Master. De Payns was now a sworn officer of the DGSE, another secret society with pledges that could not be disavowed.

They swapped stories, Templar's coarse, blunt appraisal of people in stark contrast to Shrek's quiet and intelligent observations. Templar had a full-bore energy while Shrek came out of his shell to make a joke or a comment, but then pulled back. One of his friends was plucked from university and the other from the paratroopers. But each was excellent at their job. Shrek could read anyone and manipulate them into anything, and his mastery of kung fu and sword disciplines made his small stature one of the great traps for macho men. Templar was stronger than ten men and looked it. He was like a cyborg, and was hell to drink with.

'What happened down there?' Templar asked, when they were halfway into their second beers. They'd all given their Falcon debriefings and written reports, but the official finding—with all the stories woven into one—would come from Frasier's office.

De Payns looked around and saw only locals. 'We were on-mission until Commodore told me he wanted the passports with us when we went drinking.'

'Why?' asked Shrek, keeping his voice low.

'He said Murad was in town and would pay three million euros for the passports,' said de Payns.

Templar whistled low.

'Fuck,' said Shrek, shaking his head. 'Murad, as in the Sayef Albar commander?'

De Payns nodded and his friends leaned in. 'I thought it was worth the risk to get a look at him.'

'Of course it was,' said Templar, throwing the Jack Daniel's down his throat without taking his eyes off de Payns. 'So, which one was he?'

'Shrek, you remember on the ferry, the last time Commodore took a piss?'

'You poured your beer into the carpet,' Shrek recalled.

'Yes, that was the one,' said de Payns. 'I don't know if you had the right angle to the WCs, but a tall guy—well dressed, maybe Pakistani—was at the WC door when Commodore came out.'

'I didn't see him. Was it contact?' asked Shrek.

'Couldn't confirm it,' said de Payns, not wanting to overreach. One of the first disciplines in the intelligence world was learning to identify things as they actually were rather than how you wanted them to be. He wasn't going to let a couple of beers ruin that. 'They may have swapped words but the tall Pakistani looked at me very briefly.'

'Jesus Christ,' said Shrek, leaning back and pushing his brown hair off his forehead. 'So maybe they had us in Cagliari?'

'Shit,' said Templar, knowing a lot of that fell on him. 'No fucking way.'

'Don't get carried away,' said de Payns. 'By the way, why did we call it off?'

'Jerome was around the back of the bar, saw two Mercedes pulling up,' said Templar. 'It didn't look friendly.'

'Two?' asked de Payns.

'That's what he said. They looked professional and armed. It looked like an ambush.'

De Payns nodded. 'I made it one vehicle.'

Shrek said, 'I only saw one.'

'The one Commodore got into?' Templar asked.

De Payns nodded and drank.

Templar seemed distracted. 'Tell me about Commodore and this person outside the ferry toilet.'

'It might have been an opportunity that came up on the ferry,' said de Payns. 'They saw it and took it.'

'Opportunity?' echoed Templar. 'You mean the passports?'

De Payns nodded.

'But if Murad was outside the toilet—'

'I don't know if it was Murad,' de Payns reminded him.

'Then how did he know that you had passports?' Templar finished. 'That was a surprise, *non*?'

'When did you reveal you had passports for Commodore?' asked Shrek.

'Right before he went to the WC,' de Payns said slowly.

'So?' replied Shrek, looking from de Payns to Templar. 'Murad knew about the passports before the contact with Commodore. He moved to the toilet door to tell his asset something, give him instructions.'

'His instruction was, *Get those passports and we'll find you in Palermo*,' said Templar with a nasty smile. 'But that doesn't answer the question—how did Murad know about the passports?'

De Payns almost whispered, 'How would *we* know?'

The obvious answer—that Sayef Albar had Michael Lambardi wired—hung unspoken between them. The three operatives had already leaped to their next question. If Sayef Albar and Murad were running a wire on their guy against the DGSE, they were confident about who they were targeting. And if it was as bad as they were guessing, the terrorists had planned to shoot de Payns behind Bar Luca along with Lambardi. Planned, professional, targeted and reliably informed. The Sayef Albar organisation had inside knowledge.

■

The beer mirror behind the bar had the windmill of Brasserie de Saint Sylvestre etched into it, although the mirror was so old and distressed that you'd have to know the brewery to understand what was being advertised. De Payns stared into it as he ordered another round, squinting through the whisky bottles and mirror flaws to get a proper glimpse of himself. What stared back was a patchwork of a man: part husband, part father, all spy. He wanted to be with Romy, Patrick and Oliver, but he also needed to be with people who wouldn't scold him for his occupation. He needed to unwind with the people who kept him alive. It might be contributing to the slow death of his marriage, but he needed to be with his crew—his clan—like a shark needed to keep moving. And somehow he needed to work out what he and Shrek were going to do about Manerie and the DGS. He wasn't going to spy on his friend, a person who had saved him from certain death in Sicily. But he was holding back for some reason, and it was eating at him.

He turned with the tray of drinks and the middle-aged woman on the guitar muttered something into her microphone and smiled when a drunk further down the bar yelled his approval. The accordion player squeezed out the opening bars of 'Idées Noires', the classic Bernard Lavilliers song about a depressed guy who just wants to run away from his life and wife. When the woman started singing, others in the bar joined her in a drunks' choir. Templar stretched back in his chair, eyes closed, waving his hands like a conductor as he sang.

As Templar lost himself in a haze of French accordion and American whiskey, de Payns realised Shrek was staring at him with those hypnotist's eyes.

'You okay?' asked Shrek. 'You look tired.'

'I'm drunk—is that what you mean?'

'No, I mean exhausted and worried,' said Shrek, his gaze shrewd.

'Fuck,' said de Payns, leaning back and running his hands down his face. 'Manerie came to me.'

'The DGS guy?'

'Yeah,' said de Payns. 'He had a photo of me and Mike Moran, from SIS.'

'Shit,' said Shrek. 'And?'

'I didn't register a CRE,' said de Payns, referring to the *compte rendu d'entretien*. 'I don't know what he wants to do with it, but he's a sleazy prick.'

'Yeah, he is,' said Shrek. 'I saw Mike a couple of months ago at Twickenham.'

'You know Mike?' asked de Payns. He hadn't been aware of the connection.

'Sure,' said Shrek. 'You know how it is.'

'Yep,' said de Payns, reminded of how tricky it was for spies to drink together. 'I know how it is.'

CHAPTER
SIXTEEN

The smell of coffee and warmed pastry brought him around and he squinted through a seismic hangover at the bedside clock: 6.24. His wedding ring sat on top of the clock radio, a symbol between Romy and him. DGSE operatives didn't wear wedding rings because it left a mark when removed, which could burn the legend of a 'single' operative.

Groaning, he rolled onto his back, noticing Romy was not there. For the past six months she'd been waking at five in the morning to work on her thesis before the child rituals began, but now—the thesis having been completed and accepted—it seemed early rising had become a habit.

De Payns winced against the slit of light that poured through a small gap in the curtains and tried to estimate what time he'd arrived home. He'd barely had three hours' sleep.

The scalding water of the shower felt good on his head, and after a shave he wandered into the kitchen and kissed his wife as she handed him a large black coffee. He could see through her short nightie and he lingered in the kiss, thinking of a possible return to bed before the kids got up. He dropped his hand to her rounded hip but she wasn't interested.

'How's your head?' she asked, holding two Advils in her hand and offering a glass of water.

Taking the painkillers, he leaned against the kitchen counter, looking through the main windows into the south of Paris. It was going to be a fine day, maybe rising to twenty-five, twenty-six degrees.

She slid a plate towards him on which was a warmed *pain au chocolat*. 'Eat this before you take the Advils. And we need some milk.'

He chewed as he walked to the coat rack and grabbed his windbreaker.

'Two minutes,' he yelled, letting himself out.

At the entrance portico he performed his daily habit—before venturing out he'd take a look through the glass of the main doors to see if anything was out of the ordinary, such as the presence of *sous-marins*, or subs—vans or cars used as observation vehicles—or pedestrians hanging about with no pretext. If he saw someone who looked off, he'd first clock their shoes, since footwear was the only thing a follower couldn't change in a *filature*. De Payns was always looking for a *filature*—the professional shadowing of another person.

He bought the milk at the neighbourhood *épicerie* and returned to the apartment. He drank another coffee and Romy fixed him a fresh *pain au chocolat*. She was friendly but distant, an attitude he accepted because it was similar to his own style. In Romy's mind she wasn't finished with the PhD until after the ceremony and dinner with her parents. She would be distracted until it was out of the way.

'I have a bit to do today—I'm leaving soon,' said de Payns, glancing at his plain Omega watch. For their first wedding anniversary, Romy had bought him an expensive military watch, but it spent most of its life in the bedside drawer; a shiny adventurer's watch was too conspicuous for his work.

'My parents are arriving tomorrow,' she reminded him. 'But my graduation is next Saturday, okay?'

De Payns nodded. The silence lasted one second too long.

'The ceremony starts at six, and I've made an eight-thirty booking at La Bohème,' she said, looking into his eyes.

'Sounds great,' said de Payns, standing and draining the remains of his coffee. 'I'm really looking forward to it.'

'You'll be there?'

He realised she wasn't being arch; she was worried. Hugging her, he nuzzled her hair and whispered in her ear, 'I wouldn't miss it for anything. I'm very proud.'

■

When he hit the pavement again it was 7.21 and Paris was starting to pump. Delivery vans were double parking and filling the street with West African rap as their drivers ran to building porticos with their parcels; commuters on mountain bikes shouted at drivers and hundreds of pedestrians walked the wide footpaths. The street looked safe, and he caught the crowded Metro south to the interchange then changed to a northbound line which hooked around to Odéon. Catching a bus east, he alighted at a stop in Noisy before wending through an IS into the side street, where a hidden side entrance of the Bunker was situated. He felt alert and a little paranoid, which he put down to the hangover. Even small leaks from intelligence services made people antsy, and the worst affected were the field operatives. The problems in Palermo gnawed at him, not the least because it reminded him of how he'd never resolved the torture-death of Amin Sharwaz, and how it was that the Pakistani engineer was revealed to the ISI. De Payns sometimes wondered if he should acknowledge the true extent of his concern to Romy, but he always stopped short—the day he divulged all to the mother of his children would be the day she pulled the plug on their marriage.

CHAPTER
SEVENTEEN

The vials of prototype were sealed inside polystyrene canisters, which were in turn secured within the five stainless steel capsules that resembled a construction worker's thermos, with a small combination lock on the screw lid.

'Are we in agreement?' the Doctor asked the man who sat on the other side of his desk. 'Small rural settlements, with an observable population?'

'I have the sites,' replied the man, nodding to the piece of paper he'd supplied to the Doctor. 'Operation Scimitar will be conducted as agreed and you'll get photographic evidence.'

'And stool samples and swabs,' said the Doctor, too quickly.

The Doctor didn't like this man who lounged before him. He was tall, well dressed and altogether too smooth, like a movie star or a salesman. He was Pakistani, which was in his favour, but he was a contractor with the ISI, foisted on him by the Colonel. As such he had a codename—Murad—and the Doctor knew nothing else about him, except that he had security clearance to be here, in the basement levels of the facility, which implied a certain seniority. He'd heard gossip that Murad managed an al-Qaeda cell on behalf of the ISI, giving the intelligence agency influence and control in North Africa. It wouldn't have surprised the Doctor—the ISI also operated the Taliban in Afghanistan and Northern Pakistan, using it as a tool for control over an area much larger than the Pakistani government's official reach.

It was one of the irritations of the Doctor's undeclared scientific work that all his connections to the outside world had to be managed through a secret office of the ISI, controlled by the ghost-like Colonel. Three years ago, the Colonel had directly taken over research projects at the MERC after his predecessor was found to be selling secrets to North Korea. The Colonel now had managerial control over both the MERC and the missile development programs at Noor Khan Air Base in Rawalpindi, whereas he had previously had oversight of the clandestine programs. The Colonel, for all his ignorance of science, was at least a good manager. But living in secret meant having to rely on a person like Murad, who might be competent but was clearly mercenary in his motivations.

'If this works,' said the Doctor, 'as I know it will, we'll be ready for the final stage of Scimitar as per the agreed timetable. Is that a problem?'

'Not at all,' said Murad.

'What about that business in Sicily I read about?' asked the Doctor. 'Anything to do with us?'

'It's under control.'

'Control?' echoed the Doctor, annoyed at the arrogance. 'What does that mean?'

'The French secret services were in Palermo,' said Murad, showing his gleaming teeth. 'But they were looking into a passport racket, nothing else. We're clean.'

The Doctor breathed deeply. There had been one hiccup, almost two years ago. A scientist of his with a traitorous husband. But she had been dealt with. Now he had no choice but to trust this man, Murad . . . for the moment. His sponsor was the notoriously capricious Colonel, and who knew what would happen to Murad once he had served his purpose?

'We've discussed these vials and their safe use,' said the Doctor, pointing to the canisters. 'Your team has been shown the safety video I sent? They'll need to use full protective measures when handling them. No exceptions.'

In fact, the Doctor's project team had engineered paper caps on the vials which lasted around thirty-five minutes, when submerged in water, before eroding. This meant there was little risk of spillage, but he didn't want a clumsy soldier making a mistake and infecting himself, complicating the operation.

■

When Murad had left with the canisters, the Doctor walked into the security airlock that separated his administrative offices from the laboratory. He input a security code and offered his hand to a palm-reader, which allowed him into the most covert facility in Pakistan.

The smell hit him immediately. Although this place had its own ventilation system, the smell of sickness and ordure was strong. The room was in darkness, sub-lit by dim red bulbs which gave a faint outline of the internal structures. It was quiet, thanks to the timers which shut down the main lights at 9 p.m., and the Doctor sat on the top step of the entry stairs, fishing a pack of cigarettes from his cardigan. He lit up, knowing that while smoking was not permitted on the campus of the Pakistan Agricultural Chemical Company, the discrete ventilation system in this area meant there'd be no smoke alarms going off in the security offices.

He was feeling nervous but excited about his work being allowed into the field, even if the Colonel and ISI had determined that he couldn't be present at the tests. It had been a long journey from childhood to scientific pre-eminence. His discoveries were as great as those of Isaac Newton or Robert Oppenheimer, but he would never be lauded by other scientists or feted at the United Nations. However, once unleashed, his discovery would not only right a historic wrong done against his family—it would bring to its knees one of the world's great nations and the very foundation of Western culture.

CHAPTER
EIGHTEEN

'Either way's a risk,' said Briffaut, slicing up a breakfast apple with a pocket knife. Lying in front of him was de Payns' mission plan for Alamut. The operations were briefed from the DR and authorised by the section heads, such as Dominic Briffaut. But the owner of the plan was the *chef de mission.*

'I like the simplicity of your plan,' said Briffaut. 'One team, one car. But doesn't that leave us exposed?'

The plan detailed how the Alamut team would ascertain the main arrival and departure times at the MERC and then base themselves in a petrol station located at the end of the road leading to the centre, or a cafe north of the junction, in a group of shops. They'd wait two hours in the morning before leaving to live their legends around Islamabad, then return to the access road for the two hours when people departed their workplace. All the cars coming or going from the MERC would drive past them, and if a car recurred and looked important, they'd follow it to isolate the phone number with their spinning machine. Then they'd identify the house and take a picture of the person associated with the car.

De Payns' temples were still tight from the previous evening's Jack Daniel's—left to their own choices, Shrek and de Payns drank vodka, but Templar always insisted on the American whiskey. 'We don't need a full support team; it would just draw attention. Our cover should be okay.'

Briffaut made a face. 'Palermo ended well because you had a support team.'

De Payns knew what Briffaut was saying, but he still had confidence in his plan. 'I'd rather stay low profile and slightly exposed than have teams in-country. The film company cover feels strong.'

'Film scouts in Pakistan? The police might buy that, but what about the ISI?'

De Payns nodded. 'We'll mix it up, and the legends are clever. We even have a screenplay.'

'It's all light ID,' said Briffaut, poking his finger at one of de Payns' pages. Light ID meant the names generated would pass at customs and immigration and would satisfy a cursory inspection with a call to the film company office. But there wouldn't be bank accounts in his name or credit cards that he could use. They'd be travelling with cash. 'And you'll need a car,' he added.

'We have an honourable correspondent in Islamabad—she'll make sure Hertz rents us a car in cash.'

An honourable correspondent was a French person living abroad who used their occupation or social influence to voluntarily assist the DGSE, but de Payns could see his boss still looked apprehensive. 'I want you flying in next Sunday. That gives you five straight days of recon, and then I want you the hell out of there.'

'I'll know more when I get on the ground and have a good look, but we're going to be very tight, very careful,' he assured him.

'And fast,' said Briffaut as he ate another slice of apple. 'Careful and fast.'

■

When the meeting with Briffaut wrapped up, de Payns headed into the basement level of the Bunker to see how his mission team was progressing. He found Thierry and Brent in one of the workrooms, hovering over a laptop.

Brent stood. 'You seen these new spinners, boss?'

De Payns looked down and saw a silver Toshiba laptop with a fifteen-inch screen. It looked unremarkable.

'That's it?' asked de Payns.

'Yes,' said Brent, smiling like a child with a Christmas present. 'Built-in antennas, can accept multiple cell phone signals, can isolate IMSI and IMEI, and still operates as a computer. Show him, Thierry.'

Thierry's hands flew across the keyboard, and the screen opened in a standard desktop format with apps down the side and folders on the right. There was a logo for Capital Films etched into the wallpaper.

'Let's see the locations,' said Brent, and Thierry opened a folder called *'Lake Forgiveness'*—the name of their fictitious film. It contained a synopsis, a screenplay and a document called 'Production Notes', which itself had twenty-eight subfolders, each labelled by scene.

'Open a folder,' said Brent.

De Payns reached forward and clicked the folder labelled 'Scene 22'. It opened at *22. EXT.—ISLAMABAD SUBURBS—DAY.* Below were stock photographs and maps of the city, with specific buildings prominent.

'I'm thinking we have two photographers in the car, and they're shooting for locations that we file to these folders,' said Brent, indicating the Canon DSLR kits on the neighbouring desk.

'Good,' said de Payns, liking the attention to detail. When police or intel—or even just a hotel manager—asked an agent what they were doing and where they were going, the worst thing to do was hesitate. An operator in character had to have a pretext ready to go at any moment, and it had to come out quickly, because humans were the best readers of other humans—a flicker of hesitation, a roll of the eyes up to the left or a simple *umm* could bring the whole show undone. So all operations had to start with proper preparation.

'And there's this,' said Brent, opening a folder and showing de Payns its contents—a distressed screenplay called *Lake Forgiveness*, with a pale blue cover sheet and two brass lugs in the holes of the screenplay paper. De Payns picked it up and saw the name of the screenwriter, David Keller, and in the bottom left corner the owner of the property, Capital Films, with the Paris address.

De Payns smiled, recognising the false ID. 'So, Brent, you're the writer? Where did we get the screenplay?'

'Used screenwriter software, totally untraceable,' Brent replied.

'How so?' asked de Payns.

'Thierry wrote the code.'

De Payns looked at the squinting whiz-kid. 'Code?'

'Yeah,' said Thierry. 'I trained it to find screenplays stored in the cloud from a criterion that included father–son themes, Kashmir conflict, Muslim versus Hindu, dispossession and Islamophobia . . .'

'You can do that?'

'Sure. Then we bring it into a smart database and we use some AIs we wrote to assemble a ninety-minute screenplay—in French, of course. We changed a few names and did some editing, but basically the AI put it together.'

De Payns realised they were serious. 'Is it any good?'

'Sex, violence, war . . .' said Thierry.

'And a coming-out scene,' said Brent. 'It's very tasteful.'

'I'll need to read it,' said de Payns. 'Can you courier it to the film company? What about the spinner?'

Thierry executed a series of workarounds on the keyboard, and the computer transformed from a filmmaker's laptop to a cell phone spinner, which used graphic boxes. Having locked on to an IMSI number, the number would be allocated to the box and other data such as time and connections would be filled in. Spinning machines did not operate the way they were portrayed in the movies—it was almost impossible to simply pick up someone's cell phone and 'track' them with coordinates. The spinner—in reality, an IMSI catcher—just acted as a telecom tower connection on the local network. So what the mission team would see on the spinning laptop were the IMSI numbers from nearby phones connecting to the 'tower' that sat inside this laptop. If there were a lot of people with phones around, there'd be a lot of numbers. If a phone was not moving, the number would remain on the screen, but other numbers would come and go, meaning those phones were moving in relation to the laptop. After a few days, the team would have a group of numbers which could be of interest and which would be registered in the system. That's when the team would follow the car of interest, and because the mission team's car would be following at the same speed, only the phones located in that car would stay connected to the laptop. Those numbers would switch from one antenna to another along the travel route, but the phones would always be connected to the spinning laptop, as if the laptop were a permanently available cellular tower.

Brent continued. 'We use the antennas around the screen to line up our target, and when we lock on we harvest the IMSI and the IMEI numbers.'

While IMSI was stored on a SIM card, the IMEI was the international mobile equipment identity—the identity number given to each phone, behind the battery. Most networks also stored the IMEI in an equipment identity register which contained all legitimate cell phone IMEIs, allowing the cell network owners to identify stolen or non-complying phones.

'Excellent,' said de Payns. 'Briffaut wants us in-country by next Sunday, which gives us a whole working week to do our thing. Everyone okay with that?'

'We're good,' said Brent.

CHAPTER
NINETEEN

He put the battery into his phone as he reached street level at the Metro and when it powered up there were two text messages from Romy. Both asked him to call her. He made the call as he walked with the late afternoon commuters.

'Hi, honey, how are you?' he asked as she picked up. His hangover was still substantial.

'Just wanted to check with you,' she said. 'Ana invited us to dinner.'

De Payns dodged other walkers, also with phones to their ears. 'Um . . .'

'The kids are very close,' said Romy. 'They pushed for this.'

De Payns was uncomfortable, but he was also aware that as their children grew up he couldn't control the friendships they made.

'I said we'd head over around seven,' Romy told him.

Great, thought de Payns. The whole thing was planned. One of those arrangements that was not really optional at all.

Across the road he saw Jim, obviously waiting. Jim put on his cap and de Payns walked to the pedestrian crossing and waited for the green signal. He walked westwards from the Port-Royal RER station towards Montparnasse Cemetery. Jim led them into one of the leafier streets, filled with grand Belle Époque apartment buildings with awnings over the restaurants and cafes at street level. They cut down a side alley, which de Payns never liked, although this one had old cobble pavers under foot and ended in a tall cast-iron gate, which Jim pulled back and walked through. They were now inside one of Paris's private gardens, which formed a park from the combined backyards of an entire block of Montparnasse. They wove through trees that were hundreds of years old and crossed a bridge over a brook. De Payns pulled back as they walked across an enormous lawn. He didn't know this garden and he was wary of being so exposed.

Jim must have sensed his reluctance, because as he reached the edge of the lawn he stopped and looked back at de Payns, making a small gesture with his head. Then he walked towards a brick cottage which looked like a gardener's quarters. De Payns advanced as Jim reached the cottage door.

'Come on. You walk like an old woman,' said the former soldier, holding the door open and gesturing for de Payns to enter.

De Payns paused at the threshold and looked Jim in the eye. 'This is on you, Jim,' he said. 'If I have a problem in there, then you have a problem. Understand?'

Jim laughed. 'You and I already have a problem, *mon pote*. Now get in the goddamn room.'

De Payns ducked under the mossy lintel into a low-ceilinged space that might once have housed a family. Now it was filled with lawnmowers and motorised yard equipment and shelves of chemicals. In the dusty corner was a kitchen and sitting area, and on a sheet-covered sofa sat Philippe Manerie.

'I'm in a hurry,' said the director. 'Sit.'

De Payns walked to a wooden kitchen table and pulled out a rickety chair.

'There's no need for the crap you're giving Jim,' said Manerie. 'We are all on the same side, and anything he asks of you is an order from me.'

De Payns looked at the soldier, who was standing guard at the door. 'Sorry, darling.'

'You're forgiven, *ma chérie*,' said Jim.

'Stop it, both of you,' snapped Manerie. He looked at de Payns. 'You owe me some insights. What's happening with the Falcon investigation?'

'Still no report of a body that we could confirm as Commodore. We have a name for the dead Turkish bodyguard, but we're doing more work on who he really is,' said de Payns. 'All the debrief reports are in, and when the director of operations has formed his own view of what went wrong, he'll show it to me and ask me to comment.'

'What is his view?'

'We were fucked by someone close enough to know what we had planned in Palermo that night.'

'What's your view?' asked Manerie.

'Sayef Albar knew about the passports before I left the ferry in Palermo. Maybe it was Commodore and maybe someone was wired up.'

Manerie rose to his feet.

'Just one thing,' said de Payns. 'Who's the mole? Any ideas?'

'Lots,' said Manerie, walking for the door.

■

The kids played an Xbox game on the living room television while de Payns, Romy and Ana sat around the kitchen table drinking Beaujolais. It was a comfortable apartment but not ostentatious—three bedrooms and two bathrooms was doing well in Montparnasse, but the place was compact. The husband,

Rafi, stood at the stove, tending a ceramic device that looked like a cooling tower for a nuclear power plant, but it was emitting delicious smells that filled the apartment.

'. . . so I say to this boss manager, why would I need a praying room? And he say, for your praying rug.'

At this, Rafi made the Middle Eastern version of a Gallic shrug, and Ana and Romy laughed. De Payns went along with it, but not wholeheartedly.

'So, Rafi,' he said, 'I guess you're a Christian, right?'

'By upbringing, yes,' said Rafi. 'But not so much the choirboy.'

He was a chatty engineer, enjoying his life in Paris, and his wife was a Frenchwoman, although one of her grandparents was Syrian. It was very Parisian, and if de Payns wasn't professionally paranoid he would have liked to relax and have a few drinks. However, stories that self-advertised the teller as non-Muslim simply made him edgy. And women who were beautiful, intelligent and confident—but made nothing of it—were worthy of suspicion. When he was first plucked from the Intelligence Division and inducted into the Y Division at the Bunker, he was taught the skills of counterintelligence, especially when countering female operatives. It hadn't been until de Payns was firmly inside the Bunker that he realised how devastating a female operative could be when pitted against the male ego. Even the most unappealing man, who had never been with a beautiful woman, could be flattered into feeling entitled to such beauty and intelligence. As they said in the spy game, a beautiful woman doesn't bring you undone—she makes you bring yourself undone.

Conversation moved across Macron, the *gilets jaunes*, French petrol taxes and the chances of France in the coming European Football Championship. Romy accepted a second glass of wine from Ana and then leaned back into him and de Payns gave her a quick kiss on the neck, feeling her soft blonde hair on his face. The kids came to the table when Rafi called that dinner was almost ready, and de Payns excused himself and made for the bathroom. He counted off one child's bedroom and a closed door that he assumed was the spare room. He entered a white-tiled bathroom near the apartment's front door, where there was a toilet, sink and bathtub with a showerhead above it. Two blue towels on a rack, a child's T-shirt and underwear on the floor in the corner. He moved to the vanity, opened the mirror-door cabinet and saw a tube of toothpaste, a bulk packet of toothbrushes, an unopened bar of soap, a clear plastic punnet of elastic hair ties and a bottle of head lice lotion.

Closing the cabinet, he checked the vanity counter and opened the doors underneath, where there was a spray bottle of shower cleaner and several cleaning sponges. The toilet cistern was white ceramic—he lifted it and checked for hidden items. De Payns flushed the toilet and washed his hands. As he left the bathroom, he noticed a patchouli-like scent that lingered in the house. He paused in the hallway—the door across the hallway was three inches ajar. Through the gap he confirmed it was the master bedroom. He paused and tried to get a line of sight through the gap, but as he looked to his left he realised the Homsi child had left the table to do something with his Xbox, and he was looking straight at him. De Payns smiled and walked towards the boy, who immediately stood up and returned to the table. As de Payns resumed his seat and watched Rafi serve his meal, he wondered what the child had been doing at the Xbox. Romy gave him a warning look and de Payns eased back in his chair and smiled. He drained the last of his wine and held up his glass.

Ana was ready with the bottle. 'Nice to get to know you, Alec,' she said, with a winning smile.

CHAPTER TWENTY

De Payns heated up a breakfast of *pain au chocolat* for Patrick and Oliver and made a coffee for Romy as she emerged from the bathroom wearing nothing but a towel. He ate with the boys and they had a laugh at *SpongeBob* while Romy checked her emails. He made a full round of hot chocolates, kissed his wife for six seconds and ducked out of his building's side entrance, hitting the street at 8.06 a.m. He headed east for two blocks to a small lane which ended in a stone staircase that rose under a building to a cross street. He slowed as he arrived at the stairs, and at the top of them turned to his right, giving him a view of the two hundred metres he had just walked. There was no one behind him.

He took a bus, changed to the Metro, and when he emerged in the southern part of the thirteenth arrondissement, he walked to the Company's changeover house. He removed his phone and battery, his watch and wallet, and his Ray-Ban sunglasses, and placed them in what OTs called the 'life box'—the section of his secure locker that contained his genuine effects. He looked down—he was wearing grey NB trainers and blue Levi's. They could stay. He took off his dark blue polo and replaced it with a pale green button-up shirt from the locker. Removing his black windbreaker, he turned it inside out and put it on again. Now he was wearing a cream windbreaker. He poured the contents of the Clement Vinier manila folder onto the tallboy shelf in the locker, and, checking the Vinier wallet, he found a Metro card which had around thirty euro on it, a sheaf of cash, a genuine driver's licence with his fake address and a membership card for the SRF, the Société des Réalisateurs de Films. He picked up the Clement Vinier Nokia, took a battery from the charger, and kept them separated in his windbreaker's inside pocket. He would not fire up a phone until he was well clear of the safe house.

He caught a bus to Charenton and plunged into the narrow side streets, eventually entering an unfashionable building with the sign *Café Internet* over the door. Inside he dished out five euro and asked for computer eleven, which was near the back of the shop, out of range of the security CCTV.

He manoeuvred between stacks of cell phone boxes and slabs of bottled water and dodged the backpacks that had been left in the walkway by two students engrossed in a Skype call. De Payns took a seat, checked for eyes and switched off the computer. He waited until the screen was completely blank before he rebooted it and inserted a USB key which contained a Mozilla program. He launched his internet navigation from the USB key, obeying the Company rule to never navigate from an unknown computer's browser. Now he opened his Clement Vinier LinkedIn account. It had him as a researcher, AD and director at Capital Films in Paris, with some of his industry skills confirmed by other LinkedIn users. He navigated his account and linked with people, issued 'likes' on other film industry workers who were editing and writing, and joined in a discussion among SRF professionals about protectionism in French film—a drawn-out argument that had been active for decades. Then he entered a post about travelling to Pakistan where he was scouting for a shoot on his new film, *Lake Forgiveness*. He dropped a stock picture of Islamabad on it.

He did the same thing on his Facebook account then went into the SRF website and contributed a comment in a blog featuring Frédéric Jouve. Having left a few Clement Vinier crumbs, de Payns ejected the Mozilla USB and cleared the history and cookies seven times. Any less than seven wipes and smart people with good equipment could access his shadow data.

He caught the Metro to Gare du Nord and walked to the Montmartre area, where he found an oldish building now converted to offices. He let himself into the building foyer and cleared the mail from one of the boxes. He sorted through it, binning the junk and opening the two envelopes addressed to Clement Vinier, Capital Films. One offered low-rate credit for business owners and the other was for life insurance.

There was a convenience store on the corner, and de Payns walked in and greeted the Tamil woman behind the counter. 'Hi, Ezzy, how's business?' he asked.

'Hello, Monsieur Clement,' she said with a smile. 'I got the film magazine. Let me show you.'

The short middle-aged woman led de Payns to her magazine section and put one of the publications in his hand. 'Came in yesterday, and look at date.'

'It's the current one,' said de Payns, clocking the masthead of the American *Variety* magazine. 'Well done.'

'More,' she said, showing him the English-language *Empire* and *Hollywood Reporter.*

'Great,' he said, grabbing the *Empire* and moving back to the counter. 'I'm scouting locations in Pakistan. I'll need some reading.'

Leaving the convenience store, he crossed the road to the Polish barber and took a seat while Igor finished with a customer. He read the football and boxing magazines, and shifted along the bench seat when two more customers entered. After eleven minutes, Igor took the money from the previous customer and gave de Payns the nod.

'Ah, it is my friend the Cecil B. DeMille of Paris,' said the Pole, who seemed to see the humour in everything.

The Naugahyde squeaked as de Payns dropped into the chair. 'Just the usual, thanks, Igor.'

'Steve McQueen in *The Getaway*?'

'Let's do that,' said de Payns, smiling at himself in the mirror as the white bib was clipped around his throat. 'That's my favourite McQueen.'

Fifteen minutes later, sporting his new haircut, de Payns dropped into a Ukrainian-owned travel agency down the block from the barber shop. It advertised Kiev–Odessa river cruises on faded posters. Nadja, the elderly heavy smoker who owned the agency, was happy to see her filmmaking neighbour.

'What can I do for the Frankish Ford Coppola?' she asked, making her usual joke as she motioned for de Payns to sit. She had a hairdo like the mother in *The Simpsons*, but black rather than blue.

'Four tickets to Islamabad,' said de Payns, lighting up. 'Cash okay?'

'Of course,' said Nadja, waving him away and tapping on her keyboard. 'You have hotel?'

'We don't have a big budget. We need six nights, two rooms, arriving next Sunday. You know of any nice three-stars, in the city?'

She tapped a few keys. 'I have the Pearl Continental. Is clean, is cheap and has the bar.'

'Sounds okay,' said de Payns, having already researched it and decided he wanted the Pearl Continental. 'Safe?'

'Oh, yes. Secret police make sure of that,' she said, chuckling so hard that her hair shook like a building in an earthquake. No one did secret police jokes like the comrades of the former Soviet Union.

He caught a bus north, alighted at a Metro station and descended to the platforms, where he caught connecting trains that took him west, into the Muette Sud area. He walked the leafy boulevards till he reached a *superette*, where he bought a litre of milk, two pastries and a loaf of bread, and made small talk with the owner, who knew him as Clement.

Half a block from there he let himself into the foyer of a rundown but once-grand apartment building where he'd found an unoccupied flat. It was just before midday and the building seemed quiet. He'd placed his name—C.J. Vinier—on the letterbox in the portico from which he pulled seven letters, two of which were in his name. There were credit card offers and a letter from a person in the neighbourhood with a long-term parking spot to sublet. He climbed the stairs to his assumed apartment on the second floor, where he checked his *bouletage*, a needle squeezed into the hinge side of the door. It was in place, meaning no one had been in the apartment since he last checked ten days ago. He used the key he'd had made and let himself in. The apartment looked untouched. It had a varnished wooden floor, so having shut the door he kneeled and looked across the living room floor and saw undisturbed dust reflected in the sunlight. No one had walked the floor. Next, he checked the three-point alignment he'd made between the transistor radio on the kitchen counter, the trinket box on the coffee table and the leather-bound copy of Victor Hugo's *Notre-Dame de Paris* in the bookcase. He walked to his 'bullseye', or the place the operative would stand which would be used as the reference point. From the bullseye he could define three axes, one in front of him, one on his right and one on the left. When a premises had been checked over, at least one of the three axes would be slightly changed. His alignment was intact. He remained at the rear of the main room, focusing through the gap between the partially pulled curtains and on the building opposite his apartment. He was looking for large camera lenses or people with binoculars lifted to their face.

He dropped the *Empire* magazine on the coffee table and moved to the kitchen, took the bottle of milk and loaf of bread from the fridge and placed them in the rubbish bin under the kitchen sink. He put one of the pastries in the fridge and ate the other as he moved to the bedrooms. In the master bedroom he rearranged the sheets of the bed so the turn-down was different from how he had left it, and changed the book on the bedside table from Proust to Flaubert. In the shelf under the table he put the copy of *Variety*, opened to page nine. He brushed his teeth in the bathroom, taking care to allow bits of toothpaste foam to hit the mirror. Then he washed his face and, having dried his hands, he left the towel on the vanity counter. As he was leaving he turned on the hall light in the small entryway to the apartment, and jammed a *bouletage* into the door as he eased it shut.

De Payns' light IDs had to be nurtured and attended to, so when one of his assumed names was checked by the Russians or the Saudis, the people doing the digging into his life were coming up with cafe owners and bartenders who said, *Oh, yeah, Clement the filmmaker? I talked with him last week.* The entire visit to Clement Vinier's apartment, including buying groceries, took a shade over fifteen minutes, and in that time de Payns built details into his cover that could save his life, if they hadn't done so already.

He thought about the discipline of his job, and the fact that not only did he owe his own life to observing the detail, but so did his family. This was his truth and his lifeline, and as he descended into the Metro to head back to the Bunker, he made a decision to maintain the discipline. With his right hand he broke down Manerie's burner phone in his windbreaker pocket, and without slowing his stride he deposited the pieces in two garbage bins as he approached his platform. He might be on the hook to Manerie and Jim, but he wouldn't let them undermine his basic security.

CHAPTER
TWENTY-ONE

De Payns spent the evening going over financial and logistics checks for Alamut and finally got back to Montparnasse just after midnight. When he emerged from Port-Royal Metro station he immediately saw Jim on the other side of the boulevard. Something moved in him, but he followed Manerie's offsider into a dark corner of the public park opposite the Metro stairs.

'You deaf or you lost your phone?' asked Jim, turning to face de Payns.

De Payns took an extra step, hit Jim in the solar plexus with a hard left hand. As the DGS man sagged, de Payns kneed him in the balls. He went straight for Jim's pistol under the left armpit and tore it from the jacket as Jim moaned softly, on one knee.

'Fuck, de Payns,' panted the soldier, his face a mask of agony in the dappled streetlight that came through the trees. 'Bad night?'

De Payns emptied the Beretta 9mm's magazine and actioned the weapon, making it eject the round sitting in the breech. He threw the handful of steel into the shrubbery.

'That stupid phone you gave me? It's in the garbage, where it should have been in the first place,' said de Payns, adrenaline pumping but keeping his cool. 'And this is the third time you've contacted me in public, in the same place. That's a danger to me and my family.'

'You weren't answering . . .'

'Shut it,' said de Payns, pointing a threatening finger in the soldier's face. 'You tell Manerie I might be on the hook, but I'm not walking around with some random phone in my pocket, and I won't have these approaches made around my life zone. It's not happening.'

Jim nodded slowly. 'Manerie asked me to give you a message. Wanna hear it?'

'Do I have a choice?'

Jim stood, wincing slightly as he tried to straighten. 'He hears you're about to travel. He wants to know where and why.'

De Payns could have hit him again. 'I don't know what he's talking about.'

'You sure about that?'

'Sure,' said de Payns.

'Not what Manerie is hearing.'

'Tell him you have to be careful with what you hear in public toilets,' said de Payns, feeling his pulse reduce slightly.

'Okay,' said Jim, opening his hands at de Payns in an appeasing gesture, smiling.

'Something funny?' asked de Payns, breathing through his nostrils.

'I was wondering when I was going to see the great Aguilar cut loose,' said Jim, sounding genuinely amused. 'But, shit, a knee in the balls?'

'I was improvising,' said de Payns, not wanting to get into a discussion about violence. The 'great Aguilar' reference alluded to a fracas in Cairo in which de Payns had allegedly beaten up three bad guys when a fire door in an old hotel failed to open and left him trapped. The truth was simpler—it was initially two people who came for him, but the passageway was so narrow that they could not attack at the same time. The third person was waiting in the lobby as he left the hotel. So while he did beat up three people, it was a case of one-on-one each time. But soldiers being soldiers, they'd turned him into the French Chuck Norris.

'Tell Manerie,' said de Payns, turning to go.

Jim cleared his throat. 'You wouldn't have one of those flashlights on your phone?' he asked, pointing at where de Payns had thrown the Beretta. 'You seen the paperwork if you lose a firearm?'

■

He crawled into bed at 1.07 a.m., thankful for a wife who liked a blacked-out bedroom to sleep. But his head spun: Manerie? What did he know about Operation Alamut? Why was he interested? And was his altercation with Jim going to cause trouble? It might lead to repercussions, but it was just as likely Jim wouldn't mention it; soldiers could be funny like that.

He lay in the dark, head buried in the pillows, and felt Romy turning into him.

'You okay, hon?' she whispered.

He breathed in her soap brand and felt soft blonde hair on his face.

'I'm fine.'

'You're grinding your teeth,' she said.

'I'm fine but not relaxed.'

'You're not going to make my graduation ceremony, are you?'

His heart banged against his chest. 'I'm working on it. Promise.'

'You're not looking well,' she said. 'I'm worried.'

He thought she might be starting a fight, but then he realised she was crying.

CHAPTER

TWENTY-TWO

The Bunker had three sensitive compartmented information facilities. One SCIF was for executives, another for operational briefings and the third was effectively the entire basement level, thanks to its construction. The basement was home to the Team 9 technology spies and some of France's most talented engineers, who built the gear that gave de Payns and his teams the edge on operations.

The basement SCIF was where de Payns conducted the meeting for his technology team, explaining how they were going to cleanse themselves without a support team. The Pearl Continental Hotel had a rear entrance and a standard eight-floor, elevator-hub layout. They would not be using cameras or microphones to counter the surveillance, relying instead on properly rehearsed legends. They were filmmakers, and the environment they established in their hotel would support their legend. The only IS they would perform would be conducted by Templar when he followed a person of interest to their home.

'So, just the four of us?' asked Brent, nodding slowly.

'The legend is filmmaker, so there's no illegal action, no need to go heavy,' said de Payns, who'd been expecting some questions from the techs. 'The only counter-measures will be three-point alignments in our rooms.'

'And if we pick up a follower?' asked Brent. 'Pakistan can get nasty.'

'We keep our legends and play the tourists without dropping our covers.'

'That's okay for a short period,' said Brent.

De Payns agreed. 'That's why we're on a tight timeline—arrive on a Sunday, spend all week doing the recon, and fly out on the Saturday. You're right, our covers will only hold as long as the pretext holds.'

Templar leaped in to reinforce de Payns. 'Just focus and play it out. Use the usual procedure for individual security in your rooms, but in public we'll stay in character.'

They nodded and de Payns shifted to the ground game—on the whiteboard he drew the layout around the MERC campus, which featured one road from the facility's security gate. At around eight hundred metres, the entry road hit the north–south public road at a T-junction. One hundred metres to the south of the T-junction was a service station and to the north was a small township, with shops and schools and a cafe. De Payns put crosses on the service station and cafe. He wanted to break up the way they travelled around; they would circulate in the car, but they couldn't do that constantly, so there would have to be legitimate places that a film scouting crew would stop. There were tourist stops such as the Faisal Mosque, of course, and de Payns had a list of others. But they needed staging points for their reconnaissance activities that did not look like staging points.

'We know that the lower-status scientists and technicians live on the campus, but there's enough traffic in and out of the facility to suggest that the senior people are allowed to leave. That's who we're going to identify. That's how we're going to access the MERC.'

Brent stretched, ran his fingertips through his slight beard. 'The technology will work and the plan looks good.'

'But?' asked de Payns.

'If the secret police get serious with us . . .' said Brent.

'Templar has an exfiltration plan,' said de Payns. 'We can't rely on it, though. Our best bet is still plan A—be professional, be fast and leave in one piece.'

■

Briffaut said little as de Payns ran through the final checklist—the tech was finalised and Templar was in Pakistan, scouting the layout and checking on the hotel. In a full action mission, where illegal activities or building penetration was required, a recon team would go into Islamabad a month before de Payns arrived and the team would do an *équipement de ville*, responding to the *chef de mission's* requests—it might be five ISs, three tourniquets, three *plans de supports*, one life zone, three hotels and one exfiltration. When the recon team returned, they would detail each item and the action team would have a few weeks to learn them by heart and plan the mission around those elements.

But this mission involved no illegal action, no approach, no recruitment, no house or structure penetration. It was just four of them playing their legends, moving as tourists. Without a mission team or a system of ISs, there was little to coordinate. Everyone had their job and their commitment to being in and out within seven days. It would mean a tight focus on the MERC and insufficient time for the Pakistanis to see patterns in the four-man French team. Theoretically.

'Emergency exfil?' asked Briffaut, who turned a stainless steel lighter over on the desk, not taking his eyes off de Payns.

'Shouldn't be necessary,' said de Payns. 'We'll play our legend.'

Briffaut nodded. 'Falcon was a close call.'

'Palermo was close,' agreed de Payns.

Briffaut held his stare. 'You good for this?'

'Absolutely.'

'Team all sorted?'

'They're sharp and ready.'

Briffaut. 'So, what's eating you?'

'My wife. Her PhD graduation ceremony is on Saturday.'

Briffaut said nothing.

De Payns shrugged. 'Her parents are in town.'

'Bad timing and bad luck,' Briffaut deadpanned. 'You know how it goes in this job.'

'I do,' said de Payns.

'Good luck,' said Briffaut, offering his hand. 'And if it turns weird over there, pull the pin. We good?'

'We're good,' said de Payns.

CHAPTER

TWENTY-THREE

The Pakistan International Airlines Boeing 777 landed at Islamabad International just after 2 p.m. and taxied to the air bridge. It was a fine, warm afternoon but de Payns felt frosty cool, a habit he'd developed from his first field operations—start the operation with the attitude you intend to strike for the duration; get in character, be the legend, stay alive and return with the goods. In the back of his mind was a life-saving night at the Sorbonne's Grand Hall, paying homage to his wife as she received her PhD. Patrick and Oliver on either side of him, his parents-in-law to his left, he felt blessed and proud and almost at peace in that amazing building. When the speeches started he'd glanced up to the vaulted ceilings and saw the twin spirits of the Université de Paris, looking down on the gathering. They were the marble statues of Archimedes and Homer, representing the sciences and the arts, coming together in one place. There was little academic instinct in de Payns, but seeing his wife glowing in the pride showed by her parents when they went to dinner, was something that moved him deeply. When Romy grabbed his hand and whispered *thank you* in his ear, he almost cried.

As the Boeing reached the gate, de Payns thought about the two spirits inhabiting his own body—the manipulating spy and the proud husband and father. Romy had been right about him—he did leverage families, he did use them where he could. And the look on her face—disgust—was a normal human reaction. He wondered what it meant that he needed the respect of his wife more than he needed self-respect.

The seatbelt sign was switched off and he snapped into tourist chatter with Brent and Thierry, who had been seated beside him for the almost-eight-hour flight. He reached into the overhead locker and retrieved his backpack, which contained a Canon 6D camera and zoom lens. It was a professional's camera but didn't have the size of the upscale models, meaning it attracted less attention from customs people and police. Yet it could still be operated manually to achieve high ISOs and long fields of focus, which was crucial in reconnaissance photography.

They moved through the passport gates with no problems, wheeling their cabin luggage straight to the taxi stands outside the new terminal building. A little under fifty minutes later and they were at the Pearl Continental Hotel, waiting at the reception desk as the clerk photocopied their passports. Templar arrived as they stood there and made a show of greeting his fellow tourists and filmmakers, talking excitedly about the sights around the twin cities of Islamabad and Rawalpindi, expressing his eagerness to get on the road and scout some shooting locations, especially for scenes seven and thirteen.

They adjourned to their rooms, de Payns bunking with Brent, Templar sharing with Thierry. They were good-sized rooms and very clean and comfortable for a mid-tier hotel. De Payns moved to the windows and squinted through the small crack between the heavy curtains. The room was on the second floor and the view was north-facing, taking in a park in front of the hotel and, in the distance, what looked like a very large water tower. He shifted his body to the side of the curtain gap and looked down onto a busy street. According to his map, this was Mall Road. He switched to the other side of the curtains and looked down on another angle of the street. No followers or watchers that he could detect. But that didn't mean the hotel staff weren't talking to the secret police. While de Payns checked the street, Brent checked the in-room phone, furniture and light fittings for electronic surveillance. He gave the thumbs-up after a few minutes. No surveillance.

■

They took the afternoon off and met the following morning at the hotel restaurant where they chatted over breakfast. The hotel was in Rawalpindi, the ancient side of the twin cities. Adjoining in the north-west was the capital Islamabad, which had been built to house government departments, embassies and grand hotels. Rawalpindi was more raffish and it suited the Alamut team.

They finished breakfast and walked onto the street just before 9 a.m. Templar waited at the kerb in a pale blue Nissan Maxima, rented from Hertz in cash, but with the rental papers in the name of Clement Vinier and Capital Films.

They drove south, Templar looking for tails in the mirror. It was an interesting city, with all the ancient buildings of Damascus or Amman, but with evidence of modern civil infrastructure—there were souks, but there were also bright storefronts that would not be out of place in Paris or Frankfurt.

Templar swung west and aimed for the MERC. They unpacked the camera and laptop and hooked the Canon to Brent's Toshiba. He opened the scene folders; the pictures they wanted to use in their movie would be downloaded into the laptop. De Payns took the *Lake Forgiveness* script from his backpack along with a notebook and pen.

'Take this and read me the beginning of scene seven,' said de Payns, handing the bound screenplay to Thierry.

They drove through the south-west of the sprawling city, Thierry reading the scene's opening descriptions, de Payns jotting them down as points in the notebook. Scene seven was an exterior shot of Rawalpindi's city streets during the day. The hero was going to be running down the footpath and through a souk to deliver a message to his dying mother. De Payns wrote the street name—Ganj Mandi—and made notes that would please a secret policeman: *modern clothes, no hijabs, clean streets* . . . Then he wound down the window and took his first photographs of the streetscape and people.

The team relaxed a little with the first pictures in the can. Templar drove them out of the city blocks and got them onto the Islamabad Expressway, where he accelerated into the fast traffic going south. The ability of a Western person to drive safely and inconspicuously in Asia was an underrated skill, and one that de Payns always relied on with Templar.

Templar jammed the Maxima between two overloaded trucks and settled into the traffic. 'From here, eleven minutes,' he said.

■

The Material and Energy Research Centre crouched like a provincial high school in the near distance as they took an off-ramp from the expressway on the south-western outskirts of Rawalpindi. Further west was the international airport and the M2 road to Lahore. The land around the MERC looked as if it had been put aside for government uses—there were trees and patches of grazing areas but not a lot of buildings or houses. As they slowed in a small bunch of shops de Payns noticed dogs on the street, and he took photographs. He needed his camera filled with images consistent with a movie scouting mission.

'In three seconds, look to your right,' said Templar, guiding the car out of a clutch of shops and low-rise office buildings and up a hill. De Payns looked to his right—they were clear of buildings and looking down on the MERC complex, about two kilometres away across brownish scrublands. Inside the perimeter fencing de Payns recognised a collection of low-rise, commercial structures with driveways connecting them and a single gatehouse at the lone exit and entry.

A large roundabout loomed at the western end of the road they were on. Templar took a right, so they were driving in a northerly direction on a single-lane main road with high-quality asphalt.

'Okay,' said Templar. 'In one kilometre on the right is the road to the MERC. Check out the service station on the left before the turn-off, and then we'll go through a bunch of shops which includes the cafe.'

They drove north in the traffic, doing around seventy kilometres an hour. The car was silent. On the left was a mid-sized petrol station, with a yellow awning featuring Urdu lettering across it. De Payns could see a small mini-mart and some tables and chairs at the side. Ten seconds further north, the turn-off for the MERC was on their right. The road went straight for several hundred metres, through low scrublands, and terminated at the MERC gatehouse. Having driven for five minutes past the MERC road, through a small section of shops and homes, Templar looped back and they stopped at the shops and parked where they could see the T-junction. They went into the cafe, bought coffees and small homemade biscuits, then left the small township and spent the day practising their legends. In the afternoon, they looped back to the area. They were trying to ascertain knock-off time at the MERC, when they'd have a wave of vehicles to assess and surveil.

The four of them watched the road. At 4.03 p.m., a long-wheelbase Fiat van coming from the south turned into the road and drove towards the complex. A lightweight truck with a closed-in box on the back made the same manoeuvre at 4.09.

'So it's not four o'clock,' said Brent.

Their research suggested that government departments finished work between four and six, but not on the half-hour. And government employees in Pakistan finished work en masse; there was none of the flexi-time that operated in the bureaucracies of Western Europe.

For the next thirty minutes they drove around the area playing their legend, taking photographs and making notes, and keeping away from the T-junction. They had to frequent the area sufficiently to find a pattern, but not so they'd look like they were spending too much time in one place.

They timed their return for shortly after five, making a northbound pass at 5.04 and then a southbound one at 5.08. Still no flood of cars.

'So it's six,' said de Payns.

They kept the atmosphere light and stayed in character with banter about the movie as they took a long circular route west of the MERC. Approaching from the south shortly before six o'clock, they drove straight to the service station where they made a show of getting out and stretching, while Templar filled the car with petrol. Brent went into the small coffee shop on the side of the service station and bought four bottles of water. As he emerged, a small green Peugeot sedan arrived at the T-junction from the MERC, turned into the traffic and headed north, past the cafe where they'd bought coffee that morning. It was 6.02 p.m.

'Keen to get out of there,' said Brent, sitting beside Thierry, who started the IMSI spinner in his laptop. 'Must have Mustafa Briffaut as a manager.'

They laughed and chatted, letting the service station owner see that they were a noisy film crew with nothing to hide. The T-junction started filling fast, the Peugeot's place quickly filled by a Nissan Pulsar, a VW Golf and then a white Toyota RAV4. All the cars looked newish and they all turned to the north.

Within a few minutes, traffic built up at the T-junction as a dozen cars from the MERC queued to get onto the main road, all of them turning north and driving through the small section of shops.

'We're catching IMSIs,' said Thierry quietly as he watched his laptop. 'It's working.'

Near the rear of the line-up de Payns noticed a black late-model Mercedes sedan and, right behind it, a black LandCruiser with heavily tinted windows. All the vehicles turned north, and the Alamut team slowly got back into the car.

'Well, we've got our time,' said de Payns as Templar accelerated into the southbound lane and headed back to the hotel. 'Let's get something to eat and play up the legend for the hotel workers.'

'I researched the film industry,' said Thierry. 'They drink a lot.'

'I researched Pakistan,' said de Payns. 'They'll let us drink but they don't accept public intoxication.'

'Shit, these people,' said Templar, shaking his head and reaching for a cigarette. 'Why do they want to live in France if booze annoys them so much?'

De Payns looked out of the window, saw the sun getting low in the sky as they headed for the hotel. 'We'll drink like a French film crew, but with a great deal of care.'

CHAPTER
TWENTY-FOUR

The next day was a Tuesday—their third day in Pakistan and the chance to make progress given they now had the leaving time and they knew how the roads and traffic worked. The team concentrated on the south of the twin cities, capturing images that would fit with the film's soccer-playing scenes. The hero had a sporting aspect, so they cruised some of the football fields and made a big deal of taking photographs and scribbling notes. It was a chance to interact with locals and have a friendly chat with shop owners, a legend-building exercise in itself. Templar and de Payns even discovered that the smoking bans were not strict outside the centre of the city and they could smoke with their coffees.

They ate an early evening meal at the hotel, letting the staff see them in one happy group, and just before 5.30 p.m. they exited separately. When they met up in the street, they headed west in the Nissan. They tanked at the service station with the yellow awning at 6 p.m., with the car aimed north, and waited for the parade of cars which started queuing at the T-junction at 6.06. Templar drove past the T-junction, giving them a look at the cars.

'Big Mercedes is seven back,' mumbled de Payns as Templar stopped the Nissan north of the T-junction and left it idling.

Templar kept his eye on the rear-view mirror and Brent tapped on his Toshiba keyboard, switching the machine to spinner mode. No one turned back to look.

'And . . . we're go,' said Templar, hitting the indicator stalk and easing into the traffic. As they hit the flow of vehicles, the black Mercedes was three cars in front of them.

De Payns couldn't waste time on the small fry. The Company wanted to be in the top-secret layer, not in the slops. They needed a vehicle belonging to a senior person, someone with status and probably travelling with bodyguards, and the most obvious vehicle was the black Mercedes.

'What do we have on the radar?' asked de Payns, not taking his eyes off the Mercedes.

'Thirteen IMSIs and growing,' said Brent. 'Make that eighteen.'

When a cell phone was switched on, it registered with the closest cell tower it could find: the spinner. After ten minutes of driving north, most of the IMSI numbers had dropped off the spinner's list as cars turned off the main road and connected to another cell tower.

Fifteen minutes after they started their hunt, there was only one vehicle—a white VW van—between the Alamut crew and the black Mercedes, and the spinner had just four IMSI numbers that had stayed connected since the MERC.

'That van come from the MERC?' asked Templar as they backed off slightly.

'I think it was already on the main road,' said Thierry.

The question was potentially important. If there was a senior person from the MERC in the black Mercedes-Benz, did he or she have a bodyguard. And if so, were they in the car or were they following in a van? It might not mean much the first time the team followed the black Mercedes, but if there were bodyguards in another vehicle, they'd eventually pick up the team's Nissan. The white van's indicator blinked on the right side and turned off. They now had three IMSI numbers at the top of the spinner screen and they pulled back, allowing a car to get between the Nissan and the Mercedes.

It was getting towards dusk and the car's interior suddenly filled with red flashing lights. Templar swore under his breath and pulled onto the gravel shoulder of the road, waiting as an ambulance roared past. De Payns pointed his pen ahead through the windscreen, getting his mind back on the job.

The traffic sorted itself out again, and Templar got the Nissan positioned two cars back from the Mercedes. One of the cars in front of them turned off, and there were three IMSI numbers at the top of the list.

'All the cell phones are probably in the Mercedes,' said Brent from the back seat. 'They're all connecting.'

'Scientist and two bodyguards?' suggested Templar.

'Three co-workers, sharing a ride?' offered de Payns.

'Husband and wife,' said Thierry. 'One of them has two phones—one for home, one for their lover.'

'Ha ha!' said Templar, slapping the wheel. 'Be careful with that kind of thinking—they'll put you in actions teams, right, Aguilar?'

De Payns smiled. 'Like he said, Thierry, be careful with that.'

The convoy continued north through scrub and market gardens as daylight faded. De Payns checked his watch: 6.31 p.m. They had a strict commitment to stop following at seven o'clock.

A modern-looking suburb loomed out of the scrublands, and as they closed on it the Mercedes' indicator light started blinking. The brake lights came on and the black vehicle was rolling to a stop at the traffic lights on the edge of the residential area. Templar switched on the headlights and pulled back. The atmosphere in the Nissan was tense as they rolled closer to their prey and waited for the tell-tale signs of a head in the car turning to see who was behind. The heads didn't turn.

The traffic lights turned green and they turned left into suburbia, with modern, wide streets and detached houses. The verges were green and there were established trees and acacias, suggesting this was an area that was irrigated, and not for agriculture. A status symbol in Pakistan.

They followed the Mercedes into the comfortable suburb, losing sight of it as the convoy of three cars took a long bend. On the other side of the bend, de Payns couldn't see the Mercedes.

'Side streets,' said de Payns. Templar slowed and de Payns saw the Mercedes' brake lights down a side street on their right, as it stopped and turned left into a driveway.

Templar slowed and did a U turn, circling back and into the side street. They crept down the street, keeping a constant speed as they drove past the Mercedes, parked in a driveway beside a medium-sized house. One man in a black suit was opening the rear door of the car and another man, also in a black suit, was entering the side door of the house.

Templar kept driving. They made their way back to the main road and headed south, back to the expressway and into the heart of Rawalpindi. Now they had a street and a number, and they'd seen at least two people. But neither looked like a scientist.

'Three occupants of the car,' said Templar. 'Those two are the bodyguards. Our VIP was in the back seat.'

'The one at the door was doing a security sweep of the house?' asked de Payns.

'That's what I saw,' said Templar.

'We need some surveillance and a photograph of the VIP,' said de Payns.

'Copy,' said Templar. 'I'll return tonight, confirm the house set-up.'

'Pictures in the morning?' asked de Payns.

'Consider it done.'

CHAPTER TWENTY-FIVE

De Payns was in the middle of his third breakfast coffee, but with no hangover thanks to the Islamic Republic's attitude to public intoxication. It was easier just to have two beers and call it a night. It didn't concern de Payns that much, but Templar finished most days with several glasses of something and he wasn't impressed.

Now it was after 9 a.m., the other guests had already cleared out and Brent and Thierry were upstairs, calibrating their spinning equipment. De Payns was ill at ease. He'd woken up early and stressed, thinking about Manerie and Shrek and wondering at what point he had to talk to Briffaut ... or Shrek himself? Manerie's belief that there was a mole at the Bunker was not far-fetched. Someone had sabotaged the Palermo operation—probably a Company insider, or someone being fed by such a person. He had a head filled with Murad, Manerie, Lambardi and a mole with no name. Too many loose ends. He hadn't dwelled on it since the night Lambardi was killed, but he'd woken thinking about it and the blue rats were gnawing.

'Coffee still on?'

De Payns looked up and saw Templar, dressed in jeans and a T-shirt with a Reebok backpack on his shoulder, back from his overnight recon. The waitress approached and took an order for two coffees.

'How we looking?' asked de Payns, embarrassed that his friend had caught him in a pensive moment.

Templar leaned forward on his forearms. 'The person of interest is a middle-aged Arab male with a cheap suit and shoes,' said Templar. 'But they all dress that way, even at the top of the government. He may not be running the whole MERC, but he's high enough to ride in an S-Class Mercedes. Remember, people are more modest about displaying wealth in this country. It's not like Syria.'

'Habits?' asked de Payns.

'Black Mercedes arrived to pick him up at seven thirty-six this morning, one driver and one bodyguard,' said Templar, pausing and leaning back as the waitress brought two black coffees. 'It's all on the card, but it's wiped for now.'

Templar was talking about the protocol for recon photographs in the DGSE. You took your shots amid lots of filler that supported your legend. But the photographer deleted the shots to be used back in Paris immediately after taking them. They were retrieved with special software that could reconstitute shadow data, but the trick was to wipe the shots immediately after taking them or the numbering of the shots on the SD card would reflect missing images, something the ISI would look for.

'So, a middle-aged man and two bodyguards; they all get in the car and go to work?' asked de Payns.

'They took off on the same route they used last night.'

'So now we have three people and three IMSIs,' said de Payns. 'We have to isolate the VIP's.'

'We go back?' asked Templar, draining one cup of coffee and reaching for the second.

'We go back,' said de Payns.

■

They made three-point alignments in their hotel rooms and headed out after 10 a.m. They concentrated their photography and driving in the north of the city, taking notes and using a map for directions. The mission phones were usually cheap and *démarqué*, specifically built to suit the operative's legend but not capable of being used for navigation. They'd load them with pictures of family and colleagues, and a contacts list that reflected their fake profession. French secret service operatives almost never carried smartphones on missions because they carried so much personal data that the data would give away the operative. Even the lack of data on a smartphone would ring alarm bells.

They filled up the Canon's storage cards with images and downloaded them onto the laptop, and de Payns continued to fill his notebook with observations and suggestions for locations and scenes. He even made thought bubbles for songs that would play well.

They ate in reasonably priced cafes, tipped the waitresses and engaged in conversations about the Islamabad Museum, which contained a two-million-year-old human tool, a product of the ancient Indus civilisations.

They moved southwards at the end of the day, and at 5.32 p.m. bought their coffees at the petrol station with the yellow awning. They stretched, lit cigarettes and played with their phones, waiting for the evening exodus from the MERC. They had three IMSIs listed in the black Mercedes and their job was to whittle it down to one. One person of interest from the MERC, matched with one cell phone IMSI—that's when the Company could make inroads into the facility.

They spotted the first car speeding from the MERC gatehouse towards the T-junction at the main road, and they crushed their cigarettes and moved to their Nissan. The black Mercedes drove past and the team found a slot in the traffic so there were two vehicles between the two cars as they headed north. After ten minutes, they had the same three IMSIs that they'd caught the day before. They followed the Mercedes, now staying further back and verifying the IMSIs being used in the car.

They drove back into the city and arrived at the Pearl Continental in time to freshen up and go out for dinner at a restaurant around the corner that had left discount vouchers at the hotel. The waitress brought water and menus to their table, and departed without smiling. When she was out of earshot de Payns asked Templar if everything was okay.

'They searched our room,' said Templar, deadpan. 'Yours?'

'Ours too,' said de Payns. 'They were smart enough to return the *bouletage*.'

'But not good enough to spot the three-point alignment,' said Thierry.

The four of them looked at their menus, seeing only Urdu script and what appeared to be bad English translations.

'The game is on,' said de Payns. 'Time to play.'

■

De Payns kept the pressure on the team the next day. They established that the VIP lived alone, except for a live-in bodyguard and a driver who made random circuits of the suburb while the VIP was sleeping.

Templar had been meticulous about wiping the shots of the VIP as soon as practical after they were taken. In the French secret services operatives had to be able to take a good photograph—from up close, from two miles away, from a suitcase, from a phone, from a plane and underwater. People didn't work in the field until they could do that, and do it using a range of equipment.

During the daylight hours of the fifth day, the Thursday, Templar disappeared, leaving de Payns to drive the car. In the early evening he met Templar at a cafe in the south of the city. Templar was sitting under a TV that was blaring out a soccer match because he preferred to have public conversations in an area where there was white noise. He reported that during the day a cheap and battered car was parked in front of the VIP's house and unshaven, badly dressed men were inside.

'Your conclusion?' asked de Payns.

'That house is clearly under surveillance, and by the way these guys were occupying his house, I'd say it's a common event. The place is checked every day.'

'ISI?' asked de Payns.

'Probably, but not their A-team.'

De Payns shook his head. 'We're not getting into that house then.'

'No, we're not,' agreed Templar. 'That driver does passes as well. They might even have an overwatch operating, that's why my hide is so far back.'

De Payns sipped on his coffee and thought about it—they were Day Five in Pakistan, their rooms had been searched and they had identified a VIP who was minded by the ISI. They had yet to isolate the VIP's phone number, but they had three numbers—one of which was the VIP's—and the techs back at the Bunker now had something to monitor. De Payns wasn't exactly elated with the results, but they were all still in one piece and he didn't want to push his luck.

CHAPTER
TWENTY-SIX

On Friday morning, de Payns woke early and stood in the shower for longer than he needed. He was getting his mind in gear, tweaking his attitude—a habit he learned in the air force, where they taught pilots to *navigate*, *communicate*, *aviate* as a response to all anomalies and emergencies. Not every crisis could be resolved by the pilot, but most could. And nothing ever ended well by bringing fear and panic into the equation. He often looked back on an episode where he was flying his Mirage 2000 at high altitude and had to pass over an electrical storm. Lightning fired upwards from the storm cloud, struck the Mirage and knocked out the plane's electrical generator, which he couldn't restart. He 'took the top', which meant he started the chronometer timer—he had twenty minutes of fuel, no instruments, no navigation. And it was pitch-black.

The base received a warning signal and sent up another plane to guide de Payns home. De Payns had to maintain visual contact with the wingman in order to follow him to the air base, and he could only do it by closing up to three metres on the wingman's plane—any further apart and de Payns would have lost his 'shep-herd' in the darkness. De Payns landed at Cazaux Air Base on an undercarriage that had luckily opened with gravity—in the absence of power—with enough fuel in his tanks to fill a Zippo lighter.

He wasn't brave or a hero—he stayed calm and followed the training. And that's what was in his mind on the morning of the final full day in-country. Palermo had reminded him that there was no such thing as too much caution, that no procedure was so trivial that it could be overlooked, and he wanted his team to slip out of this country as coolly as they arrived. He watched Brent and Templar pick warm croissants from the buffet and head back to the table. Thierry peeled a mandarin.

'That's it for the spinning,' said de Payns as Brent and Templar landed in their chairs. 'Let's go sightseeing.'

'Seen plenty of sights,' said Brent with a smile, only to realise it wasn't a joke.

'Play it out?' asked Templar carefully.

'Film guys who have done their scouting and are being pure tourists before they fly out on Saturday. Brent?' he prompted, looking at the tech spy.

'We have a load of IMSIs. It's good data and we'll find out how many calls were sent and received by those IMSIs once we're back in Paris. We're good to go.'

De Payns switched his gaze to Templar.

'Good shots of the VIP and the two bodyguards, and we've got the car rego, the residential address and a working routine for our VIP. I'm happy. That good enough for you?'

Forensic work on the phones and faces would only occur once they were back in Paris. That's where the jigsaw would be put together and they'd decide how to access the MERC. 'I think we have enough for now. Those hard drives been swept?'

Templar and Brent nodded.

'Okay, let's play it out today. No more patterns for the ISI to follow.'

De Payns' central concern on these operations was avoiding patterns, especially around places like the MERC. It was precisely the kind of thing that he would look for—a group of outsiders driving around a classified site. They do it once, it's a coincidence; they do it twice, it gets your attention; do it three days in a row and you're on them like flies on shit.

They'd entered the VIP's world for four days in a row, at different times and different angles. They'd been smart, patient and professional, never entering the route at the same place at the same time. If there was an overwatch on the VIP, de Payns was certain they hadn't given themselves away. It was now Friday morning and with the recon product in the can, and seats booked on a flight the next day, there was no reason to push their luck.

'Okay,' said Templar, biting into the croissant. 'You want us to split up, blend in?'

'Yeah, why not,' said de Payns, knowing that his friend was sensing something. Templar's gaze shifted to look over de Payns' shoulder, and then there was a smile on his face so gormless it could only be for public effect.

De Payns turned slowly. Two official-looking Pakistani men stood over them. Not friendly, not hostile, just watching.

'Nice day, gentlemen,' said the slimmer and taller of the two, in fairly good English. He was a hawk-faced forty-year-old in a well-cut brown suit and mid-price shoes.

'Good morning, *monsieur*, how are you?' replied de Payns, not offering his hand. 'Parlez-vous Français?'

'*Un peu*,' said Hawk-face. 'But English is better.'

De Payns kept his smile. 'You from the government? Did we ask too many times about how drunk we're allowed to get?'

The Hawk paused slightly but then smiled. 'We are used to our French friends wondering about our alcohol laws.'

De Payns offered his hand. 'Don't mind my friend,' he said, nodding at Templar. 'He's a piss-head.'

Hawk's English wasn't that good. 'Major Dubash,' he said, offering de Payns a card.

As he took it, de Payns saw the green shield of the Inter-Services Intelligence, the ISI. On the green shield was a silver markhor—a native mountain goat—with a snake in its mouth.

De Payns didn't hesitate as they shook hands. 'Were we speeding again? We did that in Poland a few weeks ago. We get carried away . . .'

'Do you mind if I sit?' asked Dubash, pulling a chair from another table. His offsider—a burly, round-faced plod with dead eyes—remained standing, unintroduced.

'You must be Clement Vinier, yes?' asked Dubash.

'That's me,' said de Payns, reaching for his coffee to prove his hands weren't shaking.

'And this is your . . . *crew*? Is that the word?' asked the ISI man.

'Yes,' said de Payns, adding with a laugh, 'though they're often referred to by less complimentary terms.'

'Because you are filmmakers, yes?'

'You can call them that, yes,' said de Payns.

'What are the names of these films?' asked Dubash, crossing his legs.

'This current one that we're scouting locations for is *Lake Forgiveness*,' said de Payns. 'We've made probably five films between us, including the short feature *Change*, which had a run in Cannes . . .'

'*Change*?' said Dubash. 'What's it about?'

De Payns remembered the hurried shoot he did with a new recruit who had a film background, along with a couple of trainee actors. 'It's about a teenage girl realising that if she can change herself, she can change the world. But changing herself is not that easy.'

Dubash made a face and looked straight at Templar. 'He's a good filmmaker, this Clement Vinier?'

'He's very good,' said Templar. 'Very funny but also sensitive.'

'He uses very good writers,' said Thierry.

De Payns introduced the group, but Dubash kept his eyes firmly on the *chef de mission.*

'Islamabad is a good place to make a movie, I think,' said the ISI man. 'So, where have you scouted?'

'North, south, east and west,' said de Payns. He had his film notebook in front of him and offered it to Dubash, who took it and flipped through the pages, pausing at a page and squinting at the bad handwriting. 'Okay, so the Raja Bazar Road, the great food and shopping, yes?'

De Payns nodded. 'We had a couple of great pizzas down there.'

'Excuse me for my poor reading of the French. But I believe this says that the girls—the women?—in Raja Bazar are very sexy. No hijabs. Great place for Ravi to lose his innocence?'

De Payns shrugged but Dubash wasn't smiling. 'Explain to me this *innocence*?'

'Well,' said de Payns, treading carefully, 'Ravi is young and has had a sheltered upbringing—he has never seen girls like this before.'

Dubash looked confused. 'These are *Pakistani* girls? You mean like teenagers?'

De Payns tried to smile. 'It's part of the coming of age, when a fourteen-year-old boy discovers himself . . .'

'Fourteen? That's not marrying age in Pakistan. We're not in Afghanistan.'

'No, no,' said de Payns, trying to rescue the conversation. 'Not coming of age so he gets married.'

Dubash and his sidekick stared at de Payns, waiting.

De Payns tried to play it out. 'You know, teenagers, love, sex, experimenting . . .'

Dubash looked genuinely embarrassed. 'You have the camera?'

Templar produced it from his bag, powered it up and switched it to viewing mode.

Dubash scrolled through the hundreds of shots, not seeing anything sexy. He gave up after forty seconds and handed the camera to his number two.

'You do know that along with alcohol, we don't have pornography in Pakistan?' asked Dubash, focusing on de Payns. 'You don't have daughters, yes?'

De Payns was caught off guard. 'Ah, no. No, I don't.'

'It is obvious,' said the ISI man, shaking the notebook. 'No one with daughters would disrespect women with this filth.'

De Payns searched for something light to say but the intel man was on his feet. 'Your notebook says you were in the west of the city?'

'You mean the airport?' replied de Payns.

'I was thinking further west and a little south of the airport,' said Dubash, smiling. 'See any *sexy* young girls out there?'

'No, afraid not,' said de Payns, his heart banging in his chest. Had they been spotted around the MERC?

'You see anything out there that might fit in your movie?'

De Payns thought fast. The best lie was always eighty per cent of the truth. 'We liked a petrol station with a yellow awning. It had a great coffee shop on the side of the building. We like it for a scene. Liked the coffee too—it would pass in Paris.'

Dubash weighed the notebook as if deciding on a verdict, and then handed it back to de Payns.

'I think you're leaving tomorrow,' said Dubash. 'But you keep that card, Monsieur Vinier, because if you want to make your movie here, I can give the script to the right officials, and I can tell you what to keep out of it, yes?'

'Thank you, Major,' said de Payns, offering his hand again.

When the ISI men had left, the team stayed in character with their legends and moved towards the street. De Payns noticed, as they filed past the hotel desk, that the ashen-faced manager looked scared enough to cry.

CHAPTER
TWENTY-SEVEN

The hot water washed away the traces of Clement Vinier and the odour of Pakistan. He stepped out of the shower at the safe house, dried off and dressed in the Alec de Payns clothing that he'd left home in a week earlier. He splashed on some cologne, collected his home-life watch, keys, wallet and phone, and headed for the street. It was mid-afternoon in Paris, thanks to the time difference with Pakistan. De Payns used two changes on the Metro—where he put the battery back in his phone and fired it up—finally coming out at Port-Royal. He was very careful when coming back from countries such as Pakistan or Iran, because of the reach of their intelligence services and the number of well-trained people they could mobilise in Paris. He'd already used one Company-run IS to clear him to his safe house—as insisted upon by the Company with returning OTs—and remained vigilant as he made for home.

He picked up a bunch of flowers from the woman who ran the local cafe-bar and carried the peonies in the crook of his arm as he made his way up the stairs. His heart pounding as he got to the door of the apartment that Romy's savings was helping them to afford. The Ministry for Defence owned residential properties all over Paris to allow people earning government wages to live in one of the world's most expensive cities, but the best apartments went to the 'Hot and Cold Waters', the military and intelligence officers who awarded themselves the red collar pip of the *Légion d'Honneur* and the blue ribbon of the National Order of Merit. They dominated the Ministry-subsidised apartments in the seventh, fourteenth and fifteenth arrondissements. Such apartments were referred to as the Hot and Cold Water buildings, in reference to the red and blue strings worn around the occupants' suit collars, when not in military uniform.

He unlocked the door and pushed through, holding the flowers in front of him. He padded down the hallway and started talking, hoping to surprise Romy and the boys. But there was no one in the kitchen and the TV wasn't on in the living room. The curtains were drawn, making it quite dark.

'Romy!' he said, dropping his pack on the floor. His heart picked up and his breath rasped in his own ears as he checked the bedrooms and bathroom. No one. He checked wardrobes and the broom closet in the hall. Picking up his phone, he hit Romy's number and waited. It rang out, ending with her voice asking him to leave a message.

'Fuck!' he said, casting around, his mind buzzing with possibilities. Grabbing his keys, he walked to the elevator and caught the lift to the basement, where their VW Polo was parked. He walked around it, looking for damage. He touched the hood—it was cold—and looked through the windows to see if there was anything out of place in there. Romy had the car keys.

He took the elevator back up to the ground floor and burst out onto the footpath, making another call to her. Still no response.

He walked the block and a half to a collection of neighbourhood boutiques and cafes. Romy and the boys weren't in their usual cafe and Valerie, the woman who ran the small *épicerie* where they bought newspapers and milk, hadn't seen the de Payns family that afternoon.

He walked the block, trying Romy's number again. Nothing. His blood pressure rose, the fear rising along with it. He paused as he walked north through a leafy street behind their apartment, and above the traffic he heard the chanting of young kids. He followed his ears to an open door at the church hall. It was a Saturday afternoon, which meant karate with sensei John. Inside the hall parents were sitting around the walls on fold-down wooden chairs, and in the middle of the floor a bunch of young kids in white canvas *gi* yelled in unison as they ran through their kata on blue and white mats. In the first row of kids he caught sight of Patrick's blond head. His son had that serious look on his face, lips pursed as he concentrated, mouth wide as he roared back at sensei's prompts. A spitting image of de Payns himself at the same age. A hand waved from along the watching parents and de Payns' eye was drawn to his wife, smiling and beautiful, while his youngest—dark-haired Oliver—mimicked the kata from the sidelines.

He tried to make his legs move towards Romy and Oliver, but his thighs felt like jelly. He was frozen, a wave of emotion moving up and through him like a drug. He was overwhelmed—he'd been running through a list of plans and contingencies for dealing with his kidnapped wife and here they were, and here he was, stranded in the midst of his neighbourhood life. It was too much. He longed to be elsewhere—to be sitting in Big Nose's bar with Templar and Shrek, drinking in a place where he belonged and he could be himself. Before he could make himself leave the doorway, Oliver was in his arms, yelling, '*Papa!*' so loud that the mothers laughed.

He picked up his son and swung him around so no one could see his emotional state.

'I love you, Ollie,' he whispered, as he held him. It was the best he could do.

'Dad, can I do karate and soccer?' asked his five-year-old. 'Mum won't let me.'

CHAPTER
TWENTY-EIGHT

De Payns dimmed the lights of the top-floor SCIF and switched on the projector. In the room were Frasier, Briffaut, Lafont, de Payns and Garrat. The Alamut team had worked for the past week and put in an eleven-hour Monday to assemble the package that de Payns hoped would green light the next phase.

He started with the MERC itself, the images coming up nicely from deleted shadows on a CF card. He pointed to the double security fences, the barren ground and scrub between the MERC fences and the roads. He also had some good shots of the 6 p.m. queue of cars leaving the MERC, and with a laser pointer he indicated the black Mercedes-Benz waiting to enter the T-junction and turn north on the main road. Templar's photographs of the VIP and his house were excellent. They showed a medium-height man in his late forties, with middle-management clothing worn shabbily. He had a greyish beard clipped close to his olive skin and a full head of hair, also greying and cut short.

'We don't have a name or a position for our person of interest, but as you can see, he is well protected.'

He clicked between the shots of the bodyguards—one was bigger in the chest and arms than the other, but they were both in their late thirties, wore black suits and white shirts, and gave themselves away with black tactical boots on their feet. Operators required to do the physical stuff liked a solid footing.

'One bodyguard stays in the car and does random loops and circuits,' said de Payns, clicking to a close-up of the more slightly built man. 'The other lives in the house with our VIP.' He brought up a photograph of a heavy-jowled man. 'The car is registered to the Pakistani Ministry of Agriculture and the house is owned by a government agency that validates pesticides and herbicides for farm use.'

'Anyone else of interest from the MERC?' asked Lafont.

'Not really,' said de Payns. 'This was the most expensive car exiting the facility, and from the beginning we were tracking three IMSI numbers from it. We can say this person is senior at the MERC, he's guarded and under surveillance.'

De Payns switched tack. 'I asked the DT to do an *environnement téléphonique* on this number,' said de Payns, referring to the Technical Directorate, which along with Operations, Intelligence and Administration, made up the four directorates of the DGSE. 'We know that on the Thursday of our operation, there was a call from one of the three IMSIs that lasted exactly ten minutes. It seemed like a trained thing to do. The DT went back for two years and found that the call occurs every Thursday at the same time, for ten minutes.'

'And?' asked Garrat.

'This,' said de Payns, flicking through the images until he reached a list of phone calls under the number associated with the IMSI that made the ten-minute call. 'Most of the other calls from this phone were junk. They were internal and seemed to be government-allocation cell phone numbers. His average call is three minutes and nine seconds. He's not chatty.'

'So a ten-minute call stands out,' Frasier observed. 'Especially a regular one.'

De Payns clicked to a new page of phone calls, this time with the ten-minute calls highlighted in orange.

'We went over these calls and, as you can see, all the ten-minute calls were to the same cell phone number, and they all occurred just after 6 p.m. Islamabad time, on a Thursday.'

De Payns knew his audience was transfixed. It was important to get the narrative right if you wanted to push forward to 'actions'. The raw product had to be made to mean something, especially to Frasier, the man who could make big things happen.

'For the last seventeen months, every Thursday, at the same time, for ten minutes, never more.'

Lafont smiled. 'Are you going to tell us who this scientist is calling?'

'I'm afraid I can't—but our tech teams estimate the recipient is in Mons.'

'In Belgium,' said Lafont, eyes wide.

'Just over the border,' snarled Frasier. 'And the answer's yes.'

'I'll need a full support team,' said de Payns.

'I said *yes*—get on it.' The director of operations shook his head. 'Belgium! Holy fuck.'

CHAPTER TWENTY-NINE

The climbing frames and bright plastic tubes were a vast improvement on what de Payns remembered playing on as a child. The playground to the west of their Montparnasse apartment even had a bouncy rubber mat running under the length of it, making the daredevil antics of those girls who swung upside down by the crook of their knees a little less scary. De Payns was starting work late, taking Oliver to the park while Romy had a meeting for a potential job. Given her academic qualifications she was looking for work with the IMF or the OECD. UNESCO and the European Union also had operations in Paris. That's where de Payns wanted her to be—something with a big salary that would challenge her intellect and enable them to pay the rent on their apartment without tapping into her savings. Instead, she was interviewing at a global economic think tank that he'd never heard of.

She'd texted him fifteen minutes earlier, suggesting they meet for coffee. She said nothing about how the interview had gone, from which he surmised that it had gone well. Romy wasn't one for emotional declarations. When she had found out she was expecting their first child she'd merely smiled and said, *We're pregnant*, then asked if he wanted the extra garlic in his mussels.

Oliver, standing on the bridge of the playground's 'ship', pointed and yelled, 'Maman!'

De Payns caught sight of Romy through the trees, walking along the path with a coffee in each hand. She was smiling and so was the woman beside her—Ana Homsi. Ana's son, Charles, ran ahead, calling to Oliver.

Shifting along on the park bench, de Payns made room for the women and took his coffee from Romy.

'Hi Alec,' said Ana, letting Romy sit next to her husband. 'Sorry to gatecrash. Charles really wanted to see Ollie.'

De Payns smiled as he got a kiss on the cheek from Romy. She'd come from her interview so she was dressed like a typical Parisienne in summer—sleeveless and classy.

'So, how did it go?' he asked, taking a sip of coffee.

Romy beamed. 'We got along well. I really liked them.'

'Who is them?'

Romy said, 'The Tirol Council.'

De Payns hadn't heard of it. 'Tirol, like schnapps and lederhosen?'

'No,' said Romy, laughing. 'They're based in Geneva, former World Bank economists and thinkers.'

De Payns didn't bite at that. In his world a *thinker* was either a bullshitter or a Communist. 'What do they do?'

'Policy work and research with the OECD and EU. They want someone to work on the historical drivers of wealth disparity between Western and Eastern Europe. It's my thing.'

De Payns raised his coffee cup in a toast while Oliver and Charles argued about who was going down the slide first. 'I knew that PhD would be useful.'

Ana leaned forward and looked at him, her dark hair falling across her face. 'Talking of useful, you wouldn't have a cigarette, would you, Alec?'

'Not officially,' he said, fishing his Marlboros and lighter from his windbreaker pocket and handing them over.

'Oops, sorry,' she said, wincing at Romy.

'It's not a big deal,' said Romy, a little peeved. 'I just don't want the boys to see their father smoking.'

De Payns held up his empty hands as Ana lit a cigarette and handed back the pack.

'I feel terrible,' said Ana, biting her bottom lip. 'But I can't drink coffee and not have a cigarette.'

Her cell phone sounded and Ana looked at it, excused herself and stood to take the call.

'So, happy about the interview?' he asked Romy.

'It went really well,' she said. 'They asked all the right questions.'

When Ana was back on the park bench de Payns looked at the two women. 'So how come you guys are together?'

'We bumped into each other at Port-Royal station,' said Romy.

'We were coming back from the doctor,' said Ana. 'Charles's ears play up in summer. Must be the pollen.'

'It was a real coincidence,' said Romy.

■

De Payns checked his watch. He had twenty minutes before his scheduled meeting with Templar and Brent. The two men had spent the day over the border in Mons, doing an initial recce and getting a feel for the area that was covered by one of the three cell towers that the Pakistani VIP's phone connected to when he made the calls every Thursday afternoon. They'd already gone over it on the maps—the area that could be served by all three towers was slightly to the west of the city, outside the old medieval walled precinct, and north and south of the leafy area of the Rue des Compagnons. It was what Templar called a 'look-see', a chance to scope the neighbourhood and ascertain if there were going to be obvious impediments to an operation, such as a police station in the middle of the mission zone or a primary school where parents would crowd the street with their cars every afternoon at pick-up time.

'Watch out for gypsies,' de Payns had joked before Templar left.

Two years earlier, Templar and de Payns were staking out a French Navy scientist who was meeting with his Mossad handler. Having tracked the scientist across the Pont d'Arcole, Templar was approached by a gypsy woman while her pickpocket brother came in from behind, thinking he was a tourist. When the pair wouldn't back off, Templar had taken matters into his own hands. The video footage of the scene became famous, showing Templar grabbing the man by the shirtfront and belt buckle and then, in one smooth movement, the gypsy was sailing over the bridge railing into the Seine. If you'd blinked, you would have missed it.

De Payns decided he had time to finish the *demande de criblage*, or DDC, he was working on. His first meeting with Ana Homsi, and then the subsequent dinner with her husband, had made him wary of Romy's new friend, and the meeting in the park that morning had done nothing to ease his discomfort. A week after receiving her PhD, Romy has a job offer—not from the OECD or the IMF, but a think tank operating out of Geneva. He'd researched the Tirol Council—they wanted all of Africa vaccinated and a debt-forgiveness program in the developing world.

Ana Homsi troubled him. He'd let two annoyances go by with her—one was her skilful burrowing into the de Payns family, via preschool and then karate; and second, her constant pouring of wine for the guests while barely touching her own drink. Now, Ana had intercepted Romy on her way back from her city interview before she could debrief with her husband. It was the kind of intervention that de Payns made with his assets on a regular basis.

So now de Payns completed a short screening request. It was written in the third person—as all OT-generated reports in the

Company had to be—and covered the appearance of the Homsi family in his personal life. It named the main people of interest—#ANA HOMSI# and #RAFI HOMSI#—and included their address and all the information that de Payns could remember about them, which wasn't much. He didn't know who Rafi worked for or anything about Ana's background. He included the conversations he'd had with Ana, and the more he wrote the weaker it sounded. Reading the DDC back he realised he had nothing incriminating on Ana or her family, so he requested a check of them on the basis that Ana had asked Romy about her husband's employer. By the time he hit 'send', he knew that it looked like a standard instance of new people entering an OT's life. He knew he was going to appear paranoid, but he also held to the advice given to him by an old instructor in DGSE training—better to be paranoid and embarrassed than complacent and dead.

CHAPTER

THIRTY

They were waiting for him at the kitchenette when he went looking for a glass of water—Alain Portmann, a DGS straight-shooter, and his sidekick, Julien Laval.

'Hi, Alec,' said Portmann in that awkward tone between authority and collegiality. 'Can you join us for a chat?'

De Payns smiled. Portmann was what they called 'very FBI'—dark suit, plain white shirt, unremarkable tie and a taupe trench coat, even in the middle of summer. They'd been in the same intake year for French intelligence, and had done a number of rotations together at Cercottes, including firearms proficiency and locks. Portmann had taken the DGS route and de Payns was where he was.

'Sure,' said de Payns.

They adjourned to an interview room which featured a white rectangular laminated table, two fabric-covered office chairs on either side and a mirror down one wall. There was a glass dome in the ceiling for the cameras and every word was being recorded.

Portmann started straight in, reading from a page in his folder rather than looking at de Payns. 'Are you aware of the national security waiver you signed in relation to legal counsel?'

'Yes,' said de Payns. If you worked in the French secret services you did not have the right to an attorney and you did not have the right to remain silent. You got to sit in a room and have your colleagues throw accusations at you. It wasn't personal and it certainly wasn't open to lawyers.

Portmann recited his first few questions in a robotic tone. 'Have you told the truth in regards to the destruction of five French passports in Palermo?' 'Is there any reason why you cannot speak honestly?' 'Have you discussed this matter with any person outside of the DGSE?'

It was a standard opening, but then Portmann got to the point. 'Three million euros is a lot of money for a commander at the Company, *n'est ce pas*? Could you do with that kind of pay-day?'

De Payns shrugged.

'You were offered three million euros for five French passports,' said Portmann, holding up a printout of de Payns' report on Operation Falcon. 'And you declared them destroyed.'

'I did destroy—'

'They were real French passports, Alec,' said Laval, his slab-sided face making him look like a farmer without a tan. 'They had to be good enough to pass muster with Sayef Albar . . .'

'. . . and to keep your head on your body,' Portmann finished, with an unnecessary flourish.

'I know what Falcon was all about, thanks, gentlemen,' said de Payns.

'Good to hear,' said Portmann. 'So when Falcon was a bust, what did you do?'

'I destroyed the passports at the wharf adjacent to the Palermo ferry terminal.'

'How?' asked Portmann.

'Tore the pages and the covers into thirty or forty pieces, ensured they went into different garbage bins.'

'Who was with you?'

'No one.'

'Who saw you?'

'No one.'

'You can confirm that?'

'No.'

'You didn't sell them to this Murad?' asked Laval, blue eyes narrowing with suspicion as he looked down at de Payns' report. 'Three million euros. *Pas dégueulasse!*'

'I don't need three million euros,' said de Payns, instantly realising the conversation had been herding him there.

'Really?' snapped Laval. 'What about that apartment of yours?'

De Payns sighed. 'What about it?'

Laval sneered. 'You don't have a Ministry-subsidised apartment.'

'No, I don't,' said de Payns, suppressing his desire to say, *Because cocktail-sipping cocksuckers like you spend your careers jockeying for the best government-owned Paris apartments.*

'Paris is expensive,' Laval remarked. 'Especially when your wife wants to live in the fourteenth.'

De Payns said nothing.

'Three-quarters of your income goes on housing,' Portmann said. 'Your wife doesn't work.'

'And she spent the last year doing a doctorate at the Sorbonne,' Laval added.

De Payns knew what they were saying. 'My wife's smarter than all the IQs in this room added together, and she's got a piece of paper from the Sorbonne to prove it. So what's your point?'

'My point, *Alec*,' said Laval, 'is that you have one government income, you're living in Montparnasse and your wife's tuition fees must hurt.'

'And then an Italian migration agent offers you three million euros for a packet of genuine French passports,' said Portmann. 'Passports that you conveniently have to throw away anyway because an operation went sour.'

De Payns levelled a flat, dangerous gaze at Portmann. 'Two people died that night—"convenient" might be the wrong word to describe what happened.'

Portmann broke the eye contact and cleared his throat.

De Payns continued. 'I know what Commodore offered and I declared it.'

'Who pays for the Montparnasse apartment?' asked Laval.

'I have a living-in-Paris allowance,' said de Payns.

The DGS men chuckled at that. The Paris living allowance was two hundred and eighty euros per month. Some agents called it the 'Grigny allowance'—referring to a far-flung suburb south of the city—because you sure as shit couldn't live on it in Paris.

Laval grinned. 'So how does it work? Wifey has a rich daddy?'

De Payns stood, the scraping chair legs seeming very loud. He could feel himself flexing into an assault stance.

There was a knock on the door and it opened to reveal Philippe Manerie. He smiled at a wide-eyed Laval, then turned to Portmann. 'I'll take it from here, thanks.'

When the two DGS agents had left the interview room, carefully avoiding de Payns, Manerie inclined his head and they walked, without talking, down one flight of stairs and through the doors that opened onto the lawns around the old fort.

'I heard you were overseas,' said Manerie as they strolled east. 'Anything you'd like to share?'

'Jim needs to stand back. I don't shit where I sleep.'

'Okay,' said Manerie. 'I'll have a word. So, where were you? Turkey? Syria?'

'You know I can't talk about that. By the way, have you shared that photo of me and Moran?'

'No, but *you* are the one answering *my* questions at the moment. Did Shrek see where you disposed of the passports? Are you protecting him?'

De Payns shook his head. 'What is it with DGS and the fucking passports?'

'Three million euros is a lot of money, Alec. I've seen with my own eyes what some OTs will do if they can get away with it.'

They stopped at the old copse of trees by the fort's eastern wall.

'Forget the passports,' said Manerie, lighting a cigarette. 'I want to know who sold us out in Sicily.'

'It wasn't Shrek,' said de Payns reflexively.

'You know that for a fact?'

'I know that better than I trust you,' said de Payns.

'If I put a red flag on you, it's desk duties,' said Manerie. 'And by the way, you owe me for stopping all that shit with Laval. If you'd punched him you'd be on weekly head checks. So no more dodging me, Alec. I want to know who Briffaut and Frasier are fingering for the mole. There's a bigger game being played and I need to be in front of it.'

When Manerie had left, de Payns walked quickly to the foyer of the Bunker, his head spinning with Operation Falcon, the unsolved leak and the three million euros.

He used his swipe card to go to the top floor, Briffaut's office. He had to head off any attempt by Manerie, Portmann or Laval to sabotage him and eject him from Operation Alamut. The MERC investigation was important and he had to keep up the momentum, no distractions. As he rounded the corner into a wood-panelled area he paused. Briffaut was in the antechamber, where the executive assistants sat, talking to Frasier and a second man. De Payns stayed hidden behind a credenza and watched as the three men nodded, as if agreeing on something. A few seconds later, Briffaut returned to his office with Frasier, and the other man walked away. Shrek.

CHAPTER
THIRTY-ONE

They started with the technical environment, established by the DT in Mons. It had to start from scratch because the phone number that received the ten-minute call every Thursday was also *démarqué* and therefore carried no data on the owner or an address. The receiving phone was not even Belgian. The DT people confirmed it had been bought in France and used a French network. From the back of the sub, the techs used the IMSI spinner to find which three cell towers the phone of interest was connected to, searching at night to find the general zone where the person lived. With the phone not moving, the IMEI of the phone could be established and tied to an address. They were able to trace it to a modern apartment block in the north-west of Mons, in the old city. De Payns covered the operation from a nearby hotel room, through a radio headset. When the owner of the phone went to work, the phone moved and the team followed and took pictures of the people moving at the same time the phone moved, often on a nature strip in front of the identified apartment building. They put a team of followers in front of the building, and one of the techs in the sub rang the phone of interest. One of de Payns' team saw the target—a woman answering a phone when no one else was in the vicinity.

She was in her mid-thirties, a well-dressed Arab woman, and she was walking with two girls, aged around nine and twelve. De Payns was happy with the progress but he wanted to confirm a phone call from the Mercedes-Benz in Islamabad. A call from Islamabad at 6.15 p.m. would be received in Mons at 3.15. The woman stayed in her apartment on Thursdays until 3.25 before leaving for the school to pick up her children. So they had the phone that was called from Islamabad and the owner of the phone, but the Alamut team was yet to see the woman actually taking the call from the MERC employee.

They followed her. Having dropped her children at school, on foot, the woman went to a cafe and one of de Payns' technicians followed her in and sat at the neighbouring table with a spinner the size of an iPhone to confirm that the woman was carrying the phone.

De Payns also had a *filature* planned for when she left the cafe. The *filature* entailed a team of five people putting the woman under surveillance and reporting in real time back to the sub, where de Payns sat with the DT operatives.

Before she left the cafe, de Payns checked everyone was on the net.

'Y radio check,' he said into the mic on a necklace under his T-shirt. The activation button was in his pants pocket.

The confirmations came back, one after the other. 'Jéjé'; 'Danny'; 'Paulin'; 'Vehicle'.

De Payns confirmed he was hearing them. 'Okay Y. Loud and clear. Jéjé, you have the alert.'

'Jéjé. Copy.'

Jéjé was a former naval diver who'd been recruited into the DGSE in his late twenties. He was smart and tough and the operation would start at his lead.

After forty-five minutes of radio silence, Jéjé broke into de Payns' earpiece.

'Alert, alert, alert,' he said. 'Target. Brown jacket, jeans, black handbag. Just exited the cafe, walking south towards Place de Vannes, on Borgnagache, odd number side of the road. Coming towards you, Paulin.'

'Aguilar copy,' said de Payns. 'We're moving to de Vannes.'

As the sub started moving, the *filature* actively communicated.

'Danny copy. Visual. On the other side of the road. Keeping visual.'

'Paulin. Copy. I'll take Echelon 1 when she walks past.'

'Vehicle copy, on standby,' said the driver of a small Citroën. Her passenger was ready to alight from the car and pursue on foot.

'Jéjé. Going to the Mons Metro. Danny, you stay at Echelon 2 after Paulin takes her.'

'Danny, copy.'

'Paulin. Visual. I'm on it. Turning right from Borgnagache onto Place de Vannes, opposite way of the car flow, even numbers side of the street, level with number forty-two, walking slow.'

'Danny, visual.'

The sub was now heading towards Boulevard Charles Quint, which looked down towards the Mons Metro station.

'Aguilar. Boulevard Charles Quint, anticipating target.'

Twenty seconds later they could see the target in her brown leather jacket leaving Place de Vannes. She was into Boulevard Charles Quint and turning left for the Metro.

'Aguilar. Visual on target. Walking south on Charles Quint towards Mons Metro. Odd numbers.'

'Jéjé, pre-positioning Mons Metro,' said the former frogman.

De Payns said, 'Aguilar for vehicle, drop one pedestrian at the Mons Metro on south line.'

'Vehicle copy,' came the response.

De Payns had constructed the classic *filature* for train travel. They would follow her to the station, where one of his team was waiting on the opposite platform. When the woman descended to her own platform, the team member watching from the other platform radioed another team member waiting at the previous railway station, telling him the woman's position on the platform. That follower would take the next train and sit where the target was most likely to enter, so that when she entered the train she suspected nothing. The job was to identify which station she travelled to two days in a row.

De Payns' team followed the target one station north, into an area of low-rise corporate suites and medical centres with good stands of trees and parks between them. The shops were fairly upmarket without being high-end. They followed her to a modern white building with management consultants, engineers and bioscience firms on the tenant board. One of the *filature* team reported that she got off the elevator on the second level, where the only tenant was a Belgian bioscience company called GrowTEK.

While the *filature* team tracked the target's daily movements, the DT set up the gear to make a *trombinoscope* of the building she lived in. The *trombinoscope* was basically a gallery of images, names, associates and habits of the main players and locations in an operation, collected in an operations room, and eventually converted to a book.

Having established which door was hers—2206, which translated to the second block, second level, number six—the tech team placed cameras in the green exit sign in the hallway in front of her door, so that de Payns and his team could see who was living with her or visiting. The persons of interest were followed and photographed until they could be identified.

Back at the Bunker in Noisy, de Payns used the incoming pictures and intelligence to build the body of knowledge—the *dispositif*—on a corkboard in one of the operations rooms.

De Payns worked on identifying the woman's name and her work, not hidden as evidenced by a name on the letterbox and on the apartment doorbell, and confirmed by the field team's checking of her mail. An identity not covered up could mean a deception, so the team cross-checked the declared name with utility bills and the Belgian driver's licence.

■

His team moved fast, and within two weeks de Payns was sitting in his office at Noisy, re-reading the brief he'd written for Mattieu Garrat. Garrat, Briffaut's 2IC, was running the operation in Mons. They had confirmed to ninety per cent certainty that the woman with the phone of interest—the one receiving weekly ten-minute calls from a senior figure at the MERC in Pakistan—was Anoush al-Kashi. The team had her migrating from Pakistan two years earlier with her husband and two children. No trained intelligence behaviours were detected in her. But the team had not seen a husband after two weeks of solid surveillance, which was a missing piece that de Payns and Garrat would rather have in place. Spouses who could not be sighted or investigated raised uncertainties and risks. Regardless, de Payns was ready to go to the 'contact' phase and show his face. No more hiding in a hotel room, huddling in a van or building pretty pictures on a corkboard. It was time to go and do what he was trained for. All he needed was Garrat's green light, and he'd be entering Anoush al-Kashi's life.

He made a final check of his report and pushed 'send', waited for thirty seconds then shut down his computer. It was summer in Paris, and de Payns wanted to kick a football with his sons and drink wine with his wife.

CHAPTER
THIRTY-TWO

Mattieu Garrat's office sat on a corner of the Bunker, giving a southerly view across Paris's trees and rooflines. De Payns took it in as he paused at the door, coffee mug in hand and Advils in his belly.

'Alec, Alec,' said Garrat, gesturing for him to enter. 'Come in. Sit.'

De Payns took a seat and Garrat regarded him with shrewd, intelligent eyes. 'Great work on Operation Alamut. You got a team?'

'Templar's leading the support team,' said de Payns.

'Excellent,' said Garrat, his shaved head glinting in the morning sun. 'You look ready for a contact environment.'

'We're ready,' said de Payns. 'We have to stay on her—she's our only connection to the MERC.'

De Payns didn't have to push it too hard. Frasier, Briffaut and Lafont wanted Alamut to go to the next level and Garrat would not stop it.

'There's nine of you at the moment,' said Garrat, tapping on his keyboard and peering at the screen. 'What am I requisitioning?'

'A continuation of the current Alamut team. That'll give us enough people to form a PEC if we need it.'

'Okay, sounds fair,' said Garrat. The PEC was *prise en compte*—a controlled zone where the team could conduct meetings and surveillance activities with a lot of unseen security.

'What are we calling the person of interest?'

'Raven,' said de Payns.

'Okay,' said Garrat, typing. 'What's the approach?'

De Payns took him through the operation—Templar's team would continue surveillance on Raven, while the tech team infiltrated her computer and her email and put a tracking device on her car. De Payns covered the research and he took Garrat through the pack—she was of Pakistani origin, married to a pharmacist, also Pakistani; her daughters were nine and thirteen years old. She was a freelance translator from French to Urdu, not an uncommon profession so close to Brussels, and she also listed Pashto and Punjabi as languages she could translate into French and English. There was a report on her phones. She had a Belgian cell phone number that seemed to be her daily usage phone, and also a *démarqué* French-network phone—the phone of interest—that she used every Thursday afternoon and at no other time. The seemingly lone Pakistani woman with kids could mean a divorce but it could also be a soft exile, in which case that might be used as leverage to recruit her. The translation business could be another leverage, if she needed clients.

'We'll pick up what she's emailing and who her friends and family are,' said de Payns, 'and I should be able to give you a plan for contact in a couple of weeks.'

'Don't be a stranger,' said Garrat. 'With the budget we're burning on this I need ammunition to keep it going. Understand?'

De Payns smiled. 'Sure.'

'I mean it,' said Garrat. 'Lafont is pushing for this, and because it's bioweapons it has some political goodwill, but you have to keep giving me the good stuff—you know what the bean counters are like around here.'

'You got it,' said de Payns.

Garrat leaned back, stroked his tie. 'By the way, the DDC came back.'

'Oh, that,' said de Payns, remembering the vetting he'd requested on Ana and her husband, Rafi. 'I got back from down south and my wife had a new friend. Just being too careful.'

'Can't be that,' said Garrat. 'Too careful, I mean. Anyway, the Homsi husband and wife checked out—no flags.'

Garrat smirked slightly and de Payns could sense a comment forming.

'If a dame like that was pushed my way, I'd think twice about blowing the whistle on her, know what I mean? Maybe blow a whistle *at* her?'

De Payns felt embarrassed for the guy, but Garrat wasn't picking up on it. He turned the computer monitor to face de Payns. 'Now that lady could get *undercover* with me any day of the week, *non*?'

The picture was one that the DGS had sent when they'd cleared Ana Homsi of being on a French government database or watchlist. They'd appended a digital photograph from the personnel files of an accounting firm where she'd worked before becoming a full-time mother. It verified that the agent and DGS were talking about the same person. It showed a woman with long dark hair and big round eyes, not unlike Claudia Cardinale in her heyday. He reckoned the picture had been taken eight or nine years ago.

'She's not my type,' said de Payns, standing.

'You lying bastard,' laughed Mattieu Garrat, as de Payns retreated down the hallway. 'That dame is everyone's type!'

CHAPTER
THIRTY-THREE

De Payns started with a run around the Bunker, and just before 10 a.m. he entered the gym in the basement, where he was alone except for someone sitting on a weights bench peering at their phone. He slurped at the bubbler, grabbed some boxing gloves from the gear cupboard and went to the heavy bag. He hit the timer on the wall and it started counting down from three minutes. He took a boxer's stance, balanced his weight and began slow, throwing jabs, hooks and straight-rights and, keeping his weight evenly distributed on the balls of his feet, bobbing and weaving, making his legs and hips throw the punches.

When the timer buzzed out, de Payns was panting, his legs almost jelly. He gasped for breath, wondering why he didn't do this three times a week and keep his fitness at a constant level. He was psyching himself into completing two more three-minute rounds, when he heard a voice behind him.

'Call that boxing?'

Turning, he found Shrek, dressed in a tight-fitting Brazilian jujitsu shirt and shorts.

'I call that rusty,' said de Payns.

'Don't tell me—you have your annual next month,' said Shrek, openly amused. 'I warned you, didn't I? You can't be a natural all your life, *mon pote*. Have to put in the work.'

'Yeah, yeah,' said de Payns. He looked like a one-time rugby player who'd once flown fighter jets, while Shrek looked like an academic who would take you to the cleaners in a game of chess. But Shrek had done the work and was a black belt and instructor in Wing Chun kung fu, and de Payns was getting through a pack a day and trying to get fit for his annual check-up. Shrek was right. Any natural ability with his fists probably belonged to a younger version of himself.

'Come on, let's see what you've got,' said Shrek, walking to the gear cupboard.

'I'm not doing one of your sparring sessions,' said de Payns. 'You kidding me? I can barely hold my own against the heavy bag right now.'

'You'll be fine,' said Shrek, throwing a pair of black MMA gloves at de Payns. 'I won't hurt you.'

'Yes you will,' said de Payns, replacing the boxing gloves with the MMA mitts.

'Okay, but I'll spare your feelings,' said Shrek, walking to the blue martial arts mats in the northern end of the gym. They kicked off their shoes and walked onto the hemp-packed mats, de Payns dreading what was about to come.

'So, did I see you talking to Frasier the other day?' asked de Payns innocently while he did his shoulder stretches. 'Outside Briffaut's office?'

Shrek smiled. 'That's fairly specific. Not a spy, are you?'

That was classic Shrek. Seamless dissembling wrapped up in humour. If de Payns pushed, it was he who had the problem.

'I thought you were going for a pay rise—at least, that's what everyone's saying.'

Shrek's eyes flashed. 'Who's every—?'

'Ha! Got you!' said de Payns. 'Smug bastard.'

'You prick,' said Shrek, fist-touching with de Payns' glove.

They stood back from one another and de Payns raised his hands in a defensive posture, crouching into a fighting stance. Shrek twisted sideways, backed up with fast reverse shuffle steps, and unleashed a back kick that caught de Payns in the solar plexus, lifting him off his feet and onto his arse. He coughed and looked up at Shrek.

'So much for not hurting me,' said de Payns, catching his breath and realising this was going to be a painful return to sparring.

'I'm a spy,' said Shrek, shrugging. 'I lied.'

Leaping to his feet, de Payns regained his composure and effected a stance.

'Oops,' said Shrek. 'Not going all jujitsu on me, are you?'

'Bring it,' said de Payns, and they circled one another, Shrek more careful now, knowing his sparring partner would go to the ground if he had the chance.

De Payns feigned a lunge to the torso, and when Shrek countered with a stamp kick and a punch combination, he was ready. He slipped the left-hand punch and blocked the right-hand with his elbow, extending his arm and barring Shrek's twisted right elbow so Shrek was lifted off the ground. To avoid breaking his arm, Shrek twisted downwards and away, and de Payns used the momentum to take them both to the ground, where de Payns drove his forearm into Shrek's neck and then positioned himself into a chokehold on his friend, which he tightened.

Having tapped out, Shrek stood and the two faced one another, the score one-all. They could have left it there, but Shrek raised an eyebrow, so de Payns called game on. Shrek let go a fast roundhouse kick into de Payns' thigh then followed through with a punch. De Payns slipped inside the extended arm and hip-rolled him onto the mat, only for Shrek to roll free from the slamming and come to his feet again. De Payns was onto his partner as he regained balance, trying to hook him into another arm hold, but Shrek leaned away and lashed out with a right-foot side kick, hitting de Payns in the floating ribs. As Shrek followed through with a left-hand punch, de Payns ducked under it and threw his friend to the ground, pinning him once more with a forearm to the throat. This time, Shrek twisted away and slammed a fast left-hand elbow into de Payns' right ear, stunning the larger man. They rolled away from each other and jumped back to their stances, panting heavily.

De Payns could feel the sweat running down between his shoulder blades. He was not in shape. 'That's not a bad warm-up, old man,' said de Payns, trying to get oxygen.

'Beats a stretch,' said Shrek, voice rasping. 'Let's do this.'

■

He gasped as he reached for the wineglasses in the dresser. A rib on the left side of his chest felt like it wanted to spring straight out of his bruised skin.

'You okay, honey?' asked Romy, watching him from the sofa.

'It's fine,' he said, pouring two glasses of riesling. 'I sparred with Shrek.'

'You always regret that,' she said.

'I didn't have a choice. He cornered me in the gym.'

'Where are you hurt? I have some tiger balm.'

'Ribs, legs, stomach, arms,' he said, delivering the glasses.

'You need a massage,' she said, sipping at the wine.

He noticed she was wearing the red trackpants that made her look like the genie from *I Dream of Jeannie*. 'It might have to be one of those massages where I touch you at the same time,' he said with a wink.

'You get the boys out of the bath, and you have a deal, *monsieur*.'

De Payns put down his glass and leaped to his feet, crying with pain as a muscle gripped in his thigh.

'Easy does it, tough guy,' Romy said, chuckling. 'We have a deal, remember?'

CHAPTER THIRTY-FOUR

De Payns sat in the operations SCIF at the Bunker, listening to Brent and Templar run through their plans for establishing 'environment' around Anoush al-Kashi, now known as 'Raven'. When the environment was established, de Payns would make the contact with Raven. The team leaders were selling the strength of their plans, assuring the *chef de mission* he would not end his days in a shallow grave in the Calmeynbos. To be certain of no counter-measures from the Pakistanis, the team would collect as much environment information as possible on Raven, including family and friends, workplace and leisure habits. The first phase had been establishing identity and a connection between the caller in Islamabad and the receiver in Mons. The full environment was deeper and had to give the Alamut team enough life detail to enable de Payns to infiltrate Raven's world in a plausible manner.

Brent went through the tech plan. It included cameras at the entrance of Raven's home, with a lens in the eye of a teddy bear in the back of a car, alternating with another hidden in the streetscape to monitor Raven's building entry. Brent would have his people mark her car—a small silver BMW—with a device which allowed for the tracking of the target's cell phone traffic as well as vehicular movement. They now knew she used Gmail on a Toshiba laptop, and intercepting her email traffic was not difficult. Brent's team had already cracked the target's two phones, which were being listened to, and the woman's activity on social networks was being observed.

Templar also had enough people to rotate three teams of male and female agents who would take turns dividing and squaring Raven's different routes, whether it was taking her daughters to school, bringing them home in the afternoon, going to dance classes or travelling to her translation appointments, including regular visits to the GrowTEK offices. Using several teams to divide and square the target's routes would give them accurate data but without the risk of easy detection should there be an ISI overwatch program in Mons.

'We'll make her mail,' said Templar, meaning her mail to the apartment would be cleared and opened and returned when she wasn't around. 'We've already cut our own key to the foyer. Also, we still haven't seen the husband, but he's part of this environment. We'll identify him as well as all her contacts.'

They talked through the logistics of it. A decent environment could take a month and the support teams would have a certain amount of rotation—which would mean travelling back to Paris—but the surveillance would be occurring at all hours, so the teams would have to disperse to hotels and pensions, pay in cash and assemble where their gig started each day or night. De Payns noted the sombre atmosphere—they'd been in Islamabad together, escaping detection, but this was slightly different. They were now surrounding a target who had a direct connection to a VIP from a Pakistani bioweapons facility. If there was counter-surveillance around her it would be professional and ruthless.

'It'll be fully sanitised,' said Templar, nodding. 'They'll need a Ouija board to know we're in town.'

■

When Templar and Brent had left, de Payns turned his focus to the fictive ID of Sébastien Duboscq. Duboscq was not a new ID for de Payns; he'd used it around Europe and in the United States. The legend was that of a pharmaceutical consultant through his company AlphaPharma Consulting, which had offices in Paris—so named because a generic corporate moniker made it harder for opposing intelligence agencies to search for the owners of it. He'd done monthly 'gardening' of his corporate front, including visits to his office in the ninth arrondissement, email responses to prospective clients and attending conferences in Germany and the Netherlands. Duboscq's approach would be a request for Raven's translation services. He wanted to ensure his clients in Pakistan and some neighbouring Stans could understand his website, so he needed Urdu and Pashto versions. His Sébastien Duboscq persona was well dressed and smooth. He dressed in smart suits and good shoes and appeared unconcerned by money. De Payns had gone through all the photography from Mons and, judging by her expensive taste in handbags and accessories, Raven's MICE might include ego. She looked like a bourgeois subcontinental woman who might be persuaded to step up to some romance with a sexy Parisian professional. He made a note to get a better haircut and perhaps wear a men's fragrance . . . Paco Rabanne, maybe—something that suggested Sébastien Duboscq might be up for some fun but wasn't desperate.

■

He took the Metro east, had a shower at the Company flat and selected the dark blue suit in his locker's wardrobe, matching it with a new white shirt and a pair of brown Bowen shoes from

England. Placing his Alec de Payns collateral in one manila envelope, he poured out the Duboscq wallet, effects and phone from another. He put on a slim gold watch and slipped a vintage-looking gold confirmation ring onto his finger.

The Metro journey to the Duboscq apartment took twelve minutes, during which he assembled Sébastien's Nokia. He cleared the mail at the foyer of his vacant apartment above a restaurant on Rue Godot de Mauroy, and then crossed the road to the offices of AlphaPharma Consulting. He climbed the stairs and entered the tiny serviced space. There was a desk with two chairs and a sofa, and a phone and computer on the desk. Not much, but enough.

He turned on the lights and moved around. He could hear the insurance broker down the hallway yelling into the phone. He sat behind the desk, turned on the computer and leaned back in the cut-price executive chair as he tried to get into his Sébastien Duboscq mindset. He had two of the best field teams in Europe, led by Templar, and they already had Mons wired. If they burrowed deep into Raven's private life and could confirm the environment was clean of ISI minders and overwatch, de Payns could be there in two weeks. His thoughts drifted to Operation Falcon and the disastrous interview with DGS about the three-million-euro passports. It meant Palermo was still lingering, and Frasier still hadn't released a final report, meaning there was nothing to give Manerie. He wondered again why it had turned so bad in Sicily, pondering the mystery of the sleek, well-groomed man on the ferry. Had it really been Murad? And if so, what had dragged him out of hiding into what was essentially a field matter? Murad allegedly had ties to Osama bin Laden's executive and he was suspected of financing sleeper cells in Paris, London, Madrid and Frankfurt. And he'd emerged from his safe haven—wherever that might be—to personally oversee Michael Lambardi on the ferry and then at the bar? Why?

Heels clicked on the parquet floor outside his office and then stopped.

'Sébastien?' came a woman's voice. 'You there, *chéri*?'

'Claire! Come in,' said de Payns, reverting to Sébastien Duboscq, the suave single guy.

The frosted-glass door swung inwards and Claire, the blonde employee who did 'all the work' at the insurance brokers, leaned on the doorjamb. She wore a dark pencil skirt and a loose red blouse that looked like it was meant to conceal her curves but failed.

'Thought that was you,' she said, pulling a soft pack of cigarettes from her waistband. 'You been off adventuring again, Seb?'

'If you call hard work "adventuring". In this business the clients are everywhere,' said de Payns, accepting a smoke. 'I never stop travelling. You know how it is.'

'Poof!' she said, dismissing de Payns' complaints. 'Give me one week as a man, I'll take it. Running around out there, doing whatever I want.'

'It's not that great,' said de Payns, accepting her light.

'Bullshit,' said the blonde, as she lit her own smoke. 'Only a man would ever complain about his own freedom.'

CHAPTER THIRTY-FIVE

Before heading to his 9.30 a.m. meeting, de Payns made breakfast for the boys and watched *SpongeBob* with them. They talked about girls and bullies as they made the waffles—'Papa's way' with extra sugar and cinnamon—and de Payns lowered his voice when Patrick wanted to know when he could play rugby.

'Why rugby?' he asked, not wanting Romy to hear the conversation—she hated rugby. 'I thought you liked soccer?'

'You played rugby,' said Patrick. 'I saw your school photos.'

'Okay, we'll ask your mother,' said de Payns, as he poured maple syrup.

'I already did,' said Patrick.

'And?' asked de Payns.

Patrick smiled, 'She said *never*. You'll have to tell her, Papa.'

'Oh, *I* have to tell her?' replied de Payns, laughing. 'How do you think that will turn out?'

'Maybe ask her nicely?' suggested Oliver, eyes wide.

By the time they'd watched two *SpongeBob* episodes, de Payns didn't want to move. In the first week of September, Patrick would be back at school and Oliver would be starting his first year. He remembered when Oliver couldn't talk; now he'd be learning to read and write. He was conscious of the years racing by, not purely in age but in family time. While he got lost in his latest subterfuge and manipulation, his sons did their karate and played football and hung out watching *SpongeBob Square Pants*—proud of the fact they could follow it in English. He thought about his family and wished he could walk on a higher moral ground. In his world, family was leverage; family was a weak point to be exploited, and given that most rational people would do anything to spare their families, kids were part of the game. He'd avoided facing up to it until the night he'd returned from Palermo and Romy had asked: *That's what* you *do to people? Get to their families?*

Yes, he thought, as he sipped on his coffee in front of the cartoons. That's what I do.

He kissed the boys, suggested they let their mother have a lie-in, and slipped out of the door just before eight-thirty.

■

They sat in Dominic Briffaut's office, de Payns and Mattieu Garrat briefing the head of Y Division on why they felt the operational environment was ready to be upgraded to contact. The three-week environment phase, run by Templar, had not disclosed anything special about Raven apart from the fact that in emails and phone calls she criticised her husband a lot, and she wished for more freedom. The phone calls to the mystery man at the MERC had been monitored and played back for the cryptographers at the Cat, who couldn't find a code in the dull conversations about shopping, traffic and school lunches. It was not unusual in countries such as Pakistan and Iran for classified government workers to train their family and friends never to ask about their work or refer to it. So Raven wasn't asking, and the person of interest at the MERC wasn't telling. Briffaut had a file of the transcripts between Raven and the POI, and he flipped to a random page which contained the conversation:

POI: How are you?
RAVEN: Good.
POI: How are the kids?
RAVEN: Happy.
POI: How is the weather?
RAVEN: Fine.
POI: How is work?
RAVEN: Busy.

Briffaut sighed. 'This is it?'

De Payns nodded. 'The conversations are so banal that we should at least consider the possibility that Raven is trained.'

Briffaut shrugged at that possibility. In the intel game you also had to accept that people conducted uninspiring communications.

They went through the photographic surveillance, which demonstrated Raven's ego, a potential MICE leverage. She had a pretty face and a voluptuous body. In one of the shots, she wore silky parachute pants and a tight bodice that was less modest than a typical Pakistani woman would wear.

'One of Templar's female team-members followed Raven to a Latin club,' said de Payns. 'She reported that the dance leader at the club was a good-looking man in a sleazy sort of way. It's in the reports section.'

Briffaut made a face as he scanned the photographs. 'We picking up any counter-measures?'

'We've found nothing,' said de Payns. 'The environment is clean.'

Garrat directed the meeting to emails Raven had exchanged with other female Middle Eastern migrants living in Europe. In them, she complained about wanting to get away from Fadi—the absent husband—whom she accused of controlling her and becoming radicalised.

Briffaut shut the ring-binder file, pushed it back towards Garrat. Then he turned to de Payns. 'If we go to contact, do you have a plan for Raven?'

'I know how to approach her,' said de Payns.

Briffaut nodded, his mind already shifting to something else. 'It's a yes from me. I'll take it to Frasier. You'll know by tonight.'

CHAPTER THIRTY-SIX

The new Gare de Mons was a sweeping temple of white concrete, as if the old LAX flying-saucer building had had a love child with the Sydney Opera House. De Payns alighted from the Intercity train he'd caught from Brussels, having taken the Thalys from Paris, and walked the clean Belgian concourse to the taxi ranks outside. He gave the address of the Hôtel Saint Georges, selected for its location off the main streets and paid for in advance with cash through a travel agent in Paris, claiming his wallet had been stolen and he'd had to revert to his emergency cash. He checked in as Sébastien Duboscq and went to the third floor, where he did his sweeps of the room. He observed the street from his window and looked for people sitting in cars and service vans that seemed to be doing more parking than servicing.

He switched on the TV, which received Belgian and French services, and lay on the double bed. He'd called Raven from Paris two days before, introduced himself and told her he was going to be in Brussels later in the week. He'd asked if they could meet in Mons to discuss some translation work for his website. His adrenaline was now elevated. This was the 'action' work that the Y Division was created to do, and de Payns had been trained specifically for the task. Yes, he could drive fast, use firearms and make bombs. But accessing a human's life, becoming part of it and betraying the trust created with that person, was on another level. It was difficult to initiate, hard to maintain and, if the target was protected in any way, it was dangerous. In order to appear calm and natural, an OT had to be meticulous and hard-working. It was like the proverbial duck on the pond—just because the effort was hidden from view, it didn't mean there was no frantic paddling beneath the surface.

He lay on the bed and ticked boxes in his head—AlphaPharma Consulting had an address known to other businesses, and a business registration; it had a list of clients and engagements that could be checked. If ISI went nosing around the Paris offices of AlphaPharma, they might not find Sébastien Duboscq behind his desk, but they'd probably run into Claire, who could tell them all about the man she'd shared a smoke with just the other day. Sébastien had a personal identity, a driver's licence, an address and a trail of social network activity on Facebook and LinkedIn. His work phone number was backed up and his two most recent clients would be verified by someone in the administration section of Y Division. This preparation was critical—if a target was being monitored by a secret service, they would test de Payns' fictive ID; if there was one loose thread, a good intelligence operative would pull at it until the entire fabric unravelled.

Raven and Sébastien were planning to meet at Café Havre at 6 p.m.—early enough to make it professional but informal enough to start on a sociable footing. It had to be a good first meeting. De Payns took a shower and opened the Paco Rabanne toilette set he'd bought, using the deodorant and splashing on the cologne after he'd shaved. He dressed casually at first and made a pass of the venue at 5.28 p.m. He wanted to memorise the global picture so when he turned up for the actual meeting he'd be able to spot if something wasn't right. The cafe was located on the corner of the main street and a well-used cross street. De Payns knew how an intelligence team would set up around and inside the cafe, and he could see nothing amiss.

He returned to the hotel, dressed in his suit and English shoes, and walked the three blocks to the cafe with a small leather satchel, arriving two minutes early. He sat against a wall so he could see the street, the entrance and the hallway that led to the WCs. There was virtually no one in the place—the Belgians ate even later than the French. As the waitress poured a water and asked if anyone else was joining him, Raven walked into the cafe, dressed in a stylish dark blue silk blouse and white flared pants with medium heels. De Payns sprang to his feet, all smiles, and she blushed.

'Hi, Anoush?' he said, putting out his hand. 'Sébastien Duboscq from AlphaPharma.'

She seemed a little flustered. 'Hello, Monsieur Duboscq.'

'Call me Seb, please,' he said, hurrying around the table to pull out the chair for her. 'You're on time. Such a refreshing change.'

De Payns found that a positive comment about a person's professionalism always worked better than flattery about their looks or clothes.

'So you've had some bad experiences with translators?' asked Raven, as she sat in the proffered chair.

De Payns explained that he sometimes required translations at short notice, and occasionally these were technical—not all translators were up to it.

'What kind of technical material?' she asked.

'Obviously, some of the writing is purely pharmaceutical and chemical, and there are trials and testing regimes to explain, which don't always translate well from European languages,' he said.

She laughed and he could see good dentistry. 'You've had some experience with scientific work?' He smiled as he looked at the menu.

'Not really,' she said. 'But some of the translations I've seen are hilarious.'

De Payns found her personable although she was heavy-handed with the Opium. He pushed on, telling her he had a website he wanted translated into Urdu and Pashto, and his main body of work was for clients in the pharmaceutical and agricultural industries who saw developing markets in Pakistan, Iran and the Stans.

'But I will have to ask you to sign an NDA,' said de Payns, once he knew she was interested and had the technical experience. 'I only have a business if my clients are satisfied that I'm not disclosing anything about them to my other clients.'

He kept things charming but distant, and when they'd finished their meals de Payns made it clear he was not ordering another bottle of wine, keeping their meeting clearly in the 'business' category. As he put her in a taxi, he shook her hand, thanked her for the meeting, and suggested they meet again in a week when he'd have the NDA and the commercial engagement paperwork ready to sign.

'Thank you for that,' she said, slipping sideways into the taxi. 'It looks like interesting work.'

As she disappeared into the long dusk, de Payns felt a rush of excitement at the first contact. It was always like this for him—out of the shadows, a ghost no more.

CHAPTER
THIRTY-SEVEN

De Payns was supposed to spend the next day in Paris tending to his five other IDs, and arranging for meetings with his contacts. At the second internet cafe he visited, he picked up an email message with Briffaut's acronym and number, and once he was three hundred metres from the cafe he used a *démarqué* phone to call a service number. When he gave his own identifier, the woman on the other end told him he had an emergency meeting at the Bunker at midday.

When he arrived at Briffaut's office, Marie Lafont was sitting on the visitors' sofa while Briffaut finished a call on his landline. As he took a seat he saw his boss had taken off his tie, usually a sign that Dominic Briffaut was going into the field.

'Anything more on that bioweapons rubbish?' asked de Payns, as Lafont looked up from her phone.

'We're about to find out,' she said.

Briffaut ended his call. 'There's a car waiting in the garage,' he said, standing.

■

They drove in a silver Mercedes van, which had seats facing one another in the back and a soundproof barrier between the rear seats and the driver. The section heads' vans were supposed to be SCIFs on wheels, but de Payns had never been convinced. They drove in a southerly direction, beyond the Périphérique, Briffaut briefing de Payns along the way about the Afghan national lying in the secure hospital of Villacoublay Air Base.

'He was picked up by an RPIMa patrol in Kapisa Province,' said Briffaut.

'Kapisa?' said Lafont. 'We still have paras operating in Afghanistan?'

'Logistics and humanitarian,' said Briffaut, deadpan.

Lafont shook her head, tired of the same old shit. 'Okay, so a French *logistics* unit discovers this guy and flies him to Paris. Why?'

'Let's find out,' said Briffaut.

■

They veered off the N118 south onto the A86, and Villacoublay Air Base loomed to de Payns' left. Having been cleared by the gate security, they drove to a large administration building, parked, and de Payns walked with Briffaut and Lafont to a rear tradesmen's entrance. De Payns felt old emotions rising. He'd never been inside this building, controlled as it was by the French secret services. During his air force career he'd been billeted at a more modern operations centre further west on the base. He paused at the door, allowing Marie Lafont to enter in front of him, and looked into the sky, where two Mirages flew in a formation of leader and wingman. As he tried to make out their markings, he was transported to another time and place—11 September 2001. They were on dogfight exercises when the ground signal came through:

'Marcou Hotel, Dijon.'

De Payns had responded, 'Marcou Hotel.'

'Marcou Hotel. Knock it off, knock it off. Report steady.'

'Hotel steady,' de Payns replied, curious about the command.

'Hotel, ready for TOP TOD?' asked Dijon Tower.

'Hotel ready,' said de Payns.

'Hotel three-two-one TOP TOD.'

After switching to encrypted radio frequency, he heard, 'Marcou Hotel, check?'

De Payns replied, 'Hotel on freq.'

'Copy. Hotel, RTB ASAP, clear speed and altitude.'

That's when de Payns' pulse had stepped up. RTB was 'return to base', and 'clear speed and altitude' meant 'do whatever it takes, just get here as fast as possible'. In the controlled environment of the French Air Force, it was almost unheard of to be given clear speed and altitude.

'Hotel copy,' said de Payns. 'Reason for the RTB ASAP?'

'Will be specified on the ground.'

'Hotel copy,' said de Payns. 'Heading to Dijon.'

Hitting speeds of over Mach 2 at any altitude that suited the pilot was a rarity and he recalled the adrenaline pumping as he was cleared for landing at Dijon and had to taxi into the 'armed' area before being pushed backwards into the bomb-proof hangars. Live air-to-air missiles were attached to the Mirage's underwings while the single engine was still running. The pilots were required to remain in their seats. It wasn't until de Payns' mechanic climbed the mobile ladder to deactivate his ejector seat that de Payns got to ask what the hell was going on.

'New York is under attack,' said the mechanic, the stress visible on his face. 'The World Trade Center is on fire. It's World War Three.'

De Payns remembered sitting in the cockpit and hearing the news, thinking that not only was there no better place to be seated for the beginning of a world war than in a combat-armed Mirage at Dijon, but that this war wouldn't be like the others and that intelligence would be the key to winning it.

The technicians reset the Mirages to activate the Magic II infrared guidance systems and MICA EM 'fire-and-forget' targeting systems which aided the twin 30mm cannons and the missiles. The radios were set to half quick and the switch from normal TOD comms to QOD—which changed frequency a thousand times per second—was locked in. The squadron was switched to a 'two-minute posture', which meant from the first scramble alert the pilots had to be wheels-up in at least two minutes—war footing. To achieve a two-minute posture the pilots had to remain seated in their planes at the end of the runway for hours, waiting for the scream of the scramble alert. Headings and orders would be given when the planes were in the air.

De Payns could still feel remnants of the stress and excitement surging through his body as he watched Lafont and Briffaut move into the building. He recalled the subsequent missions over Afghanistan and Iraq and the fatigue reignited inside him as if it had been sitting in his bones all these years. He shook it off and walked through the door, interested to see what Afghanistan had sent his way in his new career.

■

The intelligence section had its own hospital as well as its own prison, sleeping quarters and restaurant. The hospital looked 1970s American, down to the scalloped-glass partitions and the water-dispenser nooks along the linoleum-floored corridor. De Payns, Lafont and Briffaut followed a large male intelligence staffer to a private hospital room where Anthony Frasier stood over a bed, a white mask covering most of his face.

Frasier nodded at the staffer, who handed out face masks to the new arrivals and left the room.

'They're calling him Fazel,' said Frasier, pointing to a man lying in the bed. 'Arrived an hour ago.'

They drew closer and de Payns observed 'Fazel'. He looked to be around thirty, clean-shaven with cropped dark hair. He could have been from Iran, Pakistan or Afghanistan, and was connected to all sorts of tubes and machines. De Payns saw that a Middle Eastern man in his twenties was standing beside Frasier.

'French military entered a village two days ago,' said Frasier. 'Thirty-seven people dead—the only one still alive was Fazel here. The unit's medical officer attended some of the bodies and suspected some sort of agent had been used because of the extensive haemorrhaging. The unit evacuated the one survivor to hospital in Kabul, but he became steadily sicker and the medical officer suggested he be brought to France, where we might like to question him about his condition.'

'Why did he survive?' asked Briffaut, nodding at Fazel.

Frasier shrugged. 'He's been in a coma but we're going to kick him out of that and we have a translator to help us. Our DO medical team is in the lab a few doors down, testing his blood.'

The translator standing beside Frasier nodded at the group as Frasier walked to the door and called in the doctor. 'We're ready,' said Frasier.

The military doctor entered the room and walked to the patient, checked the vital signs on the monitors, then produced a large syringe.

'Give it about two minutes,' said the doctor to Frasier.

They waited as the patient opened his eyes, blinked several times and gradually focused on his surrounds. The doctor checked him with a torch in the eyes and then Frasier cleared his throat.

The doctor looked up. 'All yours,' he said, and he left the room.

Frasier turned to the translator. 'Tell him we're friendly, he's in France and he is safe now.'

The translator rattled it off and Fazel shook his head as he responded.

The translator said, 'He asks what happened to the village.'

'The village? Doesn't it have a name?' asked Frasier.

The translator repeated the question, and Fazel responded in a rambling monologue. The translator nodded a lot and asked his own questions. 'He says he was travelling to Kabul from the north, and he was dropped by a truck driver at a crossroads near the village. This is just east of the Nuristan Forest, near the Pakistani border. He walked into the village around four-thirty a.m. and used an old cistern to wash himself. He didn't drink the water from the cistern because he had his own bottle. He was going to wait for the village to wake up and try to buy food, but after waiting for an hour he felt very sick. He'd washed his face with the cistern water and he assumed it was a bad supply. His sickness got worse and he vomited three times. He didn't see it at first, because it was dark, but as dawn came he realised he'd vomited blood. He panicked and went into the village, but no one was around. He knocked on doors, no reply. He looked in a window and saw three people, including one child, lying on the floor in a circle of blood. He pushed the door open and went in, and found they were dead, bleeding from all orifices. He realised he might have the same illness and drank all his bottled water. By now he couldn't walk very well, he had diarrhoea and it was blood. He checked other houses but everyone was dead. Massive blood loss from the mouth, nose and rectum. He was feeling weaker and unable to move and he must have passed out. He was woken by foreign soldiers at what he thought was around six-thirty or seven.'

'What then?' asked Frasier.

The translator asked and Fazel responded.

'He says he remembers thinking that the soldiers weren't American or Australian, so maybe they were French. He thought he was dying and then he woke up here, just now. He wonders what the date is. He thinks he's lost some days?'

The intelligence section of Villacoublay had its own secure communications system and SCIFs, and the DGSE team adjourned to the serviced offices where the DO team was waiting. Frasier conferred with the lead scientist, took a sheaf of papers and returned to the group who were sitting around a meeting table.

'It's clostridium,' said Frasier, shaking his head. 'Now where have I heard that name recently?'

'This is the bacterium the Russians think is being made at the MERC?' asked Briffaut. 'This is what it does to people?'

Frasier raised his hand slightly, as if asking people to slow down. 'Clostridium can be naturally occurring, outside of bioweapons labs. We'll do more tests and see exactly what we're looking at.'

Frasier turned to de Payns. 'I'm not asking you to cut corners on Alamut, but if there's a fast way and a slow way, you're to take the fast way, understand? I have a feeling time is not on our side.'

CHAPTER
THIRTY-EIGHT

De Payns closed the latest DR file sent to him via Marie Lafont. It was depressing reading—French teams had taken control of the poisoned village in Afghanistan, testing the ancient water cistern and the dead bodies. It had been a week since Fazel had been delivered to Villacoublay and the DO science team had now concluded that the samples taken in Afghanistan were manipulated strains of *Clostridium perfringens* suspended in drinking water. Manipulated because the strain detected was epsilon toxin type D—ETX-D—a type of *Clostridium perfringens* not found naturally in humans. There were no animals or animal organs found in the cistern or upstream of the cistern. The bacterium had caused massive internal haemorrhaging in the victims and multiple organ failure, and at death the body was filled with gassy pustules. The Company could not isolate where it came from, but through intercepted military communications the DGSE knew the Russians suspected a weaponised clostridium was being developed at the MERC.

De Payns put down the report and rubbed his face. The photographs of the deceased were hideous and he had only been able to look at a few before pushing them aside. He had to accelerate

Alamut. During the week de Payns had conducted a second meeting with Raven in Mons and the Company wanted him to push harder and faster than he normally would. He checked his watch, then headed for a meeting with Garrat, Lafont and Templar.

■

Garrat summarised de Payns' second meeting with Raven. The important milestone was getting Raven's signature on an NDA and engagement contract. As de Payns' association with Raven became stronger he would ask for information and insights that took her into the grey areas of legality and loyalty. This escalation should lead to an upgraded contract to reflect greater secrecy. It was that second, grey-zone documentation that could eventually propel the target into the black zone. It was easier to ask someone to break the law if they had already bent it. And it was the second contract that contained the clauses that could later be used to blackmail the target: *What do you mean we tricked you? That's your signature, isn't it? And this is a picture of you signing the contract with a French spy?* Having got that far, a person like de Payns—when faced with a pull-back from a target—could waive the contract and discuss the facts of life: *I wonder if the head of counterintelligence at the ISI would be interested in your contractual agreement to deliver us classified material from the Pakistani government? He can even read how much we paid you.*

The entrapment was driven by money. Escalating amounts of it for darkening shades of grey. Up to a point. The French secret services were notoriously tight on the purse strings, and having taken a target 'black', the Company usually withdrew the money and made it simple blackmail: *Keep it coming, my friend, or we go to the ISI.*

De Payns wasn't going to do it that way initially. He wanted Raven to trust him and like him; he'd use that to discover who was calling her from the MERC.

Garrat moved to the subject of electronic surveillance in Mons. The reports showed Raven's emails to friends saying she'd met 'a cute French guy'. In phone calls on her non-MERC phone she made it clear to one of her friends that she'd have an affair with Sébastien Duboscq, if he was keen.

Garrat shook with mirth as he read aloud from a transcript: '*It's not just his looks—he's a real gentleman.*'

'And look at this,' Garrat continued. 'The friend says, *But he is French—is he not arrogant?* And Raven says, *He is sure of himself, yes, but he is also very funny.*'

'Enough with the jokes,' said de Payns. 'Has she shown those contracts to anyone else?'

Garrat shook his head. 'She hasn't emailed the documents and she hasn't used either of her two cell phones or her landline to ask about signing the docs.'

Turning to Templar, de Payns asked, 'Does she have surveillance around her?'

'No,' said Templar. 'We've been on this for more than a month and we're clean.'

It was one thing to have established contact with Raven, but she was only a stepping stone. The point of Operation Alamut was to discover the identity of the senior person at the MERC and attempt a contact on him. De Payns wanted to hasten things along without entangling himself too much with Raven. He knew what the agents at the Bunker wanted him to do but he wanted to maintain his record of no sex.

'It's a go,' said de Payns. 'We'll take it to the next level. Mattieu?'

'Green light from me,' said Garrat. 'Can you get up there tomorrow?'

■

The Thalys train to Brussels left Gare du Nord on time at 9.25 a.m. and de Payns eased back in the airline-like seat as the train picked up speed. After the Garrat meeting, he'd called Raven with a last-minute request to have lunch and talk about projects. Raven had said yes and now he was Sébastien again, dressed in a good suit and travelling to Belgium with a waft of Paco Rabanne.

The acceleration of Operation Alamut forced him to delay meetings that his other identities were having. He didn't like to do that, because his Paris-bound weeks were fairly structured, with each day committed to a different identity. He would usually fix an appointment with a target by phone or email and, having set up a meeting, he would plan his trip with logistics and decide whether he needed a team. The DGSE didn't like to waste money, so resources had to shrink and expand with the operational needs. With Raven, the team had shrunk from nine to four, including a long-range photographer who was shooting footage of Raven and de Payns at the cafe.

Although he wasn't prepared to sleep with Raven, he was prepared to make the contact more romantic. Raven's private conversations revealed she had feelings for Sébastien, and he would capitalise on that without betraying his wife.

The previous evening he and Romy had enjoyed two glasses of wine and an early night. It was never going to be the way it was when they met—he a dashing air force pilot and she a policy worker at an economic think tank. Their single, child-free selves had been very different. He smiled remembering how he'd met Romy at a bar when she was with her boyfriend. He'd manipulated the man into drinking too much—so much that he vomited. He'd then approached Romy at her workplace and told her that since she was a real Frenchwoman, she needed a real Frenchman, one who could hold his drink.

'I actually have a boyfriend,' she'd said.

'And yet, here I am.'

They'd never lost their shared sense of humour but romance had not been easy to maintain once they had kids. The standard longevity in the field for a Y Division *chef de mission* was five years before he or she flamed out with exhaustion or alcoholism, or was promoted to a desk, as Garrat had been. Five years of field work at the Company was all it took to wreck a marriage. De Payns had been in the field for seven years and his workload was extreme. He had to keep alive five fictive IDs at a time, which meant constant gardening, constant pretending and lying, constant breaking down of phones and powering them up again to assume another identity. He couldn't talk to Romy about what he did, and he could only divulge half of what he was doing to his clan—and even then, only once the operation was over. It was isolating, and the policy of the DGSE was to keep the *chefs de mission* apart, to prevent them from talking and comparing notes.

Templar was divorced. Shrek was still married, but he didn't have kids. There was only so much he could talk about with them. So his marriage had become an anchor, even as it had to sit like a psychological island, divorced from the mainland of his career. Romy was his rock, his trigonometry point for sanity. He was going to entrap the Pakistani woman they called Raven, but he wasn't going to screw her.

CHAPTER
THIRTY-NINE

The phone call came in the middle of the night, a function of different time zones and his associate being unable to make calls from his high-level job. The Doctor took the call and listened intently, not saying much.

'The person of interest just returned from Pakistan and I understand he has briefed the CP office.'

'CP?' asked the Doctor.

'Counter-Proliferation. Nukes and bioweapons. I haven't seen the briefing reports but we can assume they're looking at Scimitar.'

'They were in Islamabad?' asked the Doctor.

'Yes,' said the voice. 'When I have more details I'll let you know.'

The Doctor thanked the caller and hung up. He walked into the kitchen and told his bodyguard they were going out. They drove to the MERC, where he let himself into the vast research facility that employed some of the smartest minds in Asia.

He descended to level B5, walked the long corridor and opened a door at the end of it. He hit the lights to reveal an enormous laboratory. It was equipped with the latest digital equipment from the US, Germany and Japan. Some of the autoclaves, centrifuges and particle accelerators had been sourced illegally and were so advanced that they were not yet used in this lab because they didn't have the requisite computing power to run them.

During the day, a team of thirty-five scientists separated bacteria, grew it, enhanced it and then allowed it to reproduce under different scenarios and conditions. Over the past twenty years, the MERC had hosted experts from South Africa and Iran, North Korea and Russia. They had destroyed thousands of batches of bacterium culture that hadn't made the grade, perfecting and pushing and then developing the strains to the point where they could both be stabilised—for certainty of transportation—and where, upon introduction to water, they would flourish, waiting for their introduction to the all-important receptor cells that just happened to reside on the intestinal walls of mammals such as goats, sheep, cattle . . . and humans.

The *Clostridium perfringens* bacterium produced a painful and deadly condition called 'gas gangrene', and it was one of the oldest bioweapons known to man. Gangrenous humans and livestock had been routinely thrown into rivals' water supplies, usually a well or cistern.

The last known time it was used militarily was the US Civil War in the 1860s. It wasn't a subtle or clever pathogen—when ingested it simply triggered a bacteriological war inside a digestive tract, attacking the vital organs and quickly leading to internal haemorrhaging, massive blood loss and a painful death. It didn't kill everyone it touched—it didn't have to. Even if it could render thousands of people incapacitated from one poisoned water supply, it destroyed morale, diverted resources to sick people and generated societal panic, whether an army camp or a city.

Yousef's achievement was to isolate the strain that could be stabilised—as far as such an aggressive pathogen could be stabilised—and manipulate it so that when it met water it would thrive rather than degrade.

He walked the length of the underground lab, pondering his quest. His journey through high school in Pakistan and then university had led him to America, to Stanford, where he finished his PhD in bacterial engineering. His PhD was funded by the US Army, and he was offered a position in one of their labs. Little did they know that the gifted Pakistani was the son of a farming family from southern Iran. Yousef's mother had been orphaned in the mid-1950s, when a French oil company had disposed of its drilling chemicals in a dry channel. That wadi was also a recharge for an ancient aquifer used by farming communities. His mother had watched her parents die in a crappy hospital, from internal injuries, because of French greed. His mother's sister—the Doctor's beloved Aunt Lavi—was brain-damaged from the poisoning and lived out her days in her sister's house, singing childish ditties for her nephew and niece. His mother's once-proud landowning family had been torn apart by the Westerners, their lives diminished, reduced to living in their adopted country of Pakistan. His immediate family wasn't sold on vengeance. His sister was influenced by their kindly and entitled father—a man who had walked away from his Pakistani culture and thought nothing of adopting Western mannerisms. Yousef, meanwhile, had increasingly aligned himself with his Iranian mother and her rage towards the French. He had a good mind and a spectacular education, and he had vowed to humble the arrogant Franks with his greatest weapon—his superior intellect.

The day came when, as an associate professor at the National University in Islamabad, he'd returned to his office after teaching a class on bacterial toxins to find a suave but dangerous-looking man waiting. The man, whom Yousef would only ever know as 'the Colonel', offered him a job with his own lab and staff.

At the rear of the long lab, he unlocked a heavy, soundproof security door and locked it behind him. He descended two flights of stairs and came out in a large room filled with cages. The soft glow of red stand-by lights cast an eerie pall over an enclosed area that he knew held around a hundred and thirty people.

He walked past them to his office, turned on his desk lamp and sat at his secured computer. The computer had no connection to a public or even a Pakistani government network. The B6 level of the secret facility held a server farm with a manually upgraded scientific research database uploaded by ISI cybersecurity officers once a week. In the encrypted section of the internal computer system lay the secret to Operation Scimitar—scientists knew that while *Clostridium perfringens* produced a dangerous bacterial toxin in its own right—more deadly than the *Clostridium botulinum* and *tetani*, and a hundred times more lethal than the *Clostridium septicum* toxin—that wasn't the end of the story for this vicious bug. Working off stolen North Korean clinical papers from the 1960s, the Doctor had reassembled the experimentation on *perfringens* that had been abandoned decades ago, and identified where those earlier scientists had faltered. The North Koreans had isolated the most virulent strain—the epsilon toxin, or ETX—which, when injected into or fed to a goat or sheep, would kill the animal within one to three hours. Liver, kidney, heart, lungs and brain—as well as the central nervous systems—would collapse with a rolling thunder of oedema, lesions, loss of blood–brain barrier and cellular damage. It meant massive internal bleeding and the breakdown of bodily functions, and an agonising, thrashing death characterised by diarrhoea. There was no vaccine for ETX and no antibiotics strong enough to arrest it. If a strong enough dose was administered to a human, the victim would be dead inside three hours.

As soon as ETX had been isolated, and Western intelligence learned of its development, it immediately went onto the banned bioweapons list because of its specific danger to humans. Human-only cell lines such as G-402, HRTEC and ACHN were highly susceptible to the epsilon toxin and it was classified as a

Category B Biological Agent by the United States Centers for Disease Control and Prevention and also by the French government. But the original researchers, while impressed with the potential of ETX for a widespread biological attack, became—in the Doctor's opinion—sidetracked on a quest to deliver it effectively. Those scientists had tried to deliver it via aerosol or bomb, but had faced the ever-increasing need to concentrate and potentise the epsilon toxin in order to make it effective over large areas and populations, an expensive and resource-consuming task if it was going to be properly weaponised.

The Doctor's innovation had obviated the need to make the ETX dose so strong at the source. Instead, he focused on building a strain of ETX that was ready to start acting internally as soon as it landed. His innovation was to isolate the sialidase enzymes—the presence of which allowed the ETX proteins to readily connect to cells in the intestine—and promote their production from the ETX itself, thereby ensuring that even with a lower quantum of ETX in the introduced load, infection rates were even higher because the ETX was optimised to work. As his younger scientists put it, with the ETX primed to produce sialidases, it was 'locked and loaded' and could succeed with relatively small concentrations. The most important aspect—the ETX would now hold its full lethality in water.

Yousef thought about the phone call he'd just received and considered his dilemma—to release the enhanced pathogen in Operation Scimitar, and avenge his mother's family; or to keep testing it until it was perfect. He was a perfectionist but he had to listen to his source in Paris. If the French were closing in, it was time to act. Scimitar would have to begin.

He padded along beside the cages and some of the people stirred, sticking their heads up and looking through the bars. They were Communists and insurgents and some of them were Christians and Jews. Mostly they were university students seized from protests and illegal political meetings and sent to the Doctor to assist in the national effort. Their religious or political designation was irrelevant, thought Yousef. Science was agnostic.

Walking from his office into the main gallery of the lab, he turned on the lights and in front of him was a large window that looked into the test cell. It was painted white, and in a pile on the floor was a bloody mess of naked young people. No one moved. They were dead from a teaspoon each of ETX-infected water.

He walked back to his office, the eyes of the prisoners following him. He accessed the encrypted service run by the ISI and selected the 'To' tab that identified one of his project partners. From this console, his messages were sent to the ISI office in the MERC, and they would relay the email via their own secure systems.

He paused, thought of his mother and his aunt, and then typed: *Activate Scimitar.*

He hit send.

He was ready.

CHAPTER
FORTY

The first thing de Payns noticed about Raven when she walked into the cafe was that she'd just had her hair and nails done. He could smell all the product from the salon, and her dark hair was big and piled up on top of her head, exposing her neck and giving him a look at the small silver hoops in her ears. She wasn't his type, but she dressed for what she had.

'Hi, Sébastien,' she said, smiling brightly. She gave him the French greeting of a hug and double kiss.

They made small talk as she handed over the sample translations he'd asked her to prepare.

'It's not like I can check them,' said de Payns, chuckling, but noticing her translations were both in the European alphabet and Urdu script. 'Did you have any trouble with the material?'

'No, it's not too bad,' she said, putting a napkin on her lap. 'When I hit a word I don't fully understand, I search it.'

De Payns smiled and pushed an envelope across the table.

'What's that?' she asked, eyebrows raised.

'Your payment, one thousand euro,' said de Payns. 'It was easier to do it in cash. Please count it.'

She extracted the notes and fanned them, and somewhere through the western window of the cafe, one of Templar's team was recording the entire transaction on HD video.

'It's nice to be paid so quickly,' she said. 'Government clients make me wait sixty days.'

They ordered and de Payns started what he hoped would be a fruitful escalation. 'Once we get some of these foundation documents done, and printed and uploaded, I have something more specific for you.'

'Yes?' she replied.

He handed over the next level of translations that had been given to him at the Bunker. 'The pharmaceuticals side of this business is well developed as a channel, and I know exactly who we have to target and service,' said de Payns. 'But the agricultural side—the biotech and agritech and chemicals research—is more diffuse.'

'I'm sorry,' she said. '*Diffuse*?'

'You know, not defined, not concentrated?'

'All over the place?' she suggested, smiling.

'I should just speak in plain French,' he said, and explained that the supplies and machinery his clients wanted to push in the Middle East did not always have a central market, because the R&D groups were tucked away in facilities and campuses attached to universities and government departments, and it was hard to market to such a *diffuse* group of people.

Anoush nodded, indicating that she understood the problem. But she gave up nothing.

'We might have a research facility on our list of potential clients, but are they developing pesticides, or herbicides, or GMO crops or fertilisers? Or are they working on vaccines for chickens or better yields for dairy cows?'

Anoush shrugged. 'Could be anything.'

De Payns changed the topic to a man outside the window—he was allowing his dog to urinate on a chained bike.

'That's very nice of him,' said de Payns, winking. 'I bet he wouldn't allow that if it was his bike. This man could be Parisian!'

She laughed and agreed, and as the laughter died down, she asked, 'So which research facilities are we talking about?'

De Payns kept it casual and listed four, in Saudi Arabia, Iraq and Kuwait. Then he said, 'We can't forget your country. Pakistan has some of the best scientists in the Middle East.' De Payns watched her face.

'I don't know much about that,' she said.

The food arrived and de Payns shifted the conversation to personal topics. He asked about her kids, and allowed her to skirt around her husband without stating that they were estranged. By the time they were on to coffees, de Payns went for the social escalation. 'I'm in Mons for a couple of days this time. What does a visitor do around here?'

She looked down at her coffee and then addressed him with a hopeful smile. 'Perhaps I could show you?'

'Sure,' said de Payns, showing all his teeth. 'Let's do something.'

CHAPTER FORTY-ONE

De Payns used the afternoon break to contact Templar and inform him of the evening plan; that Raven wanted to take him to the Latin club, and they were meeting in another bar first.

Templar laughed knowingly. 'You know she was at the beauty salon before she met you?' he said. 'It's getting serious, *mon pote.*'

'Don't start,' said de Payns.

'So just fuck her,' said Templar. 'You got performance anxiety or something?'

■

De Payns spent an hour walking the main streets, discovering there was a small, medieval core to the city, and more modern sections further out. He found a quaint bookstore, bought a 1954 first edition of *Huit affaires pour Biggles*, and napped at his hotel in the late afternoon. Then he showered and dressed in casual clothes, and at 6.58 p.m. he walked into the bar Raven had told him about, ordered a light beer and a glass of riesling—her favourite—and took a small round table near the door. Raven walked in three minutes later and when he stood he could tell she was nervous. They drank and laughed, and when they were finished they walked the two blocks to the Latin Bar, where Raven had reserved a table with a banquette, two tables away from the stage. De Payns ensured he took the seat on the edge of the banquette and allowed her to sit in the middle. The waitress arrived with a tray containing two margaritas and they clinked glasses and drank.

De Payns took it slow, pouring his drink between his feet when Raven was looking the other way. They ordered Cuban pulled beef and more drinks. By the third margarita, which arrived during the meal, the band was hitting its first number, an instrumental piece heavy on the bongos, leavened with high-pitch trumpet.

Raven leaned in to talk when making a point, her warmth and perfume enveloping him. By the time de Payns had finished eating, the lights went down and the dance leader stood in a spotlight on a parquet dance floor in front of the stage. The crowd—Raven included—whooped and applauded.

The dance leader's accent was so heavy that de Payns struggled to understand what he was saying, but the other diners seemed to have no trouble, because they rose as one and headed for the dance floor. And then his hand was in Raven's and he was being dragged into a Latin dance night.

Half an hour later, he collapsed into his seat, sweaty and panting from the work-out. Raven ordered a pitcher of margarita and now she wanted to talk. A female singer took the stage with the band, and Raven leaned in so her lips were on his neck.

'What would you do if someone in your family became very religious?' she slurred.

'It would be difficult,' said de Payns.

She made a groaning sound, sat up, rolled her eyes and leaned back into de Payns. 'My husband.'

'You don't have to explain,' said de Payns.

'I know. But it's so hard, living in Belgium with all this freedom and women having their own lives, and . . .'

De Payns sipped and waited.

'My husband and I moved here five years ago, and it was great. He had a good job.'

De Payns ears were now pricked up and he leaned towards her slightly as the singer and the band performed a rowdy Latin American number.

'But our mosque was filled with radicals, and Fadi fell in with them,' she said. 'Suddenly, he doesn't want me drinking and he wants to go back and live righteously in Pakistan. But I don't want to give up my freedom.'

'He doesn't live in Belgium?'

'His clothes are still in the wardrobe and the kids live in hope that he'll walk in the door, but he went back to Islamabad, where he belongs.'

'Did he find work back at home?' he asked. Perhaps the middle-aged man from the MERC was her husband, he speculated.

'Yes, but now he spends a lot of his time working out of Dubai.'

That ruled out the man from the MERC.

He topped up her glass but not his own.

She leaned in again. 'Women in Europe can be independent, if they have education and they have a way to make money.'

'That's about it,' said de Payns. 'Or come from a wealthy family. That's also a good strategy.'

She sighed. 'I know all about that.'

'Yeah?' prompted de Payns, interested again. This gave him an opening to play at the ego end of MICE. She was at a point of great candour.

'But it's also a prison.'

De Payns let a moment go by, nodding his head to the band's beat. He didn't want to appear too keen. 'You mean in Pakistan?'

She nodded. 'You get privilege, but they have you in their pocket the whole time.'

'Who's *they*?' asked de Payns.

'The government, the police,' she said, waving her glass.

'So, your family is political?' asked de Payns. 'That's why you speak English and French?'

'No,' she said. 'My family is academic, *scientific*.' She was drunk now, her words not flowing. 'I didn't tell you the truth about those facilities.'

'Which facilities?' asked de Payns. 'In Pakistan?'

She tried to swallow her drink. 'Yes, I know a bit more about them than I told you.'

De Payns shrugged.

'There's a place outside Islamabad which is the kind of research institute you were talking about.'

De Payns frowned as if he didn't know what she was talking about.

'It's called the Pakistan Agricultural Chemical Company, and it's supposed to be about fertilisers and pesticides, but they do a lot of high-level research for the government—actually, for the army,' she said, looking around her.

De Payns could feel his heart thumping. 'You mean the military?' asked de Payns, keeping his voice calm. 'What do they have to do with agriculture?'

Her laugh was a bleak rattle. 'Agriculture? I'm not so sure.'

De Payns' guts twisted. If the ISI caught her talking like this, they'd kill her.

'Well, okay then,' he said, bringing it back to his legend. 'That's good for our marketing materials, but how do you know this?'

'My brother is the head scientist of all the weapons programs at this place,' said Raven, hiccupping. 'I talk to him once a week.'

'Right,' said de Payns, his tone offhand. Meanwhile, his mind was doing somersaults. *The person of interest is her brother and he runs the MERC!*

He was very careful with the next sentence. 'Well, that might help us target our marketing, do you think?'

Raven shook her head and turned her body towards de Payns. 'You don't understand. Yousef runs a weapons program, I'm sure of it. He's completely controlled by the government and he's allowed to speak to me for just ten minutes, once a week.'

De Payns mimed confusion.

Her face changed very suddenly, as if in panic. 'You can't ever mention this to anyone. You have to promise.'

'I promise,' said de Payns, putting up his hands as she poked him in the chest.

'I mean it,' she said. 'If they knew I was telling you these things, we'd all be dead.'

CHAPTER
FORTY-TWO

The Thalys train got into Gare du Nord just before 11 a.m. and de Payns walked with the commuters through the famous vaulted concourses. He was mercifully free of a hangover, a fate he wouldn't guarantee for Raven. She was sloshed by the time he loaded her into a cab and dropped her at her apartment. She was too drunk to make it to the door so he escorted her in and paid off the babysitter.

He had a quick look for followers in the Gare du Nord then ducked down the escalators to the Metro platforms and waited seven minutes for a train south to the Gare d'Austerlitz. As he took his seat in the lightly populated car, his Sébastien Duboscq phone trilled. This was the part of the journey where he'd normally break down the phone in preparation for a change of ID at the safe house. It was Raven.

'Anoush,' he said. 'You're up early.'

She groaned the groan of a person who'd had one drink too many. 'Don't laugh at me. Oh, and thanks for dealing with the babysitter.'

'No problem,' said de Payns. 'You wanted that sofa for a bed.'

They made small talk for a few minutes, and then her tone changed. 'Some of the things I told you last night, I . . . I really shouldn't have.'

'Don't worry about that,' he said. 'I promised you it wouldn't go further than me—and I may change jobs shortly, so it's not of any importance to me. What *is* important to me is that you gave me your trust, and I'm very touched. Go back to bed and see you in a week.'

He could hear her chewing her lip. 'Really?'

'I'm trying to remember exactly what you told me,' said de Payns, jollying her along. 'Now you have me all intrigued.'

'Maybe I'm overreacting,' she said. 'I just really shouldn't talk about him, and now you'll have to shut up about it.'

'I understand,' said de Payns, laughing. 'Are you okay?'

'I'm fine, really. But please, forget about last night?'

'Anoush . . .'

'Let's meet again next week when you're in Mons. But no mention of this in emails, okay?'

De Payns could almost feel the fear down the line.

She finished the call, and he broke down the phone as they closed on Austerlitz.

■

He spent most of the day writing his report. His night with Raven was a major breakthrough—the person of interest at the MERC was Anoush's brother, a former professor in bacterial engineering named Dr Yousef Bijar. De Payns was happy to have the information, but he believed he was not the man to carry the operation further. The next step would involve getting closer to her family and she was now scared of her relationship with de Payns—or scared of the consequences of their association for Sébastien Duboscq, at least. If she was scared of what her brother or the ISI could do to her new friend, she could easily clam up and not allow any further incursions into her life or family.

He'd called ahead and notified Briffaut, Garrat and Lafont that he was ready to brief them. He had twenty minutes before the meeting started, so he grabbed a large black coffee and headed out into the morning sun, where he lit a smoke and walked the lawns around the old fort in search of a park bench where he could relax and stretch his legs. The end of summer was a time to savour the warmth before the cold winds of autumn started. He felt tired but not exhausted, a state that affected his brain more than his body. But he focused on the events of the night before and Raven's call to him that morning. She was an abandoned woman, in a foreign country, quite vulnerable and expected to shut up about her brother, while talking to him once a week. He knew from Poles and East Germans that the true victory of the secret police was imposing self-censorship. He sucked on the smoke and sipped at the coffee. He wondered about Romy, Patrick and Oliver. What danger was he bringing into their lives on a daily basis? If his family knew who and what he was, would they live their lives in a similar state of fear?

He saw Briffaut exit the double doors down by the gym entrance and walk towards him holding his own coffee mug. Dominic Briffaut was fifteen years de Payns' senior, but he still walked strong.

'One of those for me?' asked Briffaut, sitting on the bench. 'Saw you with that damned smoke and suddenly I needed one.'

De Payns handed them over, and when he got the pack back he lit another for himself.

'Saw your report on Raven,' said Briffaut, sucking on the cigarette. 'Nice work. How do you want to do it? Work Raven to contact Bijar? Or go to Islamabad and push for a contact directly on Bijar?'

'It has to be through Raven,' said de Payns. 'And it has to be in Islamabad; he won't leave that city. But I don't know if I'm the one to do it.'

Briffaut dragged on his smoke and regarded de Payns. 'That's not what Frasier wants to hear right now. He thinks there's some credible good news for the President.'

De Payns agreed. 'I'm not terminating the operation, but I'm probably not the person to take the contact where it might have to go.'

'Gone far enough with her?'

'Something like that,' said de Payns. 'She's shitting herself about saying too much last night.'

'She's worried about your welfare?'

De Payns nodded. 'I've seen this before. She's scared that her association with her brother is a negative for me. There's panic about divulging too much.'

'Okay,' said Briffaut. 'And then she stops communicating because she doesn't want you running a mile from her?'

'That's a real possibility.'

'Why?' Briffaut chuckled. 'Because she's got a crush on you?'

'Don't make fun of me.'

'You going to tell Marie this?' asked Briffaut, shaking his head. 'She's a hard thing.'

■

De Payns took them through his report and made his case early.

'The relationship is getting very close,' he said. 'Too close. It could wreck any chance of a contact on Bijar.'

'We got a pseudo for Bijar?' asked Briffaut.

'Timberwolf okay with everyone?' asked Lafont, to nods. De Payns could see her tensing up, wanting to argue with him. 'Can I ask you, what is *too close*?'

Briffaut leaped in. 'If a target says too much, they'll sometimes back off because they want to keep the frisson the way it was. We might be in that position.'

Marie Lafont gave a wry smile. 'So, Alec, how close?'

'Drinking together, laughs, friendship,' he said.

'Did you fuck her?' asked Lafont.

Garrat and Lafont started laughing and de Payns joked along rather than take offence. 'No, I haven't done that.'

Garrat said to Lafont, 'I told you so.'

'Come on, people, cut it out,' growled Briffaut.

'Okay, okay,' said Lafont. 'I'd like to make the point that *too close* generally means you've fucked, and now the relationship has changed, become complicated, and it might be harder to manipulate the target because the leverage is gone.'

'Then I haven't got too close, and perhaps I maintain some leverage?' asked de Payns, regretting it as he said it. Female agents were regularly expected to include sex in a contact.

'How nice for you,' said Lafont sarcastically.

'The aim of Alamut is to find a human access to the MERC,' said de Payns. 'We're doing that through Raven, but if Raven is worried about her admissions to me, I don't think a sexual relationship is going to help us.'

'I'll do it,' said Garrat.

There was a pause for two seconds and then the meeting broke into laughter. It got so bad that Briffaut had to thump his own chest against his smoker's cough, even as Garrat blushed with embarrassment.

'What's wrong?' he asked, clearly not enjoying the ridicule. 'I'm divorced, it's okay.'

When the laughter had stopped, Lafont turned to Garrat. 'You've seen her horny emails, right, Mattieu?'

He nodded. 'Sure.'

'Those emails were about that,' she said, pointing at de Payns.

Lafont turned back to de Payns. 'Nice try, Aguilar. The sex part is optional, but you're not bailing out of this contact. We're almost there.'

De Payns looked to Briffaut, who shrugged. 'Like she said, *mon pote*. Maybe read those emails again?'

CHAPTER
FORTY-THREE

Lafont followed him back to his office. 'Sorry about that,' she said, as de Payns secured two files in his safe. 'If you have a better way to Timberwolf and the MERC, I'll listen. But Mattieu hasn't been in the field for five years—on something this sensitive, he'd absolutely screw it up.'

'I'll do it,' said de Payns, sagging back in his chair. 'It's okay.'

'It's not okay,' said Lafont. 'I did this when I was single. You're married with kids.'

De Payns opened his hands at her. 'Any ideas?'

'You could try some hot and heavy kissing and then pull away, tell her you have an admission to make—you're married and now you're torn between the lust you have for her and the vows you made to your wife?'

De Payns scoffed. 'You kidding me? That works?'

'If you want her to pull you in, not push you away—yes, it could work.'

'Or she thinks I'm a married sleaze, having an affair . . .'

Briffaut appeared in the doorway. 'Frasier's called an emergency meeting for Alamut. We'll take my car.'

■

There were five of them in the smallest of the executive SCIFs, on the top floor of the Cat. De Payns and Briffaut, and Lafont and her chemicals genius, Josef Ackermann, also from the CP division. Frasier sat at the head of the table, in a hurry as usual.

'As some of you know, I've delayed issuing the final report on Operation Falcon because, candidly, I wanted more details,' said Frasier. 'That's no reflection on Aguilar or his team—we had to pull the plug and I guess we weren't hanging around interviewing people.'

Frasier caught his eye and de Payns nodded.

'So five days ago I tasked Shrek to go to Sicily, retrace what we know and see what else might present itself. Well, Shrek got back from Sicily yesterday, and along with his report he had some samples.'

Frasier distributed a brief report featuring photographs of pale granular items on dark backgrounds. De Payns flipped the pages and saw wide-angle shots inside old warehouses and a square drain covered with an iron grille.

'He backtracked Commodore's movements—and, we think, Murad's—to a warehouse behind the Palermo docks. The warehouse was abandoned but he took samples of some unusual granules in a drain,' said Frasier. 'They're mainly chlorine but with very faint traces of *Clostridium perfringens* on them. Our lab says they match with the Afghan village samples, so they're the manipulated . . .' He glanced at the CP pair for help.

Ackermann obliged. 'Epsilon toxin type D, sir.'

'Afghanistan?' asked de Payns, slightly stunned by the Palermo connection. 'What's this got to do with Afghanistan?'

Frasier handed over to Ackermann, who said the samples had been tested six times. 'Every test has come up with the same result. The chlorine samples are now sealed in an infectious diseases vault, but I can confirm they've been exposed to a virulent strain of *Clostridium perfringens* that is not consistent with natural formations.'

'Which means?' prompted Briffaut.

'It means it's been enhanced, manipulated,' said Ackermann. 'These samples are the epsilon toxin, which occurs naturally in goats but is death to us—humans have no defences. It turns our insides to mush and results in gas gangrene.'

Briffaut stared at the anxious scientist. When he became serious his large physique seemed to expand. 'It was found in Palermo? What the hell has Operation Falcon got to do with this gangrene bioweapon?' He turned to de Payns. 'Tell me—how does a fake passport operation get its hands on a bioweapon?'

De Payns shrugged. 'I have no information that connects Commodore with something like this. He was a useful idiot who sold fake identities to terrorists, that's it.'

Briffaut asked, 'Do we know who made this toxin?'

Ackermann shrugged and Lafont stepped in. 'Only a handful of countries have ever developed ETX as a weapon. The Russians and South Africans stopped their programs in the eighties, and the North Koreans have developed it in the past but they're now focused on nukes. That leaves Pakistan and Iran, but Iran's programs are predominantly sarin and ricin, and they're also throwing their resources into nukes.'

Briffaut nodded. 'So we're back to Pakistan? That means the MERC?'

Lafont continued. 'Can't confirm, but most likely. That's certainly where Russian intelligence is looking.'

Frasier looked from one face to another. 'So we are fairly certain there's a bioweapons program at the MERC in Pakistan and the Russians think it's clostridium. We've got weaponised clostridium testing in an Afghani village, and now we have weaponised clostridium confirmed in Europe—the same strain we found in Afghanistan.'

'How do they use it?' asked de Payns.

'It seems to be optimised for water,' said Ackermann. 'The lab people need some outside help, because they say the epsilon toxin type D strain they can identify has itself been modified.'

'What does that mean?'

'We're finding out.'

'Looks like the game just got bigger,' said Briffaut, looking at Frasier. 'Any theories?'

Frasier started gathering his papers. 'That warehouse was cleaned out the day before Shrek arrived. So whatever was there is now somewhere else.' He pointed at de Payns. 'We're on a clock—find me some answers.'

CHAPTER FORTY-FOUR

It was Friday afternoon and de Payns had an operation to get back on track. He'd let Raven drink too much and perhaps he'd been too friendly. Whatever the combination, she'd divulged too much about her brother at their last meeting and then suddenly pulled back.

She was scared, justifiably so, and if he couldn't palm off the contact to someone else he'd have to find a way to resurrect it himself. He trained across town and found an internet cafe in le Marais from where he sent an email to Raven, telling her he was in Belgium again and asking if she would be available to see him. Then he took the Metro to the Left Bank and, after three stops, ducked into another internet cafe. He opened the Sébastien Duboscq webmail and found a response to his email, logged at eighteen minutes after he'd sent it. She was keen, and his heart sank as he read her suggestion that they borrow a friend's boat on Saturday and explore the canal. He'd wanted to spend the weekend with Romy and the boys, walking through the markets, watching Patrick play soccer, buying new school gear for Oliver. But if the Raven situation wasn't rescued now, they might be too late to stop whatever the Pakistanis were cooking up.

He sent an email: *See you at 11, at the marina? I'll call as I approach, Seb.*

He headed home earlier than usual, picking up flowers on the way. It was a cliché but sometimes it worked. As he opened the apartment door he could hear kids yelling and running. He intercepted Oliver and got a hug, then continued to the kitchen, where he found Romy, wineglass in hand. He got a tipsy kiss from his wife, a little wetter than usual. Ana Homsi was on the Juliet balcony, finishing a smoke. She stepped in and gave de Payns a one-two on the cheeks.

'I hadn't realised before,' said his wife's new friend. 'Romy says you were a fighter pilot in the air force?'

'A lifetime ago.' He smiled while Romy poured him a glass. 'I'm a pen-pusher now. It takes a lot of managers to keep one plane in the sky.'

'A pen-pusher who gets to wear comfortable shoes,' she said, raising her glass.

'Casual Friday.' He returned the toast.

They took the kids to one of their local cafes and ate an early meal, which mainly consisted of feeding the children the most expensive cheese toast in Paris. De Payns knew that when they got home, the boys would want bowls of cereal anyway. When Ana snuck onto the footpath for a cigarette, de Payns broke the news that he had to work over the weekend. 'I'm sorry. I wouldn't do this unless I had to.'

Romy handled her disappointment better than most, resting her chin on her hands and looking at him with those green eyes that saw more of him than anyone else. 'Patrick's playing striker. He'll be sad that you're not there to see it.'

'Really?' he replied. 'That's fantastic. I wish I could be there.'

'I'll film it.'

De Payns felt deflated. Some of the privations of his occupation could be offset against the greater good, but he would never retrieve the moments lost with his boys. He changed the subject. 'What's this about my flying?'

'Oh, nothing. Ana wondered what you do to stay in shape, and I had to point out that you'd served—you know, in combat.'

He didn't say anything. He smiled and reminded himself that the DGS had no flags on this woman or her husband. He had to relax, let his family life be a family life.

CHAPTER
FORTY-FIVE

De Payns arrived early for his boating date and walked to the west of the Grand Large, where the launches and yachts were moored. This artificial lake had access to the North Sea via the Nimy Canal. He stopped beside the marina, where boat owners were crawling over their vessels, readying themselves for a Saturday on the water, perhaps the last blast of summer. He took out his Sébastien Duboscq phone and called Raven.

'Hi, I'm here early,' he said, adopting a cheery tone. 'Wow, this place is fantastic. Which one are we on?'

She told him it was *Marianne*, a big motor launch on the most northerly arm of the marina.

'I'll see you in thirty minutes,' she said, sounding excited. 'I'm just picking up our picnic.'

De Payns walked north and found *Marianne*. It was a forty-foot gin palace near the end of the marina arm; the only other boat owner was busy with a vessel closer to shore. He clambered onto the wooden duckboard and reached over the transom, unhitching the gate. He padded across the afterdeck, noting there was dew on it from the overnight chill. No footstep marks. He made a cursory tour of the boat, looking in the windows for signs of someone waiting in there, but saw nothing. He took a seat in a recliner on the afterdeck.

Raven arrived at the agreed time, and he sensed a change. Her hair was pulled back in a ponytail and she wore a white hoodie and a pair of white trackpants. In leisure clothing she was all curves, and more confident than he'd seen her previously.

'You put those away and I'll get the engines started,' she said, handing him two grocery bags, one of which contained two bottles of Mumm champagne.

She unlocked the cabin and walked through to the bridge, while de Payns put the picnic and booze in the galley fridge. Her scent was different, he decided. Something lighter than her usual Opium—perhaps Arpège?

The engines growled to life beneath him as he poured two glasses of the champagne and walked them through to Raven.

'Thanks,' she said, taking her glass. 'You're the deckhand, time to cast off.'

When he got back to the bridge, she was easing the launch out of its berth and into the Grand Large. They headed north for the Nimy Canal, and turned to the west, the water sparkling in the sun. She clinked glasses with him and they sipped as they motored.

'I didn't see you as the maritime type,' said de Payns, genuinely impressed. 'I thought you said your background was academic?'

'My father was a boating enthusiast,' she said, smiling. 'He raced yachts, built boats. My brother wasn't interested so that left me.'

'Nice,' said de Payns, drinking. 'Tomboy?'

She laughed, almost wistfully. 'I don't know about that. I guess when a father has a daughter who loves the outdoors and a son who likes books, then he starts to spend a lot of time with his daughter.'

De Payns noticed something a little deeper but decided not to push. 'So you sailed in the Persian Gulf?'

'Yes, he had his boats in Karachi and we'd tour around Shomali Island and across to Bahrain and Abu Dhabi. We went on a holiday once to the Maldives and toured around the islands. I got all my certificates before I turned twenty.'

De Payns felt happy for her and relieved that she was resourceful. On a boat she was in her element, less a victim, more capable of bouncing back from what was coming.

'You look surprised,' she said, laughing at him.

'Honestly, I had an image of women in Pakistan not being allowed to skipper a boat like this. Maybe I was wrong?'

'Well,' she said, 'you're basically right. But if you have a great father, then you have a great life.'

'And then you marry your husband?'

She laughed so hard that she breathed in her champagne and de Payns had to pat her on the back. She was warm and soft through the fabric and he could feel her hip against his crotch.

'That,' she said, as she regained her composure, 'is the story of my life. My dad told me I could be whoever I wanted to be, and then my husband finds Allah and he didn't know who I was. Still doesn't.'

They motored west for an hour, laughing and drinking and waving to other boats, some with families, others blasting Guns N' Roses from their stereos. She pulled up at a small quay at a waterside park, adjacent to a bike path. He hopped off *Marianne*, secured the boat and joined Raven on the afterdeck, where she was laying out cheese and bread, olives and hummus.

She paused while she helped herself to hummus. 'I was thinking about our chat the other night.'

'Oh yes?'

'About my brother.'

De Payns could see her discomfort and decided to take the lead. 'You know, I've been thinking about that too.'

'I didn't want to scare you . . .'

'No, no,' said de Payns. 'I want you to know that I'm not judging him—you know, because his lab might have a military role. He must be a very, very intelligent man. Conversations with him must be fascinating.'

She relaxed visibly. 'You sure?'

'Absolutely,' said de Payns. 'I think some of the great scientific minds have devoted themselves to military projects. Wasn't it Archimedes who invented a more powerful catapult, at the siege of Syracuse?'

'I'm so happy you said that. He is such a great man, and I'm really proud of him.' She paused. 'I'm sure the two of you would get on really well.'

De Payns tried not to look too interested. 'You think so? Why?'

'Because you're interested in his field of science—and you said yourself you want to have better marketing channels into Asia and the Middle East.'

De Payns nodded casually, but his mind was spinning. He had to close this. 'Well, who knows, Anoush? Given where I travel, maybe our paths will cross.'

She lit up. 'Are you planning a trip to Pakistan?'

De Payns smiled, sipped on his champagne. 'Well, I travel through these countries, but all I ever see are hotel rooms and offices. It would be good to have more leisure time there. I love ancient history, and I've wanted to visit some well-preserved Moghul sites in your country. It's apparently like time travel.'

Raven beamed. 'That would be great. I'll be going back there for a visit myself soon. You could stay at my place.'

'And your husband?'

She smiled and shook her head. 'Oh no, not there. I have a little flat owned by my family. You could stay there.'

De Payns could feel the opportunity looming. 'That's a generous invitation, but I don't want to bother you or put you in any kind of bad situation with your family.'

'Don't worry, you won't.'

'Well, then, it sounds like a plan. Will your brother be around?'

She looked confused. 'Why?'

De Payns pulled back; he couldn't afford to blow this. 'You thought I would get on well with him, *non*? I'd like to meet him.'

She nodded, relaxing again. 'He doesn't have a lot of freedom to move around, because of the nature of his work. He's mostly limited to his lab and his home. I'm the only person he's allowed to see socially. Perhaps I can invite him for dinner?'

De Payns smiled. 'That sounds great. When are you leaving for Islamabad?'

'In three weeks,' she said.

De Payns realised this might be the only chance. 'That's perfect. I'll be in New Delhi around then and I have a client in Lahore. Islamabad is just up the road–I could hire a car, come up and see you?'

'I'll let you know,' said Raven, raising her glass.

De Payns raised his own and clinked it against hers. 'To science,' he said.

CHAPTER
FORTY-SIX

The Alamut mission team had a short window in which to meet. Lafont was in Germany and couldn't make it, so Briffaut convened in the top-floor SCIF with de Payns and Garrat. The atmosphere had become rushed, which usually indicated that Frasier had briefed a member of the government and now results were expected yesterday.

Briffaut worked with his shirtsleeves rolled up. 'Right now, we have two lines operating at once—the DO have a team working on the comings and goings at that Palermo warehouse, determining what was there, how much there was and where it has gone. It could have left by ship or plane, or, if it was a small enough quantity, it could have been walked off Sicily in a couple of backpacks.'

De Payns had already helped the DO team get started. They were led by Louis Blanco, who was a good operator; if there was a logistics trail for whatever had been in that warehouse, Blanco would find it.

'The second line is Alamut, and that's what we're here to discuss,' said Briffaut. 'We have to get close to the MERC and confirm the source of the *Clostridium perfringens*. That's our only chance—to get to the source of this crap.'

There was one game in town and that was de Payns' relationship with Raven.

'Your report says you've been invited for dinner with Timberwolf and Raven in Islamabad,' said Briffaut. 'Are we sure it's not a trap?'

De Payns knew his role—he couldn't be sure the dinner wasn't a trap, but Briffaut did not want that evaluation on the record. He wanted de Payns to be sure enough to accelerate what was a very dangerous operation. He wanted to hear that de Payns could be dining with Raven and Timberwolf in Islamabad very quickly. He didn't want to hear the doubts and the 'ifs'.

De Payns placed two copies of his briefing on the desk, the result of an early-morning meeting with Templar. 'The email and phone intercepts suggest Raven's protective of me, so I think we're safe on that front. The test comes when she's in Islamabad, organises a dinner with her brother and acknowledges me as a guest. That's when Timberwolf and the ISI will respond.'

There was silence. The three of them knew that attending such a dinner date—under the noses of the ISI, in Pakistan—was very dangerous, not only for de Payns but for the rest of the mission team.

Briffaut cleared his throat and grabbed his copy of de Payns' mission briefing. 'You're aware we have to speed up this operation, but this better show me how you're dealing with the risks.'

De Payns walked them through it. A recon team from the Company was flying into Islamabad that morning, to spend a week setting up the *équipement de ville*, that included ISs, tourniquets, support plans, hotels, exfiltration plans and the dating games—the *jeux de rendez-vous*. Once the recon team had set up the *équipement*, the mission team would spend a week learning and practising it. Then the mission team—consisting of Templar, Danny, Jerome, Paulin and Simon—would go in to Islamabad, and two days later de Payns would arrive for his dinner date with Raven and Timberwolf.

De Payns took them through the basics—the support team would number only five, but they would be in and around the environment, which was largely Raven's flat and de Payns' hotel, as well as travel routes to and from the international airport. Special attention would be paid to Raven's flat—de Payns would not be wired, so the team would have to be close enough to give assistance to de Payns while staying inconspicuous. Templar had suggested wireless mics placed around the flat and its approaches—his thinking was that the ISI would sweep inside the flat for listening devices but probably not the exterior. The hotels would consist of tourist three-stars for the support team and de Payns would stay at the Marriott, chosen because it was a fit with the Duboscq legend and because it had several entry/exit points. Hotels with multiple exits were chosen for DGSE operations because it gave the team options for the exfil, which was also designed before de Payns arrived in-country.

'What about the car?' asked Briffaut. 'You probably don't want to use the Hertz contact again.'

'Templar will buy something from a backpacker hostel. The cars are not a problem; the main issue is the flat itself and the assumption that Timberwolf will be accompanied by ISI minders. The team loses sight of me at six o'clock or thereabouts, and then I'm in a flat with Dr Death and his ISI bodyguards.'

'I don't like it,' said Briffaut, leaning forward. 'Surely we can get some comms into her flat?'

'If the ISI do a sweep of the place just before I arrive and find the intrusions, I'm fucked,' said de Payns.

'It's worth the risk,' said Garrat.

De Payns shook his head. 'Not to me it's not.'

■

They were waiting for him near the exit of the Port-Royal RER station. De Payns could see Jim Valley through the century-old glass-panel doors that had recently been renovated. Jim saw him and exited through another door, putting on his cap as he left: *Follow me*. They walked north for five minutes—with a decent gap between them—until they were in the Jardins des Grands Explorateurs. Jim walked past the famous fountain featuring the women holding up the world, taking off his cap as he did: *Stop following me*. De Payns saw Philippe Manerie seated on a park bench, walked over and took a seat, leaving a big gap between them.

'Still too close to my neighbourhood, but an improvement,' said de Payns, lighting a smoke. 'What do you want?'

'Nice to see you too, Alec,' said Manerie, who was wearing a dark grey felt hat in the Paris sunshine. 'Perhaps I didn't clarify our relationship—you were to report to me on this hunt for the mole in the Y Division.'

'I told you, Manerie, I'm not privy to that investigation, and—as your own people will tell you—I'm suspected of selling passports to Sayef Albar for three million euros.'

'Nice deflection, Alec. But you missed an important fact about your friend.'

'Shrek?'

'I'm told he was sent back to Sicily.'

De Payns hissed out a plume of smoke and looked at the fountain. 'I haven't seen his report.'

'I didn't ask for his report.'

'So?'

'So, why was Monsieur Tibet in Palermo?'

'You work in the same building as Lafont—why not ask her?'

De Payns watched Manerie's face change. The pale eyes hardened and for a second de Payns saw the mask of the special forces soldier. 'Lafont, you say? So, this is not Operation Falcon?'

De Payns knew he'd made a misstep. He now had to tread carefully. 'I don't know. I haven't seen the report.'

'Stop with the fucking report,' snapped Manerie. 'Falcon is not Lafont's operation. What's her interest in Palermo?'

'I don't know, Director. I haven't spoken to Lafont or Tibet about the Palermo job.'

'But you know he was working for Lafont? What would she be looking for down there?'

De Payns shrugged, but Manerie was on to him. 'Marie Lafont is Counter-Proliferation. She would not deploy someone like Guillaume Tibet unless it was important. It's not like he's a scientist or an engineer. So tell me, what is the Y Division doing snooping around in Palermo?'

'I don't know,' said de Payns, feeling the eyes of his tormentor boring into him.

Manerie sighed and stood slowly. 'You know what I used to tell the Marxist guerrillas we captured in Africa?'

De Payns shrugged, squinting as he looked up. 'What?'

'You lie—you die.' Manerie crushed his cigarette under his shoe. 'That was generally the last conversation those Communists ever enjoyed.'

De Payns watched Manerie walk away, the waters of the fountain now seeming very loud.

■

He woke shortly after 1 a.m. as the rain started. He usually slept lightly before an operation, and he left the bed and padded around the apartment, checking on the boys and the front door. He checked the windows and made sure the security latch on the Juliet balcony was where he'd left it when he went to bed. On the street below he looked for vehicles that were new or unusual, or had people in them. It was dark on the street and, as on most Paris streets, his view was blocked by trees. He stared into the night, questions erupting in his brain. Who had sold them out in Palermo and how much did that person know about Operation

Alamut? He wondered about Raven and her motive for inviting him to dinner in Islamabad. Was he really going to walk into that flat with Timberwolf and his ISI thugs? Was he going to go up against the ISI right in the middle of Islamabad?

He shook off the pre-operation nerves and headed back to Romy. He wanted to hold her, as if this could be the last time, but he wanted to do it without scaring her. In the end he lay against her shoulder and listened to the Paris rain and her breathing. He wanted to enjoy the moment, but his mind was racing over the week ahead.

CHAPTER
FORTY-SEVEN

De Payns arrived at Indira Ghandi International at midday and took a shuttle into New Delhi, where he booked into a three-star local hotel that he'd paid for in cash in Paris. He was dressed in sneakers, jeans and a windbreaker, with a sports jacket, trousers and good shoes in his wheelie suitcase. Having checked in, he walked to the quiet greenery of the Mughal Gardens in the downtown area. He built up his Sébastien Duboscq phone and just after 2 p.m. local time called Raven and told her where he was. She sounded excited and he was relieved that her voice didn't have any of the tightness that indicated coercion.

'I'm just finishing up in New Delhi,' he said. 'Who knew that they speak Urdu and Punjabi up here? I thought it would all be Hindi, but there might be some more work for you, Anoush.'

'Well,' she said, 'there are more Urdu speakers in Pakistan, but there's still a lot in northern India.'

'Well, thank God for your translations. I had them in my computer and printed them out to show our marketing partners.'

She was bursting to talk about their dinner date. 'Yousef is coming over to the flat on Sunday evening. Please tell me you can make it.'

De Payns told her he'd be there. 'I might go out to the Taxila ruins on the Saturday and see you on Sunday?'

He ate a meal in a cafe down the street from his hotel and flew out the next morning, landing in Islamabad in time for lunch. He checked into the Marriott in the north of the city; it was within a twenty-minute walk of Raven's flat.

He got a room on the fifth floor, looking eastwards to Rawal Lake and beyond to the uplands of Pir Panjal in the distance. He checked his room for listening devices and cameras. Then—having put a needle as a *bouletage* in the doorjamb—he walked north-east along Aga Khan road. After two minutes of walking he came to a bus stop and waited as the traffic sped past. When he was sure he was unobserved he put a white *gommette* on the side of the glass covering the timetable. This was the *plan de support* of his infiltration. He kept walking and explored the city, passing the parliament building on his way to the Lake View Park, where he checked the time. He walked back to the bus stop exactly two hours after depositing his white *gommette* and searched for the response to his signal. There were four *gommettes* arranged around de Payns' white one, meaning the support team was in place and had acknowledged the arrival of their *chef de mission*. De Payns 'cleaned' the *plan de support* by removing all the *gommettes* and placing a new one in the top right-hand corner. The 'arrived safely' stickers were some of the most important because they signalled the entire team was in place and ready to get into the operation. For de Payns it meant he could now start to live his legend. If he needed to contact his support team, he'd put a yellow *gommette* on the bus timetable then come back in an hour. If there was a second yellow *gommette* on the board, that meant he would meet Templar in the hotel's ground-floor toilets in one hour. A white *gommette* with a black cross would mean there was a complication or a setback and he needed six hours to set it right, after which he'd put a plain white *gommette* on the board.

As part of his legend, he was now a travelling businessman with a day off, which was a chance to do his own discreet reconnaissance of the *équipement de ville* that he'd learned by heart, but from afar. In the lobby of the Marriott he picked through the tourism packages and found one for the ancient ruins of Taxila. He booked a 9 a.m. pick-up and asked for a 6 a.m. wake-up call. Tourist interactions were a good thing, especially as he noted a mid-thirties local man sitting in the lobby, dressed conspicuously like an American and pretending to read a newspaper. He saw the second secret policeman as soon as he emerged onto the street. He was heavier than the man in the hotel foyer and wore a black leather sports coat and elastic-sided riding boots. De Payns relaxed—he'd spent so many years doing this dance of followers and targets that it almost felt normal. De Payns was fine with these public displays. The hotel time, spent alone, was when isolation crept in. Hotel time was when he wondered about Romy and the boys but couldn't look at any photographs of them. Company operatives were searched before leaving to ensure they carried nothing of a personal nature that could tie them to their real life.

He ambled slowly down the street, stopping to buy Pakistani knick-knacks at a souk and joking with the vendors. After thirty minutes, the follower gave up, having been put to sleep by a man with absolutely no anomalies in his behaviour. It made for terrible movie scenes, but the truth of espionage was that the ability to put a follower to sleep had saved more people than kung fu. That, and a decent three-point alignment, and nothing worth finding in your luggage.

When he felt reasonably certain the secret police had lost interest, he walked the tourniquet that he'd rehearsed back in Paris, except he did it in reverse so that when he walked it for real, the followers would not recognise his route. The tourniquet covered a specific route from Raven's apartment to the Marriott. It would begin with a green 'ready' *gommette* on a street landmark, which de Payns would only observe and not touch. Templar would have support team agents—'candles'—placed along the fifteen-minute walking route, and if they detected no followers, the *plan de support* at the end of the route would show a green *gommette*. If the support team detected followers, they would place a red *gommette*; if the followers looked intent on arresting or physically grabbing de Payns, the *gommette* would be red with a black cross through it. This would be the signal to activate the emergency exfiltration, also created by the support team and rehearsed by de Payns in Paris.

He walked back to the hotel using a different route to the tourniquet and ate a meal at a cafe across the road from the Marriott. His phone rang and he picked up. This was his Duboscq phone, only used to contact Raven, never his support team.

'Hi, Anoush,' he said, smiling as he answered.

'Yousef likes strong, traditional cooking,' she said, with a hint of mischief. 'Do you mind a strong taste?'

'Okay,' said de Payns, going along with the joke. 'I guess I need to arrive with a fire extinguisher for my mouth.'

She shrieked with laughter. 'We're Pakistanis, not Tamils! Don't worry, it will not burn. I promise.'

'Sure,' he said. 'As long as there's something to wash it down with.'

'I've got something very nice cooling down as we speak.'

When de Payns walked into the Marriott, a new secret policeman was sitting in the same chair as the previous follower. De Payns smiled at him as he walked past and went straight up to his room. The *bouletage* was on the ground and the three-point alignment was way out. He was expecting this. A heavily guarded bioweapons scientist was going to meet with his sister for dinner, along with her mysterious French friend. At the very least the ISI would have a look at him, search his room and his bags and see where he went during the day. De Payns knew this and knew that his job was to hypnotise them with banality; almost annoy them with how boring he was. It was about regulating movements and gait, limiting his gaze to innocent tourism, and never letting a follower see that he had tradecraft.

CHAPTER
FORTY-EIGHT

The minibus ride to the Taxila ruins was notable for the friendly patter from the driver and his expert commentaries on farm sizes, agricultural production and the role of irrigation in the Islamic Republic. The driver's music selections leaned heavily on Helen Reddy, Dionne Warwick and Demis Roussos—none of them known for their piety, thought de Payns, but perhaps they were on an approved list for tourism operators.

They walked around the ancient compound of settlements, the oldest of which had been inhabited in 1000 BC. De Payns fell in with an American couple who had been in Israel, Turkey and Jordan and were now doing the Peshawar Valley. They were funny, and the wife—Amy—even had some French. The husband, Quentin, showed de Payns a flyer he'd picked up at the souk. In jumpy English it advertised 'American Karaoke', which, according to his new friends, was code for 'serves alcohol'.

De Payns laughed. 'So they gave this to an American who thought a Frenchman could use it more?'

He was dropped back at the hotel as the sun went down, and after a meal de Payns walked to the elevators, noticing that the follower's chair in the lobby was no longer occupied. Within only two days they were bored with him and had been unable to find anything of interest in his room or his travels. Operationally, he felt good.

Having showered, he realised he wasn't tired. In fact, he was wound up. He felt like a glass of beer and fished the American Karaoke flyer out of his jeans. Looking over the map of Islamabad in his room, he realised the place was two blocks away. It wasn't even 9 p.m., so he dressed again and stepped out.

The karaoke bar was in the basement level of a small hotel off the main boulevard. He showed the flyer to a doorman and was allowed inside. It looked like a Paris student bar, with rock music playing and a long bar overlooking twenty-five round tables. He looked around, adjusting to the gloom, and saw people of European background, in Western clothing, drinking beer and wine—an activity usually confined to foreign hotels in Pakistan. If de Payns took a wild guess, it looked as though the Islamabad police didn't care about foreigners drinking alcohol, so long as locals weren't doing it. Especially not local women.

De Payns sat on a stool at the far end of the bar, from where he could see the door. Old habit. They served Budweiser and Heineken, and he went for a cold Heineken as a song by Richard Marx started. He sipped and consciously brought down his emotional brain. It wasn't healthy to be on the verge of ruining a person's life and to start worrying about it. He'd had to deal with those misgivings when he flew over Kosovo, and he had to get on top of it now. The mission was to access the MERC through Timberwolf. He had to stay focused on Raven as the channel for a successful operation, not as an individual with a life in jeopardy. He went over lists in his head—the following actions, the tourniquet and the exfil. He sipped at the beer and thought of all the *cas non conformes*, the 'what-ifs'. What if they arrest me when I go into the flat? What if they arrest Anoush and ask me to talk while they torture her? What if I make it through the dinner but they're waiting for me in my hotel room when I return? What if one of my support team has already been arrested? And the biggest *cas non conforme*: What if I rushed this? What if we needed three weeks more for recon and planning?

This, thought de Payns, could be my last beer . . . So he finished the Heineken, raised his finger at the barman and got another.

As the barman took his euros, Roxette's 'Listen to Your Heart' started pumping out of the speakers.

'Never worked out what year this was from,' said a voice, very close to him. 'Was it eighties, nineties, noughts? Could be any of them, know what I mean?'

De Payns snapped out of his reverie. There was a man in his early forties—American by the sound of him—standing at the bar, a fifty-euro note held between his fingertips. 'I'll have what he's having,' said the man.

The barman opened a Heineken and took the money. The American continued. 'I think it's nineties, but is this Berlin or Roxette?'

De Payns laughed. He also confused the two bands occasionally, and the timeless nature of the song made it very hard to nail down to a year.

'Definitely Roxette,' said de Payns. 'But I don't know what decade it's from.'

The barman slapped down the American's change. 'Narek,' said the American, 'what year is this song from?'

The barman gave a quick nod of thanks as the American pushed his tip towards him. 'I don't know,' said Narek, who was maybe twenty-five. 'It's, like, classic rock. It's, like, *old*.'

The American turned, and for a second de Payns saw a flash of himself. The same professional openness, the practised ease of meeting new people, the conservation of movement in public that makes a person less conspicuous. He was slightly shorter than de Payns, and he wore a pair of chinos and a dark blue polo shirt. He was groomed to be forgettable, right down to the suburban haircut and fresh shaving. Like de Payns, here was a man who shaved twice a day so he was always unremarkable, always in the background. De Payns would bet his pension on this American having no tattoos, no jewellery and no piercings. De Payns couldn't even smell him—there was no aftershave or cologne, and unlike most Americans, his polo shirt was logo-free.

'Peter, from the US,' said the man. 'Sales.'

'Sébastien, from Paris,' said de Payns. 'Consulting.'

They raised beers in the direction of each other but didn't touch.

'Roxette are strange,' said de Payns. 'They wrote and sang in English, even though they're Swedish.'

'Like ABBA,' said Peter.

'Yeah, but ABBA recorded in Swedish. I think Roxette only recorded in English and Spanish . . .'

'And Portuguese,' said Peter. 'I heard them once in a taxi in Rio. Least, I think it was them. Could have been Berlin.'

'Ha!' said de Payns, liking this guy's humour. 'Rio? Nice down there.'

'I sold a bunch of data switches to a Brazilian company and they comped me for a few days in Rio during the Olympics. Saw some boxing and high jump. A bit of javelin. It's a very cool city.'

'I've never been to Brazil,' said de Payns.

'First time in Pakistan?' asked Peter.

'Fourth or fifth,' said de Payns, actually relaxing. 'But the first time I've drunk a beer outside my hotel.'

Peter chuckled. 'The owner is Narek's dad. The police leave him alone if he's only selling to Westerners.'

'American Karaoke?' added de Payns. 'That's a bit harsh. I thought it was the French who were labelled as drunks?'

'He wanted to call this place The Speakeasy, but he thought he'd better not invite the cops to his door. So, the Yanks get tarred as drinkers. We've been called worse.'

'You sell telecoms gear?' asked de Payns, assuming it wasn't true.

'Yep. Boring as bat shit, and you?'

'I'm a consultant in the pharma and chemicals industries, currently working on translations,' said de Payns, sure that Peter didn't believe him.

'Translations for their brochures?'

'For everything,' said de Payns. 'If you're a French or American chemicals maker and you want to be selling in the Stans, you want your websites and your marketing materials to be in Farsi or Urdu or Pashto, or whatever your customers are fluent in.'

'Fair enough,' said Peter, raising two fingers at the barman. 'How's business?'

'Busy.'

'I get exhausted,' said the American, looking at the pile of money in front of him.

'They overworking you?'

The American shrugged. 'It's the constant travelling, always meeting people but never really knowing them.'

'It gets tiring,' said de Payns, now convinced they were talking about the same thing. 'Getting close to someone, but always for an ulterior motive.'

The beers landed and the barman took a note from Peter's pile of cash, obviously used to American bar etiquette. De Payns remembered the first time he'd sat at an American bar, in New York, and the barmaid's hand reached out to his friend's pile of money and his first reaction was to stop her.

'Lonely too,' said Peter. 'You might have loved ones back home, but you're putting all this energy into people you don't know.'

'And it's false energy,' said de Payns, sipping. 'But your loved ones back home aren't getting any of your attention.'

They looked at one another. Were they going to discuss family? Tell each other lies about their loved ones?

Peter's face closed. 'Hear that?' he asked, raising a finger, as 'Hungry Like the Wolf' started playing. 'That's Duran Duran. Genuine eighties.'

CHAPTER
FORTY-NINE

The walk to Raven's flat was deliberately slow. He stopped at a shop and bought a bunch of blue flowers, and saw a selection of Turkish delight in a deli service area. He bought a cardboard tray of the white-dusted sweet, paler in colour than the European version, then continued on to the flat along streets lively with cafes and restaurants.

The building was a three-storey apartment block with two units on each level. Raven was on the first floor.

At exactly 6 p.m. he pressed the security buzzer.

'Hi, Sébastien,' came Raven's voice. 'I'm up the stairs, in number four.'

There was a buzz and the sound of a bolt sliding and de Payns pushed through the door. He'd managed to turn his nerves into excitement, and he felt pretty good as he bounded up the stairs. Before he knocked on the door of number four, he checked his palms—they were dry, a good sign.

Raven opened the door and greeted him with a kiss on each cheek. He was glad of his dry palms because she was wearing a sleeveless purple chiffon top, and he touched her briefly on the bicep.

'Ooh, for me?' She smiled as he presented the flowers and the cardboard box.

'I hope you like Turkish delight,' he said.

'I love it,' she replied, walking to her kitchen, from which a delicious smell was emanating. 'And by the way, it's not Turkish, it's Persian.'

It was a clean and tidy two-bedroom flat, about twenty years old. There was no sign of her kids, nor of a husband, which made him think that this was one of those gifts that Middle Eastern fathers give to their daughters, so they have some independence and their own asset. A bolthole for Muslim girls.

She emerged with a bottle of riesling, fresh from the fridge.

'I thought there was no drinking in Pakistan,' said de Payns.

'You mean like there's no pot-smoking in Belgium?'

She poured and he took a glass.

'So, what have you told your brother about me?' asked de Payns. 'Anything I should know?'

'I just told him the industry you're in and what I'm doing for you. He was happy for you to join us for dinner.'

They drank and Raven asked him about his sightseeing. He also told her about his clients in New Delhi and the hassle of trying to remember all the languages that were spoken in this part of the world. She suddenly remembered the flowers, and walked into the kitchen to get a vase. He followed her and saw the rear exit that Templar had briefed him on. The kitchens of these apartments had a door leading onto fire escape gantries and stairs. He looked down and saw that the fire stairs dropped into a concrete car park, just as the team had briefed him.

Raven placed the flowers in a vase, opened the oven and stirred the contents of a ceramic pot.

There was a movement below, and de Payns looked down and saw a black LandCruiser with large aerials pull into the parking area. Two heavies in outdoor leisurewear emerged from the vehicle, leaving the driver in his seat. The larger of the two heavies wore a black windbreaker and slate-coloured hiking pants, and his 9mm handgun was evident on his hip. He looked up and straight at de Payns.

De Payns attempted a smile. 'I think your brother's arrived,' he said, a voice in the back of his head asking, *What the fuck am I doing here?*

Raven joined him at the window and rolled her eyes. 'He's such a drama queen.'

They returned to the living room and de Payns peered over the windowsill. On the street, there was another black LandCruiser and the black S-Class Mercedes that he'd got to know pretty well. Men who looked similar to the ones out the back walked routes up and down the street, talking into their lapels.

The buzzer sounded in the flat and it gave de Payns a start.

'Ha ha, it got you too!' said Raven, pressing on the door release. 'That ringer is heart-attack material.'

A few seconds later there was a knock at the door and Raven opened it. The doorway was filled with a male shape that instantly reminded de Payns of Templar—large but athletic; trained and dangerous. The heavy walked into the room, leaving a small figure standing just outside the doorway—Dr Death, codename Timberwolf.

The scientist was as small-featured and bespectacled as any stereotypical professor. He wore a brown sports coat, khaki slacks and a mustard-coloured cardigan under the jacket, confirming that scientists had the same sartorial elegance wherever they lived. The first bodyguard walked past de Payns and did a check of the flat while Timberwolf stood beside a second bodyguard. The bodyguard at the door stared at de Payns while the first guy made a commotion opening wardrobes and pulling back the shower curtain.

'We just have to wait,' Raven said to him apologetically. 'Sorry, I forgot to tell you.'

'At least I didn't bring that whisky,' said de Payns, aiming for a joke. He smiled at Timberwolf, but the scientist showed no sign of having heard. The minder at the door simply glared.

The fire stairs banged and clattered, as one of the people from the car park checked the back exits, and they could hear the first bodyguard talking loudly somewhere in the flat, meaning he was probably communicating with the guy on the fire stairs. De Payns couldn't pick it, but it would be something like *clear* or, *Check out this French pansy—let's put a hood on him right now.*

When the minder came back from searching the flat, he motioned for Timberwolf to enter and touched de Payns on the arm, asking him to follow. They stood in the spare room—with one single bed and some storage boxes—and the minder searched him thoroughly, looking for weapons and electronic devices. He found the Nokia and, having looked at it, asked de Payns in halting French, 'You need this for to eat the meal?'

De Payns shook his head, and the minder broke down the phone very expertly and handed de Payns the pieces.

When they returned to the living room the second minder left to stand in the hallway, and the bodyguard who had searched de Payns stood post at the door. De Payns turned to Timberwolf and greeted him with his best smile. But the scientist offered only a reluctant handshake and a glowering face. 'So,' he said, dark-eyed and humourless, 'you are the Frenchman.'

CHAPTER
FIFTY

Dr Death took a seat at the table. 'You are a friend of Anoush, visiting Islamabad?'

'Yes,' said de Payns. 'I'm interested in the old trade routes and ancient cities between the Middle East and the subcontinent, so since I've come all this way for forty-eight hours of work, I thought I'd take the opportunity to visit the ruins at Taxila.'

'That's interesting. And you and Anoush work together, yes?'

De Payns shrugged. 'More or less. I'm a consultant and Anoush is a translator for one of my clients. That's how we met.'

Seeing that the discussion had started and was about her, Anoush went back to the kitchen. Alec played his role of innocent guest.

'And you, Doctor—are you married? Do you have children?'

The scientist made a surprised face. 'I'm afraid not. Given how I intend to influence the world, I prefer not to have children.'

De Payns could have killed him where he sat, but he had to laugh at the atrocious sentiment, to create empathy. It occurred to him that Dr Death was playing with him, and as soon as Anoush was out of earshot, the scientist leaned forward and said in his slow, sibilant voice, 'You know that Anoush's husband is one of my best friends? We did part of our studies together and it was I who introduced them.'

De Payns was careful in his reply. 'No, I did not know that. Unfortunately I have never had the chance to meet him.'

Timberwolf held a long silence, staring into de Payns' eyes, before resuming. 'I do not understand who you are. I do not understand what you are doing here. I do not understand your relationship with my sister,' he said. 'I find it very dishonourable for her and our family, and I feel that something is wrong.'

Alec could feel the rope tightening around his neck. Timberwolf was being deliberately ambiguous, fishing for a reaction rather than accusing. The lack of urgency in the Doctor's tone was actually more dangerous to de Payns' ears than an outright denouncement. The man was skilled—he thought he was playing with this Frenchman and de Payns knew he had to get out of there, and quickly. Quickly, but without being arrested. He had to disrupt Timberwolf's rhythm and the best defence might be attack.

'Excuse me?!' de Payns retorted, feigning outrage. 'What exactly are you insinuating? I'm here at the invitation of a friend and colleague. I gather you are someone important, but that does not give you the right to speak to me that way.'

Hearing that the tone of the conversation had changed, Anoush emerged from the kitchen to see what was happening. De Payns leaped in quickly.

'Listen, Anoush, your brother has accused me of behaving dishonourably and I don't appreciate it. I'm sorry, but I'm going to leave you now. I'm not here to create a scene. I hope you enjoy your dinner—we can catch up some other time.' He rose from the table. 'Goodbye, Doctor,' he said stiffly. 'Please accept my best wishes. It wasn't my intention to intrude.'

De Payns headed for the front door under the amused gaze of Dr Death, who obviously appreciated the situation. Moving deliberately, avoiding any jerky actions that would cause the bodyguard to react, he collected his windbreaker from the coat hook beside the kitchen door. For now he had only one play—act embarrassed and get onto the street. His palms had turned clammy as he put on his jacket, the pieces of the phone rattling in the pocket.

On the other side of the door the second bodyguard stood his ground, not moving when de Payns passed him. De Payns tracked his movements without staring at him. If the bodyguard went for a weapon, de Payns would crush his throat, take the pistol and deal with the man in the hallway. His heart was not racing yet, but the room was feeling very small and he could feel his pulse jerking in his throat. He was ready for violence, yet he had to avoid a confrontation at all costs. Just get onto the street without mishap, he reminded himself. Once his team had eyes on him, he trusted Templar's guys against the ISI. Templar had once exfiltrated a blown agent from Cairo, keeping her safe for thirty-six hours while the secret police searched every corner of the city. He'd got her back to Paris at the cost of a bullet in one French operative's leg, and a lost finger when an operative's hand was slammed in a car door, which was a pretty good result.

He turned to say goodbye, rotating into the bodyguard, not away, so he could keep tabs on him. Raven stood in front of him, tears on her cheeks, her great head of hair suddenly flat and limp. She wanted to hug him but de Payns reached out a hand and offered a handshake.

'Thanks for a wonderful evening, Anoush,' he said. Over her shoulder, a man who could kill millions with his bioweapon looked at de Payns and smiled.

'Good evening, Dr Bijar,' said de Payns.

The other man didn't reply.

De Payns headed towards the stairwell—to get down the stairs and into the street would take forty-three steps—if he wasn't stopped by a hood over his head or a bullet in his back. He was at their mercy. The sweat on his scalp was ice cold.

He took the first of what would be the longest forty-three steps of his life.

CHAPTER
FIFTY-ONE

In the Cercottes training they'd been taught to regulate their breathing when fear made the breaths shallow. If you let fear take over your physical self, oxygen in the brain dropped and decision-making capacity reduced. They'd undergone similar simulations in the air force, to show the pilot trainees what happened to cognitive function when the brain was deprived of oxygen. The lower the oxygen intake, the worse they'd become at breaking down a pistol or doing basic multiplication.

De Payns kept that in mind, counting steps and breathing deep through his nose as he descended the stairs. He had to make good decisions over the next half-hour—good, professional decisions. Romy and the boys belonged to another life at this moment. Behind him he could detect at least one of the bodyguards, following him but not close enough to attack. A decent backhand fist to a point just below the kneecap might give him enough time to dispossess the bodyguard of his weapon. But while keeping himself alert to the possibility of violence, he wasn't going to start a fight. He was going to do what he had been taught—play it out, let the followers follow and never let an adversary see that you're trained.

He opened the lobby door at thirty-eight steps. The second bodyguard was visible in the reflection of the glass as he pulled back on the handle. The minder wasn't holding a gun, but his hands were held in such a way that the gun would be very close.

He pushed onto the street and found the black S-Class Mercedes parked directly in front of the building, in a no parking zone. He knew this car well. Behind the car was the LandCruiser and leaning on it were two ISI thugs, one of them carrying an MP5 machine pistol over his shoulder on a black strap.

The thugs stood up straight and watched de Payns as he exited the building. Behind him, the second bodyguard said something to his colleagues, and across the road, the orange glow of a cigarette flipped through the air and another bodyguard—this one carrying a shortened assault rifle—stepped away from a lamppost and joined the watching.

De Payns nodded to them as he passed the LandCruiser and started his long walk back to the hotel. It was a moderately populated street, just north of the main CBD and west of the diplomatic enclave. He realised the locals were taking one look at the LandCruiser parked beside the Mercedes before electing to walk on the opposite side of the street.

His job was to follow the tourniquet, giving his team—his candles—a chance to find his followers and give him their verdict on the *plan de support final*. If he reached the advertising on the bus stop and there was a red sticker with a cross drawn through it, de Payns was to move towards the hotel as if nothing was wrong. This was the critical part—there would be no rupture through the established *passage obligé*, no car chases. There'd be no *bang-bang*, as the Company referred to the use of firearms. If he was being followed, he would have to do one of the most difficult things an OT could be asked to do. He'd have to walk with the mannerisms of a man who was not stressed, not scared and who was not taking every step as if a van was about to stop beside him and scoop him up. He would have to behave as if everything was fine, as if he wasn't in Islamabad and the head of the bioweapons program had not all-but accused him of being a spy. The followers would have to be put to sleep.

He walked, taking a pack of smokes out of his windbreaker and lighting one. He consciously kept any preparedness out of his step; he knew that a certain stride was what Templar usually clocked when he was picking those in the game out of a crowd. That and their footwear.

At the first main junction, he turned right at the pedestrian lights and was now walking at ninety degrees to the road that Raven's flat was on. It was 6.27 p.m. local time as de Payns passed a corner cafe on the other side of the road with a notice-board outside—the starting *plan de support*—and saw the green *gommette*. The tourniquet was ready to be played, which meant Templar and the team were in place and ready. It calmed him a bit.

He kept walking slow and easy, while his heart flipped like a pancake. He readied to cross the road to go west again on the cross street, glancing left as he did to see if there was oncoming traffic. He was quite sure he saw a green van pull into a no parking zone eighty metres back the way he'd come. He had to stop looking for things that weren't there, he told himself.

He crossed the road, looking around like a tourist, willing the walk to be over and to see a green sticker on the bus stop hoarding. As he reached the other side of the road, he walked past a double-fronted store with hundreds of clothes racks, being picked over by seemingly half the women of Islamabad. Beside it was a cafe—this was the start of the tourniquet, and if de Payns was running it he'd have put a candle in that cafe to see who was following around the corner. But he didn't look for his team. He walked past, flicking his smoke in the gutter, and shoved both hands into his jacket pockets. He wrapped his hands around the pieces of Nokia, not wanting to reassemble it in public for fear of being provocative.

This leg was two blocks. Two teenagers whooshed past him on skateboards and a family with a gaggle of loud and unhappy kids spilled out of a restaurant, the father using the universal body language of *shut up and get in the car.*

He got to the end of the final leg and stopped to cross on a traffic light. The first candle would now be watching him at this turn, while candle number two was heading for the *plan de support*, waiting for a radio instruction from Templar about which sticker to place on the bus stop siding. In reality, a good support team knew if their agent was being followed at the first candle. The next two were confirmation and double-confirmation. A well-managed tourniquet didn't just establish surveillance, it gave the candles a chance to get a sense of the followers' tactics and numbers.

He waited for the pedestrian light to turn green, his throat dry as he tried to swallow. It was a cool evening in Pakistan's capital, but the back of his neck felt clammy. The light went green and he crossed, entering a less populated side street that curved slightly. The bus stop was on the other side of the road. He walked to the kerb and looked to his right and left. A van turned into the street and parked. He waited for a gap in the traffic, crossed the road and walked along the pavement, dodging the pedestrians. The bus stop loomed. Unlike European bus stop advertising, this one had no back-lighting. He created a side-step situation with a woman coming the other way, and ended up directly beside the *plan de support*. He looked down briefly, hoping for a green sticker.

But it was red, with a cross.

CHAPTER
FIFTY-TWO

He'd just spent twelve minutes finding out that he wasn't clean and now he had around seventeen minutes of natural walking to get to the lobby of the Marriott. From there he'd have a three-minute turnaround, in which time he'd pretend to be going back to his room for the night but instead get into a car and clear the Pakistan border.

The job was to do nothing, to act as if nothing was wrong, when his brain was running several dozen scenarios that involved basements, tractor batteries and pliers. He focused on his breathing once again, keeping the oxygen high and using his brain to put the followers to sleep.

After an eternity he arrived at the Marriott, and checked the time: 6.59 p.m. He had three minutes to make his exfil rendezvous, with a hard cut-off of five minutes. His team was now running a clock and he went straight up to his room. The hotels they used always required rear exit points, which at the Marriott was a long corridor down the side of the kitchen and administration areas, ending in a rear lane with a loading bay, his pick-up point. Now he mentally focused as he quickly packed his suitcase. He thought about the corridor, the fire stairs, and the hallway to the hotel's rear entrance. He would hurry but not run, and it would take one hundred and thirty-five seconds, from room to pick-up. He knew this because he had walked it in a dry run the day he arrived.

De Payns closed his wheelie case and stood by the door. He checked that his Nokia pieces were in his windbreaker, and he checked he had his wad of euros in his Levi's pocket. His case was in his left hand, leaving his right free. Breathing out, he opened the door. The corridor was clear. He slipped out, shut the door carefully, and walked to his right, past the elevators, where he dropped the Nokia pieces in the rubbish bin, saving the SIM card. For all his urgency to get out of Islamabad, he might need to contact Raven again.

De Payns walked through the fire door, closed it quietly, and moved down the concrete stairs, the sound of his sneakered feet and his breathing deafening in the echoing space. He concentrated on rhythm rather than speed, which reduced sound, and he covered the ten flights without tripping or shoes squeaking. De Payns felt trapped, as if at any moment he would round a corner and come face to face with the ISI who—according to his red sticker with a cross—were following him with intent.

At the bottom of the stairs he paused in front of the ground-floor door. The door opened into the hallway to the hotel's rear exit, which meant it was not in the line of sight to where his followers had sat in the lobby. However, he was more concerned with a night reception woman standing at the desk as he emerged from the stairs. If she was an asset for the ISI, she would call them immediately. He couldn't control that.

He looked at his watch—twenty-six seconds till 'go'. Pulling back the fire door, he peered out into the lobby—one person checking in, occupying the reception woman. He slipped sideways into the hallway, and as he walked he saw a cleaner to his right who was looking straight at him. De Payns smiled and walked swiftly down the hallway to the door at the end, which stood like a beacon. His heart banged, every touch of his feet on the lino sounding like an alarm. He walked past an opened door which held all the cleaner's equipment, and then he hit the horizontal locking bar on the door and pushed through into the loading bay area. There was one night-light over the receiving stage, but the rest of the turning area and the rear lane were dark. As the door swung shut, de Payns looked down the hall and saw the cleaner had come into the hallway and was peering at him.

He was on time but there was no car, no support team. He walked to the kerb and looked both ways, even though it was a one-way street.

Darkness, no movement.

Behind him the door creaked and de Payns turned. The cleaner stared out. He was in his early fifties, short and fit-looking. De Payns looked the man in the eyes, and saw fear. It was a sensible reaction because de Payns was calculating whether he could reach the cleaner and incapacitate him. As de Payns read the distance—about eight metres—the cleaner smiled; he had no French and de Payns had no Urdu. De Payns edged towards him; all he had to do was get his foot in that door and get his hands on the cleaner before he yelled.

De Payns edged closer—six metres—and the cleaner found some English. 'Your bag,' he said, holding out something in his hand. It was hard to see. He got to four metres and dropped his case, ready to pounce, when he realised what was in the man's hand.

'For the bag,' said the man, offering de Payns' leather name tag from the wheelie. De Payns breathed out with so much relief that he almost choked.

'Fuck,' he said, wiping spittle from his mouth. He reached out and took the name tag, returning the man's scared smile. De Payns realised his face must have been a neon sign of impending violence.

'Thank you,' he said in English, taking the name tag.

De Payns was close enough to ensure that the cleaner never spoke to anyone, ever. But a car engine sounded behind him, and the cleaner closed the door and disappeared back into his hotel.

When he turned back, Templar was at the wheel of a white Toyota Camry, another support team operative—Danny—was at the trunk, opening it. De Payns grabbed his bag and walked to the Camry. He slid into the trunk, feeling a rubber yoga mat beneath him. Danny arranged boxes and suitcases over and around him, and pointed out a bottle of water, two apples and a bunch of muesli bars jammed up against the transom. There was also a black 9mm handgun that looked like a SIG. Danny tapped an empty bottle with a screw top, and de Payns nodded. It was going to be a long drive, no toilet stops.

CHAPTER
FIFTY-THREE

Templar and Danny had done their best to create a comfortable nest in the back of the Camry, but de Payns felt every small bump and the road noise roared in his ears. After five minutes in the trunk he decided to get comfortable and try to relax. He ate an apple and drank bottled water. There was a faint trickle of fresh air from somewhere, but no clues about direction or route.

He went through his usual checklist at the end of an operation. What did he do wrong? Who could identify him? Was the operation a success?

The last question was easily answered. Dr Yousef Bijar—chief scientist at Pakistan's foremost bioweapons facility—was not going to provide access to the MERC. He was not cooperative, he would not be manipulated. He may have been brilliant but he was also a terrible human being and possibly a bit mad. The Company training had covered the basics of psychology and, in particular, extreme personalities. These people—whom de Payns had to understand well enough to befriend, manipulate and leverage—were often possessed of very strong intellects and intense personalities that could inspire a following. But they were often lonely, isolated, crushingly insecure, petty and vindictive.

Their surfeit of confidence often came with life-altering paranoia, and their success was tempered with depravity. Timberwolf's revelation about why he didn't have children was chilling. De Payns had dealt with some terrible people in his time at the Company, but Timberwolf was unique—the first self-aware sociopath and science-criminal he had met. Most scientists and engineers who worked on weapons of mass destruction tried to justify themselves, claiming that their heightened intellect put them above morality, or that their inventions couldn't be understood by normal people lacking their education. Even the scientists turned to working for France often clung to their delusions. But Timberwolf simply told him outright that he'd never bring children into a world where people like him were on the loose. De Payns could never prove it, but he had the strong impression that Timberwolf had guessed that the Frenchman opposite him had children. It was a deliberate provocation, guaranteed to haunt the parent who had to hear it.

What had de Payns done wrong? There wasn't a list of mistakes to go over. France wanted access to the MERC, and they'd taken their best shot. They could have waited another month, another six months, another year. More intelligence, more reconnaissance and closer relations with Raven. And still they'd have run into Timberwolf, regardless of how long they delayed the contact.

Could anyone identify him? de Payns wondered. The answer was yes—Timberwolf, at least four bodyguards and his followers from the hotel had all seen de Payns up close, which was unfortunate but it was one of the drawbacks of 'contact'. One thing was certain—de Payns would not return to the apartment in Montparnasse until he'd been thoroughly sanitised. The fate of Amin still haunted him—he would not bring the ISI to his family.

The final question was the fate of Raven. De Payns had to shake that thought from his head. He had a lot of problems to deal with before he could worry about an adversary.

■

He rose three centimetres in the air and woke as he thumped down on the yoga mat. De Payns gasped, for a split second not knowing where he was. The darkness was intense and he wiped saliva from the side of his face. He must have been in a deep sleep but now the Toyota had slowed and, judging by the heavy bumps and gravel noise beneath the car, they were off the tarmac. He looked at his watch: 11.45 a.m.

The car came to a stop, and Templar's voice conferred with what sounded like an official. He spoke in a mix of English, French and Urdu and there seemed to be a lot of agreeing going on. De Payns assumed they were at a border. Templar was good at borders and they cleared this one in record time. They'd been in the car long enough to get him into India or Afghanistan, thought de Payns. It was normal security procedure for the person in Templar's position to design an emergency exfiltration and not tell the rest of the team the details.

Ninety minutes later the Camry stopped, reversed, and then the engine was switched off. The silence was beautiful and de Payns' bones were thankful for the respite. He strained his ears, listening for an aircraft or the sounds of a harbour, but all he could hear was Templar's voice through the rear seat bulkhead.

'Aguilar, hold tight, *vieux frère*,' he said. 'We're switching cars, and when that's done you'll be riding up front, okay?'

'Okay,' said de Payns.

He lay in the blackness, revelling in the quiet, and now knowing that the exfil was a cross-country drive, not a plane or a boat. He found the other apple, ate it, and then devoured one of the muesli bars, which contained bits of dried apricot and chocolate chips.

After fifteen minutes, during which Templar and Danny fiddled with the radio and laughed at the local pop music being played, de Payns heard a car engine. It got closer until it was right beside the Camry. Doors opened, there was a conversation. The Camry sagged with weight on the driver's side and Templar said, 'We'll have you out soon. Danny's checking our new car.'

Then the trunk latch popped and Templar's arm was clearing away the suitcases and boxes around de Payns. It was dark, no moon.

'Okay,' said Templar, and de Payns grabbed his arm and was pulled out of the boot. His legs almost went from under him.

They were in a park by a lake with a small building beside them that looked like public toilets—a picnic area, de Payns thought. There were two cars in the car park—the Camry and a silver Passat parked beside it.

'Need to go?' asked Templar, pointing at the building. 'Make it quick, I want to get moving.'

The Camry rolled out, Danny driving and another man in the front seat, leaving the silver Passat.

'Where's Danny going?' asked de Payns, walking to the toilet.

'He's got his own route. It's just you and me.'

CHAPTER

FIFTY-FOUR

When de Payns returned to the Passat, Templar was sitting in the driver's seat, an orange envelope in his hand.

'You're now Georges Morel,' said Templar, hitting the map light.

'Great—where are we?'

'Afghanistan.'

De Payns opened the envelope and found a French passport in the name of Georges Antoine MOREL, with his photo in it. There was an EU identity card and a French driver's licence, along with a Nokia phone and charger.

'Let's get the old ID off you,' said Templar.

They went through his wheelie cabin case and tore up the Sébastien Duboscq passport, and destroyed boarding passes, receipts and baggage barcode stickers from his flights, and a tourist map from New Delhi. Then Templar made him turn out his pockets and consigned to the rubbish bin every piece of paper that de Payns was carrying. He took his shirt and windbreaker and dumped them, and gave him a black sweatshirt and a brown leather jacket that was badly aged.

'The Company has a Facebook account for you, and apparently if you search Georges Morel on the internet, Google has you at the fourth ranking. You're listed as a journalist who is interested in social justice and climate action.'

'I like me already,' said de Payns.

'You came across the border yesterday from Turkmenistan, and you were travelling with me. I'm the photographer,' said Templar. 'You're a freelance journalist who is currently researching the effects of climate change around the region.'

'Okay.'

'If anyone asks, northern Pakistan and eastern Afghanistan have some problems with aquifer mismanagement. There's salt coming to the surface and the livestock don't like the groundwater.'

De Payns was always surprised by what his friend could pull out of a hat.

Templar asked, 'Does it sound plausible?'

'You had me at hello,' said de Payns. 'What magazine are we writing for?'

'A webzine called *Socialist Climate Action*,' said Templar. 'You'll fit right in.'

De Payns laughed. 'Have they run our stuff?'

'Brent did a thing back at the Bunker,' said Templar. 'When you search the SCA webzine, you're sent to a mirror site where our photos and stories are featured. It won't last longer than a week, but that's all we need.'

'Who wrote the stories?'

'Remember how Thierry put together our script for *Lake Forgiveness*?'

De Payns nodded.

'Well, he did his AI trick again and he came up with a story on plastic bottles in the ocean, saving the whales and how great Cuba is.'

'You've got some photos?' asked de Payns.

'Back there in the camera,' said Templar. 'Charlie's taken care of it.'

'Who's Charlie?' asked de Payns.

'The man who delivered this car,' said Templar. 'He works out of Kabul.'

'What are the photos of?'

'Sick-looking cattle,' said Templar, 'and video interviews of farmers saying the aquifer is fucked.'

'Charlie just rolled up and starting shooting?' asked de Payns. 'And they started talking?'

'Seems to be how it works,' said Templar, starting the engine of the Passat. 'Who knew journalism was so easy?'

'So we have footage. What about notes?'

'Grab that notebook I gave you and start writing about poison aquifers and low-yielding farms. And date it yesterday.'

They smoked cigarettes and drove across a landscape that was arid in some parts, verdant in others. It was physically beautiful and very rural, yet marked by burned-out trucks and piles of steel wreckage on the roadside.

De Payns let the kinks work out of his neck and back. 'So where are we? And where are we going?'

'We're south of Kabul,' said Templar, passing him a road map. 'And we're going to Zahedan, over the Iranian border, to the west.'

Zahedan was a large town in Iran. It looked like a twenty-hour drive, and they'd cross the border at Afghanistan's western boundary.

'We'll pick up a flight at six-thirty tonight, booked and paid for in Paris, and we'll fly home via Istanbul.'

De Payns needed information. 'What happened back there? At the Timberwolf meet?'

Templar shook his head, his big neck showing piano string beneath the skin. 'I think you and I have used up all our dumb luck.'

'That bad?'

Templar sighed. 'We have to talk.'

De Payns caught a new tone. 'About what?'

'We were compromised,' said Templar.

'Fuck!' said de Payns, pushing back in his seat and looking for something to punch. *'Fuck!'*

'Thankfully, not before the meeting. We managed to get a couple of wireless mics around the entry to Raven's apartment,' said Templar. 'When you said goodnight and started walking, Timberwolf walked out behind you. You aware of that?'

'No,' said de Payns, tired. 'I didn't look back.'

'So he's standing on the street with his minders around him, and I was about to pull back and loop into the candles but his phone goes off.'

'Dr Death's?'

'Yeah,' said Templar. 'He pulls a phone out of that horrible jacket of his, and answers it. And guess what he says?'

'What?'

'*Bonjour*,' said Templar.

'No!' said de Payns. *'No!'*

'He's taking a call from a fucking Frenchman!' Templar confirmed.

De Payns swallowed sandpaper. It was too much. 'What did he say?'

'He says, *Aguilar? This playboy is Aguilar?!*'

De Payns slumped. He was blown. Betrayed. Only a handful of people in the world knew—or were authorised to use—that name. 'Anything else?'

'He said something like, *I'd rather have known that an hour ago*, and then he hangs up and tells his bodyguards to follow you. That's when I knew we'd be doing an emergency exfil tonight.'

De Payns' brain roared. Not just with the possibilities of who in Paris had sold them out in the middle of an operation, but the probabilities of the ISI going after Romy, Oliver and Patrick. He couldn't contact them to tell them to get out of the apartment. And where would they run? And who could he ask at the Company to keep them safe? He could ask Shrek but that just begged the question—who was the mole?

Another thing occurred to him. 'If the operation is blown, maybe the exfil is too?'

Templar nodded. 'I booked the flight in cash, but I did it in Paris.'

'We have to change it,' said de Payns. 'We have to go back into Paris separately.'

'You want the car?' asked Templar.

'What will you do?'

'Don't ask, don't tell,' said Templar. 'There's a town up ahead—about two hours' drive—called Gardez. I'll get out there, you keep driving.'

They smoked in the dark as they closed on Gardez, through a zone that had been bombed, judging by the craters alongside the road.

'Tell me about Dr Death,' said Templar. 'What happened in there?'

'He's a nutter,' said de Payns. 'Said there was something off about me . . .'

'Imagine that.'

'Accused me of dishonouring his sister, cuckolding his best friend.'

'So we've got our guy? We had eyes.'

'Timberwolf is confirmed. He's the head scientist at the MERC and he's evil.'

Templar looked at him sideways. 'What else?'

'Don't worry,' said de Payns, annoyed that someone could know him so well.

'Tell me. What did else did he say?'

De Payns took a breath. He was feeling very anxious about his kids. 'The reason he doesn't have kids is he wouldn't want them to live in a world where he's making his bioweapons, is basically what he said.'

Templar laughed. 'Oh shit. Now I really need a drink.'

CHAPTER

FIFTY-FIVE

They stopped to relieve themselves and de Payns gasped as he twisted out of the car.

'You injured?' asked Templar.

'Still have shoulder pain since I sparred with Shrek.'

'Everyone gets beaten up by Shrek.' Templar laughed. 'How is he, by the way?'

De Payns shrugged, zipped and sat on the Passat bonnet while Templar finished.

Templar said over his shoulder, 'I mean, you and him—I don't see you together anymore.'

'He's working on something,' said de Payns, unsure if Templar was indoctrinated in Shrek's trip to Palermo.

'With Frasier?'

De Payns pricked up his ears. 'Why do you say that?'

'I saw them together at the Cat.'

De Payns mulled on that.

'You okay?' asked Templar.

'Falcon,' he said. 'Ever wonder why it went like that?'

'Only forty times a day,' said Templar, zipping up and fishing a pack of smokes from his pocket as he walked to the car. He paused as he realised what de Payns was saying. 'Oh, man. It wasn't Shrek. No way!'

'You know I was approached by Manerie?' asked de Payns. 'He wanted information on what happened in Palermo. Lots of talk about a mole.'

'Manerie's investigating Falcon? I thought they'd throw it to someone under him?'

'I know—so Manerie tries to implicate Shrek, and now Shrek has been acting strange.'

'Manerie is investigating *Shrek*? For Falcon? Why?'

De Payns lit a smoke. 'I don't know. He keeps cornering me with that gorilla Jim Valley.'

Templar nodded. 'He has something over you?'

'Yes, and it's not money. I failed to declare a meeting.'

'And he has photos?'

De Payns laughed. 'Sure does. Gotta love those DGS guys.'

'So how does Shrek get into this?'

De Payns thought about it. 'He insinuates that maybe I don't know him as well as I think. He reminds me that Shrek was the one with me on the ferry from Sardinia, and the one with me at Bar Luca. Shrek was around the passports, and he was close to the money.'

'So were you,' Templar pointed out.

'I know. But Manerie is most interested in the Company's conclusions on Falcon.'

'And you told him?'

'No, I deflect. I tell him that Briffaut has my report and the support team's briefing, but Briffaut hasn't shown me his report, which has gone to Frasier, and Frasier hasn't finalised.'

'Why doesn't Manerie just ask Briffaut?'

They looked at each other for a second too long. Templar was the first to break. 'Don't you dare. Not Briffaut!'

De Payns jumped off the car's bonnet and walked in a circle. 'I know it can't be Briffaut—yet there we were in Islamabad, in the mouth of the wolf, and Dr Death gets a phone call talking about Aguilar and the Company.'

Templar nodded. 'So if it's not me or you, not Shrek and not Briffaut . . .'

'Brent knew some of the details,' said de Payns.

Templar shook his head and a convoy of two trucks motored past. 'Brent's one of us. His grandmother's sister was tortured to death by the Gestapo for feeding Allied airmen. He's solid.'

De Payns kept pacing, a thought forming.

'What's up?' asked Templar, his tone changing. 'Your face tells me trouble.'

'We thought the tourniquet would be timed for between eight-thirty and nine,' said de Payns. 'The end of the dinner date.'

'And that's what we were set up for, but you came out early,' said Templar. 'Very early.'

'I know. When I was coming down those stairs I was praying your team was ready.'

'So?'

'So whoever made that call to Dr Death knew my schedule.'

Templar completed the thought. 'They timed the call thinking you'd still be sitting there at dinner with Timberwolf. What are we dealing with?'

'Someone who wants the Falcon team wiped off the board,' said de Payns.

■

They came over a hill and the pale lights of Gardez lay in front of them. Afghan towns didn't leave their electricity running all night like they did in Europe. There was a small camp of Afghan soldiers and armoured four-wheeler military vehicles on a spur to the side of the road, but they weren't running a checkpoint and the Frenchmen drove through.

'There's a twenty-four-hour service station on the other side of the town,' said Templar. 'Tank there and I'll get moving.'

'You got money?'

'Enough.'

De Payns pulled a swag of US notes and euros from his pocket and gave five hundred US dollars to his friend.

'You haven't told me about the ISI,' said de Payns. 'Who came for me?'

'Two professionals on foot, one sub and a car,' said Templar. 'Timberwolf took the call and was straight on to you. We were fucked.'

'Why didn't they grab me off the street?'

'Maybe he didn't want to lose face in front of his sister? Or maybe he was going to scare you, and just bank the favour.'

'Bank it?'

'You know what these people are like,' said Templar. 'At some point he'll want to be rescued by France; you'll be called out to Évreux one day and he'll be sitting in a cell saying, *Remember me? I did you a favour once, now you do me one.*'

De Payns smiled at the assumption of French goodwill. In his first year at the Company, he'd been part of a team that brought a Syrian opposition politician to Paris. The Syrian was going to give the Company all the inside information on the Assad regime, and France would get his family out, give them citizenship and donate eight hundred thousand euros to his party. When it became apparent that the politician was just jockeying for position and trying to destroy his rivals with unfounded gossip, the Cat decided to cut him loose and de Payns was instructed to deal with him. He drove the Syrian to a busy intersection in Paris, handed him the attaché case with the promised money, and told him to get out.

'But where is my family?' asked the man.

'That's your problem,' said de Payns.

'But I'm a dead man without protection,' said the panicking politician. 'I've just betrayed half the politicians and generals in Assad's regime.'

'That's your problem,' de Payns had repeated, leaning across him and opening the door.

The Syrian was found floating in the Seine ten days later. The Company was testing de Payns and he passed. There would be no quid pro quo for Timberwolf if he ever turned up asking for favours. France didn't work that way.

■

After the call from his associate, the Doctor nodded at his henchmen. 'Follow him to the hotel, but wait,' he said. 'Let's see who is working with him. No point in removing the cheese when we can also catch the mice.'

As he got into the Mercedes, his sister ran out from the building. 'How dare you, Yousef! How dare you come into my home and talk to my friend like that! And you wonder why I live in Europe?'

'Go back inside,' said Yousef, as kindly as he could. 'It's not your fault.'

'I know it's not my fault,' said Anoush, her pretty face flushing with indignation. 'It's *your* fault.'

As the Frenchman disappeared into the darkness of the evening, Yousef explained, 'You weren't to know that this man is no good. These Westerners see a married woman without her husband, and'—he shrugged—'for them it's a game.'

He willed her to go back inside, to avoid saying anything that would require him to escalate the situation. He'd suspected something was amiss before meeting the Frank but he'd wanted to deal with Anoush's indiscretion without making it the business of the state.

'It's time you were in bed,' he suggested, but he could see immediately it was the wrong thing to say.

'I'm not yours to order around, Yousef Bijar!' she shrieked. 'I'm my father's daughter, remember that.'

'How could I forget?' replied the Doctor. 'Still, it's best you were inside right now rather than out on the street.'

He could see her anger rising, and even though most members of his security detail were now following the spy, his driver and bodyguard were looking at his loud-mouthed sister.

'If anyone is to blame, it's me, not him,' she said.

'Inside. Now!' he ordered.

'I told him about your work and your position, building you up as a great man even though the world is disgusted by what you do.'

A young family scuttled past on the other side of the street, trying to pretend they'd heard nothing.

The Doctor lowered his voice. 'Last chance, sister. Get inside.'

'You could have been a great man, Yousef, but you can't talk about what you do in that place, can you? Now why is that exactly?'

He wanted to have it out with her, to damn her for adopting the soft Western ways of their father, while their mother and aunt were forced to endure the lonely hell of their forgotten history. He wanted to tell her that the maternal side of their family contained greatness and perseverance, and the French corporation had taken that from them. It was an injury that they all should have borne together, but Anoush and their father were too busy with their decadent boats and secret drinking. But he held back—his sister already knew what he thought.

He climbed into the Mercedes and shut the door. Anoush had done it again—had put him in the situation of having to choose between Pakistan's security and the welfare of his own sister. He breathed deeply, aware of the ISI man watching him in the rear-view mirror. The decision he had to make now was easier given the decision he'd made seven years ago, when his father had asked too many questions and made the mistake of judging him. His father had subsequently died from an unexpected 'heart attack'. Now Yousef had to decide about Anoush.

He thought of his youth, growing up alongside his gregarious little sister. The holidays in which Anoush and their father had skied and sailed, while Yousef looked for a quiet place to read a book. Being the clever one of the family wasn't easy. Being the one to uphold the honour of his family—to avenge the losses they had suffered—was never going to make him popular. But that was his role.

He keyed his phone and watched the number connect as Anoush stormed back into her apartment building.

'Colonel,' he said into the phone, 'we have a security situation.'

CHAPTER
FIFTY-SIX

Between them they had one firearm, which de Payns insisted Templar take. And then Templar threw a small backpack over his shoulder and walked into the shadows without even a backward look.

They were at the northern outskirts of Gardez. North of his position was the service station, which de Payns could see stayed open for all the trucks that were on their way to or from Kabul. It was 5.24 a.m. He drove into the forecourt, avoided the diesel queue and went straight to a petrol bowser. He tanked and went to the counter with euros and US dollars, then waited behind a truck driver who was paying. As he did he became aware of a couple of National Police officers standing at the coffee stand to his left. He smiled briefly and they glared at him—early thirties ANP cops with Sigma 9mm handguns on their hips and AKMs over their shoulders. De Payns got to the front of the queue, gestured to the petrol pump and asked for a large bottle of water, a pre-paid phone and a pack of Marlboros, offering euros and US dollars. The young man accepted the euros.

As he walked to the car he sensed the cops behind him. The hum of diesels vibrated around him as the trucks lined up for fuel.

'Good evening sir,' said the taller of the cops, in English. 'Far to go?'

De Payns turned. 'To Kabul.' He smiled.

'American?' asked the one with a moustache.

'French,' said de Payns.

'Ah,' said the tall one. 'Long way from the home. Why are you in Afghanistan?'

'I'm a journalist,' de Payns said. 'Morel. Georges Morel. I'm doing a story about the aquifers in northern Pakistan and eastern Afghanistan.'

'This is your car?'

'Yes,' said de Payns, as the tall cop walked to the front of the Passat and made a face.

'You staying in Afghanistan for long?' asked the tall one.

'I'm flying out in the next two days,' said de Payns, wishing they would just leave him alone.

'Okay,' said the tall one, now smiling. 'If it was more than thirty days, you'd have to change those plates. Pakistan plates no good.'

■

De Payns made good time north, hitting only one checkpoint, where he was not asked to stop. It was 7.43 a.m. when he reached the city limits of Kabul. He kept an eye out for an internet cafe. As he moved into the city he saw a place, stopped and paid for a screen. He opened a Gmail account in the name of Charles Paris and sent a quick message, with his new phone number, to Dennis London, better known as Mike Moran.

He drove for another five minutes, past soldiers in mixed uniforms lounging on armoured personnel carriers, smoking; the city was looking less bombed out than on de Payns' last visit, two years ago. He saw a restaurant with an English sign that looked open. He was happy to find the female owner was French and he ordered coffee, *pain au chocolat* and an omelette. As the woman walked away, his pre-paid phone rang.

'Hello?'

'This is your wake-up call,' said an English voice. 'Long time no see, *mon pote*.'

'Too long.'

Moran said, 'Shall we meet?'

'That would be great,' said de Payns, pouring sugar into his coffee. 'You where you always are?'

'I am,' said Moran. 'I'll wait at the gate.'

'See you in an hour,' said de Payns and hung up.

He finished the omelette and coffee, and carried the *pain au chocolat* to the Passat.

■

He arrived early at Tajikan Road, in the north of Kabul, and walked the street in front of the police special forces base. The city of four million was getting busy, a mix of horses and motorbikes, limos and army trucks. One of the biggest markets in Afghanistan was over the road from the base. There were soldiers and police on the street, and even first thing in the morning the thump of a helicopter engine was audible, hovering over the base. It was a fortress and had to be that way; a former police chief from the Taliban era had turned on his former colleagues and decided to work for the new American-backed government. That simple shifting of allegiance had triggered fifteen years of attempted assassinations, bombings and kidnappings of anyone associated with the National Police.

He walked routes to see who was around and who might be interested in him. It seemed clean, and exactly one hour after he'd spoken with Moran, de Payns walked to the main security gate. Before he could get there a local man in an Afghan *pakol* and a *shalwar kameez* grabbed his arm. As de Payns tensed, the man told him to relax. It was Moran. They walked through the crowds and down a side street where a black Toyota LandCruiser was parked in the loading bay of a laundry.

'In here,' said Moran, opening the rear door.

They clambered into the vehicle and a heavily muscled local man started the car and drove off.

Moran whipped off the hat and struggled out of the knee-length dress. 'Hate these things,' he said, as he kicked away the long shirt, revealing pale chinos and a dark polo shirt. He was a solidly built, dark-haired man who obviously exercised.

'How are you Alec?' asked the Englishman, holding out his hand.

As they shook, de Payns couldn't keep the smile off his face. 'You're looking younger. You doing yoga?'

'No, mate,' said Moran with a wink. 'Second divorce. Pure joy keeps me young.'

Mike Moran was two years younger than de Payns, and had spent all his post-university life in the SIS. They had known each other as children, when their grandparents used to meet up once a year. During World War II, Moran's and de Payns' grandfathers had fought with de Gaulle for the Free French. Moran's grandfather married an Englishwoman and lived out his days as a bank manager in Southampton. De Payns' grandfather returned to France with de Gaulle and stayed close to the President and managed his pine forest in the south of the country. For years the families would meet up in Bournemouth over the summer and the tradition was kept alive by Mike's and de Payns' parents.

'We gotta stop meeting like this,' said Mike. Then his tone changed. 'What's up? You okay?'

'Something's not right and I have to get back to Paris. Independently.'

Mike nodded slowly. 'Well, you wouldn't ask if it wasn't important. How's your mum?'

'Loving Netflix but doesn't like all the swearing,' said de Payns.

'Ha! That's her. That's exactly her.'

Then he leaned forward between the front seats and asked his driver something in the local tongue. They nodded and went back and forth, and then the driver met de Payns' eye in the rear-view mirror.

Moran sat back. 'Abed can get you on a government supplies plane, but it lands in Frankfurt. That useful?'

'Sure is,' said de Payns.

They motored west to the Hamid Karzai International Airport and swung around the back, past cells of soldiers and vehicle-mounted heavy machine guns, into the government and military annexe. They were checked at the gate with mirrored wands under the vehicle and a dog handler walking around the LandCruiser. De Payns fished the Georges Morel passport from his windbreaker and handed it to Moran, who did the talking. Abed drove them along an endless series of bomb-proof hangars, the air conditioning keeping them cool as the morning air started to shimmer with heat outside. They stopped at a collection of freight depot hangars in which de Payns could make out large pallets of plastic-wrapped boxes with European names such as Siemens and Krupp on them. Obviously this was the receiving depot for Germany.

They stopped beside a security post and Abed became all smiles for a local woman in a security uniform with no hijab. By the way he flirted—despite her *no chance, mister* look—de Payns assumed they were well known to one another. Eventually she stood and came around to the passenger seat, electronic clipboard under her arm, and climbed in.

'Which one is Georges Morel?' she asked, peering into the back seat.

De Payns raised his hand and smiled.

'You have friends in high places, *monsieur*,' she said. 'But you'll have to go on the manifest. That a problem?'

'No,' said de Payns, handing over his passport.

She brought up a screen on her iPad and input de Payns' fictive name and passport number.

'I need an address,' she said.

'Place d'Armes, Versailles, France,' said de Payns. He spelled it out for her and she hit 'enter'.

The woman said, 'Come on, then,' and got out of the LandCruiser.

Moran extended his hand. 'Good luck, brother.'

'Thanks, Mike,' said de Payns. 'I owe you.'

'All you owe me is a beer,' the Englishman replied. It was an old joke between them—it didn't matter what they did for one another, the only debt was a drink.

De Payns clambered out of the Toyota and watched it drive away. There was no breeze among the buildings and the temperature must have been high-thirties. He followed the woman through a security door and into a small lounge that shared space with more freight pallets and boxes. One set of pallets featured water filters, probably destined for Afghanistan's new water infrastructure.

The woman unhooked the radio handpiece from her chest webbing and talked to someone in German. She nodded then turned to de Payns. 'You can board, front stairs.'

He loaded up with water bottles and packets of biscuits from the lounge area and walked onto the apron towards a DC-10 with a meaningless acronym on the tail. He climbed the stairs to a small area at the front of the cargo plane which had one row of seats, right behind the cockpit. A pilot leaned through, saw him and asked, 'You are Morel?' in a thick Dutch accent.

De Payns nodded, and the Dutchman said they'd be in the air in about forty minutes. 'There are no other passengers, so spread out.'

De Payns reclined the seat and let his eyelids droop. He thought about Islamabad and Palermo and a phone call to Dr Death. And he thought about weaponised gangrene and what that evil bastard might be planning.

CHAPTER
FIFTY-SEVEN

De Payns came in to Gare de l'Est at 6 a.m., direct from Frankfurt. He walked the concourse, checking for followers, and caught the escalators down to the Metro station, where he went in search of breakfast. He then caught two trains to the Place de la République. He gave a signal with his hand and hair beside the statue at 8 a.m., and at 8.30 entered the Café Français, where the Company's team was ready to conduct the IS. By 9.16, Alec de Payns was sitting in Briffaut's office, door closed.

'I've heard the phone call to Timberwolf,' said Briffaut, taking a seat. 'We tracked it back and the most we can come up with is that it came from a French phone, and probably a tower in the north.'

'Paris?'

Briffaut shrugged. 'We have a recording of the call and we're working on a voice match.'

'Shit,' said de Payns, shaking his head. 'Someone gave up my pseudo in the middle of an operation?'

'We're on it.'

'My family?'

'DGS report they're fine. You okay?'

'I'm in one piece, but Timberwolf was hostile. He's a scary guy—he's capable of anything.'

Briffaut looked at him. 'Give me a quick report then go to bed. You're no use to me like this.'

'We need to find the mole,' said de Payns. 'We should have been in the middle of dinner when the traitor called—Timberwolf would have taken the call right in front of me. I'd have had no chance.'

'That's interesting,' said Briffaut.

'Only a very small group knew the timing of that dinner,' de Payns pointed out. 'I let Templar know and he emailed a situation update to you. And you copied it to Frasier and Lafont.'

'No one asked me for the dinner meeting details,' said Briffaut. 'I'll check on the other two.' He paused. 'Something else has come up. The DR has been searching for any other stories that have involved mass cases of internal haemorrhaging and those gassy pustules. The Red Cross reported a case six days ago in northern Burma. Thirty-five people dead. We're trying to get samples we can test, but for now the photographs look the same as the ones taken by our patrol in Afghanistan. According to the post-mortem, these people died approximately three hours after ingesting the bacteria. It's very quick, apparently.'

'So the bioweapon works?'

Briffaut nodded. 'The question is, what are they going to do with it?'

■

Nasim glanced at the clock on the wall then wound up the meeting. The project team had a major client to keep happy in the following two days, but he had other commitments that could not wait and he dismissed the five people who worked for him. When they were gone, he fished a new burner cell phone from his safe and caught the elevator to the street.

It was approaching the end of summer in Paris and he walked with crowds to the Rambuteau Metro station and took a northbound train, hopping off at République, where he lost himself in the throng. He was not a distinctive man in his native country, but in Paris his height and looks meant people stared openly. Paris was that kind of city, and he liked to blend in where he could. In the smaller streets to the south of Place de la République he found an internet cafe which only had three patrons in it. He turned his assigned computer on and off, and inserted a small USB drive on his office key ring, which ran a Mozilla browser. He opened his encrypted web-based email account, registered in a meaningless name, and looked at his watch: 2.58 p.m. He waited two minutes then sent an email which simply listed the number of his new burner phone. Then he shut down the email and the browser, and wiped the history seven times before turning off and restarting the computer.

He walked the pretty streets of what was the Jewish district of Paris. Although he'd been raised in Pakistan, his parents were not haters and he found this part of Paris very peaceful. Those who assumed Nasim's undeclared activities automatically made him an anti-Semite were wrong. He had in-demand skills that generated a lot of income—what else was a former intelligence agent supposed to do with his knowledge? Let it go to waste? It was not hate that drove him, but money.

The phone buzzed in his jacket pocket, and he answered. 'That last tidbit was well received,' said Nasim, without preamble. 'The mighty Aguilar, working in Islamabad? He's either very desperate or very good.'

'I have something else,' said the caller. 'Frasier's report on Operation Falcon just landed. He's satisfied the passports were destroyed in Palermo. Aguilar is clean.'

'Hmm,' said Nasim, as he strolled past the pizza bars and punk shoe shops. 'So they really are gone? That leaves us five passports short.'

'There's not much I can do about that,' said the voice.

'Well, given your position, I'd argue the point on that one,' said Nasim.

There was silence except for the sound of a sigh. 'I wasn't in Palermo,' said the caller, in a tone that Nasim didn't appreciate. 'The passports weren't my deal.'

'Except to tell me there was a packet of them there,' said Nasim, stopping beside a stand of trees. 'And then you forgot to tell me that our friend Aguilar was on that ferry.'

'I didn't know.'

'Well now you do, and I'm short five French passports,' said Nasim, wondering how far he could push this man.

There was a long silence, then: 'What do you want me to do?' asked the man.

'Use your position,' said Nasim. 'After all, I have a budget for five French passports, and I haven't spent it yet.'

CHAPTER FIFTY-EIGHT

De Payns wrote a two-page preliminary report on Operation Alamut and the dinner meeting. He was about to shut down his system when he saw an internal phone call on his console—it said *Briffaut, D.*

'Yes?' he answered.

'I need you in my office—now.'

■

Briffaut and Brent Clercq were looking at Briffaut's computer screen when de Payns arrived.

'Look at this,' said Briffaut, pointing at an image. 'Is this Murad?'

'Étienne got it from the ferry company,' said Brent, referring to a young operative from the Y Division. 'Is it him, Alec?'

De Payns brought his face in close and squinted. It was grainy, shot from an oldish CCTV system, screen-grabbed and emailed. It appeared to be from footage outside the WCs on the ferry, taken on the afternoon that Commodore and de Payns had arrived in Palermo from Cagliari.

'I believe that's him, but how did Étienne know who to look for?' asked de Payns, reaching for the mouse to see if he could enlarge the image.

'Your report was very specific about where you saw the man you thought was Murad—outside the toilets, as Commodore emerged, around ten minutes before docking.'

'Okay, well I think that's him,' said de Payns. 'Although we can't really see his face, so I'm going off my memory of his shape and clothes.'

The man was clearly looking at Commodore as the Italian emerged from the WCs, and their body language suggested some words were being exchanged.

'No one knows who he is?' asked de Payns.

Briffaut shook his head. 'The Arabic desk is going over it, but it basically can't be used. We have that and the sketch that was made from your description, which is more useful right now. That's all we have.'

'We don't even know if it *is* Murad,' said de Payns.

'By the way, we've had a small breakthrough on the Palermo situation,' said Briffaut. 'Shrek's main find was traces of epsilon toxin in the warehouse, but he also discovered that Michael Lambardi used his brother David's real estate firm in Palermo for some back office matters such as billing and accounts. And phones.'

De Payns raised his eyebrows. 'He mentioned David but I never met him.'

'This is Commodore's phone,' said Briffaut, pulling a sheaf of printed papers from beside his PC. 'Brent's guys have been working on his telecoms.'

De Payns looked down the spreadsheets where they'd isolated two Michael Lambardi numbers—one seemed to be business and local and they went to a spray of Italian numbers without much pattern. But there was another IMSI—a *démarqué* phone—and the pattern was immediately obvious. The secondary phone only called one number, once a day.

'We've had some work done on that recipient number, and it has used cell towers in northern Pakistan, probably Islamabad, and Europe, Italy and Spain. But the most common area it's been used has been in France.'

'Fuck,' said de Payns. 'What was Palermo really about?'

Briffaut pointed at the spreadsheet. 'Look at the dates. There's a week of those calls terminating at northern French towers—probably Paris—and then, two days before Operation Falcon goes bad, Commodore's daily calls are terminating at Italian locations.'

'We know Commodore was taking his orders from Sayef Albar and Murad,' said de Payns. 'But what's Murad doing in Paris?'

'Sayef Albar has been trying to move into Europe, and maybe Sicily is their staging point?'

'Staging point for what?' asked de Payns. 'That gangrene shit?'

Briffaut shrugged. 'I need more information.'

De Payns was driven in a Company Audi north into Paris, stopping at an underground car park in Muette Nord, where they switched cars before driving across town to the neighbourhood of the safe house just after midnight.

He let himself in and went to the bedroom, where he changed out of the George-the-journalist clothing into his Alec de Payns clothes and emptied his collateral onto the bureau in his locker. Having slipped on his watch and put his wallet and keys in his pocket, he suddenly felt the fatigue and paranoia. He grabbed the bureau to steady himself. Dr Death's eyes were seared in his brain. He didn't know if he could go home, but he knew he had to. He needed grounding.

He made fast time to Port-Royal and walked the long way to the apartment. It was almost 1 a.m. when he let himself in and tiptoed to the kitchen. The light in the extractor fan had been left on, something Romy was always telling him not to do. He smiled as he switched it off, plunging the kitchen into semi-darkness. He turned slowly, aware of a new scent. Very slight, familiar . . . and male. It smelled like Old Spice, which he didn't wear. He walked to the living room and the main window in front of the Juliet balcony, then looked down to the street out of habit.

He turned for the bedrooms and, in the half-light created by the city, saw a small pile on the coffee table—Romy's wallet and keys. He stared at it. He knew he was tired and paranoid, but it still didn't seem right. Romy's stuff was always piled on the hall table near the front door and it was a running joke between them, because to de Payns that was just asking for an opportunistic thief to stick his head in the door and take your stuff. And where was her phone? Romy was organised and her iPhone always accompanied her wallet and keys.

He pushed off his sneakers and padded quietly down the dark hall. The city's ambient light didn't reach here and he moved by muscle memory. At Patrick and Oliver's door, he paused and stuck his head around the jamb. Oliver had a Buzz Lightyear quilt and Patrick's was Paris Saint-Germain.

He crept into the room. No boys.

They'd probably be with their mother, a common sleep pattern when he was away. He went to the next room, and as soon as he stuck his head inside, he knew it was empty. No sleep noises, no sleep warmth or smell. He flipped the lights and his mind went to white noise. The bed was empty—it hadn't been slept in.

Snatching his phone from his pocket, he tried Romy's number.

It went straight to voicemail. He left a greeting and followed it up with a text. He tried to stay calm but he was flipping out.

His breath rasped as he walked the room, checked the wardrobes and under the bed. He ran through the apartment, swearing to himself, panicking, his skin crawling and his brain squawking like an old field radio. He jumped from Dr Death to Islamabad, from weaponised gas gangrene to power drills and children as he grabbed the car keys, put on his shoes and burst out of the apartment door.

He took the fire stairs down to the underground garage two at a time and headed to the family VW, which was parked in its usual spot. He walked around the car, looked under it, and then unlocked it and opened the door. There was nothing amiss—a Buzz Lightyear toy on the back seat and a book list for school on the passenger seat. He turned on the power and scrolled through Romy's recent map directions—nothing unusual. He scrolled the recent calls on the screen. She'd received a call from Ana at 3.49 p.m. the day before; Romy had missed the call and rang her back at 4.02. They spoke for six minutes.

He returned to the apartment and sat on the sofa, cycling his breathing to calm himself. He scrolled through his own personal phone, found Ana's number and texted, *Are you awake?*

The reply came twenty seconds later: *Am now.*

De Payns called her and Ana picked up immediately. He apologised for the hour and explained that he'd come home to an empty apartment. 'Do you know where Romy and the boys are? Have you seen them today?'

Ana was sleepy. 'I rang her to ask about regulation school shoes for when the boys start next week,' said Ana. 'We ran through it and agreed we should meet up at the park in the next couple of days. Surely they haven't just *disappeared*? Could they be at Romy's parents' house?'

'Not without Romy's wallet and car keys,' said de Payns. 'Oliver's teddy bear is still here. He wouldn't sleep over without it.'

He knew what he had to do—the personal security of the Company's operatives was handled by the DGS, and the protocol, when there was a breach, was to contact the emergency number and report it. Ending the call with Ana, he dialled the number which all operatives had to memorise. He was asked for his OT number by the male voice on the end of the line, who paused. 'I can't respond to you,' said the DGS man.

'What?!' replied de Payns. 'You can't—'

'There's a note; I'll connect you now,' said the man, and the line clicked and buzzed, as if he was calling a new number.

'Hello, Alec?' answered a man.

De Payns knew the voice. '*Manerie*? Christ, is that you?'

CHAPTER
FIFTY-NINE

'I've been waiting for your call.'

Cold anger welled up in de Payns. 'Waiting?! Manerie, what the fuck? Where is my *family*?'

'Be outside in ten minutes,' said Philippe Manerie. 'And as they say in the movies—don't tell anyone about this. Remember your oath.'

De Payns stared at the phone, the call now ended. What was Romy involved in? The director of DGS tells him to shut up about the disappearance of his family and reminds him of his oath, the one he took on being commissioned at the Company. That oath included total adherence to information security imposed from above. If someone with a higher rank told you something was secret, you disavowed all knowledge until you were told otherwise. No exceptions.

He was aware of his own panting. He knew how to get through situations where his life was in danger; he had the skills and personality to handle it. But the threat to his family was triggering pure animal fear.

He picked up the phone again, thought about calling Shrek or Templar. He thought about calling Briffaut. But he'd wait until after he'd seen Manerie, he decided. He would also revert to his training—if you have the opportunity, always do recon of a meeting site. Reconnaissance was always worth the effort. He ran down the fire stairs again and emerged in the parking garage. It was now 1.29 a.m. He made for the far side of the garage, where the building manager had a caged-off area containing the water meters, power meters and assorted hardware such as sump pumps and ladders. De Payns used the wires in his key ring to pick the padlock on the cage gate and moved to the corner where the pipes and conduits all disappeared upwards into the building. He shifted a stepladder into position and reached up and into the pipes cavity, and brought down an object wrapped in oilskin canvas. He removed the CZ 9mm handgun, checked it for safety and load, pushed it into his belt and replaced the oilskin. Then he left the cage, relocking the gate behind him.

The street was slick with recent rain. He walked away from his apartment for one hundred metres, looking for anomalies, then crossed to the other side of the street. He walked in the shadows of the trees, the only person moving. Ahead he saw something that triggered his brain—a blue tradesman's van parked fifty metres west of his building. Tradesmen did not generally live in Montparnasse. He was walking towards it when a black Audi SUV slowed and then stopped in front of his building. De Payns knew the occupants would be looking at the entrance to the apartment building, so he walked slowly in the shadows, watching the vehicle. There seemed to be only one occupant. He stepped into the street. A block away a truck started its engines. He looked through the window of the Audi and saw Manerie, alone at the wheel, face ethereal in the red glow of the instruments. He opened the passenger door, giving Manerie a start.

'Tell me where my family is,' said de Payns.

'Get in,' said Manerie, deadpanning de Payns with the face that once stalked the war zones of Africa.

De Payns climbed in the Audi and Manerie accelerated.

'Romy and the kids are fine,' said the director. He was dressed in chinos and a polo shirt, windbreaker over the top—the standard field wear of spies when not living a fictive legend. De Payns twisted, saw a small wheelie suitcase perched on the back seat.

'You going somewhere, Manerie?'

'Mind your business,' said the DGS man. 'Romy and the boys are in an exercise.'

'A kidnap exercise?' asked de Payns, blood boiling. 'Why wasn't I notified?'

Manerie ignored him.

'And what's this got to do with finding the mole? What the fuck is going on?'

Manerie smiled. 'At five p.m. today, I'll make a phone call to the field team and the exercise will be over. Smiles all around. Happy families in Montparnasse.'

De Payns looked at the side of Manerie's head, wanting to put a bullet through it. 'You'll make a *phone call*?' exclaimed de Payns. 'Holy shit, are you threatening me?'

They stopped at a red light, Manerie turned to de Payns, and—in a small flash of clarity—de Payns saw the truth in his eyes.

'You?'

Manerie shrugged.

'You're the mole?!' said de Payns, his heart sinking at the thought of his family. 'My God, Manerie! What have you done?'

Manerie hit the accelerator as the light went green, and before he could stop himself, de Payns had the CZ muzzle jammed in the DGS man's neck. 'Pull over.'

The Audi came to the kerb in a bus zone opposite the Café Odessa. De Payns jammed the muzzle in harder, controlling his breathing but finding it hard to quell his emotions.

'It seems we have a stand-off,' said Manerie, his head pressed against his window. 'I've set this up so it can end peacefully.'

'You used my family?'

'It's what we call leverage. You're the expert, yes?'

De Payns pushed harder, then suddenly pulled back, leaving an embossed circle just below Manerie's right earlobe. His number one priority was Romy and the boys. He had to control himself.

Manerie straightened, rubbing his neck. 'Here's the deal—you stand down, talk to no one, initiate no protocols. Maybe even take a day off work, if that doesn't raise any flags. When I'm clear, I make the call, and as far as your family is concerned, it was just an exercise, helping out France.'

'Why would I trust you, Manerie? You're a traitor.'

'Because you have no choice, Alec.'

They stared at one another, both knowing that de Payns was going to back down.

'I don't understand this,' said de Payns. 'Why me? What justifies any of this?'

Manerie laughed. 'You cost me three million euros, and you ask about justification? That's funny.'

'Cost you?' replied de Payns. 'Are we talking about those passports?'

Across the road a bakery van pulled up at the Odessa and a person emerged from the cafe.

'You sold me out for three million euros?' asked de Payns.

'You weren't supposed to be on that ferry,' snapped Manerie. 'As soon as you looked at our friend, it became a clean-up exercise. A person like that doesn't like eye contact.'

De Payns' brain roared. 'I was supposed to die that night?'

'Not my doing,' said Manerie. 'I told him there were five genuine French passports waiting in Palermo, and the handover meeting was set. Our friend decided to have a chat with Commodore on the ferry and instead finds himself being stared at by the DGSE. Not happy!'

'Cagliari was a last-minute thing,' said de Payns. 'Commodore wanted me at a meeting. I joined him from Marseille.'

'Well, he didn't tell his handlers, and I guess he paid the price.'

'But the money was going to Commodore . . .'

Manerie laughed, genuinely amused. 'Three million euros, to a knucklehead like Michael Lambardi? Commodore was never getting that money.'

Manerie checked his watch and pulled out into the street, did a U-turn and headed back to where they'd started. De Payns wasn't convinced. 'I don't see why you'd leave me or my family alive right now. What's in it for you?'

Manerie's smile was more to himself than for his passenger's benefit. 'You went and put a wrinkle in things with your little trip, and so for the next fourteen hours you're not going to poke the wasp's nest. That's good for me, and good for you. I'm sure we understand one another?'

'My little trip?' de Payns remembered how Manerie had tried to work out where he was going, unsuccessfully. 'You betrayed me in Islamabad?'

Manerie's face changed into a rictus of hate. '*Betrayed?* Don't you use that word with me, de Payns,' he snarled. 'I fought for France just as much as you and your glorious family, and I kept Mike Moran under my hat for years. Is that a *betrayal*?'

'I never sold operational secrets.'

'Fuck you, de Payns,' snarled Manerie. 'Moran is SIS. He's a sworn officer of a foreign intelligence organisation.'

'I declared the Morans when I first joined the air force and when I joined the Company. They're friends of the family.'

'You didn't declare that you go drinking with Mike Moran four times a year,' said Manerie. 'Rule number one: *Don't get drunk with foreign spies.*'

They pulled up outside de Payns' apartment. 'Five o'clock,' said Manerie. 'I'm still running security at the DGS, so I'll know if you're frightening the horses.'

De Payns opened the door, then stepped onto the road. Before he could say anything more, Manerie accelerated away.

He felt a deep dread. As he walked to his building he took a look at the parked tradesman's van. The passenger door opened and a man stepped out. It was dark, but he knew that shape.

CHAPTER
SIXTY

Briffaut and Shrek walked towards him out of the dark. The van accelerated past them.

'Shall we go up?' asked Briffaut. 'We don't have much time.'

Shrek made coffee in the kitchen while Briffaut and de Payns spoke at the table, smoking.

'Templar and Brent are in the van, running the spinners on Manerie,' said Briffaut. 'Do you know where he's headed?'

'It has to be the airport, but I don't know where he's flying,' said de Payns. 'How did you know there was a problem over here?'

Briffaut looked sheepish. 'You made a call.'

'Ana?' he asked. 'Shit, you're bugging me?'

Briffaut opened his hands. 'As soon as Palermo went bad the Company wanted to keep tabs on you. Sorry.'

'So when did you know it was Manerie?' asked de Payns.

'Something you said last night, about who knew the details of your dinner date with Raven and Timberwolf,' said Briffaut. 'You, me and Templar. We didn't leak it, so it must have been Lafont. I called and asked her and she angrily denied it. That left Frasier, the last person indoctrinated on Alamut.'

'Not Frasier?'

'I thought that. I called him and he said the update to the file had been placed in the DO's safe and he hadn't read it. He'd accepted my verbal heads-up. So who had access to that safe?'

'The director of DGS,' said de Payns, shaking his head. 'The failsafe for compromised operations.'

'I asked the night duty at DGS to check the access logs to Frasier's safe on the day of your dinner. It was accessed four times, so we checked the CCTV against those times.'

'Manerie,' said de Payns.

'He accessed the safe at eleven minutes past midday—while Frasier was at lunch—and that evening, Islamabad time, Templar recorded Timberwolf taking a call.'

Shrek brought the coffees to the table.

'Can we match the voice to Manerie?' asked de Payns.

'It's not Manerie's,' said Briffaut. 'We're working on the assumption that it's Murad.'

He pulled out his phone. 'Listen to this.' The voice file was a smooth, cultured South Asian voice with an English undertone.

De Payns nodded. 'So we have a loop between Dr Death and the epsilon toxin, and the Sayef Albar operation in Palermo?'

Briffaut's phone trilled. He took it and asked a few questions before disconnecting. 'That's Templar. They just caught a call from Manerie's car. Now we run it through the phone company systems and see where the call terminated. Could take an hour.'

De Payns sat back with his coffee and looked at his old friend Shrek. 'So where have you been lately?'

Shrek shrugged.

'He's been with me,' said Briffaut.

'With you?' asked de Payns.

'We've had our eye on Manerie and . . .'

'And me?' asked de Payns.

'Manerie told me the DGS was investigating us both,' said Shrek. 'He basically blackmailed me to leak to him from Noisy, so I went to the boss. We've been trying to backtrack Palermo, work out what Manerie was scared of us finding.'

'I know why it went bad down there,' said de Payns. 'Manerie was promised the money for the passports. When I decided to leap on the Cagliari trip, it meant I unexpectedly got a look at Murad on the ferry and he decided to pull the plug.'

'So that really was Murad?'

'According to Manerie, yes.'

Briffaut got on his phone again and told the recipient of the call to make up a pack and send it to all intelligence agencies, police stations and embassies. 'It's a crappy picture,' he said, 'but it's all we have.'

CHAPTER

SIXTY-ONE

The Audi SUV disappeared into the parking building at Charles de Gaulle airport in northern Paris and Templar told the van driver, Jean-Michel Legrand, to pull over.

'We can't spook him now,' he said, watching Manerie's vehicle move out of sight. It was just past 2 a.m. and the airport precinct was becoming busy. Templar had one job—to find Aguilar's family and return them safely. It would have a complication, because the mother and two children thought it was an exercise and Aguilar wanted them to continue to believe that, if possible. If Romy ever got wind of the fact her children really had been abducted, she would not stay married to the Company.

Behind him in the working area of the van, he could hear Brent Clercq making another call to the DT section back at the Cat. He asked yet again if there was a terminating tower for the call they'd logged from Manerie's phone. The DT was talking to a cooperative phone company but it was taking time.

Templar had been trained to wait, to conserve his energy and then to execute his orders with ruthless accuracy. It was what he'd done as a special forces paratrooper in Iraq and Afghanistan, and as a long-range recon man in Africa. It was the role he played for the Company, the forgettable man, the face in the crowd, the person you don't give a second's thought to—until the time was right, and then he acted. He was an expert at waiting but he wasn't enjoying this wait. He probably shouldn't have taken the assignment. He was friends with Aguilar and Romy, he'd been around when the kids were babies. So he had to consciously contain his ferocity. In the Angolan bush he would have caught Philippe Manerie and hurt him so badly that the traitor would have begged to take him to Romy, Patrick and Oliver. He would have pleaded for Templar to take them. But this wasn't Africa, and it was delicately poised; Manerie had the upper hand and Templar had to wait for the information.

After almost two hours of waiting, the phone trilled in the back and Brent took the call. He spoke for thirty seconds and then leaned through, 'Attigny, north-east of Dijon Tower thirteen twenty-eight. I have the coordinates.'

Templar tweaked the phone and called Briffaut, told him the news.

Briffaut replied, 'We have a Caracal at the military annexe. When you're at the tower, let me know and we'll call Valley.'

■

The army Caracal helicopter took them north in the pre-dawn over the sprawling farmlands of northern France, and when they were in the neighbourhood of the tower coordinates, Templar elected to put down in a farm paddock. The landscape was visible when they stepped off the helicopter beside a river. The pilot shut it down. 'We'll be two hours,' said Templar, hauling the assault rifles, binoculars and comms gear from their duffel bags. Templar was sure they'd arrived undetected. The pilot had flown downwind of the target area, and at less than 100 feet altitude.

The three of them—Templar, Brent and Jean-Michel—crossed the countryside towards the white cell tower that stood on a low ridge between stands of trees. There were two farmhouses to the east of the tower, and one to the north-west. Templar found a hide in the undergrowth and took his military binoculars from his pack. He sat, resting his wrists on the top of his knees. Jean-Michel did the same.

'Southern farmhouse, white with tiled roof,' said Templar.

'Copy,' said Jean-Michel.

'I see tractor, farm truck, motorbike and I think that's a harvester in the shed.'

'Copy that. Looks legit.'

Templar shifted his sights to the second farmhouse, which was further north. 'Northern farmhouse, white tiled roof,' said Templar. 'Is that a van?'

Jean-Michel responded, 'I make a black Renault van, parked at the rear of the dwelling; there's a late-model Audi parked behind it.'

Both vehicle types were used by the Company. There were no farm vehicles evident.

'Keep your eyes on it,' said Templar. He swung away to look at the farmhouse on the other side of the spur, and saw another legit farm.

They waited for another ninety minutes, monitoring the farm houses, and then Jean-Michel piped up. 'Okay, boss, we have persons outside the northern house. Looks like they're in the game.'

Templar swung his glasses back to the second farm. Three hundred metres away, a man walked to the front of the farmhouse, while another man—larger than the first and wearing a black cap—walked towards him.

'That's Valley—the big one, black cap. Brent, tell the boss we're in place, ready for that call,' said Templar, eyes steady on the two men outside the farmhouse.

Brent made the call. 'Standing by,' he said.

The men in Templar's binoculars shared a smoke; Jim Valley seemed to be making a point to the other, giving an order.

'Here we go,' said Brent, who was monitoring his laptop. 'There's an incoming call. It's to our IMSI.'

Templar peered through his binoculars: Valley fished a phone from his jacket pocket, hit the screen and put it to his ear.

'That's a lock,' said Brent. 'Jim Valley just answered a call from Philippe Manerie.'

'Unload,' Templar said, standing and shrugging his backpack to the ground. 'And remember—don't scare the kids.'

■

The three of them moved down from their position shortly after seven o'clock, but on the other side of a small ridge, which gave them cover from the farmhouse. They were each armed with a Heckler & Koch 416, an assault rifle that Templar didn't mind, although he preferred its predecessor, the FAMAS Bugle, which had proven itself in Africa. They each had a waist bag of wrist ties and duct tape, given they didn't know how many adversaries they'd have to deal with. There were some outbuildings around the farm, and Templar sent Jean-Michel further to the west, to enter from the other flank. He crept up behind the main barn—which was empty—and surveyed the farmhouse. The first, smaller guard had gone back inside, while Valley had taken a seat in the cab of the van, messing around on his phone while he finished his cigarette. It created a blind spot for Manerie's man. If Templar approached down the side of the van, he wouldn't be seen from the farmhouse.

He jogged into the open, and ran on tiptoe down the side of the van, swinging the butt of his Heckler at the side of Jim Valley's head as he reached the open door. Out of instinct, Valley bent his head away and deflected the full impact, which was still forceful enough to half tear his left ear from his head.

As Templar went for him, Valley's leg straightened into a ram, catching Templar in the solar plexus. Templar staggered back and Valley was on him with a left hook that failed to connect properly, followed by a fast elbow. Templar took it on the left cheek and was knocked onto his back. Valley leaped on him, trying for a jujitsu chokehold to the neck, which Templar countered by throwing an uppercut with his right elbow that connected so well it sounded like it broke some of Valley's teeth. They rolled from one another, Templar's rifle now lying in the grass. Valley threw a sweep kick from his prone position, catching Templar on the side of the nose, ejecting blood and snot into the air. He shook it off and caught a boot in the mouth, knocking him onto his back. Now Valley was on him, with a hand on Templar's larynx and a right hand descending fast at his face. Templar got a hand free and deflected the punch with his bicep as he punctured Valley's left eye with a claw strike. Valley recoiled, moaning in pain, releasing his larynx grip, allowing Templar to throw him off with his hips and roll into a rear-naked chokehold. He tightened his arms around Valley's neck, positioned his legs against his back and pulled back hard. He felt Valley's taps on the ground get softer as the blood stopped flowing to his head. Valley was a big, fit man but he finally went soft and Templar immediately cuffed him at the wrists and ankles and slapped a length of duct tape across his mouth.

Templar got on the radio net, telling the team *Valley down*, and asking for situation reports. Jean-Michel whispered he was approaching the house from the west, no resistance; Brent didn't answer.

Templar rose, looked around and picked up his rifle. Blood poured from his busted nose. He wiped it on his sleeve and walked to the north of the house. No one. To the west of the empty barn was a disused piggery. He padded around it and found the smaller guard holding a handgun to Brent's head, whose rifle was in the grass. As he came into sight, the guard swung to point his handgun at Templar and as he did Brent threw a fast backhand punch into the guard's face then let his legs go, dropping straight to the ground. Templar moved two paces, threw a low roundhouse kick at the guard's right knee, shattering the joint and dropping the guard like a rock. Brent seized him, stamping on his wrist and recovering the handgun.

'Cuff and gag him,' said Templar. 'I want to see who's around.'

He stalked to the west of the farmhouse, rifle held on his sightline, and keyed the radio. 'Jean-Michel, you there?'

Jean-Michel replied, 'Another guard just walked out the front of the house with a mug of coffee, he's lighting a cigarette.'

'Armed?'

'Handgun, in his holster.'

'You come in from the west, I'll approach from the other side.'

Templar circled back and ran along the eastern side of the house. From inside he could hear morning TV cartoons. At the front of the farmhouse, he paused and looked around the corner as blood dripped onto the concrete path beneath him. The guard sat on a wooden chair on the front porch, coffee in one hand, smoke in the other. Jean-Michel emerged from the other end of the porch, swiftly swinging a rifle butt into the man's head. Teeth rattled on the wooden boards, and the coffee cup bounced and broke. The guard tried to get up but Templar trod on his wrist and put a hand over the man's mouth.

'Who else is in there?' asked Templar.

The man shook his head, wide-eyed. Templar knew he had a reputation, but this was ridiculous. 'One?'

The man nodded.

'More than one?'

The man shook his head. Templar made the international gesture of *silence*, as Jean-Michel moved in to cuff him. Templar wiped the blood from his face and walked in the door, handgun raised. He could smell omelette and coffee. His stomach rumbled.

To his right was a door, which he pushed open gently to find a bedroom, recently slept in. Across the corridor was another bedroom—two single beds, also recently slept in. He checked the bathroom, ducked in and grabbed a fistful of toilet paper, held it to his broken nose and wiped his face. He moved into another room, the living area which opened into a kitchen. To his right, two boys watched *SpongeBob* on the TV. He lowered his gun, hid it behind his back. The younger boy—Oliver—looked up. 'Hi, Gael,' he said, then turned back to the screen.

Patrick deigned to look away from the screen for two seconds, long enough to say, 'Hi.'

'Hi, boys,' said Templar, scoping the room and walking towards the kitchen. He walked around the corner and in front of him, standing at the stove, was Romy de Payns, all blonde hair, green eyes and athletic. Always so glamorous, even in jeans and a T-shirt. She looked up from the pan and smiled. 'Gael!'

He smiled at the greeting, but behind her, the fourth guard was spooked and reached for his handgun. As he did, Brent materialised at his side and held his gun arm, while Jean-Michel appeared at his other side.

'Exercise complete,' said Templar, nodding to his team, who walked the guard out the kitchen door. By Templar's calculation, Romy and the boys should have no idea what just happened or how much danger they'd been in.

She came to him and gave him a hug and double kiss. 'That's a lot of blood,' she said, reaching for a roll of paper towel.

'I walked into a door,' said Templar.

'Hold that,' she said, as she positioned the paper towel under his nostrils. 'Well, the exercise was all a bit of a pain, but the boys thought it was fun,' she said.

And then Romy de Payns moved back to the stovetop. 'Sausage in your omelette?'

CHAPTER
SIXTY-TWO

De Payns lay on Briffaut's sofa, exhausted and depressed. He felt sick, with worry and guilt. He'd spent so much of his life away from his kids and now he'd introduced them to a danger of his own making. Every spy's nightmare.

At his desk Briffaut worked two phones. He hung up from a call, and asked Shrek what had happened with the shipment investigation from Sicily.

'DR is getting back to us. They were going to use Interpol. They track suspicious freight.'

'Chase them,' said Briffaut and went back to his own calls.

A television played the *France 24* news service and de Payns heard a phrase that got his attention. He grabbed the remote from the coffee table and turned up the volume—the screen was now filled with a colour picture of a good-looking blonde woman in her mid-thirties. He knew that face—or, more accurately, Sébastien Duboscq knew that face. The reporter's voice-over continued: '*The DCPJ have identified the body found in the Seine three days ago as Claire Fouchet, a thirty-four-year-old insurance broker from Paris. Her badly disfigured body was discovered by a tour boat operator, and investigators have appealed for any witnesses to come forward . . .'* The scene shifted to a detective, who referred to torture without spelling it out.

'You okay, Alec?' asked Briffaut.

De Payns collapsed back on the sofa. 'Claire Fouchet,' he said, pointing at the TV screen. 'She works in the neighbouring office to Sébastien Duboscq.'

'Tortured?' asked Shrek.

De Payns nodded, trance-like. 'Whoever we're dealing with, they're in Paris.'

'Get our police liaison on it,' said Briffaut to Shrek. 'And I need Interpol's intel on Sicily freight movements.'

De Payns' phone rang. The caller ID said 'T', but when he picked up, it was Romy.

'Wow, that was annoying,' she said, sounding happy. 'But it's made the boys' holiday. We're about to get on a helicopter. Ollie is beside himself.'

De Payns found it difficult to speak as the emotion welled up in him. He suppressed it by pinching the bridge of his nose. 'So you're okay, you and the boys?'

'Sure,' said Romy. 'Gael's got a broken nose. Apparently he walked into a door.'

'Yes,' said de Payns, laughing. 'He's known for that.'

He sagged when he got off the phone. 'I can't go back to that apartment. We're compromised.'

'I've got an idea,' said Briffaut. 'Leave it with me.'

■

They moved into an SCIF, Briffaut seated at the head of the boardroom table. Lafont and the chemicals genius, Josef Ackermann, arrived and Garrat sat with Templar and Shrek. There was a map of Europe and Asia projected on the screen in the room.

'We have a lot of information but it doesn't add up right now,' said Briffaut. 'Jim Valley is being held at the Cat. We haven't yet told DGS. We'll start on the questions soon.'

The faces all looked downwards. No one at the Company liked the topic of traitors.

'But this is what we do have,' said Briffaut. 'We have a strain of weaponised clostridium found in a Palermo warehouse, and that same strain has been tested on a village in Afghanistan, where it killed more than thirty people. Our informant—Fazel—became seriously ill just from contaminated water on his face.'

Josef Ackermann chimed in. 'We've got the results from the Red Cross on the Burmese village poisoning. It's the same weaponised clostridium that was found in Palermo and Afghanistan.'

Briffaut aimed a laser pointer at Islamabad on the map. 'Here's the MERC. We have no proof that this is where the bioweapon comes from, but we have two people connected to what we believe was produced there.'

Briffaut nodded at Lafont and three pictures appeared on the screen. 'This is the man we know as Murad,' he said, pointing to the grainy CCTV picture on the left. 'A Sayef Albar commander who has pledged to position the terror group in the heart of Europe and who was trying to buy five French passports to do just that.'

Briffaut moved his pointer to the middle picture. 'This is Michael Lambardi, also known as Commodore. Commodore was a Sicilian migration consultant working for Murad, and was killed by him. Fine traces of weaponised clostridium were discovered on chlorine granules in a Palermo warehouse leased by Commodore's brother, David Lambardi.'

Briffaut moved to the final picture. 'This is Yousef Bijar. We call him Timberwolf. He's the head scientist at the MERC in Islamabad. When Aguilar slipped out of the city after a failed dinner date, Timberwolf received a call from a voice that we believe belongs to Murad, based on intercepts over the years. Murad knew Aguilar's pseudo, and that he works for us. This phone call to Timberwolf is crucial—the MERC is an ISI-run facility.'

Briffaut paused. 'The conclusion is that the MERC, under the auspices of the ISI, is making a bioweapon, and a client organisation of the ISI—Sayef Albar—is going to use it in Europe.'

Everyone present nodded in agreement.

'The question is,' said Briffaut, 'where is this bioweapon, how much of it do they have and what is Sayef Albar planning to do with it?'

■

When they broke for the team to make their phone calls, de Payns grabbed a coffee and went back to his office with Shrek. They got the DR office at the Cat on speaker, and asked for an update on the outgoing sea and air freight logs from Palermo. But nothing really stood out. The biggest problem was the size of what they were looking for. A small canister of the weaponised clostridium could be carried by a person in their hand luggage and introduced to a small water supply. The test uses of the gas gangrene were conducted in local sources of drinking water, targeting village populations. But what would a bigger attack look like, and how would the terrorists transport the bacteriological material without being detected? Shrek's report described the Palermo warehouse as being about thirty metres by twenty. You didn't need a warehouse of that size for a few canisters carried by couriers. The ETX clostridium that had been transhipped through the Palermo warehouse had to be much bigger than a few capsules in a rucksack. Sayef Albar would not take the risk of renting such a large space unless they needed it.

There was a movement in the doorway. De Payns looked up. Templar and Ackermann were standing there.

'We're going down to the cafeteria,' said Templar. 'Any orders?'

De Payns leaned back in his chair. 'Josef, you were quiet in there.'

The scientist shrugged. 'I wait for Marie to call me in.'

'How about I call you in?' suggested de Payns. 'If we narrow this right down, the Pakistanis have developed a gas gangrene agent that works best when it's added to water, something we all need to use every day.'

'Sure,' said Ackermann.

'So if you were the terrorist, and you wanted to deploy this in Europe, what method of distribution would you use to create the biggest impact?'

Ackermann looked at the ceiling, thinking. 'The best way would be to add as much as I could to the water supply of a major city—say, London, Paris, Madrid. But . . .'

'That wouldn't work,' said de Payns.

'Well, not really. You'd need a lot of bacteria to influence a metropolitan water supply, and the major cities have filters and chemical treatments that can defeat bacteriological pathogens.'

'Even man-made, weaponised ones?'

'This one from the MERC is very strong and very resilient,' said Ackermann. 'And it has this added sialidase feature, which negates the dilutive effects of water. It can still work when it reaches the intestine.'

'But?'

'But you'd have to get it past the water treatment stations and all their chemicals. Once it was in the pipes, that would be another story. That's when you'd kill a large number of people.'

CHAPTER
SIXTY-THREE

The Alamut team went to lunch early. Briffaut wanted them to go and eat, regroup and come back with a solution.

Dominic Briffaut hit a four-numeral code on the landline console on his desk. Frasier picked up quickly and Briffaut told him that France could be a target, given the bioweapon was in Italy, and therefore DGSI—the Company's domestic counterpart—should be briefed. Frasier accepted this, and Briffaut continued. 'In about ten minutes you'll be asked for authorisation on a transaction we're making. I'd like you to say yes.'

'What am I okaying?' the director wanted to know.

'I'd like to thank Manerie in my own way.'

There was a long pause.

'The answer's yes,' said Frasier finally. 'Make it happen. I'll bring in DGSI.'

Briffaut rang the financial operations officer and dictated the details. Then he scrolled through the contacts in an old Nokia and hit a number. It was answered by a PA and Briffaut said, 'Please tell Monsieur Sharif that Monsieur Roche will see him at twelve-thirty.'

Briffaut hung up before the woman could answer. Then he stood up, adjusted his tie, and walked out into the sunshine, passing through the side security gates and heading north to the greenery of the Stade Huvier. He bought a baguette with salami and cheese and a cup of coffee, and sat at a table with an umbrella. Six minutes later a portly subcontinental man in an expensive suit and dark sunglasses wandered over to the coffee cart, bought a cup and sat at Briffaut's table. They pretended they didn't know one another.

'Monsieur Roche,' said the man in an undertone, stirring his coffee. 'It's been a while.'

'Thanks for joining me, Monsieur Sharif,' said Briffaut, as a woman with three dogs walked past. 'We had a high-level defection this morning.'

'Who?' asked Sharif.

'Philippe Manerie.'

Sharif stopped stirring and looked over the top of his sunglasses at Briffaut. 'That's a little higher than just high level.'

'He's been playing both ends against the middle for a number of years,' said Briffaut.

'France and Pakistan?'

'Yes,' said Briffaut, biting into the baguette. 'But we think he sells out both of us to the Israelis. He's disappeared as of this morning and we assume he's in Islamabad. That's certainly where all his best material has come from recently.'

'Really?'

'Yes,' said Briffaut, finishing the baguette and sipping the coffee. 'We want you to know that even as he feeds us intelligence from Pakistan, we consider it damaged goods. Just so we're clear.'

'Understood,' said Sharif.

'You might find this interesting,' said Briffaut, pushing a bank account number across the table.

Sharif took the paper and slipped it into his jacket.

'Have a good day,' said Briffaut, and he left, taking his coffee with him.

CHAPTER

SIXTY-FOUR

De Payns was not supposed to have a CZ 9mm from the Company at his residence, and Briffaut had asked him to return it. After lunch, de Payns descended to the armoury and small gun range in the bowels of the Bunker, where Zac often had interesting videos playing on his TV and all the best gossip in the building.

'Please sign it in,' said de Payns, passing over the handgun. 'It's about two years overdue.'

Zac brought out his Tupperware box of macarons and de Payns took a raspberry one. There was a handgun viced in place on Zac's workbench, lights focused on it.

'What are you working on?' asked de Payns, nodding at the gun.

'Blanks. They wreck a weapon. Put too many of those rounds through and I have to break them down, rebuild them. They go through thousands at Cercottes.'

'Blanks?' echoed de Payns, chewing on the biscuit. 'Hadn't really thought about it.'

'Well most people think there's nothing in them, hence *blanks*,' said Zac. 'But there's still a charge in the round. It has gunpowder and what have you, but instead of a bullet, there's paper wadding. Quality weapons don't like to shoot paper.'

'So it's not really a blank at all?' asked de Payns.

'No, it's more like a fraud. Everything looks normal on this side'—he held a flat hand to his right—'but what comes out over here isn't what you thought you put in.'

De Payns stood, his mind spinning. 'Thanks Zac.'

■

The team returned to the SCIF at 1 p.m. and de Payns focused on Ackermann. 'Josef, you said that a large-scale attack with weaponised clostridium would require too much of the material to be added to a city water supply, and there are too many filters and treatments at a water plant?'

'Yes, around seven stages. Water engineering is pretty advanced.'

'What's the final stage?'

Josef Ackermann rolled forward and looked at his files. 'It's one of the chemical treatments. Chlorine or, in the new plants, chloramine.'

'How do they dispense the chlorine?'

Ackermann held up a colour brochure showing large blue plastic barrels. 'They're like a cartridge that slots into the pipe at the very end of the process,' said Ackermann. 'The water is treated by the chlorine, and when it passes out the other side the bugs that weren't killed by the previous six stages are now dead.'

De Payns thought about what Zac had said about blanks being better described as frauds. 'What if there's no chlorine in the canisters?'

Ackermann seemed confused. 'Well, the water wouldn't have that final treatment.'

'Okay,' said de Payns. 'What further treatment is there after the chlorine?'

'None,' said Ackermann. 'Unless you have a filter under your kitchen sink.'

'Okay—and this is just a theory—what would happen if you took the chlorine out of the canisters and filled them with weaponised clostridium?'

Marie Lafont screwed up her face. 'That's just gross.'

Ackermann gulped.

Briffaut turned to Shrek. 'Those samples you brought back from Palermo? The clostridium was on chlorine.'

'Yes, it was,' said Shrek, eyes focusing.

'What if they were bringing in genuine water treatment canisters that were filled with chlorine, then emptying them and refilling them with the clostridium?'

'That would mean water treatment canisters arriving at Porto di Palermo, having their contents swapped, and leaving from there as well,' said Briffaut. 'Hand it to the DR. They can do this quicker than anyone. Chlorine is a reportable substance. Let's find out who was bringing it in and shipping it out.'

Marie Lafont picked up one of the conference phones in the middle of the table, and turned away.

■

The first response came back from the Palermo Port Authority twenty-three minutes later. Shrek took the call from DR on speaker phone—a company called Rotterdam Associates had applied to import fourteen containers of Scandland water filters from Australia, with a combined weight of two hundred and fifty tonnes of chlorine. The name on the authorisation form was Gina Bolaro. The DR woman cited the local address as 1625 Via Fiammetta.

'I know it,' said Shrek. 'That's the address for Palermo Commercial Realty—it's David Lambardi's firm, the managing agency for the warehouse.'

'When did this company export the containers out of Palermo?' asked Shrek.

'July twenty-eight,' the woman replied. 'Fourteen containers, on a ship called *Baltic Lady*. The freight forwarders were Global Transit Group.'

The team looked at one another.

'Okay,' said Shrek. 'Where was the ship going?'

The woman paused then said, 'Alexandria Port—Egypt.'

Briffaut had the cooperation of the Italian security services but the paperwork for the chlorine consignment departing the country was accurate and there were no flags.

'What's in Egypt?' asked Briffaut. 'Why are they shipping there? Is this a Shia–Sunni thing?'

The DR woman then said the consignment had been unloaded from *Baltic Lady* on the same day it docked.

'Thanks, keep us updated,' said Briffaut, ending the call.

He looked around at his team and they got back to Palermo. They quickly established that Gina Bolaro was a false ID, but before they could pursue it further the phone rang.

Lafont picked up. 'DR again,' she said, putting the call on speaker.

'New developments,' said their woman from DR. 'Those containers were unloaded in Alexandria and cleared into bond, and then they were loaded again via a new freight forwarder. We only picked it up because Alexandria has RFID readers and our person down there ran a check.'

Briffaut swore softly. 'Which ship did they go onto?'

'That's the thing,' she said. 'They went straight back onto *Baltic Lady*.'

'Where was it heading?' asked de Payns.

'Cadiz and Le Havre,' she said. 'It arrived at Le Havre two weeks ago.'

■

The arrival of the containers in France was sufficiently distant that there was nothing to search or seize. They enlisted French customs at Le Havre, who confirmed importation of chlorine water filters from Alexandria via Cadiz on the dates supplied. The containers had been held in bond for fourteen hours at a global freight forwarding operation called Atlas-HK, and when they checked with Atlas the forwarder confirmed that the fourteen containers had been released by a Gina Bolaro and trained to Reims. They could confirm that they were white Hapag-Lloyd twenty-foot containers. From there, the trail became meaningless, with fake names, fake paperwork and fake trucking companies. The containers had already been moved from the Reims' container hub, where they'd probably been broken down and rebirthed as other cargos, and they could now be anywhere in France or elsewhere in Europe.

There was a knock at the SCIF door, and Anthony Frasier walked in. 'We've got Valley downstairs.'

They descended into the basement of the old fort, into an area where the detention centre occupied a small space not taken up by the armoury, engineers' workshops and gym. The team walked into a room with nine chairs all facing a window—Jim Valley was on the other side of the glass, cuffed to a steel loop on the table in front of him.

Briffaut inserted a micro earpiece and pointed to de Payns. 'Alec and I will do the interview. I need the rest of you fact-checking his bullshit and feeding it to me, okay?'

Valley's face was a mess—fat lip, swollen eye socket, tape and bandage holding his left ear to his blood-encrusted head. The soldier looked up as Briffaut and de Payns walked in and sat down. 'For the record, Templar hit me from behind. I did pretty well, considering.'

'I don't have a deal for you,' said Briffaut straight up. 'You know how the Company works—traitors are traitors.'

Valley nodded. 'Sure, I know. But I served—I was following the orders of my commanding officer.'

Briffaut nodded. He wasn't going to argue the point.

'Anyone have a smoke?' asked Valley.

Briffaut lit one and handed it to him. 'No deals, but the small traitor who helps us grab the big traitor? That could only be a good thing.'

Valley scoffed, dragged on his smoke. 'Actually, I'm fucked. Let's get on with it.'

'You were in deep with Manerie,' said Briffaut.

'Eventually, yes,' said Valley.

'Eventually?'

'I was driving for him, riding shotgun, for a couple of years.'

'Can you remember how that started?'

'I served in a unit he commanded in Congo, back in the day.'

'He brought you into the Company?'

'Yeah, he did. I started with recon and support team work. But I knew Manerie wanted me in DGS. When the whole Murad bullshit started, that's when I came into this stupid shit.'

'What's the Murad bullshit?' asked Briffaut, lighting his own cigarette.

Valley stared at Briffaut and took a deep breath, like a man with some very big regrets. 'There was a Pakistani rocket engineer who was apparently working for us. Manerie sold him out to a guy called Murad—sort of ISI, but also private.'

'Manerie told you this?'

'Manerie *drinks*,' said Valley. 'He's not happy with some of his choices.'

'So why were you brought in?'

'Murad turned Manerie with money, but as soon as that engineer was blown, Murad started blackmailing Manerie—or at least telling him his career could be over.'

'How did that go down?'

Valley smirked. 'So, Manerie muscles up with me and starts making it clear that we'd worked dark in Africa and we weren't to be fucked with. It became a bit macho.'

'Macho?' echoed de Payns. 'You kidnapped my wife and kids. Nice work, tough guy.'

Valley looked at his smoke, nodding slowly. 'Not my finest hour. I was telling the boys I was going to wrap it up and we were all going home. And then Hurricane Templar struck. I was going to drive them home, I swear. But that's no excuse.'

Briffaut leaped in. 'Can we be clear? Murad is ISI?'

Valley nodded. 'He contracts to them. He created a group called Sayef Albar. He's bad news.'

Briffaut touched his earpiece. 'Do you know Murad's name?'

'Murad is a pseudo, as far as I can tell,' said Valley. 'I never met him, only saw him from a distance. He doesn't like to be looked at.'

'Where did Manerie do meetings with him?'

'Never in Pakistan. A few meetings were in France, Spain, Italy, but mainly they talked on *démarqué* phones. Manerie once told me that Murad hides in plain sight. He has a firm in a European city. Don't ask me which one.'

'What's Murad planning?'

Valley shrugged. 'Do I look like the mastermind?'

'Let me run through some names, tell me what you know—Yousef Bijar.'

'Never heard of it.'

'Anoush al-Kashi.

'Blank.'

'Michael Lambardi.'

'Lambardi?' Valley laughed. 'Shit, he was a dumb bastard. Murad goes to contact Lambardi on the ferry and fucking Aguilar is staring straight at him. That got the feathers flying.'

De Payns couldn't help himself. 'Lambardi died for that.'

Valley sneered. 'Lambardi was trying to make three million euros for trafficking terrorists with real French passports. Sorry for the hurt feelings.'

'You know they tried to kill Aguilar that night?' asked Briffaut.

'I heard that later. Shrek came up with some fancy pen-work.'

'Okay, David Lambardi,' said Briffaut.

'Owns a real estate firm in Palermo—Palermo Commercial Realty. He's a useful idiot.'

'Useful to whom?'

'Murad ran his European logistics out of the firm's systems, I believe. Some payments were made out of there, too. Not the big ones, but the day-to-day running of Sayef Albar.'

'How did he do that?'

'He had a very smart woman working there . . .'

Briffaut leaned in as Valley stumbled. 'Who's the woman, Jim?'

Valley went blank. They'd touched a nerve.

'She close to you?'

'She was,' said Valley, sighing. 'Her real name's Heidi Winnen. We sort of . . . you know?'

'What was her role?'

'They always had things coming in and going out. People had to be paid, all the paperwork needed an address. I don't know the details, but she ran all of that.'

De Payns came in, 'Winnen's her real name? What other names did she use?'

'She goes by Gina Bolaro,' said Valley. 'I actually really liked her, you know?'

■

They returned to the SCIF and within eight minutes Marie Lafont had a bio on Heidi Winnen, and a picture that she projected onto the SCIF's screen from her laptop. 'She's a chemical engineer, with a company called Rotterdam Associates. At university she had a boyfriend called Nasim ul-Huq, a Pakistani science student who was heavily involved in PLO politics.'

'Heidi was radicalised?' asked Briffaut.

'Doesn't say,' said Lafont. 'She's worked all over the world in major water infrastructure engineering and now she seems to be in charge of Rotterdam's pitch into water utilities in France, Germany and Spain. The best part? Nasim ul-Huq—her boyfriend from university—is the owner of Rotterdam Associates. It's in Paris.'

'Is Nasim also known as Murad?'

'We're getting a photo.'

De Payns asked, 'What is Rotterdam selling?'

'They install new chemical water filters. It's called chloramine disinfection.'

'Chloramine? Not chlorine?'

Lafont read out what was in front of her. 'It says chlorine and ammonia, the latest way to ensure clean water. It's the final part of the water treatment process. There's a link here to a media release. They're installing the biggest system in Europe this week.'

'Where's the installation?' asked de Payns.

'Saint-Cloud,' said Lafont.

'Saint-Cloud treatment plant? That's in Paris,' said de Payns.

Frasier reached for the landline and punched the DGSI number.

'Claude,' he barked. 'That shit I briefed you on? It's Saint-Cloud—they're targeting Saint-Cloud.' There was a pause. 'Yes, the fucking Paris water supply!' Another pause. 'Okay. Stay on the line.'

Frasier hit mute and looked around. 'Malle wants me to contact Saint-Cloud—he'll join the call. Someone get me the CEO.'

Saint-Cloud was one of six drinking-water plants owned by the City of Paris and its water company, Eau de Paris. It drew water from springs as far afield as Normandy and Burgundy, continuing a tradition of transporting water into the city by aqueduct that had begun a little more than four hundred years earlier, under the Medicis.

Lafont scrolled through her phone and called a number at the DGSE, and then leaned over, 'hung' the Malle call, and dialled in another number. They got the head of operations—Jean-Pierre Thorens—after waiting seven minutes, and explained the situation.

'Claude Malle, DGSI, and Anthony Frasier, from the government,' said Malle to Thorens, who wasn't concerned.

'Our infrastructure security exceeds the EU requirements and the Americans even tour here to see what we do,' he said haughtily. 'We are Paris's water supply. It's serious infrastructure with a national security designation, Monsieur Frasier.'

'I don't doubt it,' said Briffaut, jumping in. 'It's just there could be a saboteur in the engineering firm Rotterdam Associates. They're installing new chloramine filters this week?'

'Today, actually,' said Thorens.

'Okay. You don't know me, Monsieur Thorens, but I work for the government. My name is Dominic,' he said. 'I'll bet you there's a team of technicians and engineers listed from Rotterdam Associates, and there is one manager whose name is Heidi Winnen.'

De Payns heard a tapping on a keyboard. 'That is the case, but so what? She probably works for the company—you could have got that name from their website.'

'She's a saboteur,' Briffaut insisted.

Thorens pushed back. 'I don't think you understand. This is a secured facility. For any contractor to have access to our operations area, the company must first provide their name, and the contractors themselves have to produce their passports when they arrive. It's a totally locked-down area.'

'Passports?' echoed Briffaut.

'Yes, if the name doesn't match the passport, they don't enter,' said Thorens. 'We only accept French nationals in the security area.'

'How many?' asked Briffaut.

'How many Rotterdam contractors?' replied Thorens.

'Yes.'

The keyboard clattered and Thorens said, 'Seven. I can read them out if you'd like—Margaret Vernier, Nasim ul-Huq, Heidi Winnen, David Keller, Clement Vinier, Pierre Bastiat and Antonie Aguirre.'

The DGSE team swapped looks, eyes wide. Five of the names used by Rotterdam Associates were fictive IDs used by the Y Division.

When the five passports didn't materialise in Palermo, had Murad's gang simply turned to their contact in the DGS? What had Manerie done?

Briffaut broke the shocked silence. 'I want you to behave normally, Monsieur Thorens, but delay the contractors. We'll be there soon.'

'What is going on?' asked Thorens. 'Is this a prank?'

Claude Malle from the DGSI came on the conference call and cleared his throat. 'Monsieur Thorens, please be advised that all the information in this conversation is classified top secret and is protected information under French law.'

Thorens agreed to the terms.

'Have you heard of *Clostridium perfringens*?' asked Malle.

'It's a bacterium, a nasty one, that causes . . .'

'Gas gangrene,' said Malle.

Thorens stammered slightly. 'Well that can't be allowed in our system. Saint-Cloud serves Paris.'

'I understand,' said Malle. 'We believe these people have put weaponised *Clostridium perfringens* inside the final filtration canisters in place of the chloramine. Those canisters are what they're installing at Saint-Cloud, yes?'

The man on the other end paused. 'Yes, and that would be devastating.'

'Okay,' Briffaut interjected, 'don't frighten or approach these people. I know you have a job to do, but stand back from it until the police get there.'

CHAPTER

SIXTY-FIVE

The DGSI ordered a public action to be conducted by Colonel Tibaut Jenssins. He ran GIGN, the tactical response unit of the French National Gendarmerie, based at Satory, south of Versailles. GIGN had a chemical–biological–nuclear ready-reaction role and were supposed to be the first responders. The GIGN unit would be supported by the *Commandement des Opérations Spéciales*—special forces—commanded by Colonel Laurent Francisci.

Claude Malle from the DGSI reluctantly allowed Briffaut's DGSE to accompany the operation, but required they take up the rear and not join in.

'You two, with me,' said Briffaut, pointing to de Payns and Shrek.

As they left the SCIF, Lafont handed a printed photograph from the printer to de Payns.

'You're the only person in Western intelligence to have eyes on Murad. Is that him? In the background, white shirt, black tie.'

De Payns took the A4 page. The shot was of an Indian politician cutting a ribbon at a facility. In the background were three men, one of them standing out because of his height and well-groomed looks. He looked like a Pakistani Errol Flynn but without the moustache.

'That's the man I saw on the ferry,' said de Payns, touching the page. He looked to the foot of the photo, where the caption included the name and title: *Nasim ul-Huq—Chief Engineer, Rotterdam Associates.*

'We've got this fucker,' said Lafont, retrieving the photo and moving to a phone.

They descended to the ground floor and walked into the armoury, where they checked out CZ handguns and 416 assault rifles. As de Payns took his ballistic vest, Templar arrived, a white cast across his nose and cheekbones.

'Where're we going?' he asked.

'Did Frasier assign you?' asked Shrek.

'You really think I'm letting you go alone?'

They suited up and ran to the lawn in front of the Bunker, where Briffaut stood beside Frasier, waiting for the helicopter to land.

'Did I include you in this, Templar?' asked Briffaut as the Caracal flared and aimed for the grass.

'No, boss,' said Templar, smiling through a bruised and battered face. 'But who's gonna pick up these ladies when they trip over their high heels?'

'You're injured—I can't let you in the field.'

'I'm fully recovered,' said Templar. 'Can't you see?'

'You take longer to get over a hangover,' said Briffaut, shaking his head as the helicopter touched ground. 'Fuck it, let's go then.'

Frasier walked back into the Bunker to coordinate with DGSI. It was six minutes by chopper to the Saint-Cloud plant and en route Frasier patched them into a radio connection with Jenssins' unit. De Payns could hear it in his helmet speakers.

They flew across south-western Paris, the city going about its business as if nothing were wrong. Over the radio net, Jenssins told Colonel Francisci that his GIGN unit would land first and establish themselves. 'There're civilians in there and the terrorists have a biological agent right on our water supply. Give us two minutes.'

'Got it,' said Francisci, whose COS special forces operators were assault specialists, not bioweapons experts.

Briffaut asked his pilot to hold back and land in the car park of the plant, which was an industrial facility in the middle of a green parkland.

'Okay,' said Briffaut, muting his mic, 'remember to stay back when we land. We're observers here—spare me the paperwork.'

On the GIGN and COS radio net, Colonel Francisci from special forces was talking to Thorens. 'Can you shut it down?' he asked.

'It takes several hours,' said Thorens. 'You don't just shut down the water in Paris.'

'We're landing,' said Jenssins. 'Where are the consultants?'

'The Rotterdam engineers are already inside the security perimeter,' said Thorens, 'but I believe some of their supplies are still in the trucks.'

'I doubt they're engineers,' said Jenssins, 'so stay away from them, and stay clear of those canisters. We're landing now.'

De Payns could see the two GIGN helicopters landing on a field beside the large staff car park. A massive structure—the Saint-Cloud drinking-water plant—rose up out of the greenery like a grey behemoth. The Y Division helicopter lined up behind the two choppers carrying COS soldiers. From his window de Payns could see two Rotterdam trucks parked at the building, one of which had its side curtains raised, showing two-metre-tall blue canisters stacked one on top of another. A forklift approached the canisters.

De Payns and Shrek made to follow the special forces soldiers, who deployed along the side of the building to the loading bays, but Briffaut pulled them back. 'You're worth more to me if you're anonymous and alive,' he reminded them. 'We're not in Islamabad anymore, boys.'

The radio net sprang to life as the lead GIGN operators rounded the corner of the main building, so they were facing the loading bay. The gunfire started, echoing loudly in their earpieces—the gunfight was also clearly visible just sixty metres away. Concrete chips flew as three gunmen fired from the loading bay, partially obscured by a truck. They were good marksmen, for water engineers. One of the gunmen at the truck slumped, shot dead. Two other Rotterdam gunmen retreated back inside the facility. The soldiers gave chase and the DGSE team lost sight of them.

'Wouldn't mind a look in there, boss,' said Templar.

'Stay where you are,' Briffaut ordered as the clatter of automatic gunfire crackled on the radio, making them wince at the sudden burst in volume. The shouting between the GIGN troopers was constant and the team leader's instructions and the feedback suggested the operators were advancing through the facility towards the rear of the building.

Shrek nudged de Payns and pointed. From the main corporate entrance of the building, a tall middle-aged man with a crown of pushed-back silver hair approached the helicopter.

'Be nice,' said Briffaut, as he slid out the helicopter side door and stopped the man from reaching his team.

'Can I help you, sir?' asked Briffaut.

'Thorens,' said the tall man, holding out his hand. 'Jean-Pierre Thorens. I'm the CEO.'

'Dominic,' said Briffaut, taking the proffered hand. 'We spoke earlier.'

'What should I do with my employees?' asked Thorens. 'They're frightened.'

'What did GIGN say?' replied Briffaut.

'They charged straight through, told us to stay in the foyer, but it's dangerous—we can hear the gunfire, it's very close.'

De Payns looked at the glassed-in entrance—civilians milled around wide-eyed, the occasional one making a break for the car park.

'What's going on in there?' asked Briffaut.

Thorens explained that inside the loading bay was a long, open area where five different stages of filtration and water treatment took place. A gantry crane ran the length of the building and the GIGN troopers were fighting their way towards the two massive steel sliding doors at the end of the facility, where the security area started.

'That's where the Rotterdam Associates people were,' said Thorens. 'They were working on the final filtration system, where the water is cleansed by chloramine before it goes into Paris's water pipes.'

'They're behind those security doors?' asked Briffaut. 'The Rotterdam engineers are in the water system?'

'Well, yes,' said Thorens. 'They had their passports, which were all cleared by our security check. I don't know how your guys will get through those doors—I believe they're bomb-proof.'

What sounded like a grenade barked in their earpieces. De Payns wasn't too concerned about those security doors—the GIGN trained in this sort of critical infrastructure and they had master keys and manual override codes that the CEOs of these places might not even be aware of. He was more worried about bullets going through the epsilon toxin canisters or toxin being spilled deliberately into the water system, even as the GIGN operatives approached.

De Payns turned back to the building itself, where the sounds of a gun battle were pushing crowds of employees out of the main corporate lobby and into the parking area. Others clustered in groups inside the foyer. Whichever way they went, they were sitting ducks for one of the gunmen, and de Payns didn't like it.

He turned to Briffaut. 'Some of those folks need a hand.'

Briffaut was not happy, but he could also see the panicking crowd. 'Okay, but no *bang-bang*.'

De Payns leaped out of the helicopter, Shrek and Templar behind him, and they ran to the main lobby. A man of around thirty raced out of the lobby, straight into de Payns.

'Is that *gunfire*?' asked the man. 'What's happening?'

'Stay calm,' said de Payns, grabbing the man by the upper arms. 'Are there any armed people in there?'

'No,' said the man. 'The soldiers went into the building and the shooting started on the other side of the wall. Am I safe?' he asked, looking at the rifles.

'Safer with us standing here,' said Templar. 'What's going on in there?'

De Payns turned back and saw Briffaut staring at them from the helicopter doorway—he decided against going into the building even as the automatic gunfire rang out and voices screamed in renewed terror.

As he turned back from Briffaut, he was struck by how orderly some of the employees were in their departure. 'Follow those people,' he said to the man, pointing to the people making their way calmly across the car park. 'Get out on to the footpath,' he said, pointing to the main road beyond the Saint-Cloud campus. 'But take it easy—no panicking.'

The car park was now awash with people, many of them running, but amid the crowd he noticed a woman in a yellow hard hat and a hi-vis vest. She was walking away from him, across the car park, but in a very controlled way. De Payns was intrigued—how could someone turn their back on a scene of armed conflict without so much as a glance over their shoulder? It was loud, it was confronting; a gun battle *demanded* your attention. You couldn't not look at it.

The woman made a left turn, seemingly to get to her car, and de Payns' heart jumped slightly, like he'd woken up. He'd seen that profile, that blonde hair, just recently—it was Heidi Winnen.

'Christ, it's Winnen,' he said, lifting his rifle to a two-handed grip and accelerating away from Templar and Shrek.

He raced across the concrete car park, triggering screams from the employees as they realised there was an armed man in plain clothes running among them. The commotion alerted Winnen and she turned, thirty metres away from de Payns, and as she pivoted she raised a handgun from her belt. She aimed at him and de Payns stepped behind a Peugeot, keeping his rifle sights on the blonde woman.

'That's enough, Heidi,' he shouted, sights on her as she shuffled sideways behind a van, loosing two shots in his direction.

'Well, if it isn't the secret service. How the hell did you find me?' she yelled.

'Some hard work, some luck,' de Payns shouted as Templar joined him. Shrek was using a car to the left as a hide. There was another car between the Y Division guys and Winnen, and he thought about running for it, but when he stuck his head out to assess the distance another bullet pinged into the Peugeot.

De Payns ducked back to safety. 'You know, Heidi, this is sick what you're doing,' he said, as Shrek continued to outflank her. 'Putting that shit in drinking water.'

'It's science, Monsieur Dupuis. Or should I call you Aguilar?'

'Really?' he replied. 'You're smart, you're an engineer, you could do anything. But you're poisoning Paris? Think about what you're doing.'

Winnen didn't pause. 'Oh, I've thought about it *a lot*, thanks Aguilar. I'm where I want to be.'

'Poisoning a whole city? Your parents must be so proud.'

'You know something?' she replied. 'The West is a virus—a disease that is killing every other culture.'

'It's assisted most cultures to improve their standard of living and their life expectancies. Raised expectations for girls and women, too. Not a bad CV.'

'It's a cancer and we're right here in the middle of where it all started,' shrieked the Dutchwoman. 'Every disease has its starting point and the origin of the Western plague is Paris.'

Templar moved to the car to his right as more gunfire shook the building behind them. De Payns attempted to keep Winnen talking, buying time. 'You know, I met the architect of this bioweapons program, in Islamabad.'

'I heard,' said Winnen, shuffling to check on the other side of her van.

'Bijar was a most unimpressive human being,' said de Payns. 'With leaders like that, who needs criminals?'

Winnen laughed. 'You're a funny guy, Aguilar. But he's a genius—what would you know about that?'

'Not much,' admitted de Payns, keeping his gun sights on the back of the van, where her booted feet told him she was looking to where Shrek was creeping closer. 'But an hour ago I was smart enough to work out Murad's true identity.'

There was a pause, no longer cocky. 'I doubt that.'

'Nasim ul-Huq, a campus radical at the University of Amsterdam,' said de Payns. 'Must have made quite an impression on young Heidi, with all of that horseshit about Palestine, while Arafat gets rich on Iranian oil money.'

'What would you know about Palestine?' she yelled, betraying anger. 'You French! Oh my God, you're worse liars than the Israelis!'

'You really think Nasim cares about Palestine? He's Pakistani intelligence.'

There was silence again. 'Liar!'

'Well, he recruited you, Heidi. Tell me, did he ever share with you the millions he makes from the Taliban's heroin sales?'

One row behind Winnen, a silver Iveco van accelerated for the car park exit, and Winnen turned and ran to it. De Payns looked at the vehicle and locked gazes with the driver—the former campus radical, now known as Murad, the terrorist he had first laid eyes on months earlier, sailing to Palermo.

Winnen ran towards the van, but rather than slow for his lover, Murad hit the gas and kept driving.

'Stop,' yelled de Payns, as Winnen almost comically ran after Murad and the van. She slowed, confused, and suddenly turned to face her pursuers. 'No!' said Shrek, but Heidi Winnen started shooting and Templar opened up with his rifle, killing the Dutchwoman before she hit the concrete.

CHAPTER

SIXTY-SIX

De Payns heaved for breath, standing over Winnen's bloodied body. 'We got her.'

'But Murad's on the run,' Shrek pointed out.

Templar hadn't given up—eleven cars away, he crouched over a parked motorbike, his fingers working under the petrol tank. Shrek and de Payns ran to him, but as Templar got the engine turning over he fell to the ground, clutching his leg.

'Shit,' he said, gasping in pain.

De Payns kneeled beside his friend and saw the bleeding bullet wound in the middle of his right thigh. He tore the trouser fabric apart and saw a bloody hole in his muscle, but it was weeping not spurting.

'It's just a leg wound, not an artery,' yelled Templar. 'Don't worry about me—get that bastard.'

Shrek leaped onto the bike, an 1100 Yamaha, and handed a helmet back to de Payns.

'Over there,' de Payns said, pointing, and Shrek opened the clutch and surged to another motorbike. De Payns dismounted, grabbed the helmet and gave it to Shrek, who put it on and revved the bike.

'One second,' said de Payns, not getting back on the bike. A police support van had pulled into the car park and the cops were deploying in hazmat suits and breathing masks. De Payns crept into their van and unclipped two sets of plastic IDs attached to the officers' jackets, hanging from hooks in the van.

They sat on the horn, trying to carve through the rubber-necking employees, who were converging after Murad had driven through the middle of them. They finally made it onto the street, looked left and right and, spotting the Iveco van to the east, followed it onto the D907. The route was busy and de Payns hung on to the pillion position as Shrek swerved the big Yamaha through traffic at one hundred and forty kilometres an hour, ensuring they didn't lose the van. Contrary to the American movies, Paris was actually no place for spectacular car chases. There was too much traffic and too many small cross streets. The best hope was to be on a motorbike and keep visual contact. This wasn't an unusual pursuit for Shrek or de Payns—everyone in the DGSE knew how to get around Paris on a motorbike.

Briffaut burst into de Payns' earpiece. 'Was that you on the bike?'

'Yes—Shrek's riding,' said de Payns.

'Who's in the van?'

'Murad,' said de Payns.

'Shit,' said Briffaut. 'Alone?'

'Murad is the driver,' said de Payns. 'Don't know who's in the back.'

'What's your location?' asked Briffaut. 'I'll assign a helicopter.'

De Payns gave a location, and as he did Murad's van veered right through an intersection. Shrek chopped down a gear and revved the bike, just avoiding a small traffic jam and keeping contact with the van.

They swept south and then east again, and now they were on the A13 freeway and the van was flying. Shrek opened up the

Yamaha and de Payns watched the traffic flash by as they hit one hundred and eighty.

'Stay back, this is surveillance,' said Briffaut over the net. 'We have no authority here.'

De Payns was happy to hold back. They had no idea who was in the back of the van, and with the bioweapons plot discovered their job now was to see where Murad went, who he joined up with, who would give him sanctuary.

The van crossed the Seine and Shrek and de Payns stuck with it. In front of them the Eiffel Tower loomed.

The van slowed and Shrek tapped down through the gears of the Yamaha, staying back, staying smooth but fast. The van drove slowly along the right-hand side of the street, as if looking down side streets and checking on service lanes. The van sped up again, into a *rond-point*, turning at the first exit, and they watched the van dive into the right-hand kerb, where service vehicles were allowed to park. Shrek hit the brakes as he found a park in the same service parking area, behind a truck. De Payns' helmet bounced off the back of Shrek's and they turned to surveil the street and saw the entrance to the Boulogne–Pont de Saint-Cloud Metro station.

'Stay here,' yelled de Payns, keeping his helmet on as he watched Murad, dressed in a black bomber jacket and jeans, skip along the footpath and dive down into the Metro.

'I'm right here,' said Shrek.

'Be careful in there,' said Briffaut over the radio. As de Payns took off his helmet and dismounted, he could hear the police helicopter overhead.

Ensuring the CZ was tucked into the waistband of his jeans, he headed for the Metro. It was one of the main train routes west across the Seine and there were people everywhere as he got to the concourse. Crowds jostled to get through a limited number of turnstiles—a worse traffic jam than the streets at ground level.

De Payns jogged across the concourse, eyes peeled for a tall Pakistani man in a black jacket. When he reached the main turnstile, he realised he could neither get around the throng of people nor get over them. He couldn't see Murad at either end of the long concourse, so he assumed the terrorist had to be going through to the platforms. De Payns got into the shortest line for the turnstiles, figuring he'd find Murad on a platform or hiding in a toilet.

A tall person behind him wearing a white LA Lakers hoodie got too close, but de Payns shrugged him off as just another rude Parisian. The queue had stalled because an old man in front of him didn't know how to use his Navigo card; he wasn't fast enough to go through when the machine beeped. He tried again, walked through and then back, confusing the machine. Travellers in the queue mumbled about the *idiot* and the *Allemand* as the old man raised his arm for a Metro employee. Impatient, de Payns started to move to another queue, but as he did he felt the nose of a pistol push into his kidney and an accented voice whisper in his ear, 'Stay calm.' The tall man moved into his left shoulder, staying very close, and shepherded de Payns away from the turnstile, pistol in the back, a handful of de Payns' windbreaker sleeve in his hand.

'What do you want?' asked de Payns, feeling the pistol dig deep as they moved back onto the main concourse.

'An insurance policy,' said the voice from under the hoodie, and de Payns recognised the distinct tones he'd heard on the Murad voice tape. He realised this man, the man who had been driving the van and wearing a black bomber jacket, had completed a *desilhouettage*.

'Insurance for what?' replied de Payns.

The pistol dug deeper and Murad pushed him along. As they moved around an arguing couple, de Payns turned his right shoulder and swivelled on the balls of his feet, swinging the edge of his left hand into the nerve below Murad's right ear. A shot went off behind de Payns as he twisted away from the pistol, and de Payns stamped down hard with a kick and connected with Murad's instep, eliciting a scream. He grabbed Murad's 9mm pistol in a wrist lock and tore the ligaments and bone in one fast action as he took it out of the terrorist's grip. The scream was piercing and de Payns now had the man's black SIG in his hand, but a bearded man in his thirties tried to grab him and knocked him slightly off balance. De Payns instinctively struck the bearded man in the throat and without thinking drove the lanyard loop of the weapon into his face. As Beardy sagged to his knees, the crowds screamed in panic and de Payns realised the bearded man wasn't in the game—he was just a good Samaritan who'd picked on the wrong person.

Seeing his mistake, he spun to confront Murad, but the terrorist was already over the turnstiles and running, his white hoodie visible above the crowds on the platform-side concourse. De Payns ran and leaped the turnstile but as he got over it, the transit police arrived and drew on him.

'Drop it,' said the young female officer, not knowing whether to look at de Payns or the bearded man who lay crying where de Payns had left him. De Payns had the SIG in his hand, and he thought about crashing through and pursuing Murad. But as he gasped for breath, another transit cop came at him from his left, driving a baton lengthwise into his rib cage.

Gasping in pain, he dropped the SIG and the cops moved in, guns aimed and handcuffs ready.

'Got him,' said the young female officer, her knee in the small of his back as she tightened the cuffs.

'The white hoodie . . .' started de Payns, but he ran out of breath. There was something wrong with his ribs.

CHAPTER

SIXTY-SEVEN

The man-hunt for Nasim ul-Huq went on for two days, the city and its approaches were awash with police, intelligence and military people trying to trap and capture the man they called Murad. The media referred to the terrorist as the Man Who Turned Off the Water, while the intelligence and military world knew him as the Man Who Tried to Kill Paris.

The newspapers had a field day writing about the son of wealthy Pakistani professionals who earned an engineering degree but went into the ISI and then left to become a contractor, setting up Sayef Albar, an al-Qaeda affiliate with a central ideology of making money for Murad.

Parisians endured the water being turned down to a trickle while the damage was fixed and all pipes checked for contamination. The true nature of the attack—that Murad and Operation Scimitar was designed to pump an enhanced *Clostridium perfringens* epsilon toxin type D into the Paris water supply—was a tightly held secret. The poisoning of water and food supplies had always had its greatest effect in the psychological impacts. Once humans could not trust the water they drank, the city could not last for long. So the French security apparatus did what it had done for centuries—it lied to the people of Paris, for their own good.

De Payns watched the media circus from his hospital bed as they patched his broken ribs. He pondered the paradox of having chased Murad for so long, only to have his ribs busted by an over-eager transit cop. He also wondered where Murad could possibly hide. Paris was a big place, but he'd never seen the intel and policing world so focused on one individual. The DGSE, DGSI, military intelligence, all the French police forces, Interpol, Europol and the French Customs service all joined the effort. Foreign intelligence services lined up to help, too—the Americans, British, German and Israeli. One in particular—the ISI—was among the first to visit the Cat, offering every assistance.

The DGSE executives had smiled sweetly at the Pakistani intelligence envoy, but Dominic Briffaut continued to drive Operation Alamut, tasked with finding Murad and Yousef Bijar. The aim was to render the terrorists to French control and not only take these monsters out of the game but to apply whatever drugs and torture was necessary to root out every contact they had ever made. The Company had the expertise to extract such information, and it certainly had the will. Word of the de Payns family's abduction had filtered through the organisation and Murad and Timberwolf lived with targets on their backs. But Murad was in the wind, and while Yousef Bijar was known to be living in Islamabad, the Pakistani government closed ranks around its favourite scientist and his research centre. The Russian, US and French governments complained that Islamabad was harbouring terrorists, but Pakistan disavowed knowledge, just as they had with Osama bin Laden.

In Paris the DGSI took possession of around ninety thousand litres of the MERC's weaponised ETX clostridium, contained in five-hundred-litre tubes with an ingenious paper seal on each. They'd been inserted into the chloramine canisters in place of the chlorine chemicals, and rather than clean the water, they would have poisoned it with the most lethal bacterial toxin known to man. As the military scientists commented when they had studied the haul, it was enough to kill at least two million people and severely incapacitate the entire city.

While Templar and de Payns recovered from their injuries, Shrek was on Operation Alamut duties, and three days after the attack at Saint-Cloud, he responded to a strange sighting in Palermo. The owner of a private hotel in the old part of the city had a guest—a tall, suspiciously acting Pakistani. The proprietor thought the guest was not who he pretended to be, and he also looked like the terrorist who was all over the European TV news services—the man they called Murad.

Shrek visited the hotel in Palermo and inquired about the guest. The owner showed him the photocopy he'd taken of the man's passport—it was a Pakistani passport in the name of Amin Sharwaz.

Shrek pocketed the photocopy and vowed never to tell Alec de Payns what he'd found in the hotel. The people of the MERC would simply have to go on The List: those who would be dealt with in the future.

Terrorists come and go, but the DGSE never forgets.

CHAPTER
SIXTY-EIGHT

Philippe Manerie emerged from the arrivals terminal at Islamabad International Airport and squinted at the sunlight. He'd been on and off planes for twenty hours, given he didn't have the time to wait for a direct flight from Paris. He'd touched down in Rome and spent several hours in transit, and now he had found sanctuary. He had money in a British Virgin Islands account and his luggage held twelve vintage wristwatches collectively valued at around half-a-million US dollars.

He didn't feel hard done by, and he didn't feel proud. The choices he had made had cost him his marriage and landed him in a compromising position in Macao. He could blame the drinking and gambling, but he knew in his heart how young that girl was and he hadn't said *no*. And when Murad, the Pakistani intel contractor, came knocking with the photographic evidence, the rest was just a formality—a mix of blackmail to keep him on the hook, and money to egg him along.

A blue Jeep Grand Cherokee pulled up outside the terminal building and the door was pushed open. He got in with his small suitcase, and was driven to a compound in the north of Islamabad, on the border of the diplomatic section. The two men he'd driven with walked him to a motel-like quarters at the back of an office building, and when he ducked out for a cigarette he realised that the ring fence of the compound might be designed to keep people in as much as keep people out.

He was fed well, and the next day a thick-set, silver-haired middle-aged man with a military bearing but plain clothes interviewed him in an air-conditioned room.

'Call me the Colonel,' he said with a smile, and they debriefed for most of the day. Manerie was cooperative, but he realised the Colonel—who was otherwise very professional—was taking no notes, a curious departure from intelligence procedure.

'So what are your plans for me?' asked Manerie after lunch, when he thought he had forged some affinity with his new colleague, whom he assumed was ISI.

'We have something special,' said the Colonel, and left it at that.

The third day came and Manerie was surprised to find that the Colonel wanted to discuss his assets.

'We have to get our cards on the table and trust one another, yes?' said the Colonel. 'You have all these watches. Are they stolen?'

Manerie wanted to say, *Keep your nose out of my luggage*, but thought better of it. 'No, not stolen. They're a mobile asset.'

'If you work for me, I have to know your bank accounts,' said the Colonel. 'You must understand this—you are a traitor to France, and so you'd understand that I am extra cautious.'

They went back and forth a few times, but Manerie was reluctant to hand over his banking details and the Colonel finally let it go.

Manerie spent that night in bed wondering how he was going to make money and live in Pakistan. He couldn't go anywhere else because the Company would find him and either kill him or lock him in a cell at Évreux for the rest of his life, slowly milking him of every piece of intelligence he could remember. It would end badly. People like him did not get their day in court.

After breakfast the next day he and the Colonel were driven to the south of Islamabad, to a large security compound. Manerie saw a sign with the word 'Agricultural' in it. It looked like a research facility. They got into an elevator, but instead of going up it plunged several floors below ground, the board lighting up at B5.

'Time to meet your new colleagues,' said the Colonel.

They walked along a corridor that smelled of bleach and Manerie was ushered through a doorway. As he entered he was seized by two thugs. He hip-threw the one on his right, driving the younger man into the concrete. But another materialised and the two assailants wrestled him to the damp concrete floor. Subdued, Manerie was strapped to a bolted-down chair. He tried to protest but a piece of duct tape was slapped across his mouth.

In front of him the Colonel had taken a seat at a desk. To his right, in the shadows, was a second man, also strapped to a chair and gagged. Murad!

Manerie's heart pounded against his chest; he strained against the shackles and tried to yell through the duct tape.

A smaller, thinner man, obviously not military, walked into the room. Despite his panic, Manerie noticed the mustard-coloured cardigan and ugly pants.

'So,' said Mustard Cardigan. 'We have our conspirators?'

Murad flexed his muscles against the shackles, his face purple as he struggled to get words past the gag.

'All those years and all that money, so these two traitors could undo it,' said the Colonel.

'We have to find out how much they divulged,' said Mustard Cardigan. 'It might take a few weeks, but they *will* talk. I can guarantee it.'

The Colonel nodded to a man in a black shirt standing in the shadows, who picked up a power drill from a table and carried it over to Manerie. He revved it and Manerie could feel his bowels clenching as the chrome bit spun in the low light, inches from his face.

'First things first,' said the Colonel.

'I agree,' said Mustard Cardigan, as if he were deciding who would be dealer in their game of cards. 'I'd like a few answers.'

Mustard Cardigan tore the tape off Manerie's face. It stung.

'Who are you?' asked Manerie, one eye on the drill, the other on the man in the cardigan. He could think of nothing else to say.

'You can call me Doctor Bijar,' said the man, lighting a cigarette as he turned to Murad and tore the tape from his mouth. 'So tell me, dear friend Murad, how did you miraculously escape from the DGSE at the end of my operation?'

'I ran,' croaked Murad, as if he had a frog in his throat.

'You *ran*?' sneered Bijar.

'I lost Aguilar in the Metro,' said Murad, through shallow breaths. 'The cops stopped him—I got lucky.'

'That was your escape, but what about at the water works?' prompted the small man. 'Everyone is shot or captured, except the very lucky Murad?'

'It wasn't just DGSE at the water works,' stammered Murad. 'There were special forces, too. They made us.'

'Curious,' said Bijar with soft menace, 'that my program was dismantled by the French at the very last moment, yes?'

Murad shrugged, staying cooler than Manerie. 'I told you after Palermo that we had a new risk. My face wasn't listed with any intelligence service until this Aguilar saw me on the ferry.'

'That's true,' said Manerie, seeing a chance to build credibility. 'We had the name—Murad—but no pictures or sightings.'

Bijar smoked and looked at the floor. Then he looked at Murad. 'Tell me why you called to tell me the Frenchman's name was Aguilar only after he'd left the dinner? It was a little too late, yes?'

Murad shrugged. 'I didn't know he was in Islamabad until Manerie told me. Then I rang you immediately. Given the timing, I imagined he'd still be in the apartment with you and your sister.'

'I'm not in the Y Division,' offered Manerie, looking for the angle. 'They're in their own building and they're very secretive.'

'So how did you find out about this dinner at my sister's apartment?'

Manerie gulped. 'The director of DGS is given a list of active operation names every week. I saw a name I wasn't familiar with—*Alamut*. I dug around, found a briefing note in another director's safe that referred to a dinner in Islamabad. That's when I informed Murad.'

Bijar crushed his cigarette. 'Alamut—the Valley of the Assassins. Don't you love these clever Franks?'

The Colonel took over. 'The DGSE released a report saying the five passports that Murad would buy from Aguilar were indeed destroyed.'

'Correct,' said Manerie.

The Colonel looked at Murad. 'So how was it that you obtained five French passports to gain access to the high-security section of the Saint-Cloud water facility?'

Murad nodded at Manerie, who answered. 'I provided passports created by the DGSE.'

The Colonel, a career intelligence professional, was incredulous. 'You mean, passports used by DGSE field agents? Passports used for their *cover*?'

'Well, yes,' said Manerie, embarrassed that even the Colonel found this dishonourable. 'I had to work on short notice.'

'You would give us passports created by the French secret service, to allow a terror act to take place *in Paris*?'

Manerie slumped.

The Colonel slowly shook his head. 'I doubt we could have kept you safe in Pakistan once your employer realised what you did,' said the Colonel. 'But there's something else of interest to me. The passports would have secured you three million euros—and yet you provided them for free?'

'I imagined I'd be paid,' said Manerie. 'But I haven't seen it.'

The Colonel turned to Murad. 'Tell me, Murad, about this DKB bank account of yours in Munich?'

'Munich?' echoed Murad, astonished. 'I don't bank in Munich.'

'Interesting,' said the Colonel, reading from a sheaf of papers. 'A DKB account in the name of Nasim ul-Huq was just opened in Munich, and an amount of one-and-a-half million euros was deposited by Philippe Manerie.'

'What?' exclaimed Manerie. 'That's a lie!'

'The bank statement doesn't lie,' said the Colonel, shaking it at Manerie. 'You sent it from your Turkish bank account five days ago—just as you were leaving Paris, I guess?'

Manerie's head swirled. The bastards had framed him! 'I don't have a Turkish bank account,' he spluttered. 'Given my background, do you really think I'd open an offshore bank account in my own name?'

The Colonel seemed not to hear. He skipped to a new page. 'Tell me, Philippe, how did you manage to leave France so easily? It's not like the DGSE to let a traitor live happily ever after.'

'I kidnapped Aguilar's family, told him to hold off until I was clear of France.'

The Colonel nodded sagely. 'And why did your bank account receive three million euros from the French government?'

'It didn't,' stammered Manerie. 'I mean, it's not my bank account. Jesus Christ, three *million*?!'

'The statement says you received the money and immediately sent half of it to Murad's bank in Munich,' said the Colonel. 'You two thought you could arrive here, with these financial arrangements with the DGSE, and you'd play with us without any consequences?'

Manerie looked at Murad and Murad stared back, disbelieving.

'We've been set up,' said Murad.

'Or you're setting up Pakistan, perhaps?' replied the Colonel. 'You wouldn't be the first.'

The Colonel nodded and a big hand slapped tape across Manerie's mouth. Murad said a final *no* as he was re-gagged. The two men looked at each other, bug-eyed and hopeless; they'd been fucked by the French.

'Well, gentlemen,' said Dr Bijar. 'I'm sorry to say that we'll need all of your bank details, and full disclosure about your deals with the DGSE. This is the minimum you can do in hope of forgiveness—and a quick death.'

Manerie tried to reason through his duct tape, his voice reduced to pathetic whining. Across from him, Murad's chair wobbled in its bolts as he tried to move his body against his constraints.

'Colonel,' said Bijar, rising to leave, 'I'll let you play with your toys, but please keep in mind that I need their main organs for my tests. Farewell, my friends.'

'That's fine,' said the Colonel. 'I have just advised our allies of the DGSE that we had to arrest their terrorist in the context of our cooperation. I invited them to debrief him, but they won't be here for twenty-four hours and, as usual, they might arrive too late to talk to him.'

The black-shirted thug with the power drill revved it and aimed the power tool at Manerie's left ankle bone. The drill slowed slightly as the bit dug through the flesh and into bone, but then it sped up again as it cut through.

Before he passed out for the first time, Philippe Manerie saw the Colonel flick a piece of flesh from his trousers. Then his own muffled cries for mercy filled his ears and drowned out the screaming drill.

CHAPTER
SIXTY-NINE

The baton strike had broken two ribs, and he had a scorch burn down the inside of his left thigh, where Murad had tried to shoot him at the Metro. De Payns was on a two-week stand-down but Briffaut wanted a report from him. So he travelled straight from the hospital to the Bunker, via an IS, and sat down to write his final reports on Operations Falcon and Alamut.

He had just started writing when Briffaut stuck his head in the door.

'Extra intel,' he said, placing an 'O' report on de Payns' desk. It was very short and simply stated that the Pakistani national known to the Company as 'Raven' had been tortured and killed a week ago. The whereabouts of her body was unknown and her children had been returned to their father in Dubai. The writer of the report said the understanding in government circles was that the killing was done at the behest of her brother as reprisal for bringing a French spy to meet him in Islamabad.

De Payns closed his eyes and breathed deeply. He recalled a day on the water with Raven and how she had told him that the key to a good life was to have a great father. It was a pity about her brother, he thought.

Then he wrote his final reports, filed them and took a handful of painkillers, his ribs providing a constant ache. He headed across town on the Metro, and having cleansed himself of potential followers, got to the boys' school at Montparnasse at 2.45 p.m. He greeted Oliver and Patrick and kissed Romy without hugging her. The broken ribs meant he couldn't lift his arms.

She was full of joy, which de Payns thought was a little insensitive given his injury. But she couldn't help herself.

'I don't know how you did it, but you hit the jackpot, Monsieur de Payns,' she said. 'Three bedrooms, two bathrooms, double living area. And only two thousand euros a month!' She held up a key.

■

The new apartment was a Belle Époque beauty, one block from their previous apartment, with a leafy shared garden in the back. It was one of the sought-after government apartments that were twice as good as an OT could afford.

'Who moved us?' asked de Payns, more paranoid about security than ever.

'Gael, Guillaume and Dominic,' she said.

'Briffaut? He came down here and moved our furniture?'

'He said you'd be uncomfortable with anyone else doing it,' said Romy, putting her arms around his neck. 'Said it was a work thing.'

The boys watched *SpongeBob* while they got ready for soccer practice, slipping on their boots and shin guards. De Payns sent them to have a pee before they left for the field, and he flipped the channels while they were in the bathroom. On Al Jazeera he caught the tail end of a story from Islamabad, which showed flames and smoke towering into the sky and scores of fire engines trying to contain the inferno. '*Some in the crowd are accusing the West of sabotage*,' the reporter was saying, '*but the city fire chief says the fire most probably started in a cleaner's storeroom.*' At the end of the report de Payns could fleetingly see through the smoke the words 'Pakistan Agricultural Chemical Company' on the soot-covered entry portico. He snorted.

The boys ran for the door, and de Payns followed. Romy intercepted him.

'Milk or bread?' he asked her.

'Wine,' she said, giving him a kiss on the lips. 'Housewarming tonight. You're invited.'

They peeled out in Romy's VW Polo, and turned west as Patrick fiddled with the music player.

'Dad, what's a spy?' asked Oliver.

'Why are you asking?'

'Because my friend wants to play spies at school, but I don't know what it is,' said Oliver, rearranging his sock around the shin guard.

'Well, let me think,' said de Payns, braking for a red light. 'A spy is a person who finds out things for his or her country. Things they're not supposed to know.'

'Are spies secret?'

'Yes, son,' de Payns said with a chuckle. 'You may know one, but you wouldn't know they're a spy.'

Oliver considered the answer, and Patrick piped up.

'Play the moon song, Dad,' he said.

De Payns searched Spotify and they sang 'Bad Moon Rising', even as his ribs ached. He was happy, as close to balancing his life as he could ever hope for.

The lights turned green, and de Payns floored the Polo. He had one eye on the road ahead, the other firmly on the rear-view mirror.

EPILOGUE

The hotel was smaller than the enormous Oasis Resort just along the coast. However, it provided to high-security-clearance employees such as Dr Yousef Bijar a place inside Pakistan where they could unwind and take a well-earned rest on the nation's Arabian Sea coastline. The Mercedes pulled into the covered reception area and the driver—in reality an ISI security guard—lifted the Doctor's case from the trunk and walked with him to the desk. This person would be living next door to Bijar's villa for the next week, and he'd always be somewhere in the Doctor's vicinity. It didn't concern Bijar; he'd lived like this for many years and accepted the need for personal security.

He unpacked and dressed for the beach. He wanted to wash out the airline travel from Islamabad and he needed some sunlight and sea air. The strain of the Scimitar program had been on his shoulders for eight years, and that didn't count his scientific work leading up to the point where elements in the ISI decided to fund and green light the attack on Paris. The extended rounds of debriefings and report writing he'd had to go through after Paris had been exhausting. It had been made worse by the fact that the MERC and Bijar's *Clostridium perfringens* program had been largely undeclared to the government and the generals. The Colonel was a 'cut-out'—a middle man who enabled funding, resources and strategic planning, but always off the books. So there'd been two days of concern for Bijar, when he was interrogated directly by the upper levels of the ISI and the intelligence officers of the general staff. It wasn't until the afternoon of the second day that he'd realised they were less concerned with the fate of millions of Parisians than they were with reputational damage to Pakistan, which took in billions of dollars in aid and defence technology transfers from the United States and Europe on the basis that Pakistan was a bulwark against terror. When Bijar made it clear that both Murad and Manerie were not in a position to cause further embarrassment, the ISI gave him the go-ahead to destroy the MERC and transfer his program to a new facility.

Bijar swam in the clear warm waters, watching large crude oil carriers gliding past on the horizon. He thought about how his sister, Anoush, and his father had enjoyed boating on this northern reach of the Indian Ocean, and how it enraged him to be excluded from his father's approval. These two people he'd loved so much—and who had disappointed him so greatly—had met their demise at his hands. He was not proud of it, but he knew that love for one's country, and faith, were things that not everyone understood.

Bijar dried off on the beach and nodded at his bodyguard, who stood in the shade of the palm trees that populated this coast. There were practical reasons to monitor a scientist such as himself, he thought as he showered in his villa. With the MERC destroyed, the research hard drives and the weaponised epsilon toxin cultures were secreted in a location known only to Bijar and the Colonel. And only one of them knew how to weaponise and optimise the clostridium strain that he'd isolated.

Bijar slept away the afternoon, the sounds of the waves on the beach bringing him a peaceful sleep. When he awoke shortly after 5 p.m. he was very hungry. He phoned ahead for an early dinner and arrived at six on the dot. He may have been on holiday, but he liked to be prompt. He ordered the fish curry, a tribute to his childhood visits to this part of the world, and asked for a glass of water. The Arabian Sea sparkled and rolled, its pale green colouring a natural wonder. He thought about Scimitar and what he'd do differently next time. Paris was so close to success that he'd been shocked to watch the events unfold on CNN, the shoot-outs and the involvement of French special forces. Saint-Cloud was part of one of the largest water supply systems in the world and it had been mere minutes away from becoming the deadliest piece of public infrastructure on the planet. Even those who survived the dose of ETX would have overwhelmed the French hospitals and driven people from that city in their millions. Chaos, societal meltdown, distrust in the French government and endless insurgency. They'd come so close.

Bijar wouldn't fail again. He had a working bioweapon secured in a secret location and he wouldn't again use a commercial operator such as Murad, whose connections in Sicily had been the loose thread that, when pulled, brought the entire operation undone.

And Aguilar. The French spy they called Aguilar. Bijar could feel his pulse quicken just thinking about how that arrogant, entitled Frank seduced his own sister and walked into the heart of Islamabad to meet him for dinner. The gall of the French secret services was quite something, and when he and the Colonel were ready to relaunch a new version of Scimitar, they would do so in a way that eliminated any exposure to France or the DGSE.

The waiter poured a glass of water and Bijar thanked him, noticing his lighter skin shade—a feature of the Pakistanis on this coast.

He remembered how his sister and father would toast each other; how they would cook up a plan and laugh and say, *I'll drink to that*. Bijar had never had one mouthful of alcohol in his life, but he smiled at the memory of his family and, raising his glass, mumbled to himself, *I'll drink to that.*

■

The waiter walked through the kitchen and into the loading bay area where the employees' restroom and lockers were situated. He quickly undressed, threw his waiter clothes into a locker and dressed in his street clothes. He emerged into the sunlight, where the white Toyota LandCruiser was purring in the sun. He opened the rear door and deliberately slowed his actions so as not to make a mistake—he sealed the water bottle with a wax and stainless steel lid, placed it in a military self-sealing hazardous materials bag, and then secured the bagged bottle in a bright yellow bio-chem-nuclear carry case with a seal that would hold firm at a thousand feet underwater. He wiped his hands and arms with a military-grade disinfectant wipe that army field hospital workers used to kill bacteria. He grabbed another of the wipes and cleaned his face.

He climbed into the front seat and the driver accelerated away from the resort.

'Package sent?' asked Templar.

Shrek smiled. 'Delivered, accepted and stamped.'

GLOSSARY

agent—a person who engages in clandestine intelligence activity under the direction of an intelligence organisation but who is not an officer, employee or co-opted worker of that organisation.

AQIM—North African branch of al-Qaeda.

BER (Bureau d'Exploitation de la Recherche)—a bureau or 'desk' in the DR of the DGSE that specialises in a geographic area, e.g. BER-Europe.

blue rats—sign of extreme paranoia in the mind of an OT; believing everyone is an enemy.

bouletage—a small object jammed in a door that will tell the OT if the door has been opened in their absence.

candle—backup team members doing the surveillance on a tourniquet.

Cat (Centre Administratif des Tourelles)—headquarters of DGSE in Boulevard Mortier, Paris.

chef de mission—senior OT; leader of a mission team in the DO.

Company—slang term for the DGSE.

CP (Counter-Proliferation)—a division of the DR, responsible for nuclear, conventional weapon and bioweapon trafficking.

DA (Direction Administratif)—Directorate of Administration responsible for special funds management and OTs' payrolls.

DDC (*demande de criblage*)—internal request for a background and security check on a person.

dead drop (*boîte aux lettres morte*)—a secret location where materials can be left for another party to retrieve.

démarqué—unmarked phone with no associated identity; also known as a 'burner'.

desilhouettage—simple disguise, such as putting on a hat or turning a jacket inside out; to rapidly change appearance.

DGS—division of DGSE that is responsible for internal affairs; in charge of detecting moles or security breaches.

DGSE (Direction générale de la Sécurité extérieure)—Directorate General for External Security. French foreign secret service (or intelligence agency/intelligence service); French equivalent to CIA, MI6.

DGSI (Direction générale de la Sécurité intérieure)—French internal secret service; French equivalent to FBI, MI5.

DO (Direction des Opérations)—Directorate of Operations, the division of DGSE that runs operations.

DR (Direction du Renseignement)—Directorate of Intelligence, the division of DGSE that is responsible for human intelligence and synthesising and analysing the intelligence gathered by other means; DR tasks the DO with operations to further its intelligence-gathering. Personnel of the DR are not operatives, and act abroad under a diplomatic status.

DT (Direction Technique)—Technical Directorate, the division of DGSE that collects and analyses cyber, comms and signals intelligence, or creates specific equipment; operates with NSA and GCHQ.

environment—gathering of all the details on a person of interest, their home, family, phone, email, work, habits, friends etc. Environment is established by the mission team. If the environment is satisfactory, the next stage is the approach and then the recruitment. An environment can also be done on a structure of interest.

équipement de ville—portfolio of clandestine meeting methodologies required for a mission in a city; the location of *plans de supports*; routes for tourniquets; places for rendezvous, etc.

exfil—to exfiltrate an OT or other target.

filature—a team or an individual following a person or a vehicle; also known as a 'tail'.

GIGN—tactical response unit of the French National Gendarmerie.

gommette—sticker used to communicate with other members of the mission team by putting it on a *plan de support*. The colour or the markings on it convey different meanings to the mission team.

IMEI—international mobile equipment identity; the identity number of a phone.

IMSI—international mobile subscriber identity; an identifying code sent to a cell tower that identifies the user's SIM.

IS (*itinéraire de sécurité*)—basic security conducted by an OT in the field to determine if they are under surveillance, or being tailed. Also called 'dry cleaning'.

ISI (Inter-Services Intelligence)—Pakistan's intelligence service.

jeux de rendez-vous—various ways of organising a meeting between two OTs, or an OT and another trained person. The time tolerance to arrive on the meeting point is –1/+2 minutes.

legend—a spy's claimed background or biography, usually supported by documents and memorised details; a false life.

liaisons clandestines—clandestine liaisons. All the techniques that allow secret meetings, contacts and observations.

MICE—stands for money, ideology, coercion, ego; the main leverages of manipulation that will make someone work for a secret service against their own country.

mission team—the group that works under the orders of the *chef de mission*, sometimes for support, sometimes as a part of the operation.

OT (*officier traitant*)—a handler, case officer; commissioned intelligence officer of the DGSE.

plan de support—a piece of public street furniture (e.g. a pole, bus stop, etc.) that will be used by the mission team to communicate without collusion. It is defined before the mission and all team members have an allocated spot on which to put their stickers.

point de passage oblige—choke point; a narrow passage through which a follower has to pass in order to keep visual contact with their target, thus revealing that they are following.

prise en compte—a controlled zone where a team can conduct meetings and surveillance activities with a lot of unseen security.

RER—a rail system that covers Paris and surrounding suburbs.

rupture—a place known to the OT that will allow them to lose a tail.

Sayef Albar—splinter group of AQIM.

SCIF—sensitive compartmentalised information facility; an enclosed area within a secured building that is used to process or exchange sensitive and highly confidential information.

subs (*sous-marins*)—surveillance vans in which some mission team members will spend hours observing, using various types of cameras and electronic devices. They are usually disguised as construction vans.

three-point alignment—a visual trick for an OT staying in a hotel to know if their room has been checked or tapped by someone else. By aligning three objects on three different axes that point to a single place in the room (the 'bullseye') the OT can tell if the objects have been moved.

tourniquet—a counter-surveillance measure performed by the backup team, who will establish a specific route that the OT has to walk, to assess if the OT is being followed or not. A sticker (*gommette*) on a *plan de support* at the end of the route will inform the OT of the result.

trombinoscope—collection of portraits taken by the DGSE mission team that captures a target and all the people around the target during their environment.

Y Division—a subdivision of the DO in charge of clandestine illegal/illicit operations for the DGSE.

FRENCH EXTERNAL AND INTERNAL
MAIN INTELLIGENCE AGENCIES

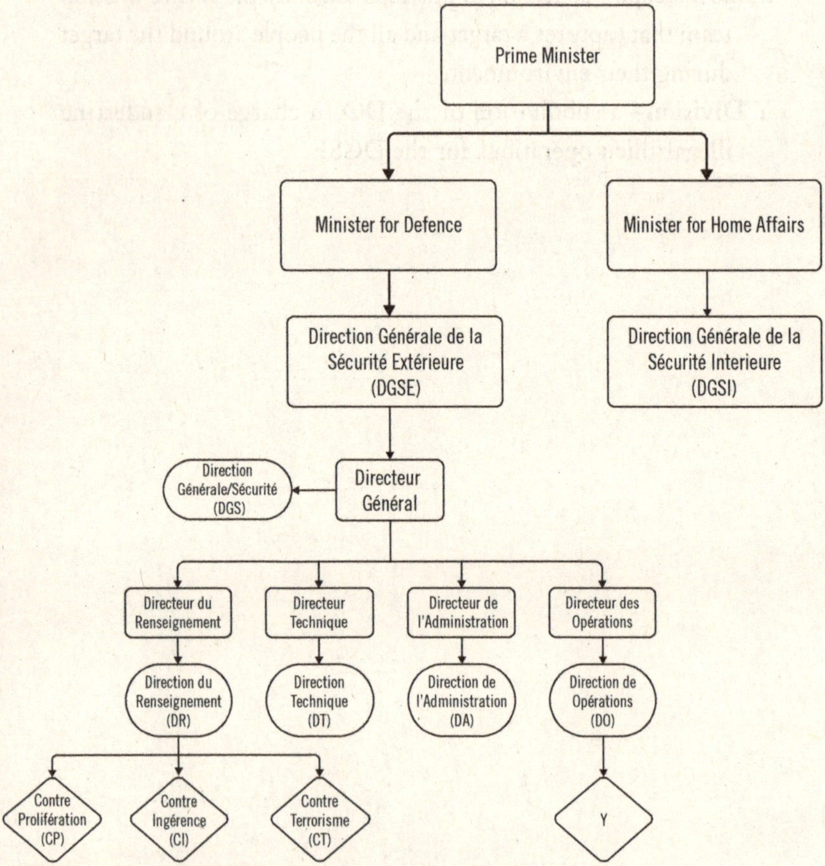